the Summer of Secrets

A former English teacher, Barbara Hannay is a city-bred girl with a yen for country life. Many of her forty-plus books are set in rural and outback Australia and have been enjoyed by readers around the world. She has won the RITA, awarded by Romance Writers of America, and has twice won the Romantic Book of the Year award in Australia. In her own version of life imitating art, Barbara and her husband currently live on a misty hillside in beautiful Far North Queensland where they keep heritage pigs and chickens and an untidy but productive garden.

barbarahannay.com

PRAISE FOR BARBARA HANNAY'S BESTSELLERS

'It's a pleasure to follow an author who gets better with every book. Barbara Hannay delights with this cross-generational love story, which is terrifically romantic and full of surprises.'

APPLE IBOOKS, 'BEST BOOKS OF THE MONTH'

'Barbara Hannay has delivered another wonderful book . . . For me no one does emotional punch quite like Barbara Hannay.'

HELENE YOUNG

'Gripping tale of outback romance . . . Her most epic novel to date.'

QUEENSLAND COUNTRY LIFE

'Lovers of romance will enjoy this feel-good read. Hannay captures the romantic spirit of the outback perfectly.'

TOWNSVILLE BULLETIN

'Get your hands on a copy of this book and you will not be disappointed.'

WEEKLY TIMES

'Barbara Hannay has delivered a fantastic story with beautiful characters and a lovely backdrop.'

1 GIRL 2 MANY BOOKS

'An engaging story of joy, tragedy, romance and heartache set within the dusty landscape of the Australian outback.'

BOOK'D OUT

'In beautiful, fluid prose, Hannay once again puts together all the ingredients for a real page-turner.'

THE CHRONICLE

'Everything a romantic reader could want . . . A brilliant piece of work.'

NEWCASTLE HERALD

'Bound to become a new favourite.'

THE AGE

'A breathtaking read. Once again, Barbara Hannay manages to knock this reader over with a feather.'

TALKING BOOKS

'Barbara Hannay writes beautiful visuals of rural and remote Australia . . . This is a remarkable book.'

READING, WRITING AND RIESLING

ALSO AVAILABLE FROM PENGUIN BOOKS

Zoe's Muster
Home Before Sundown
Moonlight Plains
The Secret Years
The Grazier's Wife
The Country Wedding

BARBARA HANNAY

the Summer of Secrets

MICHAEL JOSEPH
an imprint of
PENGUIN BOOKS

MICHAEL JOSEPH

UK | USA | Canada | Ireland | Australia
India | New Zealand | South Africa | China

Penguin Books is part of the Penguin Random House group of companies whose addresses can be found at global.penguinrandomhouse.com.

First published by Penguin Random House Australia Pty Ltd, 2018

Cover design by Louisa Maggio © Penguin Random House Australia Pty Ltd
Cover photographs: woman by Nikki Smith/Arcangel; landscape by Mark Owen/ Trevillion Images and Sommai/Shutterstock; bottlebrush by Myszka/Shutterstock

Typeset in Sabon by Midland Typesetters, Australia
Printed and bound in Australia by Griffin Press, an accredited ISO AS/NZS 14001 Environmental Management Systems printer.

A catalogue record for this book is available from the National Library of Australia

ISBN 978 0 14378 347 3

penguin.com.au

To my readers . . .

Whether you've been with me from the start, or we're meeting between the pages for the first time . . . thank you.

CHAPTER ONE

Friday night was going perfectly to plan for Chloe.

The faded flat in Coogee looked almost romantic by flickering candlelight and Jason was in a particularly mellow mood. He'd achieved some sort of coup at work and the chief marketing consultant had been full of praise. Now, with his glass refilled with his favourite shiraz, Jason's smile for Chloe across the dining table was fond and playful.

He even raved about the deliciousness of the fall-off-the-bone slow-cooked ribs she'd prepared. A huge relief. This night was incredibly important for her, so it had been worth getting up early to start the spare ribs and then rushing home from work at the end of the day to thicken the sauce and make Jason's favourite dessert.

She would wait until she served the choc pot before she shared her news.

At least, that had been Chloe's original plan, but just as Jason plunged his spoon through the chocolate brownie topping to the warm, gooey pudding, she wondered if it wasn't foolhardy to jump in too soon. She didn't want to spoil the pleasant mood they were enjoying. It might be wiser to wait till the meal was over and they were snuggled on the sofa.

Of course, she knew she shouldn't wait till they were actually in bed. By then, Jason might be too impatient to listen to her point of view, and it was important to be completely honest with him before she found herself pregnant.

With that thought, a thrill, both excited and nervous, shimmied through Chloe. Parenthood was a touchy subject in this household, but tonight it was the Very Important Subject she needed to raise with her boyfriend. In another week she would turn thirty-seven and her biological clock wasn't just ticking, it was clanging louder than bells on New Year's Eve.

Chloe didn't want to wait any longer. She couldn't wait any longer. She wasn't going to wait.

The time had come.

After all, she and Jason had been together for seven and a half years and almost all of their other friends were parents. Some of their friends had even married, although Chloe wouldn't push Jason to go that far. The subject of marriage had never surfaced, actually. It hadn't been necessary. They were perfectly happy as they were.

Or rather, Chloe would be perfectly happy once they'd cleared the air regarding the other, more pressing, subject.

Sadly, in the past, whenever she'd tried to bring up the possibility of starting a family, Jason had shrugged and yawned and fobbed her off with some lame excuse. Usually, he complained about the timing, or the costs of children and how they would need a bigger flat or a move to a less desirable, but more affordable, suburb.

The last time he'd thrown up one of these excuses Chloe had burst into tears and suggested that he mustn't love her.

She had to admit he'd been incredibly sweet then. Taking her in his arms, he'd vowed that of course he loved her. He was crazy about her, but he was simply too busy to think about babies at this point in time. Too overworked and stressed. He couldn't consider parenthood during the next few months.

But now Chloe's patience had finally run out. She'd reached the end of her rope two weeks ago when she visited their best friends Josie and Zac and their new baby girl, Eve.

She'd bought the sweetest little growsuit for Eve and wrapped it in pink tissue paper, and she'd called at their house in Ashfield after work. It was dusk and as Chloe mounted the steps, a golden light had shone out into the twilight through the glass panels in the front door.

Chloe could see through the glass to inside the house. Zac was in the lounge room, dressed in jeans and a shabby old T-shirt and walking slowly with his back to her.

Over his bulky shoulder peeped his tiny baby daughter. Eve had a fuzz of dark hair as black as Zac's and beady little eyes that stared unseeingly towards the porch where Chloe stood. Zac was jigging the baby gently and whispering to her as he paced slowly, patiently, across the room. With one big masculine hand he supported her bottom and with the other he patted her back gently. He might even have been singing softly to Eve and twice he pressed the gentlest of kisses to the side of her little head.

Ohhh.

The scene was so cute, so heartbreakingly poignant, Chloe's throat tightened painfully. There was no sign of Josie, and she imagined that her friend must have been resting in bed, or taking a bath while her thoughtful partner cared for their baby.

In that moment, it was all too easy for Chloe to see Jason in a similar role, to picture him being equally sweet with their own little one. So easy to imagine Jason fondly holding their tiny blanket-wrapped bundle, offering gentle pats and soothing whispers.

Chloe was so touched by that thought she was blinded by tears. Horrified that she couldn't stop their flow and afraid she might break into noisy sobs, she had set her gift on the doorstep and turned and quietly scarpered. The very last thing she'd wanted was to cause an embarrassing scene.

Josie had rung her the next day to thank her for the gift and Chloe had made up an excuse about being in a dreadful hurry. But the beautiful possibilities inspired by the sight of Zac with tiny Eve had haunted her ever since. For the past two weeks these possibilities had filled her head, kept her awake at night and in a daze of fierce longing during the day.

And now, as Jason rose from the table and took his replenished wineglass to the sofa, she knew the time had arrived. She had to speak before he switched on the TV and tuned in to his latest Netflix obsession.

'Jason.'

With the remote in one hand, his glass in the other, he looked up at her with a somewhat distracted, but good-natured, frown.

Chloe ran her tongue over suddenly dry lips. 'Before we start watching TV, there's something I need to tell you.'

Jason's frown deepened. 'What is it?'

'I —' Chloe swallowed. 'I thought you should know I've stopped taking the pill.'

'You've *what*?' The question exploded from his lips.

Defensively, Chloe threw up her hands. 'Don't be angry. Please.'

'Don't be angry?' her boyfriend echoed sarcastically and he was scowling at her now. 'You've made a drastic decision like that behind my back and you expect me to stay calm?'

He made no attempt to hide his anger as he dropped the remote and thumped his wineglass on the coffee table so roughly it was a wonder the stem didn't snap. 'It's bloody Friday night, Chloe, and I'm trying to relax. You can't drop a bombshell like that on me.'

'Well —' Chloe swallowed, tried again. 'You know I've tried to talk about starting a family plenty of times in the past, but you've never been prepared to discuss it. Not seriously.'

Jason thrust his jaw stubbornly forward. 'That doesn't give you the right to make such a huge decision without telling me.'

She knew he had a point, but for once she wasn't prepared to back down or to start apologising. Instead, she lifted her chin. 'Well, I'm telling you now.'

Jason shot her a narrow-eyed, piercing glance. 'When did you stop taking them?'

She swallowed. 'Not quite two weeks ago.'

'Fuck.' His attractive jaw dropped in appalled disbelief. 'You mean we've been screwing and you've known —'

'It's okay,' she jumped in quickly. 'I couldn't get pregnant straight away.'

'Are you sure?'

'Yes,' she responded stoutly, even though, in truth, she wasn't absolutely sure – although most websites claimed that pregnancy was highly unlikely to happen so quickly. 'The thing is, Jason, I might not be safe for much longer. Tonight – for example – there could be a remote possibility —'

Jason swore again as he glared at her.

'That's why I wanted to tell you now.'

'After priming me with food and wine first?'

Oh.

It was true that Chloe didn't normally put in such a big effort on Friday nights. If Jason wasn't going to the footie, they often opted for pizza or some other takeaway. Perhaps she had been a tad unsubtle.

Then again, desperate times required do-or-die measures.

She spoke as steadily and carefully as she could. 'I really, really want to have a baby, Jason. And as you know, I'll be thirty-seven next week. When it comes to pregnancy, I'm already considered geriatric. I'm running out of time.'

She had hoped for signs of sympathy, but Jason's face remained scarily hard and tight. 'And what if I really, really don't want a kid?'

Chloe flinched as if he'd hit her. She stared at him in shocked dismay, wondering if she'd heard him correctly. 'Not – not yet, you mean?'

Jason didn't respond.

'You don't mean —' Chloe fought off an urge to whimper. 'You don't mean . . . not ever?'

Jason still didn't give an answer to this.

Horrified, Chloe forced out the appalling but necessary question. 'You have to tell me. Don't you ever want to be a father?'

'No,' her boyfriend said simply and without a hint of apology.

A wave of dizziness swept over Chloe. She reached for a dining chair and managed to sit rather clumsily. Now she didn't care if her voice sounded plaintive. 'Why haven't you ever told me this?'

He shrugged. 'I thought you must have worked it out by now.'

Fighting tears, she blinked as a nightmarish picture of their childless, empty future loomed before her. Impossible. She'd been prepared to go to any lengths to start a family. IVF, whatever it took.

She might have sat for ages in a miserable daze, but her own anger was gathering steam. 'We've been together all this time. More than seven years. And you knew I wanted a family.'

Jason simply let out a sigh, as if he was already losing patience.

'You know this isn't fair.' Chloe made no attempt now to curb her pleading tone. 'It's not fair to me at all.'

He merely scowled. 'So it's fair to lump kids on me? Have you given any serious thought to how our lives would change? No more relaxing dinners like this, or trips to Bali – just a whole lot of crying and sleepless nights.'

'Only for the early months.'

'And what about the expense? We can't even afford to buy a bloody house. Why would we want kids as well? We'd never get ahead.'

This probably wasn't the moment to remind him that they would pay much lower rent if they moved away from Coogee to a less trendy suburb of Sydney, or that Josie and Zac were still renting half a house in Ashfield and were perfectly happy.

'I'd be prepared to keep working,' Chloe said instead. 'I could freelance, or maybe I could do a deal with Tina Jenkins and keep working for *Girl Talk* from home to save on childcare.' She crossed her fingers. Surely Jason would relent when he realised that she'd thought this through and was totally prepared to pull her weight?

The look he sent her, however, was chilling. There was a protracted, awful silence before he spoke. Then, in an icy voice: 'What makes you think you'd be such a great mother?'

Chloe couldn't have gasped louder if Jason had punched her in the stomach. The cruelty of his question shocked the breath from her. She was appalled that he could ask this. Stung to the core by the truth it revealed about his feelings for her.

What makes you think you'd be such a great mother?

Such a knife twist to the heart. How could he say something so brutal? Wasn't her longing for motherhood evidence enough that she would do her utmost to be the best mother ever?

Was the love she'd imagined – no, the love she'd believed in – a lie?

Chloe sat there, dumbstruck, agonisingly aware of the suffocating death of her dreams, of her hoped-for babies tumbling into the huge abyss that had opened up between herself and her boyfriend.

How could she have been so dumb? How could she have missed all the obvious clues to her boyfriend's true feelings about fatherhood? Which, ultimately, included his feelings about her?

Behind her, on the dining table, a candle spluttered and went out. She caught a faint whiff of smoke as Jason, stony faced, pressed the remote. The television flashed on with a bright ad for cheap flights to America. And already, a distant but persistent voice was whispering in Chloe's ear.

So this was what breaking up felt like. This was the beginning of the end.

CHAPTER TWO

Far North Queensland

The soft white mist on the surface of Lake Tinaroo began to lift as Emily paddled with one oar and skilfully turned the scull to head for home. It was almost seven o'clock in the morning and the sun had risen above the trees that rimmed the lake. Soon the silvery water would be awash with rose and gold, and the mist would be gone.

Emily, now ready for her morning coffee, rowed a little harder, her seat sliding forward as she feathered the oars' blades and then dipped them lightly into the water in the familiar rhythm that she'd learned years ago in her boarding school days. Since she'd come back to live at the Lake House five years ago, rowing was again part of her daily ritual and it was only on mornings when the rain was at its heaviest that she stayed home in bed.

Her rowing habit wasn't so much a matter of fierce self-discipline, but more that she simply loved being out on the water. She loved the silence and the solitude of the lake at this hour when the only sounds were a background symphony of bird calls and the splash and hush of her oars as they dipped and skimmed.

Most days Emily rose early, just before dawn broke, and she loved to watch the daylight gently arrive, filtering through the tree trunks, soft and pearlescent grey at first, then gradually rising, spreading and brightening, till it filled the lake and the sky with pink and blue glory. She loved the breeze on her face and the glow of physical exertion.

This morning, as she once again neared the reeds at the lake's edge, a family of ducks shot out, a small V-shaped flotilla, quacking a gentle protest. Emily smiled. Surely they must be used to her by now?

In the shallows, she stopped rowing, gripped the oars in one hand, keeping them level so that the narrow boat didn't rock as she climbed swiftly and neatly out. She didn't moor at the small jetty. Some of her friends liked to pop over in motorboats, so she left it free.

As she alighted, her dog, Murphy, a grand and elderly golden lab, was there to greet her, his tail wagging as gleefully as a puppy's.

'Hey there, old boy.' Emily couldn't pat him or greet him properly until she'd attended to the boat, but he waited patiently, his dark eyes devotedly watching her every movement as she unscrewed the row-locks and lifted the long, slim oars free. Then she dragged the boat a little higher onto the grass above the sandy bank, set the oars down and knelt to give her dog a proper welcoming scruff behind the ears. 'I know you always worry until I come back, you dear old thing.'

Lately, the dog's devotion had felt like the only stable and reliable element in Emily's life. With Murphy once again content, she stood, shouldered the oars, and carried them up to the house.

The Lake House, a rather stunning example of 1950s modernism, had been built by Emily's parents, Izzie and Geoffrey Galbraith. They had hired an architect from Sydney and, all these years later, the house built from stone and timber and glass still looked modern and exciting, but also welcoming and safe.

Emily had always loved this place, set back amid an open forest of pine trees and gums on an extremely private peninsula overlooking the water. Even as a child, Emily had been conscious of its comfort and beauty, and the magic of its lakeside setting.

During her primary school days she'd been everyone's favourite friend and, no doubt, much of that had been due to the wonderful parties and sleepovers her mother had organised at this house.

So much fun they'd had, with barbecues and campfires down by the lake, cooking sausages or toasting marshmallows on sticks. And later, camping on the living room floor with pillows and sleeping bags scattered over the white shag-pile carpet.

Emily could remember so well, lying there with her girlfriends, looking up at the timbered cathedral ceilings, giggling and whispering in the glow from the enormous stone fireplace. Then, waking at first light as dawn streamed through the huge picture windows, the girls would find her mother already in the kitchen, making massive pots of porridge with generous sprinklings of brown sugar, followed by mountains of bacon and eggs and hot buttered toast.

Even after Emily had gone away to boarding school, there'd been parties at home during the school holidays, so that she'd never really lost touch with her old friends. In those days, the Lake House had frequently been filled with excited voices and laughter.

So very different from the silence and loneliness now.

Emily shivered and a wave of dark despair threatened. *Don't be weak*, she warned herself.

If only she could be more like her mother.

Such a strong, energetic character, Izzie Galbraith had always been. Widowed before Emily was born, Izzie had continued to run the *Burralea Bugle,* the newspaper she'd started with her husband, into her old age. Emily, on the other hand, had devoted most of her life to supporting her husband, Alex, at Red Hill, their cattle property in western Queensland.

Her mother's fall and broken hip had brought them both back to dutifully care for her. Eventually, Izzie had moved into a nursing home, but while her mother's body was growing increasingly frail, her wits were as sharp as ever. Consequently, Emily felt a huge responsibility to keep her parents' small country newspaper afloat.

Especially now, with her life in a mess – with Alex deserting her and their son Robbie gone – the paper's success was even more important. Emily needed something in her life to go right.

She stowed the oars carefully in racks at the end of the garage, then removed her wet rowing shoes and set them to dry on the step by the back door.

Hanging her peaked cap on a peg in the back porch, she pulled off the elastic that tied back her silver-streaked dark hair and shook the tresses free. She dried her feet on a rag mat and padded barefoot into the sun-filled kitchen.

Here, she filled the kettle and set it to boil, spooned coffee into a glass plunger jug and checked her phone for messages. There was something from Moira Briggs about a Burralea Progress Association meeting, and she was excited to see another message from Chloe Brown, the Sydney journalist she was hoping to employ. But after almost a fortnight, there was still nothing from Alex.

Unsurprised, but nevertheless disappointed, Emily sank onto a kitchen stool. She was more or less resigned to Alex's silence, and yet she scanned through the list of messages, just to make doubly sure she hadn't missed anything.

But no, not a word, which could only mean one thing. Her husband really did mean to punish her.

CHAPTER THREE

It was a perfect Tablelands summer's morning, cool and clear with a trail of mist rising from the creek, but as soon as Finn Latimer turned into Burralea's main street, he sensed something was wrong. A small crowd had gathered outside Ben's Bakery and the usually affable locals looked distinctly unhappy.

As Finn drew nearer, an old pensioner shuffled away up the street and a grim-faced couple returned to their parked car. All these people were empty-handed, without a single pie or loaf of bread between them.

Curious, Finn ducked his dark head beneath the lavender bougainvillea that framed the bakery's front awning, and saw immediately that the shop's doors were still firmly closed.

Such an occurrence was unheard of at ten minutes past nine on a Monday morning. Ben's shop was usually open by seven. Stepping closer, Finn peered through the plate glass window, searching for any sign of activity within. He knew for a fact that Ben actually started baking his much-loved loaves, buns and pies at some ridiculous hour like four or five in the morning. Today, the shelves within the shop were bare.

'No sign of anyone,' old Ernie Cruikshank proclaimed dolefully as he sidled up beside Finn. 'I've already checked out the back. Kitchen's closed, too. Waste of time hanging about.'

Ernie looked up at Finn, his faded blue eyes still canny beneath shaggy white brows. 'Not even the courtesy of a sign in the window. *Back in five minutes* or *A death in the family*. Thought the government might've changed another public holiday without telling us, but I saw plenty of kids running around in the school yard.'

Finn nodded. 'It's definitely not a holiday.'

'Looks like we'll have to get our bread from the supermarket,' grumbled another whiskery old chap, his tone conveying quite clearly that the supermarket's offerings would be distinctly inferior to anything produced by their local bakery.

'There'll certainly be no bread here this morning,' Finn agreed, although he realised, somewhat guiltily, that he didn't sound quite as disappointed as the others.

He had, of course, already sensed a possible story for this week's edition of the *Burralea Bugle*. As the newspaper's editor – a grand title that camouflaged the fact that Finn was, in actuality, the tiny township's one and only journalist – he was, as usual, scrounging for print-worthy stories.

With a nod and a wave, Finn continued up the street, but a few doors along he discovered that the hairdresser's shop hadn't opened yet either. Now his curiosity was well and truly piqued. Tammy, the hairdresser, was Ben the baker's girlfriend.

Tammy and Ben weren't just a hot item, they both ran highly successful businesses and were counted among Burralea's most popular residents. For both their shops to be shut at this hour on a Monday morning, and without prior warning, something had to be amiss.

The police station, which could quite easily be mistaken for another of Burralea's small cottages, was located just a little further along the street. At least the door to this place was open, but as

Finn turned in through the gate, the town's reasonably new sergeant emerged, buckling on his gun holster as he hurried down the steps.

Finn greeted him with a nod. 'Morning, Cameron.'

'Can't talk now.' Sergeant Cameron Locke shot Finn a glance that was both impatient and wary.

It was a look Finn recognised. As an experienced journalist, he'd known plenty of occasions when habitually friendly and chatty coppers clammed up faster than a speeding ticket. Something was definitely on the go. Something serious. And right now, Sergeant Locke didn't want a pesky journo sticking his nose in.

But Finn Latimer had spent all his working life asking questions that people didn't want to answer. 'Is this about Ben or Tammy?'

When there was no response, Finn watched the policeman hurry to his vehicle and take off, and was hit by twin reactions of exhilaration and dismay. Like any journalist, he loved the whiff of a good story. At the same time, he hated to think that Ben or Tammy might be in trouble.

It was an age-old editor's dilemma. Most attention-grabbing headlines were a double-edged sword, selling news of gut-wrenching personal tragedy to the masses.

Before that thought had barely formed, Finn was slugged by his own dark memories. Raw, agonising memories of his final weeks as a foreign correspondent.

Thailand, oh, God.

Sarah and Louis.

No.

He couldn't, *mustn't*, think about any of that now.

Resolutely drawing a lungful of fresh morning air, Finn turned and headed back to his office, which was also in Burralea's main street. Hands sunk in jeans pockets and his head down, he once again fought the horror and guilt, steering his thoughts away from the past.

This was an endless struggle, a battle he faced every day. It was why he, Finn Latimer, a highly respected foreign correspondent, lived here in this sleepy, backwoods country town in Far North Queensland.

Most folk around these parts knew next to nothing about his past, and those few friends who did know – like Emily Hargreaves, his employer and owner of the *Burralea Bugle*, or the young cattle breeder Seth Drummond, or Mitch Cavello, the previous copper who'd recently moved to Brisbane – had been considerate enough not to pry.

Now, Finn pushed his thoughts to the present circumstances, to Ben Shaw, the cheerful, joke-cracking former surfie who'd arrived from the Gold Coast almost two years ago and whose mouth-watering pies had become an instant hit with the locals. And Tammy Holden, the town's much-loved hairdresser, with her multiple ear piercings, pink and aqua hair, and a huge fan base of customers from all over the Tablelands.

What could have happened? Finn felt sick as he considered the possibilities. Then he chastised himself. Worst-case scenarios were always counterproductive.

Setting the key in the lock, he opened the door to his office. Given the policeman's sense of urgency, Finn knew he would have to be patient. Perhaps in an hour or so, he would give the coppers a call.

Till then, he had the weekend sporting results to collate. Not exactly headline news, but in a small-town rag, getting an under-14s swimming result wrong was still catastrophic.

***

An hour had passed when Emily Hargreaves appeared in the doorway. A tall woman, somewhere in her sixties, she had thick dark hair that swung to her jawline and a dramatic silver streak that skimmed her right eyebrow. In slim jeans, a red linen shirt, silk scarf and dark lipstick, she looked elegant as ever, in good nick for her age.

Finn got on well with his employer. He liked and respected her, especially as she rarely intruded into his day and gave him free rein to run the paper as he saw fit. Emily understood that Finn's move to the *Burralea Bugle* had been a huge step down from his previous high-profile career, a necessary retreat after the trauma he'd been through.

'Morning, Emily,' he said to her now as she came into the office and crossed to the seat by the window.

'Good morning, Finn.' After her initial smile of greeting, her expression became serious and Finn wondered if anything was wrong.

She picked up a couple of brochures that he'd left on the chair and used them to flick at something – dust, or crumbs, or a dead moth – before she sat. Housework wasn't Finn's forte. It had been a while since he'd dusted or swept the office.

Emily smiled, a tad nervously. 'Do you have time for a chat?'

Finn glanced at the bottom of his computer screen where the time was displayed. He'd been about to give the police a call. He frowned. 'What's up?' She still looked nervous. 'Is there a problem?'

'Yes, I think there is,' Emily said carefully.

'Not with the paper?'

'Well, yes, I do think there's a financial issue.'

Finn's frown deepened. He sat a little straighter. 'We've maintained circulation. I think the numbers were even a shade higher last month.'

'That's true. You're doing a good job, Finn. A great job in covering the news. It's not so much the circulation that worries me.' Emily crossed her legs, crossed her arms as well. Her neatly groomed appearance looked a little out of place in the dingy office.

Finn noticed a cobweb dangling on the window behind her, its delicate weaving backlit by golden morning sunshine.

She said, 'It's the advertising that's worrying me.'

'Ahhh.' Finn grimaced. 'I'll admit I don't pay much attention to the ads. That's not really my field. I pretty much leave it all to Don and Karen.' These were two casuals – a retired farmer and a young mum who worked a few hours a week while her kids were in school. 'You want me to have a word with them? Keep a closer eye on things?'

He was a realist, after all, and he knew damn well that newspapers relied on advertising, especially small weekly newspapers in country towns. Country rags were an endangered species. Hundreds in regional Australia had already fallen by the wayside. Many more had been bought out by either Murdoch or Fairfax. It was a minor miracle that the *Bugle* had retained its independence for so long.

Emily's smile was gentle. Sympathetic. 'I'm not asking *you* to do anything, Finn. I don't think you could work any harder than you already do. God knows how many hours you put in doing everything here on your own. Gathering the news, editing, layout.'

Finn shrugged. He never kept track of the hours he worked. Staying busy was the best way to fight his demons. 'You know I don't mind.'

'But we don't want you burning out.' Emily drew a deep breath, almost as if she were gathering courage. 'I've actually given this a lot of thought, and I believe what we need is another journalist.'

'Seriously?' Finn knew he sounded shocked. After a beat, he said more evenly, 'How does that work? You've already said the news coverage is fine. With another journo, you'd be adding an extra wage to your costs.'

'That's true, but I'm thinking of someone who could back you up, and also write the kinds of stories that attract more advertising.'

She waved a hand as she expanded on this. 'Stories about new local businesses, new products – lifestyle stories.'

'Advertorials?' Finn said bitterly, not even trying to hide his distaste.

'Is that what you call them?'

Finn nodded, pulled a face. 'I'm not sure you'll find a decent news journalist who'd want to concentrate on that kind of writing.'

After a beat, Emily said, 'Actually, I think I may have found someone.'

Finn had difficulty covering his reaction of surprise. 'You mean you've already employed someone?'

'Nothing's been finalised. I wouldn't go that far without speaking to you first. But I admit I have put out feelers. And I've interviewed a young woman who's had plenty of experience working on women's magazines.'

Women's magazines? Emily had to be joking. Finn had thumbed through the odd women's mag when he'd been hanging out in waiting rooms, and he couldn't believe the rot they published. Ridiculous diets of cabbage soup, or consuming nothing but green juice. Bizarre beauty advice like cupping the lips with a shot glass to make them fuller, or using haemorrhoid cream to de-puff the eyes.

The last thing this paper needed in this strictly rural town was a bubble-headed female writing that kind of crap. The *Bugle*'s customers were farmers and their families, practical, hard-working, no-bullshit folk. If he printed diet and beauty nonsense, the paper would tank in a matter of weeks.

'Don't look like that,' Emily said.

Finn continued to scowl. 'Sorry,' he said dryly, but it's hard to smile when you come up with such a crazy suggestion.'

'I thought you'd be more open-minded.'

This hit home. Finn prided himself on being free of prejudice. 'So you expect me to be pleased when you're sending me a *Dolly* reporter? Probably so lightweight, she'll have to stay away from ceiling fans.'

'Finn, be serious.'

'I *am* serious. You want me to stand aside while the front page is taken over by recipes and fashion tips?'

His employer dismissed this with an impatient huff. 'I'll rise above that comment. I didn't think you'd be so foolish about this.'

Finn drummed his fingers on the desk. Was he being foolish? Surely his reaction was justified. He'd brought a wealth of professional experience to this little country rag and he'd given it his all.

If he was honest, though, he couldn't totally explain why the prospect of sharing the office with a city-girl magazine reporter annoyed him. Was it dented pride? Irritation at the extra work required to train her? Or was it fear that she might try to shake him out of the safe, hermit-like hole he'd dug for himself here?

Emily was frowning as she watched him. 'Are you really angry with me?' she asked. 'Or is there something else bothering you?'

Finn grabbed the opportunity to change the subject. 'Something else. I think there's actually something very serious happening right now, under our very noses.'

'Really?'

'You didn't notice that the bakery and the hairdresser shops are both still shut?'

'Well, no. I suppose I've been too busy plucking up the courage to broach this with you.' Even as Emily admitted this, the implication of Finn's words must have sunk in. Her dark eyes widened. 'Goodness. Do you think something's happened to Tammy and Ben?'

'It seems so. I put it on Cameron Locke this morning, but he wouldn't speak to me. Just took off like a bat out of hell. I was about to call him when you came in. There's a chance he'll have some news by now and he might be prepared to talk.'

'Well, yes, of course. Ring him. We can finish discussing this later.' Emily waved a hand in the direction of Finn's phone. 'We certainly need to know about Ben and Tammy.'

This time, when Finn posed his question, the sergeant was prepared to oblige.

'Ben Shaw's missing,' he said. 'He left for a jog on the Possum Ridge track near Lake Barrine yesterday afternoon and he hasn't been seen since. Looks like he might have stumbled on a little drug-cooking operation. About five kilometres in, there's a burnt-out camp not too far off the track. No one there now, of course, but we found the remains of a gas cooker and traces of chemicals.'

'What about Tammy Holden?' Finn asked. 'She's Ben's girlfriend and she hasn't opened her salon this morning.'

'That's because she was over at Possum Ridge at first light searching for Ben. Seems she found his cap near the hut. She's pretty shaken.'

'Shit.' This didn't sound good.

'That's all I can tell you at the moment,' the sergeant said. 'I've contacted Mareeba and the CIB, of course, and we're in the process of setting up a full-scale search.'

'Yeah, I'm sure you're busy, mate. Well, thanks for the update.' As Finn hung up, he shot a glance in Emily's direction. 'It's entirely up to you whether we need a *Dolly* reporter for the *Bugle*. In the meantime, I have some serious news to chase.'

CHAPTER FOUR

Sixteen hours earlier . . .

Ben Shaw had never expected to love the rainforest. He was a surfer. Three generations of his family had lived on the Gold Coast and a love of the ocean was in his DNA. His earliest memory was the salty smell of the sea and the excitement of small waves slapping over his chubby toddler toes. No question, the hardest part of moving north had been giving up his morning board-riding ritual. Luckily, Ben's desire to start a new life had held an even stronger allure.

These days, his mornings began in the bakery when it was still pitch black and the roads were empty. Long before dawn he was hefting heavy bags of flour, measuring out live yeast, sugar, salt and water, and pouring them into the huge mixer. Breakfast was several cups of tea drunk on the hoof while dividing up the various doughs and rolling them into loaves or buns.

He would add extra seeds to some, cheese to others, or rosemary and olives. And then there was the pastry to be rolled for meat pies, his customers' favourites.

Ben didn't mind the hard work. The satisfaction and honest toil of owning a successful business made up for some crazy mistakes in his past.

Just the same, he was striving for the whole work-life balance thing, which wasn't easy given that his partner, Tammy, was also busy with her hairdressing business. Ben had settled on an afternoon run to replace surfing for his fitness fix. By then, his shop's shelves were almost depleted and he could leave young Melanie Frith to serve behind the counter.

Jogging through a rainforest track could never replace the thrill of riding a perfect wave, but Ben had learned there were definite rewards to this new lifestyle. The birdsong in the forest was amazing, and the run took him beneath a massive green canopy arching metres above, where shards of light reached through branches, making patterns with shadows, and small creatures such as pademelons scurried off the track.

This afternoon, however, new tyre tracks leading off into the scrub snagged Ben's attention. He stopped jogging. The tracks had probably been made by forestry blokes, or researchers. There was a team from James Cook University looking for giant quolls, the ones with the spotted tails.

Two of the researchers had become regulars in his shop. Both lean, bearded fellows – one always ordered a curry pie and his mate preferred the vegetarian chilli. Interesting blokes to have a yarn with. Ben had discovered all kinds of fascinating folk on the Tablelands, and he liked mixing with them. Anyway, whether or not these new tracks were made by these scientists, they were worth a quick gander.

He wouldn't go far.

He didn't have to. About three hundred metres in, Ben skidded to a stop. Just ahead, a mud-splattered four-wheel drive was parked. And beside it stood a small demountable shed, the sort that could be flat-packed and assembled with a spanner and a screwdriver. The shed was about the size of a small room and covered with the green shade cloth normally used for garden nurseries.

Whoah. The mesh looked more like camouflage than shade.

Suspicion slithered down Ben's spine. He was pretty damn sure this wasn't a scientists' hideout and his instinct was to get away from there. Fast.

But before he could move, he heard a footstep behind him. When he spun round, he came face to face with a middle-aged man with long, greasy greying hair. The guy was wearing green overalls and he was pointing a shotgun at Ben's chest.

Shit. Ben threw up his hands. 'Steady on, mate. No problems.'

The guy in overalls stepped forward, glaring, still aiming for Ben.

'I know this is none of my business,' Ben said. 'I'm just on a jog.' *Don't do anything stupid*, he begged silently.

Panicked possibilities flashed through Ben's mind. He could try to run. Perhaps not a great idea when he was covered by a shotgun.

He could grab the gun and disarm this prick. Yeah, and that would be sure to result in this crazy bloke pulling the trigger.

Maybe this was a simple misunderstanding that could be sorted out quickly?

Maybe not.

Keeping the gun still levelled at Ben, the guy in the overalls yelled, 'Hawk, get out here.'

'Wha-a-at?' called a muffled voice from inside the hut. 'I'm busy.'

'We've been sprung.'

Fuck. Now Ben was gripped by real panic. This was no small misunderstanding. As a second man ambled out of the shed, he knew he was in grave freaking danger.

This second guy was wearing spray painter's goggles and a safety mask. He was younger, stockier, with muscular, tattooed arms and very short hair. Slowly, he lifted the goggles to reveal cold grey eyes. He pulled the mask from his mouth.

'What are we gonna do, Norman?' he asked the guy holding the gun. 'I haven't even finished the first cook-up.'

Ben's worst fears were now confirmed. He'd stumbled onto a lab producing ice. One of the worst possible drugs with highly dangerous producers and pushers.

Ben's experience with a bunch of surfies using pot and ecstasy on the Gold Coast had cost him a criminal conviction, a term on a prison farm and a police record . . . but that paled into insignificance beside this mob.

No doubt they were producing ice in various remote locations, as well as in the cities. The shed was easily demountable, so they had a portable operation. But Ben knew this sort of set-up was never a two-man operation. There were sure to be big-time crims involved.

Norman, with the shotgun, now motioned to the guy called Hawk and handed him the weapon, making sure the muzzle was still pointed at Ben.

'Here's what you're gonna do,' he told Hawk. 'This is your chance to do more than play the boy scientist with your chemicals. It's time to show you're really one of us.'

Hawk's gaze narrowed as he kept the gun pointing at Ben, but it was hard to tell his reaction to these instructions.

'Take this turkey down to that old mine shaft we found,' the older man said. 'Top him and drop him down it.'

'You're crazy,' Ben cried. 'I wouldn't —'

'Shut up,' yelled the older man, while Hawk took another step closer, still keeping the gun levelled at Ben's chest.

Aghast, Ben managed to suppress another desperate urge to protest. To explain. To beg.

'We don't want to do it here,' Norman went on. 'We'd have to bury the unlucky bastard and, if you've noticed, we don't have a fucking shovel.' He heaved a sigh, as if the troubles of the world were on his shoulders and not on Ben's. 'I'm not interested in dragging a heavy bloke like this fucker through all that scrub,' he said. 'So you walk him down to the shaft and do it in one hit.'

To Ben's dismay, Hawk didn't protest. He merely stood, frowning, until Norman made an impatient, shooing gesture. 'Just get on with it and then we'll torch this place and get out. This shitstorm is all thanks to you, you know. You said you could be trusted to find a good spot.'

Ben swallowed the glob of fear in his throat. He was sure he was too shocked and scared to think straight, but he tried to comfort himself that at least he wasn't dead yet. He knew there was no point in pleading.

His only hope was to make a run for it once they were out of Norman's sight. One on one with Hawk, he might just have a chance.

If he stumbled a bit, he might get close enough to grab the gun and throw his best punch. Hawk wasn't a big bloke. Ben was fit and strong and reckoned he could tackle him easily if he didn't have a gun.

Just the same, dread settled like concrete in his belly as he and Hawk set off through the thick, trackless scrub, ducking dangling vines and hopping over tangled tree roots. Sure enough, a walk through the forest quickly lost its charm when a gun was pointed at him.

Ben waited till they were out of Norman's earshot before he started to plead. 'You know you don't have to do this,' he told Hawk. 'Think about the consequences if you get caught for murder.'

'Shut up and keep walking,' came the snarled reply.

A few metres on, Ben tried again. 'You're bound to get caught eventually. And Norman's going to blame you. That's why he wants you to do the dirty work, so he's got someone else to blame.'

Hawk didn't bother to respond to this. He simply kept Ben well covered with the shotgun. And he also kept his distance, making Ben's stumbling and punching plans impossible.

Eventually, ahead in a clearing, was a stand of well-weathered old timber posts. Some of the posts were covered with vines, but despite the overgrowth, it was easy to see the partly overgrown, gaping hole in the ground.

The mine shaft. Ben's stomach dropped as if his body had already been tossed down into those black depths. His skin was slick with sweat, but he bloody well wasn't going to just stand around and let himself be executed. He'd rather attack and fight for his life.

As he clenched his fists, however, Hawk stepped even further away. Out of reach.

Ben lunged forward. 'No, you don't.'

The note of warning in Hawk's voice brought Ben to a halt. There'd been no sense of threat in his tone.

'Listen very carefully,' Hawk said quietly. 'And keep your mouth shut. You're not going to be shot. Not by me at any rate.'

Not going to be shot. The words circled in Ben's head. Weak with relief, he grabbed at a vine to keep himself upright.

'I'm a Fed working undercover,' Hawk went on. 'I'm going to fire a shot to convince Norman I've done my job, and you're going to sneak out of here.'

Ben nodded, hardly daring to believe his bloody amazing luck.

CHAPTER FIVE

Chloe had never flown into Cairns before, so she found herself glued to the plane's window, taking in as many details as she could of the steep cloud-wreathed mountains rising out of the shining aquamarine sea. She'd always thought Sydney Harbour was spectacular from the air, but the far north was just as stunning. And yet, so different, she almost felt as if she'd arrived in another country.

'Coming home, or arriving on holiday?' enquired Chloe's plump, grandmotherly neighbour, who'd been asleep for most of the flight.

'I'm actually starting a new job,' Chloe told her.

'Aha.' The woman beamed at her. 'Welcome to the north. You're going to love it. I moved up here more than forty years ago and now I never want to have to live in the crowded, cold south again.'

'That's good to hear.' Chloe was feeling a little nervous about the huge step she'd taken.

She'd been so impulsive. Yikes, most girls had rebound romances after they split up with their boyfriends, but she was having an entire rebound lifestyle. She had resigned from her job at *Girl Talk* magazine to work on a tiny newspaper at the other end of the country.

The decision hadn't been easy, of course.

When Chloe had first realised that she must leave Jason, she'd imagined she would find a one-bedroom flat in Sydney and stay on at *Girl Talk*, while investigating her options for IVF as a single mum. But she'd felt so let down and disappointed and generally pissed off – and a bit of an idiot, too – for having stayed so long in a relationship that was obviously going nowhere. She'd decided that a clean break was needed. A fresh start with new opportunities to explore.

The hard part had been telling her family. Chloe's two sisters were both married with good jobs, super-successful husbands and two beautiful children apiece, and Chloe had hated having to reveal her disastrous failure on the relationship and family front.

Her mum had tried to be understanding, but she'd spoiled it by commenting that she'd never been sure about Jason.

'There were important little clues,' she'd told Chloe, unhelpfully. 'I always noticed that at family barbecues Jason never once offered to help your dad to flip steaks, or to help me with carrying out the salads, or carting the dirty plates back to the kitchen.'

Chloe supposed her mum had been trying to reassure her that she'd done the right thing by leaving Jason. Unfortunately, her comments had only added to Chloe's huge sense of failure. The urge to get away had been overwhelming.

Of course, Chloe couldn't be sure if she was running away or making a bold new move, and she suspected that her neighbour might have plied her with more advice or questions if the plane hadn't touched down just then. As they taxied over the tarmac, the pilot welcomed them to Cairns, while passengers throughout the plane reached for their phones.

So, this was it. She couldn't turn back now.

Chloe dug her phone out of her bag, hoping to find a message from her new editor, Finn Latimer. The newspaper's owner, Emily

Hargreaves, had assured her that he would be waiting for her in the arrivals hall, having driven down the range from Burralea on the Tablelands.

While her phone came to life, she shot another glance through the small window to the majestic green mountains that towered behind Cairns. Somewhere up there beyond those sky-piercing hills, her future and her new job at the *Burralea Bugle* awaited her.

Thinking of the journey yet to come, Chloe was aware of a tingling in her spine, and her decision to head north no longer felt slightly crazy, but suddenly more like an admirable adventure.

Her excitement fizzled a little, though, when she checked her phone and there was no message from Finn Latimer.

Oh, well. Perhaps he was still waiting for confirmation that her plane had landed.

The plane trundled to a halt and the cabin was filled with the sound of unclicking seatbelts, of overhead storage lockers being opened as passengers scrambled to collect gear. Chloe, hemmed in next to the window, checked her phone again but there were no new messages.

That was cool. Perhaps Finn Latimer was running a bit late. It was probably quite a long, windy drive down the mountain.

Chloe was determined not to start worrying. Nothing would hassle her today. Over recent weeks, she'd already been through the worst.

This was the start of a brand-new chapter in her life. Positivity and optimism were her watchwords.

By the time Chloe reached the baggage carousel, there was still no message from Finn Latimer. While the suitcases and boxes trundled past on the conveyor belt, she scanned the faces of the men in the crowd, but it wasn't a lot of use when she didn't really know what her new boss looked like. She hadn't spoken to him during the interview process, which had been conducted via email and Skype with Emily Hargreaves.

Emily had been very warm and reassuring, but later, when Chloe had looked up her new editor on the internet, she could only find photos and information about a foreign correspondent. This guy was a tall, commanding figure with a lot of shaggy dark hair and a longish face that was rugged rather than handsome. Chloe could remember having seen him on television. He was a hotshot reporter who covered the world's major trouble spots. No way would he be working on a tiny country newspaper in Far North Queensland.

Chloe had come to the logical conclusion that the *Burralea Bugle*'s editor must almost certainly be the foreign correspondent's father. It wasn't unusual for fathers and sons to share names and career choices, and it made sense that her boss at the *Bugle* would be an old codger. Emily had mentioned his vast experience, so he'd probably been working on newspapers since before computers, in the days of hard copy and hot metal. Maybe when the crowd around the carousel dispersed, she would see him waiting patiently off to one side.

Chloe's suitcase arrived and she managed to heave it successfully from the flowing luggage stream. With the handle extended, she hitched the strap of her laptop bag over her shoulder. Great. She was organised. Ready and raring to go.

She turned, scanning the thinning crowd of tourists and locals, searching for a lone figure, probably a man around her father's age, nudging retirement. His hair would no longer be dark like his son's and, after years of staring at computer screens, he could well be wearing glasses. If he was a rural type, he might be a bit red and wrinkled. *Lost a bit of bark*, as her dad might say. He might even wear jeans and an Akubra . . .

Unfortunately, Chloe couldn't see anyone who fitted any version of this imagined persona. In fact, apart from a couple of earnest fellows holding up placards with other people's names, she couldn't see any man – old, young, dark haired or bald – who seemed to be standing alone and waiting.

As the passengers from her flight filled their luggage carts and drifted away, she allowed herself a small moment of worry. Perhaps Emily Hargreaves had forgotten to pass on her phone number to Finn Latimer, although that seemed rather unlikely. Perhaps he'd been held up on the road for some reason. Apparently, it was more than an hour's drive down from Burralea to Cairns.

It was even possible that an important news story had broken and he hadn't been able to get away. But under those circumstances, wouldn't any reasonable editor have sent his new journalist a message?

Really, Chloe knew she only had one option. She texted her new boss.

Have arrived in Cairns. Awaiting instructions. Kind regards, Chloe Brown.

An hour later, having received no reply and then having tried to ring through to Finn Latimer, only to receive a growling voice message, Chloe stood in line at the car-hire desk. It was a move she probably should have taken much sooner. If she was honest, she'd never really felt comfortable with the idea of her boss driving all the way from Burralea to collect her from the airport, but she had supposed it must be the way things were done in the country.

Now, she could only assume that the well-meaning Emily, who hadn't shared her own phone number and wasn't answering emails, had got her wires crossed. At least the hire car queue wasn't long, but Chloe wished she felt more confident about driving solo up into those big green mountains.

In Sydney, Jason had hardly ever allowed her to drive his car and she'd mostly used public transport to get to and from work. At work there'd been taxi vouchers. In fact, the last time she'd driven a car had been last Christmas, when she'd taken her parents home from a party at her sister's place, using their vehicle, because they'd had a few drinks.

Of course, in her new job, Chloe would be required to drive about the countryside to gather stories. Emily had told her that the *Bugle* had its own vehicle, which she could share with Finn. That prospect had been a tad daunting, until Chloe told herself it would be pleasant to drive on rural roads, even with the odd pothole, far better than fighting heavy city traffic.

As the queue shuffled forward, Chloe smiled at the woman behind her. She was young, with a wide-eyed baby in her arms – a cute little girl with dark hair and a round face and rather solemn grey eyes. The woman was tall and slim, with tawny hair pulled tightly back from her face into a ponytail. She had a luggage trolley beside her piled with suitcases and a folded pram and what might have been a dismantled high chair bandaged in bubble wrap. She had the kind of unremarkable face that signalled common sense and reliability, until she smiled back at Chloe, and suddenly she seemed to light up and look unexpectedly pretty.

'It's even warmer up here than I expected,' she said conversationally.

'Yes,' Chloe agreed. 'I've already shed two layers. Where have you come from?'

'Sydney.'

'Me too.'

They smiled in the way strangers do when they discover a small coincidence.

'I'm heading up to the Tablelands, though,' the woman said next. 'It probably won't be as hot up there.'

'I hope not,' said Chloe. 'I'm going that way, too. To Burralea.'

'No way.' The woman laughed. 'So am I.' She looked down at her little baby, then grinned at Chloe. 'Perhaps we should share a car?'

It seemed, quite simply, the obvious thing to do.

CHAPTER SIX

Chloe's travelling companions were Jess and Willow. Jess was going to start a new job in Burralea, too, as a waitress in the Lilly Pilly café. Willow was her daughter, but Jess made no mention of Willow's father and Chloe didn't like to ask. Given her own postponed plans for motherhood, however, she was a little envious.

Willow, clutching a garish purple and green–spotted elephant, settled quite cooperatively into her special seat in the back of the hire car. As they headed out of the city, she stuck her thumb in her mouth and obligingly nodded off to sleep. Before long the road wound upwards, climbing through semi-open eucalyptus forests that were replaced, as they got higher, by monstrous rainforest trees, giant ferns and clumps of ginger.

Between patches of surprisingly comfortable silence, Chloe and Jess – who was driving, much to Chloe's relief – enjoyed a quiet chat. It seemed neither of them knew a great deal about the town they were heading for. Jess had accommodation organised: she and Willow would be sharing a house with another woman called Hannah who worked at the café.

'Have you been able to find childcare for Willow?' Chloe couldn't help asking.

'Amazingly, there was a vacancy at the centre right in the middle of Burralea,' said Jess. 'I was so lucky. And I'm hoping that by sharing the house, I'll be able to afford to work just three days a week.'

'Sounds perfect.' Chloe said this with perhaps a little more enthusiasm than was warranted, but the idea of a single mother and her little daughter settling down and making a new life in a country town seemed incredibly appealing. Again, she felt a twinge of envy. 'So what made you choose Burralea?'

To her surprise, a tide of pink rose up Jess's neck and into her cheeks. 'I searched on the internet and it – it just looked like such a pretty place. A nice size. And Hannah, the woman I'm sharing with, is a distant relation. Her grandmother and my grandmother were cousins.'

'So you won't be living with a complete stranger. That's even better,' Chloe said warmly.

'Yes, fingers crossed it all works out. What about you?' asked Jess. 'Where will you stay?'

'I don't have anywhere permanent yet. I'm going to be working at the little Burralea newspaper.'

'Really? As a journalist?'

'Yes.'

'That's so cool. Emily Hargreaves owns that paper, doesn't she?'

'Yes,' Chloe said, surprised. 'Do you know her?'

'No.' Again, Jess's face grew quite pink. 'I – I met someone who mentioned they knew her.'

Chloe waited, expecting Jess to expand on this, but instead she tightened her lips and stared rather glumly ahead, almost as if she wished she hadn't spoken up. Which was rather puzzling.

When it was clear the topic of Emily was closed, Chloe said, 'I'm just booked into the pub for now. I thought I'd suss out the job before I look around for somewhere to rent.'

Jess nodded. 'Fair enough.' Then she flashed Chloe another of her unexpectedly brilliant smiles. 'So we're both making fresh starts.'

'Good for us.' Chloe was grateful, actually, that her travelling companion was as cautious as she was about sharing too much info about the whys and wherefores of their decisions.

If Jess had been the *super* chatty kind, she might have wanted to offload her personal history, and Chloe might have felt compelled to share some of her sorry saga with Jason. The arguments and tears, the hurt of Jason's final, brutal admission that he probably didn't totally love her.

In many ways she'd been grieving. Breaking up was a kind of death.

Now, Chloe was leaving behind everything that was familiar, as well as everything she wanted to forget. So she was relieved that Jess was happy to chat about their conventionally boring families instead. Jess's father had been in the Air Force, so they'd moved around a lot.

'I've had plenty of experience at being the new kid,' she said with a rueful smile.

'And I've had no experience,' Chloe admitted. 'I've always lived in Sydney. I went to the same school for twelve years. This is my first big move.'

'A big move to a very small town.'

'Yeah.'

Before Chloe had time to wonder afresh if her decision had been way too rash, the winding road emerged from the rainforest, opening out to a vista of rolling green farmland.

'Wow,' Jess exclaimed. 'Look at that.'

'Isn't it lovely?' If Chloe had been driving, she might have allowed herself a moment to pull over, to stop and drink in the spectacle, the rippling spill of tablelands, the sweep of cattle-dotted pastures, of ploughed fields, of valleys and hills and a distant cluster of rooftops where a small town nestled.

'Toto,' she said, in a fake American accent, 'I've a feeling we're not in Kansas any more.'

'And we're most definitely not in Sydney, thank God,' said Jess.

Chloe tried to imagine the red-tiled rooftops of Sydney filling every gap in this tranquil rural landscape that stretched before them to the far green horizon.

No way.

Right in this moment, she was more than happy to swap busy city suburbs for winding back roads and paddocks of black and white cows. 'I think I just might be able to manage living in a place like this,' she said.

'Yeah,' Jess agreed with a grin. 'Me too.'

Chloe might have felt completely relaxed if she hadn't been concerned about the unexplained silence from her new boss at the *Burralea Bugle*.

Burralea's main street consisted of a row of quaint shops, circa 1920s, many of which were painted in pretty pastels and fronted by footpaths adorned with pot plants and hanging baskets that spilled bright flowers. The *Burralea Bugle*, housed within one of these shops, was like no other newspaper office Chloe had seen.

Her previous office at *Girl Talk* had been on the fourth floor of a multi-storey glass and steel building and protected by a huge Polynesian guard at the front door, while the inner doors had coded keypads. By contrast, the *Bugle*'s pale blue and white–panelled door was closed but not locked, and when Chloe gave it a tentative push, it swung open with an ominous creak, not unlike the sound effects in a horror movie.

A tremor whispered down her spine. She turned back to Jess who sent her a cheery wave and drove off.

So. It was early afternoon, a grim, grey afternoon. The clouds had rolled in as Chloe and Jess approached Burralea, bringing a misty, drizzling rain that created a sense of gloom. To add to the weirdness, there were no lights on inside the newspaper office, but Chloe could see a lone figure in the middle of the room. A man. Slumped at a desk, folded forward, his head resting on his arms.

Dear God.

Alarmed, she flipped the nearest switch and light flooded the otherwise empty office. Instantly, an agonised groan erupted from the apparently comatose man. 'What the —!'

Chloe's spirits, which had been rapidly sinking, now took a headlong dive through the floorboards. What the hell had she got herself into? Cautiously, she closed the door, set down her suitcase and laptop and unhappily stepped forward.

The room reeked of alcohol, probably whisky, and, to make matters worse, she recognised the slumped figure. There was no mistaking the shock of black shaggy hair and the forbidding, stubble-covered visage that somehow seemed threatening even when he appeared to be asleep.

Somehow, some-*crazy*-how, Finn Latimer, the famous foreign correspondent, was here. At the *Burralea Bugle*. Dead drunk, judging by the almost-empty bottle of scotch, plus the greasy tumbler on the desk beside one of his outstretched hands, as if he'd passed out before he could pour the final snifter.

Chloe's first instinct was to turn and run. This was also her second instinct, which was damned disappointing considering the gusto with which she'd embraced the whole idea of heading north to a new job and a new life.

She might have acted on her new escapee impulse, if Finn Latimer hadn't stirred at that moment. With another groan, he lifted his head and squinted as if the light was blinding.

From beneath an untidy fall of black hair, he took a cautious sideways glance in Chloe's direction and winced, as if any small movement hurt. 'Who are you?' he growled, his voice as deep as a gravel pit.

Chloe lifted her chin and pushed her shoulders back. 'Chloe Brown.'

He shook his head and winced again. 'Doesn't ring a bell. What do you want?'

'I believe I'm expected to start work here today.' She was probably foolish to have admitted this. Surely a wise woman would have left immediately, while she still had a fighting chance.

Frowning at her, Finn Latimer took his time to respond. 'So you're Dolly?' he said at last.

'Um – no. My name's Chloe. Chloe Brown. Emily Hargreaves interviewed me for a job as a journalist with this paper.'

'Yeah, yeah.' He let out a heavy sigh, then rubbed at his grizzled jaw with a large, long-fingered hand. He was wearing scruffy blue jeans and a white business shirt, rather crumpled and grubby, with the sleeves rolled back to the elbows. 'Emily warned me, of course. She said she'd signed up a reporter from *Dolly*.' He glared at Chloe through dishevelled strands of hair. 'You *are* from one of the women's magazines, aren't you?'

'Yes,' Chloe said, although she was rather proud of the fact that *Girl Talk*, despite its frivolous sounding name, catered for a far more serious and mature audience than this man obviously imagined.

'I'm sorry,' Finn Latimer said next. 'You've caught me on a bad day.'

The apology surprised Chloe. She wondered how many bad days Finn Latimer normally experienced in any given week. If he had a drinking problem, she supposed that might explain why he'd left his high-profile post as a foreign correspondent to work on a tin-pot weekly in a tiny country town that no one had ever heard of.

Perhaps he'd had no option?

Finn was now looking glumly at the bottle and glass on the desk in front of him. 'Shit,' he said, almost, but not quite, under his breath. 'Is it —' He paused for a moment and frowned again, as if he was struggling with a difficult problem. 'Is it Tuesday?'

'Yes,' said Chloe.

'Shit,' he said again. 'Was I supposed to collect you from the airport?'

'I – I think so.'

'Damn. How did you get here?'

'A hire car.'

Finn closed his eyes, propped his elbows on the table and let his head sink into his hands. The pose seemed to draw inappropriate attention to how wide his shoulders were.

'How late is it?' he asked.

'Well, it's afternoon.' Chloe pulled her phone from her jacket pocket. '2.53 p.m. to be exact.'

He let out another ragged sigh, ran a large hand over his face. He looked terrible, his face too pale in contrast with the midnight hair, his cheeks lined by deep parallel creases that disappeared into dark stubble flecked with grey. 'I've got to get this bloody paper out.'

Chloe was aware that the *Bugle* was a weekly, but Emily Hargreaves hadn't mentioned which day it came out. 'When's your deadline?' she asked.

'Tonight. Six o'clock.'

Gulp. Chloe had no idea how much work still needed to be done, but after almost a decade at *Girl Talk*, her instincts to meet a deadline were deeply ingrained. Pushing aside any lingering tiredness from her early start and long journey from Sydney, she said, 'Perhaps I can help?' Not that this oaf deserved her help.

'Thanks. Be a good girl and get me a coffee?'

At this, she bristled and, again, she was tempted to walk out. Her days as a junior and general office dogsbody were well behind her, although this probably wasn't a useful time to try to set Finn Latimer straight.

Still smarting, she scanned the office, but she couldn't see anything that looked remotely like coffee-making facilities. 'Is there another room with a kettle?'

His mouth tilted in what might have been a grotesque attempt to smile. 'Café on the corner. They know how I like it. Put it on my tab.'

'Oh. Right.'

'And make sure you get a coffee for yourself, too.'

'How kind.' This time, the sudden gleam in Finn's dark eyes showed that he hadn't missed her sarcasm. 'Would you like anything to eat?' she asked as her stomach gave a small rumble. It felt like ages since she'd had a coffee and croissant at Cairns airport.

Finn placed a tentative hand against his stomach, which Chloe couldn't help noticing was surprisingly flat. But then, alcoholics didn't eat much, did they? He grimaced. 'No, no food, just coffee.'

CHAPTER SEVEN

I'm an idiot, Chloe told herself as she unearthed an umbrella from the outside pocket of her suitcase and headed down the street through the drizzling rain. Why on earth had she even dreamed it might be fun to work on a little country newspaper? Shouldn't she have known that no self-respecting journalist would want to take up such an ignominious post? Of course her boss would be a Neanderthal. Or a drunk. And no woman in her right mind would hang around in this job.

Emily Hargreaves had conned her well and truly, waxing lyrical about the wonderful community spirit in Burralea, the beauty of the surrounding countryside, the wide range of activities to report on, the opportunities to focus on women's stories. Pity she hadn't mentioned the alcoholic, misogynist editor. Working with Finn Latimer would be about as pleasant and fulfilling as walking the plank.

Chloe didn't have time to give full vent to the depth of her distress before she reached the end of the street and discovered the café on the corner, another quaint building surrounded by greenery and pot plants. It was, in fact, the same Lilly Pilly café where Jess was going to work.

Delicious smells of coffee and baking, along with hearty gusts of laughter, greeted her as she entered through a side door.

Half the space inside the café was taken up by an open-plan kitchen where smiling women in floral aprons were madly gossiping or telling jokes as they made sandwiches, cut up freshly baked quiche slices or worked the coffee machine.

Perhaps the stories about friendly country folk weren't just urban myths after all? At least Jess would have a cheerful workplace.

The counter that separated this noisy kitchen from the customers' tables and chairs held large glass jars filled with tempting cookies and beside these a framed sign: *Unattended children will be given an espresso and a kitten.*

Chloe laughed, surprising herself. She hadn't laughed nearly enough in recent weeks.

Yet another smiling woman standing at the counter asked, 'How can I help you?'

'I'd like a coffee for Finn Latimer,' Chloe said. 'I believe you know how he has it?'

'Sure.' The woman took an extra not-so-subtle look at Chloe from beneath long mascara-darkened lashes, before writing a few hieroglyphics on a pad. 'Takeaway long black, two sugars.'

'And I'll have a flat white,' Chloe said. 'No sugar, but perhaps I might also have —' She turned to look at the tempting goodies beside her.

She'd had no lunch so she knew she should choose something sensible and nourishing like a piece of spinach and feta quiche, but the thought of returning to the *Bugle* office to a boss with a very sore head somehow weakened her resolve. 'And I'll have a chocolate brownie.' Chocolate was supposed to be good for lifting a person's mood and her mood obviously needed a huge boost this afternoon.

'I'll have them for you in a jiffy,' the woman said.

'How much do I owe you?'

'No need.' The woman grinned. 'The *Bugle*'s got you covered.'

She laughed and Chloe noticed a poster on the wall behind her which said exactly the same thing – *The Bugle's got you covered.*

Finn Latimer was awake with his computer turned on and he was typing madly when Chloe got back to the office. The whisky bottle and the glass had disappeared and the place didn't reek quite so badly of alcohol.

'Here's your coffee,' she said, setting a cardboard mug down beside Finn. 'I thought you might like these, too.' She slipped a packet of aspirin onto the desk. 'I was passing the chemist.'

His eyebrows lifted. 'Thanks. That's – good of you.'

He didn't invite Chloe to sit down, but she helped herself to a chair at another desk where a second computer had been turned on. She turned to face the screen and took a reviving sip of coffee. 'Mmm, good coffee.'

'You sound surprised,' Finn said with the barest hint of a smile. 'You know they grow coffee up here.'

'Really? No, I didn't know that.' Chloe tucked this info away as something she might investigate later. It could make a good story – coffee from tree to cup. *If* she decided to stay here. Which was still highly unlikely. 'Now,' she said in her most businesslike tone. 'What would you like me to do?'

'Well, if you could cover the rounds, that would be very useful.'

The rounds. Chloe experienced a moment of panic. Her brief from Emily Hargreaves had been clear. She was to leave the hard news to Finn and concentrate on colour stories that would attract new advertising. She had only the vaguest idea what 'rounds' on a small country newspaper might involve.

At *Girl Talk* she'd had experience in gathering regular snippets of gossip, but the focus had been on celebrity news. Baby bumps and relationship breakups. A friend who worked in television had been a handy source for these insights, while an old school friend, who was now a GP, had kept Chloe up to date on the latest issues in women's health. And a barista friend had passed on tips about the latest foodie trends.

What counted as crucial news in a small country town?

'There's a file on that computer with all the phone numbers,' Finn told her.

'Oh? Great.' But rather than jumping to the task, Chloe took another sip of coffee and opened the paper bag that held the mood-boosting brownie. 'So are you still on the lookout for breaking news?'

'I doubt you'll pick up anything of major importance, but the locals will be sure to complain if we miss anything obvious. There's an ongoing story about a young local baker who went missing in the rainforest, so any updates on him are important.'

'A baker? Oh, yes, I was curious about that. I passed the bakery and I saw that the shop was shut and all the shelves and display cases were empty. But there were flowers on the doorstep. I wondered —' Chloe had supposed there'd been a death, but someone missing was almost worse. 'When did this happen?'

Finn frowned. 'It's more than two weeks now.'

'Gosh.' So this was really serious. 'Is there a chance he was murdered?'

'There's always a chance,' Finn said grimly. 'The rainforest's very dense and people do get lost, but I'm afraid, in this case, the police suspect foul play. Looks like Ben stumbled on a drug set-up. There have been extensive searches but no real clues so far.'

'I imagine the whole town must be worried.'

'Absolutely.'

'What's the baker's name?'

'Ben Shaw.'

Chloe found pen and paper and quickly made a note of this.

'Anyway, you'll find that all the people on the rounds list know what I'm looking for.' Finn gave a brief nod in the direction of her computer screen.

'Ohh-kaay.' Chloe deliberately drew this response out, trying to sound far more confident than she felt as she clicked on the file entitled *Rounds*.

A list of phone numbers loaded onto her screen. She drank more coffee while it was still hot and took a bite of the brownie, which proved to be delicious. At least the Lilly Pilly café had her tick of approval.

The first phone number on the rounds list was for the Burralea police. The helpful sergeant expressed only mild surprise that someone other than Finn was calling. He told Chloe about a break-in at the pharmacy in Burralea's main street. Alarms had gone off and the police had responded quickly, so the culprits were frightened off and escaped empty-handed.

'Obviously they were after drugs,' the sergeant said. 'It's worth spreading the word. Yet again. Can't say it too often. Anyone hoping to find drugs in this town is out of luck. The pharmacy has alarms and time-lock safes. That goes for all the pharmacies in this district.'

Chloe conscientiously noted this down. She would turn it into a little news item to present to Finn later. She enquired about Ben Shaw, but unfortunately, there was no news on that front. Then she rang the ambulance, but there'd been no call-outs in the past twenty-four hours. Things had been quiet at the fire brigade as well.

The fellow at the fire brigade sounded intrigued, though. 'So you're new on the *Bugle*, are you?'

'Yes,' said Chloe and then, because there was no point in hiding it, 'just started today.'

'We're not losing Finn, are we?' He sounded dismayed.

'No, no. Mr Latimer is still the editor.' She chanced a glance in her new boss's direction, but he had his broad back to her and he seemed intently engaged in laying out pages on his screen. He certainly showed no sign that he was listening to her end of the conversation.

'Well, you can tell Finn from me that if there's no decent rain in the next couple of weeks, there'll be widespread fire restrictions.'

'At least it's raining today,' Chloe said cheerfully, remembering her dash to the café through the cold drizzle.

The fireman snorted. 'You call this rain? It's nothing more than angel's piss. I'm talking about decent rain. At least a hundred millimetres in twenty-four hours.'

Well, that was telling her. Chloe allowed herself a wry smile as she made additions to her notes and, when she rang the Water Resources number, she was prepared for a similar story.

'Tell Finn the lake's at fifty percent.'

'Fifty percent capacity?' Chloe clarified.

'Of course,' he snapped impatiently. 'And as Finn knows, we've still got quite a few months to go before we can expect the proper wet season.'

'So fifty percent is bad news?' Chloe hated asking the obvious, but it was important to check.

Her question was met by silence before the voice on the end of the line responded in a tone of quiet exasperation, 'You've seen the lake, haven't you?'

Chloe supposed she should explain yet again that she was new to the job. Brand new. At one point on her journey today, she'd caught a brief glimpse of silvery water in the distance, but that was all she'd seen of a possible lake.

She realised now that she should have done more research before she'd left Sydney, but her final weeks in the city had been a whirlwind of packing and endless farewells with her family, her friends and her former colleagues, all of whom had expressed despair that she was going to travel so far away. To the ends of the earth.

'We'll worry about you,' her mother had said dolefully, but her dad had laughed at this.

'It's not as if she's heading for Outer Mongolia,' he'd said as he'd given Chloe an extra warm hug.

And yet, her knowledge of Far North Queensland was almost as limited as her knowledge of Mongolia. Perhaps the fellow from Water Resources guessed her situation.

At any rate, he relented. 'Lake Tinaroo is actually a dam, a big one, with two hundred kilometres of shoreline,' he explained with excessive patience. 'It's still full of trees and stumps from when the country was initially flooded. The farmers need to draw on it for irrigation, so without rain, the farmers keep drawing and the water level keeps dropping. But if it drops too far, we have to ban motorboats and water skiing. It's too dangerous. Problem is, that's bad for tourism.'

'Right,' said Chloe. 'Thanks very much for your explanation. Much appreciated.'

'No worries.' He sounded happier again, so she hadn't pissed him off too badly. 'Glad to help.'

Again she made notes, pleased that she had a few little stories to write up for Finn, who was continuing to ignore her, leaving her to sink or swim. The next number on her list was the Burralea Progress Association.

A woman answered, introducing herself as Moira Briggs. 'How lovely to have a woman journalist on the *Bugle*,' she said, her voice bubbling with gossipy warmth. 'Where have you come from?'

'Sydney,' Chloe told her.

'Really? The biggest of all the big smokes? Well, I daresay you'll notice things are a little different up here.' Moira chuckled. 'When did you arrive?'

There was little point in trying to hide the truth. 'Not too long ago, actually.'

'Ha! Finn's thrown you in at the deep end, has he?' This comment was accompanied by another chuckle. 'What do you think of our Finn?'

Chloe gulped. 'Um – I'm supposed to ask you the questions, Moira.'

Moira roared with laughter. 'He's hot stuff, isn't he?' A beat later, she said, 'Sorry, love. I couldn't resist that. I have a soft spot for Finn, even though I'm twice his age. Some men just have that certain something.'

Like a drinking problem? Chloe wanted to ask.

'I'm sure you must know I'm teasing,' Moira added.

'I guessed,' said Chloe. 'But do you have any news from the Burralea Progress Association?'

'Nothing new since I spoke to Finn a few days ago.'

'All right. Thank you.' Chloe was about to hang up when Moira jumped in again.

'Come down to the office and visit me, won't you, Chloe? I'm only a few doors away. Have a cuppa. It's always good to put a face to a voice.'

'I will,' Chloe said. 'Thank you.' To her surprise she was smiling as she hung up.

CHAPTER EIGHT

In Springbrook House, a Townsville girls' boarding school, set amid enormous and shady rain trees, Bree Latimer was at her desk in the two-bed dorm that she shared with a classmate, Abbey. Abbey was wearing headphones, listening to something on her computer, while Bree was rushing through her homework.

Bree was a weekly boarder, unlike Abbey or the other boarders whose families lived out west on cattle properties, or in far-flung places like Papua New Guinea or Hong Kong. On weekends, Bree went home to her grandparents, who lived just a few suburbs away.

She hadn't accepted this arrangement easily. She'd been devastated when her father announced that he was taking a job in a tiny Tablelands town called Burralea, and leaving her behind. She'd kicked up a terrible stink. How could her father abandon her when he was all she had left?

Bree's gran had done her best to explain. 'Your father's in rather a deep hole and he needs time to get over everything that's happened before he can look after you properly.'

Bree hadn't taken this well. She'd clung to her father and cried horrendously when it was time for him to leave. And her acceptance of the inevitable had come slowly. But now, eighteen months later, although her father's absence remained a permanent ache in her heart, Bree had settled into school and each weekend she happily lapped up her grandparents' loving and conscientious attention.

All their married lives, her gran and grandpa had lived in the same house, which seemed amazing to Bree, who had lived in many places in at least four different countries. Her grandparents' house was an old Queenslander in North Ward, just one block back from the sea. It had a latticed front verandah covered in pink bougainvillea and it seemed utterly perfect to Bree.

They had created the most adorable bedroom for her, with pale-lemon walls and a bright bedspread in tropical hues of deep aqua and coral. It also had a roll-out bed so that she could invite a friend home on special weekends. A desk and a computer had been installed, as well, and there were plenty of shelves for her precious collection of ornamental dogs, which was far too vast and sentimental to take to school.

The collection had started with a patchwork puppy that Bree had loved since her toddler days. The poor pooch was now minus an eye and had a badly chewed tail, but it sat proudly on a shelf next to her assortment of plaster and porcelain dogs. These ranged from super ugly to adorably cute, and included a skinny copper dog Bree's mother had bought in Africa and an exquisite glass poodle that her aunt had brought back from Paris.

Of course, what Bree truly longed for was a real dog to love and to play with, to take for walks and to have lying at her feet while she did her homework and then sleeping at night in a basket at the end of her bed. Her grandparents had drawn the line at this, however. They weren't keen on all the extra work a dog would require and said they were too old to start again with a puppy, especially as Bree was away at school for five days of the week.

Even without a real dog, Bree loved her bedroom. It had French doors painted gloss white and curtained with lace that opened onto a corner of the latticed verandah. Here, Bree had her very own little sitting area, with a cane table and chairs lined with comfy rose-coloured cushions where she entertained her friends when they visited. She felt terribly grown up serving them afternoon tea of lemonade with ice cubes and sprigs of mint and a selection of yummy goods from the bakery, as her gran had never been one for baking.

Lavished with her grandparents' love and affection, Bree knew she was lucky. And mostly she was happy.

This evening, with her dreaded maths homework rushed through and finished, Bree reached for the diary she'd kept ever since she'd started at this boarding school. Initially, it had been one of the school counsellor's suggestions.

'You have a gift for writing, Bree,' Miss Groves had said. 'So you shouldn't find it a chore to keep a diary. I think you might enjoy jotting down your thoughts, or recording things that happen. Why don't you give it a try?'

The idea had appealed. The very next week Bree had used her pocket money to buy a book with gorgeous butterflies on the cover and a special lock for keeping the contents secret, and she was quite regular about adding entries.

Mostly she wrote about school and her friends or her weekend outings, and sometimes she even made up little stories, usually ones with a dog as the hero. Miss Groves was right. She hadn't found it a chore to write. She liked her diary entries and secretly she knew that some of them were quite good. She wondered if one day she might be a journalist like her dad.

Homework dispensed with now, she pulled the diary towards her, took the little key from her pencil case and unlocked it, then selected a favourite pen.

Tuesday
Today Mrs M gave us the strangest assignment. She asked us to write a letter to ourselves. It's not an assignment that she will read and mark. She told us that no one else will read our letters. They're to be locked away safely and handed back to us to read at the end of next year, our first year in high school. But as this school covers Prep to Year 12, high school's not such a big deal. Or at least, I don't think it is.

The letter is kind of a fun idea, though, a bit like keeping this diary, I guess. But the end of next year? So far away!!

Mostly, I just wanted to ask myself questions. Lame stuff like how long is my hair now? How tall am I? Have my boobs grown? Has Joshua Cook even noticed that I exist yet?

Of course, the really big question is will I feel any better about Mum and Louis by the time another year has passed?

Bree stopped. She felt sick just writing her mother's and her little brother's names. Especially today.

By a horrible coincidence, Mrs M had chosen the one day of the year when Bree tried desperately hard not to think about any of that horror. In truth, she tried not to think about it most days. She knew that if she gave in to those saddest of memories, she would only end up bawling and then *everyone* in the school would know why she was upset and she would be sent back to Miss Groves for further counselling.

It wasn't that Bree didn't like Miss Groves, but she didn't like feeling different from the other girls – a 'marked' child. She had learned the hard way that she was better off toughing it out than letting her heartbreak show.

The problem was, the only way she could remain tough was to try to forget. And there were two problems with forgetting. It was virtually impossible. Worse than that, trying to forget felt wrong.

Especially today.

Today her gran would be remembering, of course. Gran would have visited the cemetery, taking white lilies for Bree's mum and a spray of cheeky yellow orchids for Louis, just as she had on each anniversary since the incident three years ago. And if today had coincided with a weekend, Bree would have been expected to accompany her.

The very thought brought tears to her eyes, but she didn't want to cry. She picked up her pen, added a little more to her diary.

Today's a sad day for Gran, too, because Mum was her daughter-in-law and Louis was her grandson, but Gran seems to like visiting cemeteries. I hate it. I can't help it. I just hate seeing those head-stones. I hate having to think about what they mean, and that Mum and Louis are under there. I just want to think about how they used to be.

Bree had barely added the full stop to this sentence before her memories rushed in, like a fierce wind gust. Without warning, she was back in Bangkok in the house decorated with wonderfully carved furniture and silk lanterns and beautiful antique floor tiles, and she was reliving those last days before her world fell apart.

Her dad had been busy chasing a story with an important Australian politician who was only in Thailand for a few days. Back then, he'd always been busy with reporting assignments and Bree had seen almost as little of him as she did now. But her mum had made a fuss of Bree's birthday. She had made her a special swimming pool cake with chopped green jelly for water, a licorice ladder down the side and tiny plastic dolls on a chocolate-wafer diving board.

And Louis had stuck his grubby little fingers into the jelly on the top of her cake before Bree had even finished blowing out the candles.

If only she hadn't yelled at him! She'd made him cry and her mum had gently reproached her.

'He's only little, Bree. He doesn't understand.'

I wrote about yelling at Louis in my letter today. I hope that by time I'm in high school, I won't be so mad with myself for being such a crappy big sister. But then, yelling at your little brother just before he dies is probably one of those things you can never forgive, isn't it?

I think Dad understands how I feel about cemeteries and remembering. He doesn't talk about it much either, not the way Gran does.

He didn't ring me tonight, but that's okay. I was almost hoping he wouldn't ring, because I know I would have bawled my eyes out and I didn't want to. I know he hasn't forgotten me, because he sent me three books for my birthday last Sunday and he rang me then and we talked about all the cool things we can do up there in Burralea where he lives, like swimming and canoeing on the lake. He actually talked about me going to visit him in the Christmas holidays, instead of him coming down here as usual. I can't wait.

The books he sent are totally cool, about witch wars and bad mermaids and a babysitter who's an alien in disguise. They look so much more fun than the boring books Mrs M gives us to read.

Bree stopped again as footsteps and voices sounded in the hallway outside. Girls called to each other.

'Goodnight.'

'See ya!'

'Hey, Kelly, don't forget you promised to lend me your iPad.'

The school choir was coming back from their rehearsal, which meant it wouldn't be long till lights out. Bree closed the diary, locked it and stowed it in the drawer of her desk, anxious to continue reading one of her birthday books right away. She was halfway through the one about bad mermaids.

Her roommate, Abbey, was still wearing the headphones, so she didn't hear Bree's goodnight. Climbing into bed, Bree snuggled down with her book. It still had the lovely 'new' smell and it came with a special colouring-in bookmark decorated with mermaids and fish of every shape and size. So far, Bree had coloured in three mermaids and half a fish, but now she set the bookmark on her bedside table and escaped into her favourite place – a world of make-believe.

CHAPTER NINE

By the time the paper had been emailed off to the printers, it was quite dark outside and still raining. Finn, looking pale and drawn, with his hair more tousled and untidy than ever and his jaw shadowed by more than a day's growth, somewhat grudgingly thanked Chloe for her assistance.

She didn't expect effusion. She hadn't really done much except fetch more coffee and turn those few snippets of news into usable stories. And she'd seen enough of Finn's work to know that he was extremely competent. Perhaps he was used to working with a hangover.

'I – er —' He shot a frowning glance to her suitcase, still standing where she'd parked it near the door. 'I forgot to ask. You do have some kind of accommodation organised, don't you?'

'I thought you were organising that.' The obvious chance to tease him had been irresistible and the stricken look on Finn's face was priceless.

'Is – is that what Emily told you?'

Chloe was tempted to drag out his suffering, but she relented and grinned. 'No, you can relax. I've booked a room at the pub.'

His relief was so patent it was almost comical. He managed a quarter-smile. 'Well the pub's on the next corner. You can't really miss it. I'd offer to walk you down there except —'

He didn't finish the sentence, but he didn't need to. Chloe guessed he was embarrassed about accompanying her with his haggard visage, crumpled clothes and a lingering aroma of whisky.

'I'll be fine,' she said.

He gave a brief nod. 'I'll say goodnight then. And I'll lock up after you.'

'All right.' She began to gather up her things. 'What time do you start work in the morning?'

'Nine o'clock.'

'See you then.'

'Goodnight.'

Chloe opened the door, shivering at the unexpected drop in temperature that had arrived with nightfall. Then, juggling her suitcase, her laptop and her umbrella, she set off into the night. She was quite exhausted, she realised. She'd risen at some ungodly hour to arrive at Mascot airport well ahead of her departure time. Then there had been a three-hour flight, another hour or more spent hanging around at Cairns airport, followed by the winding drive up the range.

The day had already been long enough even before she'd arrived at the *Bugle*, but the subsequent meeting with her new boss and the work she'd put in had drained the last of her reserves.

At least Finn had been right about the Burralea Hotel's location. It was on the next corner, so within easy walking distance of the *Bugle*'s office. Now, Chloe only hoped the hotel was comfortable and warm and that there was a cosy bed waiting for her.

She wasn't disappointed. The two-storey timber hotel was large, old-fashioned and rambling, with the tempting smell of roast lamb drifting through from the kitchens beyond the dining room. When

Chloe climbed the rather magnificent old staircase, she discovered a room with air conditioning, a huge bed covered by a luxurious white broderie anglaise quilt, a well-upholstered armchair with a foot stool, a desk with a lamp and an ensuite bathroom that provided plenty of hot water. *Bliss.*

Tomorrow she would worry about the likelihood of her future in Burralea. For now, these creature comforts were enough.

***

Finn woke with a start, sure that his phone was ringing.

In the darkness, he groped on the bedside table, feeling for his phone, as he'd done so many, many times during his ten years as a foreign correspondent. He knew from experience that a midnight phone call required instant alertness. Any one of a number of disasters might have occurred – an earthquake, a tsunami, a military coup, a plane crash.

His heart juddered as his fingers closed around his mobile, thumping so loudly that the beats almost blanked out the noise of its ringing. But despite the speed of his reaction, the phone seemed to have stopped.

Finn heard nothing but silence within the house and the soft whisper of rain falling outside. He stared at the device cradled in his palm. The screen wasn't alight and when he flicked it on, he saw that it was 2.05 a.m., and there was absolutely no indication that he'd missed a call.

Had he imagined the phone call? *Damn.* He knew what this meant. He'd been dreaming again, and almost certainly he'd been dreaming about Thailand.

With a heavy sigh, he dropped the phone onto the bedside table and sank back onto the pillows, staring through the darkness to the shimmer of a streetlight outside that showed as a fuzzy glow around the edges of the bedroom curtains. He knew, from the tension drumming through him, from the wired alertness that now gripped him, that he was wide awake. And after the previous night's bender that had rendered him unconscious for most of the day, he also knew that his chances of getting back to sleep were sub-zero.

What a spectacular stuff-up.

This year he'd been planning, had desperately hoped, that he would get through the anniversary without falling apart. He'd deliberately stayed back at work, typing away late into the night, fighting the dark memories, trying to bury them by writing an entire month's worth of editorials for the *Bugle*.

He'd written a commentary about the disturbing spate of recent burglaries in the district, as well as Ben Shaw's disappearance, reinforcing a plea from the police for the community to be more vigilant. He'd followed with a tribute to Burralea's junior soccer clubs and the hard work of the coaches that had resulted in two Burralea Primary School boys and one girl being selected to represent North Queensland in their age groups.

He was sure he'd also started another editorial, but he couldn't remember what it was about. It was somewhere around then that Finn's cruel memories had prevailed. Eventually the horror had overwhelmed him, tormenting him beyond endurance until a trip to the pub and a large bottle of Scottish single malt had been the only way to drown the brutal onslaught.

Of course, he'd been well aware of the foolishness of such a tactic. And, yeah, he'd known that this year's anniversary coincided with the final twenty-four hours before the newspaper's deadline, as well as the imminent arrival of a new journalist at the *Bugle*.

Regrettably, his pain and guilt had outweighed his sense of professional duty.

But what a fucking disaster – for him to wake in the middle of the afternoon, with a raging hangover, only to be confronted by the

Dolly reporter from Sydney, staring at him like a scared rabbit, as if she'd walked into the Chamber of Horrors.

Recalling this encounter now, Finn gave a disbelieving shake of his head and discovered to his relief that it was no longer splitting. At least that was one thing he could be thankful for.

He thought about the new girl. Not Dolly, but – damn it, he'd already forgotten her real name. Her surname was Brown, he remembered that much. Brown to match her eyes.

He supposed it was rude of him to have called her Dolly, but he'd mentally applied the name weeks ago when Emily had informed him of her high-handed decision to employ the woman whether he wanted her or not. He supposed, in time, he would learn to remember her real name. If she stuck around.

If he didn't sack her.

He had to admit, though, Dolly wasn't quite what he'd expected. She was older, for one thing. Somewhere in her mid thirties, he guessed, and her looks weren't nearly as trendy and citified as he'd expected. Dressed conservatively in black trousers and a white shirt, she was of average height, slim, with shoulder-length curly hair of a nondescript, light-brown shade that was surprisingly free of the hairdresser's tints and highlights that most women found essential.

She might have been rather ordinary looking if her brown eyes hadn't shone with unexpected warmth and intelligence. Wonderful eyes, really. And weren't eyes the windows to the soul?

She'd brought him aspirin. Without any accompanying comment or lecture, she'd simply set the packet on his desk beside his coffee and after that, miraculously, between them, he and Dolly had put the paper to bed.

And Finn couldn't deny she was observant, which was an important requirement in a journo. She'd already noticed that the bakery was closed and had wanted to ask questions.

In other words, she hadn't been quite as hopeless as he'd feared, although he still had grave doubts about her long-term usefulness.

With another heavy sigh, Finn threw off the covers. He now had Buckley's chance of getting back to sleep, so he might as well go through to the kitchen, make himself a cuppa and read for a bit in the lounge room.

Soon he was settled in a corner of the sofa with a steaming mug of well-sugared tea and a page-turning crime thriller. Ian Rankin was one of Finn's favourite authors, a master storyteller who could always be relied on to draw him in to a world of mystery and intrigue and adventure.

Okay, man, relax. The worst is behind you. Let it rest now. Let it go.

Finn took a deep, scalding sip of tea, picked up the book and turned to the first page, ready for the opening lines to work their magic.

It was only when he turned over to the third page that he realised nothing had sunk in. His eyes had been skimming paragraph after paragraph without absorbing a single detail.

Annoyed, he went back to the start and tried again. The book was *Even Dogs in the Wild* and two villains were about to bury someone. Finn winced at this, but he told himself he could deal with a burial scene. The setting was the Scottish countryside and Inspector Rebus would soon be on their trail. An intriguing mystery would unfold at any moment. He just had to concentrate.

Tonight, however, the author's magic simply wasn't working. Finn's mind drifted again. Shrinking from the threat of more sadness, he allowed himself to think about Bree. His daughter loved reading, too, and he wondered if she'd started any of the books he'd sent her for her birthday. He wondered how she'd survived the past twenty-four hours and with that thought came a fresh slug of guilt. He hadn't rung her last night. And now it was too late.

Poor kid. She deserved so much more than he was able to give her.

Draining his mug of tea, Finn was aware that he was in perilous danger of losing it again, of sinking into maudlin misery and self-flagellation. Like a drowning swimmer, grasping for a lifesaving, outstretched hand, he fought off the despair, forced his thoughts away from the dreaded southern Thai city of Betong.

Far better, surely, to comfort himself with recollections of happier days. He looked about the humble lounge room of his rented cottage, decorated with bits and pieces he and Sarah had collected during stints overseas. The red and beige floor rug was from the Congo, as was the collection of African water jugs on the dresser. The silk and batik cushions scattered on the sofa and armchairs were from Cambodia. Each piece carried a fond memory. His marriage to Sarah had been a very happy one.

From the start, they'd both been adventurers.

Not that Finn had realised this when he'd first met Sarah Hughes at a swanky party held in the grounds of a mansion overlooking Sydney's glittering harbour. A lovely, elegant blonde, Sarah was the daughter of a highly successful merchant banker and Finn had been invited to the party by one of his mates, a financial journo who hobnobbed with the big end of town.

Finn hadn't expected the glamorous beauty to notice him, let alone engage him in conversation, but Sarah gave every appearance of being genuinely interested in him and his work. When he'd told her he was on leave from an overseas posting in Africa, she'd seemed quite excited by the idea.

As he started to relax and to feel more confident, he might have even puffed out his chest a tad, until he learned that Sarah wasn't merely a beautiful heiress, she was also a highly qualified doctor. At that point, her stunning combination of beauty and brains had seemed a hurdle too high for a little-known journalist who had scored a job as a foreign correspondent because he was young and cheap and prepared to go anywhere.

Looking back, Finn couldn't actually remember how he'd found the nerve to ask Sarah out. Of course, he'd expected an automatic knock-back, but to his astonishment, this beautiful woman had accepted his invitation.

Not only had she gone out with him, but three months later, after a dizzying whirlwind romance and a flurry of phone calls and email exchanges between Sydney and South Sudan, she'd also accepted his rash proposal of marriage. Without any apparent reservations.

By then, of course, Finn had glimpsed the real Sarah. He knew she was so much more than a society darling who happened to have a degree in medicine. The girl he'd fallen in love with was a gritty woman with a sense of purpose, who had already worked overseas. In Ethiopia, in fact, and not in the relative comfort of Addis Ababa, but in rural villages where she'd lived in tents or mud huts with thatched roofs.

Dealing with weather extremes without the aid of fans, air conditioners or heaters, and coping with long-drop toilets and bucket showers by candlelight had amounted to a grand adventure for Sarah, rather than her worst nightmare. In that regard, Finn and Sarah had been kindred spirits. They'd shared a yearning for adventure, a need to step out of their comfort zones and to make a difference.

And there could be no doubt, Finn had loved his work as a foreign correspondent. He'd relished the adventure and the opportunity to be in the thick of big stories.

In those early days, he'd been a solo video journalist, carrying his own kit, including a camera, tripod and microphones, plus a laptop and personal backpack. Sometimes he'd also had to lug a tent and sleeping bag, as well as a fold-out satellite phone for sending stories back to Australia.

No matter. Finn had found the experience empowering, taking off into the African wilderness, knowing that the success or failure of his project depended on his own resourcefulness.

It wasn't too long after their marriage, however, that he'd been promoted to travelling with a team. The downside was that with a cameraman, a producer and interpreter in tow, he'd been required to travel further afield, which had meant more time away from Sarah, but she had never complained.

His team had reported on the frustratingly drawn out border conflict between Ethiopia and Eritrea. They'd also been on the spot when a huge locust plague invaded Senegal and Mali, destroying precious crops. And they'd balanced the horrendous news of the genocide in Dafur with the good news that eighty million African children were being immunised against polio.

Finn had been based in Nairobi, where Sarah had found work in several hospitals, sometimes voluntary, sometimes paid. She hadn't really minded. She'd always claimed to be happy as long as she felt useful, and as long as Finn came back to her.

They'd both been sensible, though. When Sarah realised she was pregnant with Bree, they'd returned to Australia and Finn had settled to work in Melbourne. Here, he and Sarah had lived in a brick suburban house with a red-tiled roof, in a quiet, tree-lined street with level, concrete footpaths. They'd enjoyed visits from their families, and weekend barbecues and dinner parties with friends.

Sarah, with baby Bree in her pram, had joined other mothers at a nearby park, or in a café for a morning coffee. Their lives had been exceedingly pleasant, wonderfully safe and convenient.

And before a year was out, both Finn and Sarah had been bored.

Finn smiled now, as he remembered Sarah's shamefaced admission that she missed the chaos and challenge of their life overseas. He understood. Those faraway places got under your skin.

The responsibilities of fatherhood had made him cautious, however. He'd waited another six months before he had finally given in and accepted another overseas posting.

To their families' dismay, they'd taken off for Thailand when Bree was just eighteen months old.

'Bangkok might be okay for a short visit, but how could you possibly want to live there?' Sarah's mother had protested. 'It's so noisy and busy and crowded and dirty.'

'I know,' Sarah told her with a cheeky grin. 'I can't wait.'

Despite his heartbreak, Finn could still remember those years in Southeast Asia as the golden years. He'd been ridiculously relieved to leave Melbourne, to escape the tightly controlled 'message of the day' world of modern media and to once again get back to the basics of journalism. He'd loved getting out of the office, talking to people who were doing extraordinary things.

In Southeast Asia, he'd witnessed the aftermath of a terrible super typhoon. In Myanmar, he'd interviewed Aung San Suu Kyi. In Laos, he'd spoken to the brave band of women risking life and limb to destroy the explosives that still littered their precious land forty years after the Vietnam war. He'd reported on the injustice of people evicted in Phnom Penh by ruthless developers.

Now, in Burralea, a night owl hooted, interrupting Finn's reverie. He let out a sigh as he heaved himself off the sofa. He could use another cuppa. Or maybe he'd scramble a couple of eggs. Actually, come to think of it, a proper post-hangover fry up was in order. He couldn't remember the last time he'd eaten.

With bacon sizzling alongside eggs, mushroom and tomatoes, Finn felt his spirits lift. It might still be dark outside, but dawn was only an hour or so away and a new day beckoned.

A new day that included finding a role for the *Dolly* reporter. As he dropped two slices of bread into the toaster, he wondered what had brought that girl with the mousy hair and remarkable eyes scuttling all the way up here from the bright lights of Sydney. What did she hope to find in the far north?

Finn had a string of suspicions, including the possibility that she had run away from unhappiness. If that was the case, she was an escapee, just as he was.

CHAPTER TEN

Chloe arrived at work a bit before nine, expecting to spend an annoying amount of time hanging about on the footpath, twiddling her thumbs, or reading the *Burralea Bugle*, which had already hit the news stands, while she waited for her reprobate boss to show up.

To her surprise, the *Bugle*'s door was already unlocked and Finn was inside, standing by his desk and talking on the phone. He was dressed in jeans and an open-necked white shirt, as he had been yesterday, but Chloe was relieved to see that these clothes looked fresh. The shirt might even have been ironed and Chloe wondered if he had a wife – a long-suffering one, no doubt – who had done this task for him. At any rate, he showed no signs of yesterday's pallor, stubbled jaw or bleary eyes.

Finn Latimer was, on the surface at least, a new man. With the benefit of thick, dark hair – much tidier today – and a rugged jawline, he could, no doubt, look quite attractive if he smiled.

He didn't smile at Chloe. Although he glanced her way, he didn't even send her a welcoming nod. His attention was entirely committed to the person on the other end of the phone.

Chloe helped herself to a seat at the same computer she'd used yesterday and turned it on. While it was loading, she took out her own phone. She hadn't upgraded phones as regularly as most of her friends, but this one was still fine for recording interviews and filing notes.

She'd already added the 'rounds' phone numbers to her contacts, but today, she hoped she could skip the rounds. Her task would be to start looking for her own news stories, unless Finn had other plans.

With the computer ready, she typed in the password Finn had given her yesterday and clicked on a search engine, wondering where she should begin.

'So, was the pub satisfactory?'

It took Chloe a moment to realise that Finn's phone call had ended and this question was directed to her. 'Yes,' she said. 'My room was very comfortable, thank you.'

He nodded. 'The meals are usually quite good, if you don't mind pub food.'

'Yes, they're fine.' Last night's roast lamb had been delicious, and breakfast this morning substantial, much more than Chloe could eat, but she was pretty sure Finn didn't want details.

'So.' His dark gaze narrowed and he shot a curious glance to her computer screen. 'What plans do you have for today?'

'Well —' Was she supposed to have plans? On her second day? Chloe was still coming to terms with the dramatic change in the man. He'd looked so wasted the night before, but now he showed no apparent signs of a hangover. Or remorse. And he obviously had no intention of apologising or offering a guilty explanation for yesterday's less than commendable condition.

She swallowed. She was surprisingly nervous and she wished Finn would sit down instead of continuing to stand, more or less towering over her. 'I wasn't sure. I thought you might already have jobs lined up for me.'

A glimmer, the merest *hint* of a smile shone briefly in his eyes. 'Seems neither of us knew what to expect then.' He lowered his butt to the edge of his desk, a move that wasn't as helpful as it should have been, as it managed to draw Chloe's inappropriate attention to his low-slung jeans and lean hips.

Folding his arms over his chest, he frowned at her as if she was a problem he had to solve.

'As I understand it,' he said. 'Emily hired you to write colour stories. She wants you to attract more advertising.'

'Yes, that's what she told me.'

'So I'm assuming you already have a few ideas?'

'Well – I —' The fresh challenge in Finn's gaze sent Chloe's thoughts scattering unhelpfully. She knew so little about this part of the world, she really had no useful ideas. Clearly, she should have prepared more conscientiously for this job, instead of wasting far too much time feeling sorry for herself over the whole Jason fiasco.

Nevertheless, she had come here to the far north in the hope of a fresh start, and that would only happen if she stopped hankering after broken dreams.

Time to suck it up, princess.

Straightening her spine, she offered Finn Latimer a brave smile. 'I thought I might start by taking a look at a few of the businesses around here. Keep an eye out for an interesting angle or two.'

To her relief, his response was a nod of approval.

'I was about to do a little research. I thought Moira at the Progress Association might be a good source.'

'Oh, for sure, for sure,' Finn said with a mock Irish accent. 'Moira can tell you anything and everything you want to know, even the things you don't want to know.'

'Is she a gossiper?' Chloe had heard about the dangers of small-town gossip.

'I wouldn't brand her as a gossiper exactly. She'll only tell you harmless stuff, at any rate.' Finn actually smiled as he said this and his face was transformed. And Chloe found herself responding with more speed and warmth than was strictly appropriate. 'She'll probably tell you that she doesn't repeat gossip, so you need to listen closely the first time.'

Chloe grinned. She liked the sound of Moira.

'There's an interesting mushroom farm at Upper Barron,' Finn said next. 'They grow a host of varieties, including the gourmet ones like oyster and shiitake. Could be worth checking out.'

Perhaps she shouldn't have been surprised that her boss had offered her a lead. 'Thanks. That sounds like a great possibility.' Hoping she hadn't sounded too excessively grateful, she typed *Upper Barron mushroom farm* into the search engine. 'Okay, I can see that the farm is open for visitors today. Perhaps I should get straight onto that?'

Then she remembered there was only one vehicle. 'Unless you need to use the car, or there's anything else you want me to do?'

Finn shook his head. 'Go for it. But stick to the colour story. I don't want you hitting them up for advertising. Leave that for our sales reps to follow up for a future edition.'

Phew. As a 'working journalist', Chloe was certainly relieved to hear that she wouldn't have to chase ads. That was a professional line she preferred not to cross.

'I'd better ring the farm first to see if it suits,' she said. Scant moments later, she had her first appointment booked. She was welcome to head out to the mushroom farm straight away.

'You can take the *Bugle*'s camera,' Finn offered, crossing to a built-in cupboard and extracting a camera in a rather expensive-looking brown leather case.

'Thanks.' At *Girl Talk*, Chloe had always used a professional photographer, so she hoped she'd be able to manage. 'Does it have special settings?'

'It does. But it works just fine if you simply point and click.'

This was another relief.

Finn indicated a row of keys hanging on hooks on the far wall. 'The car key's on the left there and you'll find the vehicle out the back. A blue Subaru Forester.'

Oh. Foresters were all-wheel drive. Chloe supposed it was a sensible choice of vehicle for a country newspaper, but she'd only ever driven small city sedans. 'Is – is it automatic?'

'Sure.' Again, a flicker that might have been amusement briefly showed in her boss's eyes. 'And it's very easy to drive.'

'Good. Right.'

Finn might have given her extra instructions, but his phone rang, and he turned and picked it up. 'Good morning. *Burralea Bugle*. Hi, Harry, what can I do for you?'

Chloe rose, slipped her phone back into her bag, crossed the office and found the car keys. In the doorway, she turned back to her new boss, raised a hand to let Finn know she was leaving.

He gestured for her to wait. 'Hang on a sec, Harry.' He held the phone against his chest. 'Do you need directions?' he asked Chloe.

She shook her head, gave her shoulder bag a pat. 'I can use Maps on my phone.'

With a shrug, he waved her off and resumed his conversation. Chloe closed the door behind her and followed the cement tracks down the side of the *Bugle* till she found a mud-splattered, dark-blue Forester in a carport.

Taking a deep breath, she pressed the central locking device and heard a satisfying clunk. She climbed in. The floor of the Forester was fitted with rubber mats that were caked with red mud and there were at least three ancient takeaway coffee mugs dumped on the passenger's seat.

She keyed the mushroom farm into Maps on her phone, grateful for the lovely purple line that appeared, marking her route. Buckling up, she turned the key in the ignition. The engine hummed to life and the petrol gauge showed that the tank was three-quarters full.

It was silly to feel nervous, but Chloe couldn't help it. The Forester felt big. Man-sized. Letting off the handbrake, she gingerly pressed the accelerator and the vehicle edged forward. The space for the tracks between the *Bugle* and the next shop seemed incredibly narrow and she drove super carefully, wondering fearfully if she was going to have reverse down this driveway when she got back.

At least when she reached the street it was almost completely free of traffic. That was one very good thing about country towns. She put her foot down with a little more confidence and took off.

Today the sky was wide and blue, with no hint of rain, and the Forester, to Chloe's delight, was as easy to drive as Finn had promised. Her route had her heading for the hills, smooth green hills that had, no doubt, been cleared decades earlier to make way for dairying.

In no time, the road was climbing higher and higher and slopes were falling away on either side. As Chloe skimmed a narrow ridge, the view was fantastic. Farmlands spread beneath her like a giant patchwork tablecloth, stretching all the way to the blue line of mountains that fringed the coast. A flock of cockatoos swooped down a hillside, stark white and fluttering against the green.

She felt unexpectedly exhilarated. A road sign announced that this was the highest road in Queensland. She was, pretty much, on top of the world.

Now the route on her map seemed to take her back down a hillside, which seemed a bit weird, but the previous times she'd used this app on her phone it had never let her down. Chloe pushed on, loving the spectacular vistas, the sense of adventure. The freedom.

It was only when she got to the bottom of the hill and recognised the road junction that she realised she'd just driven in a complete circle. And totally missed the farm.

Chloe cringed as her soaring spirits hit the ground with a thud. She'd spent the best part of an hour getting herself lost. How on earth had that happened?

Pulling over into the dirt at the edge of the bitumen, she studied the map on her phone. It seemed she had no choice but to turn around and go back the way she'd come. She must have driven right past the farm gate. What did mushroom farms look like, anyway? And why hadn't they put up nice big signs? Didn't they want people to find them?

Her mood was distinctly less euphoric as she drove back the way she'd come, eyes now peeled, searching for vital clues. About half a kilometre along, she saw a dirt road leading off from the bitumen, which she'd obviously missed the first time. It was certainly heading in the right direction.

A cloud of dust billowed around her as the tyres hit the gravel, but she set off now, once again confident. Until she reached a fork in the road and neither of the new possibilities seemed to match the purple line on her phone.

Damn. How could it be so hard to find a well-publicised farm in all this open country? The only sensible thing to do now, of course, was to ring the mushroom farm and ask for directions – which would be fine if she knew exactly where she was.

Looking in her rear-view mirror, she saw a rather dilapidated farmhouse with peeling paint, a rusted tank stand and a yard filled with weeds. What had happened to all the pretty, welcoming farmhouses she'd passed?

After another about-turn, Chloe approached the farm and parked the Forester on the dirt track in front of a barred metal gate. She took a moment or two to work out how to undo the looped wire and chain that held the gate fast – the sudden loud barking of dogs from the house hadn't helped her concentration – but eventually she got the hang of it.

The dog barking became frenzied now as Chloe approached the house, and she might have bolted if she hadn't seen two blue cattle dogs straining on leashes that were chained to a tank stand.

'It's okay, guys,' she whispered. 'I'm just here to ask for directions.'

But already, she suspected there was no one at home. All the windows and doors appeared to be shut and surely the chaotic barking would have brought anyone in earshot?

Feeling rather desperate when no one answered her knock, Chloe went back to the gate, managed to open and close it more efficiently this time, and climbed into the car. She had no choice but to reverse down the track, drive back the way she'd come and double-check the last road sign. Then, at least, she could tell the mushroom people where she was.

She was halfway through cautiously reversing when her phone rang, identifying Finn as the caller.

It wasn't easy to sound confident, but she gave it her best shot. 'Hello, boss?'

'How are you going? Nearly finished there?'

'Well, I – ah – haven't quite found the place yet.'

This news was met by silence.

'I'm sure I've been following the right route,' Chloe said. 'I don't know what's gone wrong. I must have missed a turn.' And then, in defence, 'There don't seem to be any signs.'

'This isn't Kings Cross, Dolly.' He sounded impatient.

'Well, yes, I do realise that.' If he was trying to make her feel hopeless, he'd achieved it. 'I was about to ring the farm.'

'Don't bother. Get back here. I need the car.'

*

At least Chloe could park outside the *Bugle*'s office when she got back, so she was saved having to reverse down the narrow driveway. As she steered neatly into the parking space, she tried not to agonise too much over stuffing up her very first assignment and making herself look like a raw beginner. Instead she allowed herself to focus on the injustice of Finn Latimer's high-handed manner.

He sprang from his desk the minute she walked in.

Chloe went straight into defence mode. 'It would have been helpful if I'd known I had a time limit,' she said as she handed over the car keys and camera.

'Something's come up,' he said tightly. 'A new lead on Ben Shaw. I'm heading over to Mareeba. A CIB officer is up from Brisbane and I need to pin him down.'

She couldn't deny this sounded both urgent and important. 'Perhaps I should come, too.' After all, she had next to no experience in working with police and she could learn a thing or two from observing how Finn handled them.

He shook his head. 'You stick to your colour stories.' And with that he was gone, letting the door swing shut behind him.

CHAPTER ELEVEN

'So, that's sorted.' Moira Briggs, with a beaming smile, handed Chloe a plate bearing an enormous slice of chocolate sponge filled with cream to accompany her mug of beautifully hot tea. 'You're expected at the CWA luncheon at midday tomorrow and everyone's really looking forward to meeting you. It's a long time since we've had a female reporter in Burralea.'

Chloe, having first popped into the Lilly Pilly café to say hi to Jess, who was happily ferrying meals between the bubbling women in the kitchen and their customers, had also called into the Progress Association office. She had decided it would be a useful place to start her local research, but almost immediately she'd found herself comfortably ensconced in a brightly cushioned cane chair and being plied with tea and cake.

The office was next door to the hairdresser's, another place of interest for Chloe, as Tammy, the hairdresser, was the missing baker's girlfriend. Chloe had been careful not to stare as she'd passed, but she'd glanced through the window to see a very slim young woman with bright pink and aqua–streaked hair, chatting and smiling as she cut an elderly woman's pretty silver curls. At least

Tammy seemed to be bravely carrying on as usual while she coped with the huge stress of Ben's disappearance.

On arriving at the Progress Association office, Chloe's first impression had been of a welcoming sitting room, until she'd noticed the businesslike desk and computer that occupied one corner and the walls filled with shelves carrying tourist brochures. The place served as an Information Centre as well and there were posters of beautiful waterfalls, fern-fringed creeks with platypuses, and restaurants that featured local produce on their menus.

From her comfortable armchair, Chloe noted the glossy pictures of local cheeses and fruit and couldn't help confessing to the motherly Moira about her mushroom farm fiasco.

'Ah, well, never mind,' Moira soothed. 'Some of these farms are very isolated and it takes time to get used to the lie of the land in a new place. But usually, you'll see a rural block number on a star picket outside the property. That can help.'

'I see.' Chloe supposed Finn might have explained this if she'd given him half a chance.

Moira turned to look back over her shoulder at one of the posters. 'But if you're interested in stories about farmers and their produce, you might like to talk to Greta Fairlie. She and her husband have a red claw farm.'

'Red claw?' Chloe's mind boggled. 'What's that? Some kind of bird?'

'No, no. They're freshwater lobsters. Or is that crayfish? I get them mixed up. Anyway, they're delicious, and Greta and Mike grow them in ponds.'

'That does sound interesting.'

'Greta will be at the CWA luncheon, so you'll be able to talk to her then. I'm sure she'd be happy to have a nice little chat and invite you out to look at the farm.'

'I'll have to make sure I get careful directions,' Chloe said with a rueful smile. 'Thanks for the tip, Moira.' She sliced into the sponge with her fork, and said, carefully, 'I don't suppose Finn Latimer covers too many CWA luncheons.'

'No, I don't think we've ever seen Finn there.' Moira smiled. 'More's the pity.'

'He has *far* more important stories to cover.'

Perhaps Chloe said this a little too forcefully. Moira, tea mug poised to her lips, fixed her with a thoughtful stare. 'You know Finn's bark is worse than his bite?'

'Well, I —'

'Of course, you don't. You've only just arrived. You haven't had time to find out anything about him, or anybody else. But believe me, my dear, Finn's a softie, really.'

Chloe found this hard to swallow, but she wisely kept her thoughts to herself. 'I suppose you ply him with cake,' she said, smiling as she sent her fork diving back into the chocolate sponge. 'This is incredibly delicious by the way.'

Moira's smile was coy. 'Well, you know what they say about the way to a man's heart.'

Chloe assumed Moira was joking about trying to win Finn's heart. Grey haired and stout and wrinkled, she had to be, at the very least, twenty years older than him. And yet, when Moira talked about the man, she had the starry-eyed look of a teenage Justin Bieber fan.

Having now seen her boss sober and smiling – *once* – Chloe supposed she could understand his attraction. She decided it would be wise to redirect the conversation away from him. 'So, it's been a while since you had a female journalist in town?' she asked.

Moira nodded. 'I don't think there's been a woman at the *Bugle* since Izzie Galbraith.'

'Who was she?'

'The paper's original owner. Izzie and her husband started the *Burralea Bugle*. Back in the fifties, I think it was, or perhaps even earlier. I know old Gordon Herries looked after the printing press, but Izzie did everything else. For many years there, after she lost her husband, she ran the whole business more or less single-handedly. Even after she finally retired when she was well into her seventies, she kept a close eye on things. There was a shaky stretch with a few different editors. They never seemed to last long. I don't think they could handle Izzie's constant vigilance.'

'Wow.' Izzie might have been intimidating, but Chloe couldn't help but be impressed. It was amazing to think of a woman starting up a newspaper, way before Women's Lib, and running the whole show. She hadn't given any real thought to the *Bugle*'s history, but she wondered if this was another area she could explore. Only the old-timers would remember Izzie, so the locals would probably find her story quite interesting.

'She sounds awesome,' she said.

'Oh, yes.' Moira smiled. 'I'm sure awesome would be a fitting way to describe Izzie. Emily Hargreaves is her daughter, of course.'

'Really?' Chloe had been getting quite excited by story possibilities, but now she made a quick mental adjustment. She might do a little research about Izzie Galbraith, but she certainly wouldn't write anything for publication until she'd spoken to her daughter, the newspaper's current owner.

'I don't suppose Izzie's still alive,' she said.

'Oh, yes, she is, actually.' Moira gave a laughing shake of her head. 'She must be nearly a hundred, though. She's in a nursing home these days. Took us all by surprise when she finally moved in, but I don't think she plans to die anytime soon. I wouldn't put it past her to live forever.' Moira hooted at her joke. 'St Peter's probably scared she'll want his job.'

'Goodness. She does sound interesting. And possibly formidable.'

Clearly, Moira was going to be a very handy source. Chloe was glad she'd decided to check out the Progress Association after an unproductive hour or so alone in the office. Now, she couldn't help wondering if Emily Hargreaves was as tough as her mother. She'd seemed extremely pleasant during the Skype session, but it would be helpful to be forewarned.

'I've spoken to Emily Hargreaves on the phone and on Skype,' she said. 'But I haven't actually met her yet. She seems to be lying low.'

'She's probably letting you find your feet,' Moira remarked sagely. 'Emily's not one for interfering. As far as I can tell, she pretty much gives Finn free rein.'

'So she doesn't take after her mother then? At least not where the *Bugle*'s concerned?'

'Heavens, no. Emily's a different kettle of fish entirely. For one thing, she's spent most of her married life on a cattle property out west.' Moira flattened her lips and she looked, for a moment, as if she might have wanted to say more. But she must have thought better of it. 'Anyway,' she said. 'You'll almost certainly meet Emily at the CWA, if not before.'

Chloe supposed the CWA would be another useful research opportunity, a veritable gathering of who's who in Burralea. The female half, at any rate. She set down her plate. The cake had been delicious and she'd scoffed the lot. 'That was so good.'

'It's my grandmother's recipe.'

'A strictly guarded family secret?' Chloe's mum had always been incredibly reluctant to share their family's favourite lemon drizzle cake recipe.

'Oh, no, I've given it away countless times. And it's in our local CWA recipe book. Actually, speaking of recipes, you should speak to Greta about her red claw recipes.'

'You think she might let me print one?'

'You can always try. And it wouldn't hurt her business.' Before Chloe could thank her yet again, Moira leaned forward and asked with some earnestness, 'So have you found a place to live yet?'

The sudden switch in topic took Chloe by surprise and she needed a moment to answer. She was sure it was premature to be thinking about permanent accommodation. She had no intention of quizzing Moira about Finn's drinking habits, but she needed to know if the *Bugle*'s editor had a problem before she committed herself to staying.

Said editor, by the same token, was obviously sussing her out and if she didn't measure up, he would no doubt ask Emily to let her go. After this morning's effort, Chloe knew she still had a hell of a lot to prove.

'I'm staying at the pub at the moment,' she said.

'Well, no pressure, as folk like to say these days – but if you're interested, there's a nice little flat above this office and it's vacant at the moment. There'd be no one downstairs to bother you in the evenings, apart from a Progress Association meeting on the third Tuesday of the month. So you'd pretty much have the place to yourself, and it's very handy to the *Bugle*.'

'That's true,' Chloe said carefully.

'Would you like to take a look while you're here?'

'How much is the rent?'

The amount Moira named was jaw-droppingly reasonable compared with the prices Chloe was used to in Sydney. She couldn't help smiling. 'Well, I guess there's no harm in looking.'

Customers came through the doorway just then, rather earnest and weather-beaten tourists with backpacks and canvas hats and stout hiking boots, enquiring about walking tracks. While Moira attended to them, Chloe took their mugs and plates through to a little sink in the room at the back of the office. The room was beautifully lit with natural light from wide French doors that led to a back garden. She saw timber stairs leading up to the flat above and she couldn't help feeling curious.

Moira joined her just as she finished drying the plates.

'Oh, aren't you a dear to do that, Chloe? Thank you. So let's go up, shall we?' Moira kept up a running commentary as they ascended the stairs. 'Debbie, a nurse at the hospital, was our most recent tenant, but she's taken off to work overseas. Before her, Alice Miller was here. She's a furniture restorer and she lived up here and had her little shop below where we have our office now. Alice used the space out the back as a workshop.'

Moira's eyes widened significantly. 'She's married now, to a cattleman, Seth Drummond, and she lives with him on a property called Kooringal. I believe there's a baby on the way.'

A baby on the way.

To Chloe's dismay, these few words and the simple happy image they conjured still had the power to pierce her heart and flood her with miserable memories.

Stop it.

She swallowed hard. That was all in the past. Unfortunately, she couldn't have those memories electronically deleted from her brain, so she simply had to get a grip.

Blinking away the threat of tears, she straightened her shoulders and followed Moira into the flat, which was quite small, but rather charmingly furnished. Chloe particularly liked the polished timber floors, and the curvy red leather armchairs and shaggy cream rug in the lounge room. And there was a gorgeous claw-foot tub in the black and white–tiled bathroom.

'And here's the lovely big bedroom,' Moira announced with the air of a real estate agent.

The bedroom was indeed spacious and it even had a dear little bay window. There would be room for a bassinet, or a baby's cot.

Of course, Chloe regretted this thought as soon as it jumped into her head. And yet, her heart gave a queer little thud.

'So what do you think?' Moira asked, leading Chloe back into the kitchen and opening a pantry cupboard to show off the laminated shelving.

'It's lovely,' Chloe said.

'So convenient to your work and the shops.'

'Yes.' It could be quite perfect – if she was going to stay.

'You don't have to decide now,' Moira said. 'We're not being inundated with prospective tenants.'

'Well, thanks for showing it to me anyway, and thanks for the morning tea. I'll have to book a time to interview you properly about the Progress Association, but for now, I really should get back to the office.'

Moira laughed. 'So should I.'

Two hours later, Finn still hadn't returned, but Chloe had spent the time trawling through the internet and she was now totally excited by what she had discovered about Isabella Margaret Galbraith. Running the *Burralea Bugle* had been a tame achievement compared with the rest of Izzie's story.

CHAPTER TWELVE

The man in Emily's bed was not her husband.

She woke early, out of habit, just as the first light filtered through the trees beyond the bedroom's uncurtained windows, and her first thought was one of gratitude. She'd made it through the long hours of the dark night without being plagued by the usual nightmares and harrowing grief.

Then she rolled over and found him lying beside her, his bulky arm flung wide, taking up more than half of the bed. A beefy fellow, with rusty hair and a greying beard. A bear of a man.

Emily's heart gave a guilty thud as she remembered. *Everything.*

Rolf Anders' ultra-rugged appearance was deceptive. He was a considerate and intuitive lover, but now, as the pearly light of a new day drifted deeper into the house, Emily wished she wasn't privy to that knowledge. Icy fingers of doubt plucked at her skin.

She sat up, embarrassed to find herself naked. Carefully, she rose from the bed, tiptoed across the room and grabbed her dressing gown from a hook on the back of the ensuite door. With the sash safely tightened, she continued through the house to the other bathroom, which she could use without fear of waking Rolf. She needed privacy to think.

Last night, inviting an old family friend to dinner, someone she and Alex had entertained many times, had made perfect sense, especially as Alex appeared to have deserted her. He still hadn't tried to contact her since he'd left for Red Hill, the western Queensland cattle property that they still owned and where he and Emily had lived for more than thirty years.

Alex loved the west, of course. Emily knew that. In recent years, he had agreed to retire here to the Lake House and put in a manager at Red Hill, but she understood his hankering for the outback with its harsh, rugged beauty, so different from this softer, greener country near the coast. And it *was* the mustering season. Helicopters were mostly used these days, but Alex enjoyed nothing better than to be on horseback again, chasing after the mob. So it was understandable that he wanted to oversee the fate of his cattle was reasonable. However, he had a perfectly good satellite phone, so there was no real excuse for his silence.

Alex hadn't even bothered to ring back after she'd left messages on his phone, and so she'd called the homestead number and had spoken to Janice, the housekeeper.

'Oh, yes,' Janice had assured her. 'Mr Alex arrived safely, all right. He's been busy organising the muster, but he's here at the homestead right now, enjoying a beer on the verandah. Shall I fetch him?'

'No, don't bother him,' Emily had said, but she'd been shaking as she hung up. Before he'd left, she'd suffered months of her husband's silence and a chilling tension between them, and she couldn't have borne to hear his clipped, terse response if he'd been called to the phone.

So she'd welcomed Rolf Anders when he arrived yesterday evening. Rolf lived across the lake and he'd come by canoe, as he always did, just on dusk, bringing two bottles of very expensive vintage wine along with attentive and intelligent conversation.

Emily had been well prepared, with a chicken casserole in the slow cooker, and they'd sat together on the deck, enjoying the welcome breeze that rippled the surface of the lake, watching the pelicans and ducks forage in the last of the daylight.

She had produced a platter of olives and cheese to accompany the excellent red wine, while the sunset spread a cloth of crinkled gold over the lake. Rolf was a writer, a thinker and an engaging conversationalist, and he and Emily had talked about everything under the sun, from politics to the price of beef to their favourite poetry. He had made her laugh, a rare gift these days.

With the arrival of nightfall, they'd gone inside to eat dinner by flickering candlelight. A mistake, perhaps, but she couldn't really blame the romantic setting. They'd listened to a playlist that Robbie had compiled before he'd left for Syria – an interesting, poignant mix of his favourites, plus some of hers and Alex's.

The comforting glow of the candles, the rich full-bodied wine and the gift of an attentive, sympathetic listener had worked a subtle magic. Emily and Rolf had actually talked about Robbie – which was momentous – something Alex hadn't been able to do for the past twelve months.

With Rolf, Emily had even talked about the greatest taboo of all, the terrible way her son had died – not from a terrorist's missile striking his Super Hornet in an engagement with the enemy, but a mechanical failure, a cruel act of fate. As a passenger in an American helicopter spinning out of control, Robbie had fallen and crashed to the unforgiving desert, the plane bursting into a ball of fire.

Perhaps it was inevitable that the telling had taken its toll, and Emily had broken down, but Rolf hadn't retreated from her as Alex would have done. Like a fragile boat drifting dangerously close to rocks, she had seen Rolf as the steady beam of a lighthouse.

And he had taken her into his arms, offering her the comfort and solace she'd so desperately craved.

Taking him to her bed had been a very natural progression. Rolf wasn't Alex. He was totally different. Not better. No, never better, just different, and she had savoured the knowledge that he wanted her.

Afterwards, Emily had slept peacefully for the first time in more than a year. She'd even had happy dreams about Robbie, a vision of him being here at the house with a girlfriend, a girl with dark hair and dancing eyes and a beautiful smile.

In her dream, Robbie and the girl had gone swimming, laughing and flirting with each other as they'd wrestled playfully in the water. They'd cooked sausages over an open fire at the lake's edge, and Emily had watched them from the kitchen window, filled with the glow of maternal joy. Robbie was fine. He was happy. Falling in love. All was well.

Except that it wasn't.

This morning, Emily had to come to terms with the fact that she had committed adultery. She'd given in to a moment of weakness and yet nothing had changed. Robbie was still dead and Alex still held her responsible. Before he left, he had made that crystal clear.

'All that talk of your mother and her flying heroics turned our boy's head. It's your fault he joined the RAAF.'

No, nothing had changed. Alex still wouldn't speak to her and sleeping with Rolf was surely a mistake. The pleasure and comfort had been real but fleeting. This morning, she wasn't any happier.

The kitchen was still littered with dirty dishes from last night's meal. Quickly, guiltily, Emily stacked them into the dishwasher and set it humming, before wiping down the bench tops, as if, somehow, a sparkling clean kitchen might atone for her indiscretion.

With the coffee made and Murphy, the golden lab, greeted and fed, Emily was scrambling eggs when Rolf came into the kitchen, fully dressed, his thick hair damp and tamed. She was uncomfortably conscious of her nakedness beneath the dressing gown and was relieved when he didn't try to kiss her.

'Beautiful morning,' he said, looking out to the clear blue sky and its brilliant mirror image in the lake.

'Yes, lovely.' Emily poured coffee into a mug and as he seated himself on a long-legged stool at the bench, she handed it to him. Their fingers brushed. She caught the flash of awareness in his eyes and looked away quickly.

'You're not rowing this morning,' he said.

She managed a small smile. 'I don't like to abandon my guests and leave them to get their own breakfast.'

Rolf frowned and she supposed she might have insulted him by implying that he was a guest, rather than —

'Anyway,' she said quickly, as she stirred the eggs with a dollop of cream and a sprinkling of chopped parsley. 'There's a CWA luncheon today and I still have to make a quiche.'

This brought a smile. 'I can never quite picture you at the CWA,' he said. 'You seem too . . . elegant.'

In a different mood, in a different time, Emily might have been flattered by this description. Now, she said, 'And I always think of you as being too perceptive to stereotype.'

'Ouch.' Rolf's eyes, the grey-green of the sea on a cloudy day, shimmered with amusement. 'Fair enough. I know the CWA claims that it isn't all tea and scones.'

'And it's very true. I have some wonderful friends in the CWA,' she said. 'I couldn't have got through this past year without them.'

Besides, what was the point of being *elegant* when she wanted, more than anything, to be an everyday average granny with creaky knees and comfy old clothes, happily down on the floor playing Lego with her grandchildren, or covered in flour as they baked biscuits together?

Now that was never going to happen.

Emily suppressed a sigh. The eggs were almost ready.

'Shall I butter the toast?'

When Rolf asked this, she almost hesitated. She was uncomfortably conscious of the fine line they'd crossed and she wished there were guidebooks for having affairs with old family friends.

'Thanks,' she said and she tried not to think about Alex as she piled fluffy eggs onto two pieces of toast and took her place beside Rolf at the breakfast bar.

***

The CWA meeting hall was buzzing with women's voices when Chloe arrived. As she stepped through the doorway, she felt very much a stranger; a new kid in the school yard. Fortunately, Moira spied her and grinned and waved.

'There you are!' Plump and looking flushed in pink and mauve floral, Moira crossed the room, like a literal icebreaker, making small, chattering groups of women give way to her. 'Welcome, Chloe, love.' Arms out, she enveloped Chloe in a huge, smothering hug. 'Come and meet everyone.'

Chloe held out a box of peppermints. 'Store bought, I'm afraid. I couldn't manage homemade, but I thought you might be able to use these.'

'Oh, aren't you a sweetie?' To Chloe's relief, Moira couldn't have looked more delighted. 'Now, who would you like to meet first?'

Chloe scanned the crowded room. The women were of all ages and dressed in a range of attire from conservative suits complete with pearls to hippie-style layers with floating scarves. There were hardly any boring slacks and tops, but Chloe was in her usual black trousers, although today she'd teamed them with a grey jacket instead of a white top. She wondered if she stood out as a city chick.

At the far end of the room, trestle tables were laden with warming trays and casserole dishes, salad bowls and tall vases of flowers.

'I don't suppose Emily Hargreaves is here?' Chloe asked Moira.

'Of course she is. Look, here she comes now, actually.' Moira waved to a tall, slim woman and Chloe recognised Emily from their Skype session. Today she was one of the suit and pearls brigade and was making her way towards them. 'She must have spotted you,' Moira said.

'Hello there,' Emily smiled as she reached them. 'Lovely to meet you in person, Chloe.' She held out her hand. She had to be well past fifty and possibly into her sixties. But she had admirable deportment and everything about her was tasteful, from the perfect jaw-length curve of her dark, streaked hair to the slim gold bangle that encircled her slender wrist.

'It's great to meet you, too,' Chloe said, and she wished she didn't feel nervous, as if she hadn't already been through the interview process and been offered the job.

'I'll leave you two to it,' Moira said and she sent Chloe an encouraging wink as she backed away.

Emily smiled again. 'Would you like a drink, Chloe? I believe there's fruit juice, freshly squeezed from local products, of course, or a famous CWA cup of tea.'

'I'm fine for the moment, thank you.'

With another smile, Emily continued smoothly, 'I should apologise perhaps for not meeting you sooner, but I thought I'd give you and Finn a chance to get to know each other first. I trust you're settling in to the *Bugle* office?'

'Yes, thanks.' In her effort to show no sign of hesitation, Chloe answered this almost too quickly. But her answer was honest. If she overlooked her unpleasant initiation on the first afternoon, followed by the next morning's stuff-up at the mushroom farm, things *were* going okay at the office. And at least Finn had been good about letting her come to this luncheon today.

'I'm sure you've discovered that Finn likes to focus on straight news,' Emily said.

Chloe nodded, chanced a small smile.

'Speaking of which, I don't suppose you've heard any updates about poor Ben Shaw?'

'I'm afraid not,' said Chloe. 'Finn thought the police had a new lead, but it seems to have fizzled out.'

Emily shook her head. 'It's terrible. Ben's such a fine young man. He came here to make a new start and he was doing so well.' As she said this, she looked quite stricken and her face was almost haggard, betraying her age.

Then she gave a little shake and smiled again. The moment was gone. 'But Finn does understand that innovation is the key to keeping our little paper afloat, Chloe. And I'm sure you already have lots of fresh ideas.' She posed this last as a question.

Fresh ideas . . . Chloe wasn't sure that her ideas were especially fresh. 'I – I'm thinking about doing a series about local female farmers,' she said. 'I know there are a couple of women in this district who run farms entirely on their own and others who work in partnerships. I'm hoping to talk to Greta from the red claw farm today.'

'Great idea.' Emily's smile widened. 'Greta's here at this luncheon, of course. And so is Carol Frame, who has a wonderful potato farm that she's run single-handedly since her husband died. I'll introduce you later.'

'Thanks.' Heartened by this warm response, Chloe felt emboldened to add, 'I also thought it wouldn't hurt to run a couple of historical pieces.'

'Historical?' Emily gave a small shrug. 'Perhaps. Although I'm not sure that would attract advertising.'

'I'd work at finding a fresh angle. Some kind of modern connection. The schools might be interested.'

'For school projects?' Emily's eyebrows rose as she considered this. 'Well, yes, I guess that might work.' Then she gave Chloe's arm a somewhat maternal pat. 'I have every confidence that you'll come up with great ways to make these ideas work, Chloe.'

'Well, I've only done a little historical research so far, but I've come across some fascinating stories. There are amazing ones about your mother, aren't there?'

'My mother?' Emily seemed shocked.

'Izzie – Isabella Galbraith?' Chloe prompted, wondering if she'd somehow got her wires crossed.

'Yes?'

'She is your mother, isn't she?'

'Yes,' said Emily again, but there was no sign of a smile now.

Despite the disappointing response, Chloe felt she had to continue. 'Izzie sounds incredibly heroic. Moira told me how she ran the *Bugle* for so many years, but then I read about all the flying she did in World War II. She has to be an amazing role model for young girls today.'

Emily sighed and looked down at her clasped hands, beautifully manicured, the nails perfect ovals, painted in a classic nude tone. 'I don't know, Chloe,' she said. 'I'm not sure that's a great idea.'

Chloe had to press her lips together to stop herself from blurting out a surprised response.

'Most people around here already know about Izzie,' Emily said.

Chloe doubted if this knowledge extended to the younger generation, but she was silenced by the bleakness in Emily's eyes.

'If you'd rather I didn't write about her, I'll certainly respect your wishes,' she said.

'Thank you. I think, for the moment, I'd prefer it if you followed up other avenues.' This was said graciously, but with quiet determination.

'Yes, of course.' Chloe was rewarded with another of Emily's beautiful smiles.

'Now, let me introduce you to Greta.'

Chloe was happy to meet Greta, but she was also incredibly curious about Emily's reaction to her mother's story. From her research, Chloe had been wowed by Izzie. Surely she was an all-round heroine?

CHAPTER THIRTEEN

Emily could never quite rid herself of a feeling of guilt when she walked down the corridors of the nursing home towards her mother's private room. Not that she had forced her mother into this place. Quite the opposite, really. After Izzie had broken her hip, Emily and Alex had been fully prepared to try their very hardest to care for Izzie, once she'd been released from hospital and rehab.

Izzie Galbraith had, however, tackled the situation in the same manner that she'd approached everything else in her life: head on.

Never afraid of modern technology, she had used her iPad and the hospital wi-fi to research her chances of recovery. She had learned that it would be a lengthy process. Mortality rates for the elderly in the year following a hip fracture were distressingly high. Complications often set in, caused by blood clots, infection or pneumonia.

It was in her own best interests, Izzie had decided, to submit to all-round professional nursing care. Thus, a nursing home was her best option and, as with all other important decisions in Izzie's life, once this decision was made, she had faced her fate bravely and without complaint.

Well, almost without complaint. The staff at the home were

always on their best behaviour when they attended to Izzie's needs. Anyone new was quickly inducted into how Izzie liked her bed to be made, how she preferred the curtains to be drawn, where her slippers should be placed, ready when she rose, and how her wheelie walker must be parked, just so.

Everyone's life was easier if they got these details right.

Today, Izzie was asleep when Emily quietly entered her room. She was lying on her back with her mouth a little open, looking surprisingly defenceless.

Emily had given up bringing flowers. When her mother had first moved into the home, Emily had brought fresh flowers every week, until she'd been asked not to.

'I'm not sick,' Izzie had said. 'And I'm certainly not a film star. And flowers start to smell if people don't change the water often enough.'

Now, quietly, Emily went to a chair in the corner and sat, rather pleased to have a moment of privacy to compose herself. She was still terribly conscious of the 'night of sin' she'd just spent with Rolf. She knew that her lapse couldn't possibly show on her face, but she had a ridiculously childish and unreasonable fear that somehow her mother would be able to guess.

Of necessity, Emily forced her thoughts elsewhere and found, to her dismay, that they veered straight to Alex. Once again, she was remembering the dreadful fight they'd had on the night before he left for Red Hill, the atrocious things they'd said. Or rather, yelled.

The insults were awful, as if they'd forgotten the wonderful love that had brought them together, all the good years they'd enjoyed, pulling alongside each other as life partners in every sense.

The fight had been born out of terrible pain, of course. The pain of losing Robbie and the unbearable tension that had followed ever since, including the dreadful blame game.

Remembering all of this, Emily lifted her gaze to her mother as she lay looking so peaceful and innocent. *You knew he blamed you, didn't you?*

Of course, Izzie had been aware of Alex's simmering resentment. And she'd been at the Lake House on that fateful day when they'd received the devastating news.

As a special treat, Emily had brought Izzie away from the nursing home to have lunch in her old home with herself and Alex. Emily had gone to the trouble of preparing her mother's favourites, a mustard-stuffed chicken, followed by a raspberry Bakewell tart for dessert.

'You should come to lunch more often, Izzie,' Alex had told her with a grin. 'We don't usually have such fine fare.'

The comment had surprised Emily. Surely her husband must have known that he'd left himself wide open for one of her mother's digs.

Izzie hadn't missed the opportunity. 'Why do you say that, Alex? What does Emily serve you when I'm not around? Vegemite sandwiches?'

'No, no,' Alex responded with equal speed and an annoyed gleam in his eye. 'Mostly we have delicious salads.'

'But I usually don't bother with dessert,' Emily explained, hoping to keep the peace.

'Nor should you,' Izzie replied stoutly. 'Alex would soon run to fat now that he's no longer working with cattle every day.'

So they were already tense when the doorbell rang, shrilly slicing through the quiet afternoon.

Alex frowned and sent a sharp glance across the table to Emily. 'Were you expecting anyone?' he asked.

'No,' she said. She had no idea who it could be. Their place was so private, they hardly ever had callers unless they'd been invited. Most people telephoned first. Then Murphy began to bark, so she knew this was definitely a stranger.

'I'll go,' she said, dropping her napkin onto the table as she rose from her chair.

It didn't occur to her to worry, until she peeped through the glass panel in the front door and saw the two figures in Air Force uniforms.

Oh, God.

'Alex!' she called, knowing instantly what this visit must mean and that she couldn't face it alone.

Alex must have caught the panic in her voice. He was at her side almost immediately, just as the doorbell rang again.

'It's the RAAF,' Emily told her husband and she saw the colour leach from his face.

For a fraught moment, they stared at each other, frozen in terror, not wanting to hear the news that their son, their beautiful only child, had been killed. Emily didn't want Alex to open the door, but of course he had to, eventually, reaching for the knob with a shaking hand.

Two middle aged, smartly uniformed servicemen stood on the top step.

'Mr Hargreaves?'

The men were perfectly trained and they did their job well, delivering their message with meticulous care. Compassionate, sensitive and practical, they had all bases covered. But Emily, distraught, just wanted to scream at them to go away.

If her mother hadn't been there, she might have behaved very badly indeed, but she was distressingly aware that Izzie had loved Robbie too. Deeply, painfully; perhaps more than she'd loved anyone else.

Instead of weeping, however, Izzie sat alone, a tiny figure, still as a statue. No tears. Just a terrible, tragic stillness.

'Emily.'

Emily blinked, wrenched back to the present, to the room in the nursing home, to the sound of her mother's voice. 'Mum,' she said, rising. 'You're awake.' She crossed the room, kissed her mother's thin cheek. 'How are you today?'

'Fine. How long have you been here?'

'Not very long. I was happy to sit.'

'You've been brooding about Robbie again.'

'Just a little.'

Izzie frowned. 'Have you heard from Alex?'

'I rang Red Hill,' Emily said, avoiding a direct answer. 'Alex is fine.' Then, not wanting to pursue that subject any further, she pulled her chair closer and sat again. 'I have some news that might interest you,' she said. 'I've hired a new journalist. A young woman.'

This most definitely piqued her mother's interest. 'What's her name?'

'Chloe Brown.'

Her mother frowned. 'She's not a local?'

'No, she's from Sydney. She's had a lot of experience on a women's magazine. I'm hoping she'll write colour stories to attract more advertising.'

Emily was prepared for a negative response to this, but to her surprise, Izzie seemed even more interested. 'What's Finn think of her?' Izzie was, in fact, Finn Latimer's number-one fan.

'I'm not sure,' Emily admitted. 'I think, in time, he'll adjust.'

'This Chloe Brown will have her work cut out for her, trying to please him.'

'I have every faith in her.' Emily hoped she wouldn't have to eat her words.

'I'd like to meet her,' Izzie said.

'Oh.' This was unexpected. Remembering Chloe's interest in Izzie, Emily was suddenly nervous again. She was imagining the story Chloe might write about her mother, dredging up all the World

War II heroics and, no doubt, reminding the entire district of the source of Robbie's inspiration to join the Air Force. But she could hardly back down now. 'I'm sure that can be arranged,' she said, crossing her fingers.

To Emily's relief, Izzie was happy to talk about other things. The local singing group had visited as part of the home's entertainment program, and Tammy, the hairdresser, still came on Wednesday afternoons to cut the residents' hair or paint nails or generally cheer folk up, even though she was so worried about her missing boyfriend.

Afternoon tea arrived next and there was a cup for Emily as well. After they'd drunk their tea and eaten a tiny shortbread biscuit, Emily helped her mother out of bed. Izzie wheeled herself the short distance to the bathroom, but this process took quite a while and by the time she was back in bed, she was tired.

It was time to say goodbye.

'See you soon,' Emily said, kissing her.

'Goodbye, dear.'

Emily was at the doorway when her mother spoke again.

'Emily.'

'Yes?'

'You mustn't stew so much over Alex. It's not good for you and it's not going to change him.'

Her mother could well be right, Emily thought with a sigh. 'I'll try.' Forcing a smile, she wondered what her mother would say if she knew about Rolf.

As she walked out of the carefully sanitised home and into fresh air and sunshine, she wondered also about her mother's long years of widowhood. Had Izzie ever taken lovers? Emily would never ask, but she wouldn't have been surprised if her mother had spent those years in stoical abstinence.

Izzie had always been incredibly tough and independent. Emily supposed she'd been born that way.

CHAPTER FOURTEEN

Cambridgeshire, England, 1927

'Jem! Jem, wait for me!' Seven-year-old Izzie Oakshott screamed at the top of her lungs as she raced towards her big brother, tearing across the long field that stretched behind their family's home. 'Jem, don't go without me!'

Tall and broad shouldered, with red-gold hair that glinted in the morning sunlight, Jem was standing beside his beloved Gipsy Moth aeroplane and pulling on his leather flying helmet. At any moment now, he would climb into the cockpit, don his goggles and take off, and Izzie would be too late.

'Jem!' she screamed again, even more desperately. 'Wait! I want to come too!'

Izzie loved nothing better than to fly in her brother's plane. For her, it was even more exciting than driving in Jem's sports car and usually, as long as she found him in time, he was pretty good about letting her take off with him on short jaunts. He seemed to understand that his skinny, curly-haired youngest sister was as passionate about flying as he was.

'Does Mother know you're down here?' Jem asked as Izzie arrived, breathless and panting.

Izzie hadn't stopped to ask for her mother's permission, but she reasoned that she'd been yelling so loudly, someone in the house was bound to have heard her. Surely that meant that Mother would know where she was?

Izzie nodded. 'Yes, she knows.'

For a long moment that was agonising for Izzie, Jem looked doubtful, and he studied her with narrowed eyes, as if he were assessing her honesty. She met his gaze with a steady, resolute stare and behind her back, she crossed her fingers. To her relief, Jem smiled at her, making creases around his hazel eyes.

He set down his helmet and goggles. 'Come on then. Jump in.'

Izzie grinned ecstatically as his strong hands gripped her under the armpits and lifted her high. A moment later she was scrambling into her seat in the Gipsy Moth's front cockpit.

A cushion to prop her up so that she could see over the side was already in place from her last trip. So were the spare helmet and goggles and she pulled the helmet on, strapping it expertly under her chin, conscious that her beaming grin revealed a humiliating gap where her front teeth used to be. She was tired of being the littlest in the family and she couldn't wait for her new, grown up teeth to arrive.

'All set?' Jem asked as he helped her to tighten the goggles.

Still grinning, Izzie held up two thumbs.

'Righto.' Giving her a pat on her bony shoulder, he went to the front of the plane and spun the propeller.

The engine roared to life, making a clattering racket, as Jem took a quick step back then climbed into his cockpit.

Izzie sat very still, trying to curb her excited impatience as he went through his pre-flight checks. Aeroplanes were still quite a novelty, not just for her family, but for people all over England.

Her father had a successful motor car business and Izzie, along with her sisters, loved to hear their mother tell the story of how this had started when he'd taken her on a honeymoon trip to Paris.

'Your father was stunned to discover how advanced the French were with their internal combustion engines,' she would tell them with one of her pretty dimpling smiles. 'He almost forgot about me.'

The girls were sure this wasn't true. Their father might be mad about motor cars, but he doted on their mother. They only had to watch the way he smiled at her, his dark eyes shining with love.

Even so, he *had* been inspired to come home to England and start his own business. He'd opened a tiny garage with just two cars at first, but the business had taken off like a rocket. These days he had quite a grand car sales and service centre with Rolls-Royces, Daimlers and Bugattis and he planned to start selling aeroplanes soon.

With their father's huge interest in cars and planes, no one in the family, except their mother, had been surprised when Jem learned to fly soon after he'd finished his engineering studies at Cambridge. Jem had earned his flying licence just a year ago, and a couple of months later he'd bought his own beautiful Gipsy Moth.

Mother had been quite shocked when he'd flown home and landed his plane in the field at the back of the house, tethering it to a fence post, as if it were nothing more than a newfangled horse.

'I really don't like the idea of you flying, Jem,' she had said at luncheon on that very same day. 'It was worrying enough when you were racing all over the countryside in that Austin of yours. Flying has to be so much more dangerous.'

Normally, their mother was unfailingly gentle and uncomplaining, especially towards Jem, her eldest child and her only son. The girls knew she adored him, so the fact that she expressed such displeasure showed them how very worried she must have been.

Their father, however, had staunchly defended Jem's purchase. From the other end of the long dining table, he frowned at his wife. 'Now, now, Vi, you know aeroplanes and flying are the way of the future. This is a very important and exciting day for Jem. Don't spoil it, sweetheart.'

Daddy said this gently, and added one of his special smiles just for their mother. A moment later, she wiped her tears with the corner of her handkerchief and managed a small, answering smile. Their gazes held, enjoying a moment that Izzie recognised as another of those private, understanding exchanges that passed just between her parents. Seeing it always made her feel safe and happy.

Perhaps Mother might have said something more, but Daisy, the maid, arrived to clear their plates and to serve dessert of peach shortcake and cream. Mother made no further comments about Jem's plane and she hadn't made a fuss a week later when Izzie had begged to be allowed to fly with Jem as his passenger. Since then, Mother had seemed to accept the inevitable and Izzie had enjoyed the privilege of travelling with her brother on several exhilarating flights.

Now, she wriggled in her seat with excitement as the Gipsy Moth rolled forward – taxiing, Jem called it – to the far end of the field. Then, smoothly, steadily, the plane lifted off, rising magically over the white flowering hawthorn hedge that bordered the field, and climbing higher and higher.

Izzie saw the red-tiled roof of their tall white house and the orchard and tennis courts way down below, getting smaller and smaller. She saw their dog, Hector, just a tiny black and white speck, scampering back and forth and no doubt barking up at them.

Giggling, she waved to the dog and they flew on over the patchwork of neighbouring countryside that looked so different and beautiful from way up here. For Izzie, being high in the air like a bird was the best thing in the world, even when she was dressed in a thin summer frock in an open cockpit with no cover, and soon shivering.

'Everything fine in the front?' Jem called, his voice coming through her helmet's earphones, thanks to a tube that was linked from his pilot's cockpit to hers.

'Yes!' Izzie shouted back. She wouldn't dream of complaining about the cold. 'Where are we going?'

'To Newmarket.'

'Ooh, goody.' Last time they'd gone to Newmarket, a journey that happened surprisingly quickly when you flew, Jem had bought her a dish of ice-cream with chocolate sauce and a cherry on top.

They weren't away long. Jem had some banking business to attend to in Newmarket and, while he was busy, Izzie waited patiently on a little bench in the foyer. She didn't mind waiting. She had a view through a big plate glass window to the street and she quite liked to watch the people walking past. It was fun to make up stories about them.

The young woman hurrying quickly with a worried frown could be a princess in disguise, trying to escape her wicked uncle. The old lady with the hooked nose and dressed all in black was obviously a witch and Izzie was careful not to make eye contact with her when she glanced though the window. She didn't want to risk being turned into a toad.

The round red-faced man clambering down from his mud-splashed truck was most likely a farmer whose hens laid magic eggs. But before Izzie could imagine any more wondrous scenarios, Jem arrived and took her to a café where she had her yummy dish of ice-cream. After that, they flew home again, taking off from a parking spot on a little back road that no one used very much.

Again, Izzie was captivated by the thrill of take-off, by the sense of breaking free and rising, rising, watching the rooftops and tree-tops of Newmarket fall away. It was a lovely blue-sky afternoon and she could see for miles. In her imagination, she could almost see all the way to London.

She pictured Jem taking her to the big city and flying past the King's palace. If she closed her eyes, she could picture King George standing at his palace window, waving to her with a bright-red, white and blue handkerchief like the Union Jack.

What fun!

The plane was coming into land, flying lower and lower, when Izzie saw the strange big vehicle, like a van, parked in front of their house. Two men were carrying a stretcher from the house to the van and there was someone on it, covered by a white sheet.

Izzie gasped. Her chest tightened and burned. 'Who's that?' she yelled into the speaking tube to Jem. 'What's happened?'

'I'm not sure,' he replied.

He didn't say any more, but he'd sounded worried. Izzie didn't ply him with questions. She was suddenly, inexplicably, too scared to ask. Young as she was, she sensed that something bad had happened. Besides, Jem needed all his concentration to focus on landing. Even so, it was the bumpiest landing he'd ever made.

As soon as the plane shuddered to a standstill, he disembarked in record time, hauling off his helmet and goggles and helping Izzie with hers. Then he lifted her out, set her down on the grass and took off, running towards the house, not waiting for her.

Izzie had no hope of keeping up with Jem's long legs, and his haste frightened her. Clearly he was very worried indeed. He didn't go into the house, but ran around the side, past the tennis courts to the gravel drive at the front.

By the time Izzie arrived, the stretcher had disappeared and the van's big doors were shut. Izzie's father was there, looking white as a ghost, and Jem was talking to him and two other men, both strangers, while her three sisters were clustered on the front porch, clinging to each other, weeping and looking scared.

Izzie skidded to an abrupt standstill. Her heart pounded in her chest as she stood, panting, taking in this scary scene, knowing there was one very important person missing.

Mother.

Surely *she* wasn't the person on the stretcher?

At first, Izzie couldn't bring herself to move. Everyone else looked so very distressed and distracted and she didn't know who to turn to. Then Jem must have remembered her.

He looked back over his shoulder and saw her. 'Izzie,' he said softly and his eyes were round with sorrow and his mouth was all twisted out of shape, but he held out his arms to her and she ran to him. 'Oh, Izzie.'

She clung to Jem's waist, felt the metallic bump of his belt buckle, the soft tweed of his jacket, the deep shudder within him.

'What's wrong, Jem? What's happened?'

'It's Mother.'

Izzie wailed, pressing her face into his chest.

Now her sisters were there, too. Fourteen-year-old Betty was clinging to Jem's arm and sobbing on his shoulder. Vera, the eldest girl, patted Izzie's back as if she were a baby, while Jane, who was ten, stood crying, frantically twisting her handkerchief.

'The doctor thinks Mother had a stroke,' Vera said.

Bewildered, Izzie frowned at her sister. 'A stroke?' This didn't make sense to her. Wasn't stroking a perfectly safe thing to do, like patting a dog? What did Vera mean?

'She – she's —' Vera couldn't bring herself to finish. A terrible cry broke from her and she quickly jammed a handkerchief into her mouth.

It was Betty who tried to explain. 'Mother collapsed, Izzie. She was in the kitchen talking to Mrs Phipps about dinner and – and it just happened. Poor Mrs Phipps was in a terrible state. We phoned for the doctor, but it was too late.'

'Too late for what?' But even as Izzie asked this question, she realised that she could guess the awful answer.

After the van had driven away, Izzie's father went into the house and headed upstairs without speaking to any of them. His face was pale and his mouth a thin, tight, downward-curving line. He clutched the stair railing as he ascended, as if his legs weren't strong enough to support him.

Jem and the girls went into the sitting room and Vera asked Daisy, who was hovering in the doorway and looking quite sick, if she would make them a pot of tea. Jem drifted to the far window and stood, hands sunk deep in his trouser pockets, staring out. Vera slumped into an armchair and Jane and Betty flopped onto the sofa.

Bewildered, Izzie stood in the middle of the room. None of the others spoke. No one cried. They just stared blankly into space.

'Why won't one of you tell me what happened?' she demanded. 'Mother's dead, isn't she?'

It was Jem who answered her. 'Yes, poppet.' He turned from the window and he spoke gently. 'I'm afraid she is.'

'Did they put her in the van?' Izzie asked, even though she was sure she knew the answer.

'Yes.' This time Jem and Vera spoke together.

Izzie couldn't bear it. Her mother had been on that stretcher, under the white sheet, and now she'd been taken away from them in a van. Izzie would never see her again.

A vision of her life without their mother flashed before her. No one coming to kiss her good morning or to tuck her in to bed at night. An empty chair at the end of the dining table. No one to listen to her tales of woe or triumph when she came home from school bursting with news. No special cuddles.

Her mouth twisted and trembled. 'Oh, Jem,' she wailed. 'I didn't tell her. I didn't tell her I was going to Newmarket with you. I didn't say goodbye.'

As Izzie made this terrible confession, an awful noise broke from her, a noise she didn't realise she was making at first until her knees turned rubbery and she sank to the carpet sobbing. Pressing her face into the carpet that smelled faintly of dog, she sobbed so hard she was shaking.

And now she couldn't stop. She was aware of Jem and her sisters kneeling beside her, trying to calm her, to comfort her. At some point she knew that Daisy had come back into the room with the tea tray and that cups and saucers were being passed around. And she knew she was making too much noise, but she couldn't help it. She was too filled with guilt and pain and the most awful, smothering loss.

During the night, Izzie woke often and each time she remembered that her mother was dead – gone forever – and the tears came again, making her throat ache, soaking her pillow.

At one point Betty came into her room with a mug of warm milk and honey, and she sat with Izzie after it was finished, until she drifted back to sleep. But when Izzie woke again it was still dark and the tears and misery returned as painfully and noisily as ever.

Morning finally arrived. A grey, sunless morning, and Izzie stayed under the bedclothes in a miserable huddle until Vera came in, already dressed for the day, rather than remaining in her dressing gown as she usually did. Izzie remembered that her mother would never come through her bedroom doorway again, and she was on the brink of a fresh burst of sobbing when her sister held up her hand.

'Don't start crying again,' Vera warned her gently, but quite firmly.

'Why not?' Izzie whimpered.

'You'll upset Daddy.'

Daddy. Izzie's mouth was open, ready to let out a wail that promised to be even louder and more tragic than any of her previous laments. But as Vera's word sank in, she shut her mouth again.

'We all need to be very brave,' Vera said. 'For Daddy's sake.'

Having witnessed her father's white, tight face, Izzie could understand that, of course, her father was hurting, too. Everyone in the family was hurting, even Jem, but no one else was crying like a baby and making a noisy fuss.

They were all being brave. *For Daddy's sake . . .*

'All right, I'll try,' she said.

'Good girl. Go to the bathroom and wash your face, then get dressed and come down to breakfast. Mrs Phipps has kept some kedgeree especially for you. You missed supper last night and she was sure you'd be hungry.

At the mention of kedgeree, Izzie realised that she was ravenous and she hurried obediently down the passage to the bathroom, vowing to stop the tears and to be terribly brave.

To her surprise, the mere thought of being brave made her feel instantly stronger. Being brave was much better than crying and it would probably make Mother, watching from Heaven, proud.

On that grey and gloomy morning, at the ripe old age of seven, Izzie could feel in her bones that this was a lesson she would carry with her into the future.

CHAPTER FIFTEEN

'This story's great,' Finn said. 'Well done.'

It was quite late in the day by the time he read Chloe's piece about the female farmers, but as he turned from his computer screen, the respectful glint in his eyes suggested that his praise was genuine.

'Thanks,' she said, but she looked away quickly, hoping he couldn't see the heat flooding her face. Surely his praise shouldn't be so important to her?

'Our sales reps should be able to wrangle a couple of decent ads to support this,' Finn added. 'So that should keep Emily happy.'

'That's good,' Chloe replied with a wry smile. After all, it was Emily who had employed her.

Finn closed down his computer. 'Reckon I'll call it a day.' He stood, lifting his arms in an easy, unselfconscious motion above his head as he stretched.

No doubt he needed to stretch after sitting for so long and the movement should not have absorbed Chloe's complete attention. She hoped he didn't notice her checking him out, but his body was surprisingly toned for a man with a drinking problem. She made a business of sorting the papers on her desk.

'Oh, and by the way,' Finn said as he slipped his phone into a back pocket in his jeans. 'There's one thing I've been meaning to mention.' He sounded a bit awkward as he said this, not at all like her usually in-control boss. 'I – er – normally have a meal at the pub one or two nights a week.'

'Oh?' Chloe wasn't quite sure how else to respond, especially as Finn now looked quite uncomfortable.

He gave an awkward shrug. 'I get a bit tired of my own cooking.'

Somehow, she hadn't imagined Finn living alone and cooking for himself. Even though he seemed to have an issue with alcohol, he had the looks and the alpha-male vibes that usually attracted women in droves.

'So . . . you don't have a partner? A – a wife?' The question seemed to stumble from Chloe, but as soon as it was out she wished she could snatch it back. Only a total airhead would ask something so dumb.

But it was too late to retract the words and she could see that she'd hit a nerve.

Finn's face closed. A muscle twitched close to his jawline. 'Don't you know?' he asked and he sounded suddenly exhausted.

Know what? She felt sick.

'I lost my wife and son in a terrorist attack in Thailand.'

Whack.

Fire exploded in Chloe's face. *Oh, God.* She tried to imagine the horror for Finn, but her mind flinched. This was just too awful to contemplate.

Of course, she should have known about it. Actually, she realised now that she *had* heard news stories about the terrible incident, but somehow she'd overlooked them when she'd searched the internet for info about her new editor. She'd been so certain, so absolutely convinced that the *Burralea Bugle*'s Finn Latimer could not possibly be the same man who was the well-known foreign correspondent.

'I'm so sorry,' she said, not quite meeting his gaze. 'Somehow I – I didn't put two and two together.'

'Yeah, well.' He sighed heavily, took out his phone as if he needed a distraction, then frowned and slipped it back into his pocket again. 'Anyway, that's why I sometimes eat at the pub.'

'Yes, of course.' She couldn't begin to understand the depth of his loss. His grief would be overwhelming. He would have no room for anything else.

Disappointment whispered. And then she was ashamed of herself. She wasn't looking for anything else either. She wondered what he used to be like before . . .

Surely his whole life must feel defined by that tragedy, divided into before and after.

'Anyway, I just thought I'd warn you,' Finn said and his mouth tilted, showing the barest glimmer of a smile. 'It might look weird if we're sitting at opposite ends of the pub's dining room.'

'Yes, I suppose the locals might notice something like that.' Chloe was grateful that he had warned her. She might have handled things awkwardly if she'd come down to dinner and found him there. 'Should I ask Sandra to set two places at my usual table?'

'That'd be great, if it's fine by you.'

She managed a small smile. 'Of course.'

'Good. See you around seven-thirty?'

'Sure.'

He crossed to the door and stood waiting while she dropped her phone and a few pages of notes into her shoulder bag and picked up the jacket she'd left hanging on the back of her chair.

Finn locked the door and pocketed the keys. 'Catch you later.'

They parted on the footpath, walking in opposite directions. Chloe had no idea where Finn lived and she had never asked, but now, of course, her head was swimming with questions.

It was almost dusk and the temperature had dropped even though the day had been hot and humid. She pulled on her jacket and continued on her way, past the pharmacy and the hairdresser's. She saw the pink-haired Tammy still working away with her blow-dryer, making yet another elderly client look glamorous.

According to Moira, Tammy claimed that she had to keep working, even though she was worried out of her mind about her missing boyfriend. She said the work kept her busy and her customers were like family. In their own different ways, they all supported her.

Chloe reached the Lilly Pilly café and as she did so, Jess emerged, followed by a chorus of cheerful voices calling from the kitchen behind her.

'See you tomorrow, Jess.'

'Goodnight, Jess.'

'Night,' Jess called back, and she looked happy. No, she looked better than that, she looked really content. As if she'd found her tribe. She grinned at Chloe. 'Hey there. On your way home?'

'Yep,' Chloe said. 'All done for the day.'

'I'm on my way to pick up Willow.'

'How's she settling in?'

'Beautifully. And the other mums are so friendly. It's amazing really. A group of them came to the café this morning and Marj gave me time off to sit and have a coffee and a chat with them. They were *so* nice. So relaxed and friendly. There's something about country people, isn't there?'

Chloe nodded. She'd been impressed by how warm and welcoming the CWA women had been. There'd also been a time in the not-too-distant past when she'd fantasised about being part of a group of mums who went jogging with their prams and met each other for coffee. Actually, she still ached for that dream.

'So, how's your new job?' asked Jess.

'Oh, I think I'm finding my feet.'

'By the way.' Jess stepped closer to Chloe and lowered her voice. 'I got a gander at your editor when he came in for his coffee. Lucky you.'

If Chloe had heard this comment a few days ago, she might have set Jess straight by telling her about Finn's drinking, but everything was different now. She wasn't sure how the tragedy of Finn's family was connected to his drinking, but she was certainly prepared to cut her boss some slack. She gave an offhand shrug. 'He's pretty good to work with.'

'He's not married either, so I hear,' Jess added with a knowing smile. 'So . . . quite a ride, as they say.'

Jess, no doubt, wasn't aware of the reasons for Finn's single status. 'That suggestion is wasted on me, Jess. I'm taking a sabbatical from relationships.'

'Yeah, right.' The other girl didn't look convinced.

'Are you crossing here?' Chloe nodded towards her destination, the two-storey timber pub on the opposite corner.

'Sure.'

They waited for a car to pass – just one car, how amazing was that? – and then headed across the wide street together.

'Have you met the paper's owner yet?' Jess asked.

'Yes,' said Chloe. 'She's lovely. A bit —' She hesitated.

'Snooty?'

'No, not snooty.'

'Sorry. I've only seen her the once, in the café.'

Chloe had been about to say that Emily Hargreaves was rather reserved, but in a nice way. Now she stopped herself from making even a mild criticism that felt somehow disloyal. 'Mrs Hargreaves is lovely,' she said instead. 'She introduced me to some really good contacts.'

Jess nodded and asked no more questions. Then, with a grin, she announced, 'I'm thinking of getting a little second-hand car.'

'Wow. Good for you.'

They'd reached the main entrance to the pub. 'I'll let you know if I end up with wheels,' Jess said. 'Maybe we could do a little exploring together.'

'I'd love that.'

Jess grinned. 'Me, too. I'll keep in touch, Chloe. Bye.'

Chloe came down to the hotel's dining room a little before seven-thirty. The room had an open fireplace, which was currently filled with potted ferns, but she could imagine it with burning logs in winter, the crackle and dance of bright flames making a pleasant background to the hum of diners' voices.

She took a seat at her usual table in the far corner of the long room where she had a view of the two doorways guests could enter through. She wished she didn't feel nervous about dining with Finn. It couldn't be all that different from working with him.

She hadn't gone overboard, but she'd gone to a little more trouble than usual with her appearance, showering and changing into a brown linen dress, which had the potential to look dowdy, but she liked it anyway. The brown matched her eyes and she'd brightened the neckline with a scarf in autumn tones.

After filling her water glass, she studied the menu. She knew it pretty much by heart. Tonight she would have the salmon with asparagus and wasabi. She wondered what Finn would choose and guessed that he might want the steak with fries and peppercorn sauce.

Right on time, Finn arrived. His thick, dark hair looked neat, still damp from the shower, and he'd shaved. Heads turned in his direction. A few of the diners waved to him and he stopped to greet a young man with longish auburn hair and a clerical collar. At another table, he spoke briefly to a rather handsome silver-haired couple.

'Good evening,' he said to Chloe as he reached her.

'Hi there.'

She caught a whiff of his aftershave, subtle and spicy, and she couldn't help smiling. His shirt was brown, almost the exact shade as her dress.

He looked down at his clothing and then at her with a puzzled smile, a question in his eyes. 'Something wrong with my shirt?'

'No, no,' Chloe said. 'It's just that we seem to be colour coordinated. White shirts for work, brown at night.'

Now he looked mildly amused. 'The things women notice.'

'I know. So trivial.'

'But Brown is also your surname,' he said. 'So perhaps that colours your perspective.'

At this, she rolled her eyes and wished she hadn't started this weird conversation.

And now Finn was frowning. 'It was a lame joke, but it wasn't that bad, was it?'

'No, you just reminded me of – of something else.' She fiddled with the paper serviette wrapped around her cutlery. She was digging herself in deeper.

'Something brown? Come on, spill. You've got me intrigued.'

'It's stupid.' She gave a helpless shake of her head. 'But I suppose I might as well tell you. I was just remembering this guy I – I used to know – well, live with. His name was Brown too, so we were Jason Brown and Chloe Brown. And right away, on the first night we met, he suggested we should marry and become Mr and Mrs Very Brown.'

Finn lifted a dark eyebrow. 'Sounds like a smooth-talking guy.'

'Yeah.' *Way too smooth.* Chloe had ended up sleeping with Jason on that very first night.

'Is it too presumptuous to assume that you didn't marry him?' Finn asked.

'Dead right. No wedding,' she said tightly.

'You moved here instead?' Finn's dark eyes gleamed and Chloe felt as if he could see right through her.

But she had no intention of sharing any more about her ex. 'I moved here because I wanted to expand my horizons.'

'Of course.'

To Chloe's relief, Finn was happy enough to turn his attention to their meal selections, which didn't take long. He was as familiar with the menu as she was.

'I'll go for the steak with peppercorn sauce,' he said.

She bit back another urge to smile. 'I'd like the salmon.'

They ordered wine as well. Chloe wondered if Finn might get stuck into the alcohol, but he simply asked for a glass of red while she had white to go with her fish.

He told her about some of the other diners. The fellow in the clerical collar was a popular young Anglican priest who had worked on cattle properties, and had even been a rodeo clown, before he'd joined the church. The elderly couple were childhood sweethearts who'd only met up again recently. Now they were married and the whole town was delighted.

'So have you interviewed them?' Chloe asked. 'Both those stories sound quite fascinating.'

Finn gave a smiling shake of his head. 'You have to remember this is a very small town. Not everyone wants their personal life plastered all over the paper.'

'No, I don't suppose so.' Chloe remembered Emily Hargreaves' reluctance to have her mother's story published. 'I guess the world's divided into people who are cracking their necks to hit the headlines and those who hate the thought of being in the limelight.'

'And for journos,' added Finn, 'there's the whole issue of finding and publishing the stories that need to be told whether people like it or not.'

One story Chloe knew people were hanging out for was good news about the missing baker. Unfortunately, there wasn't much to report. The coppers kept running into dead ends.

'I suppose the magnifying glass seems so much bigger in a tiny country town,' she said.

'Exactly. And it's not possible to keep everyone happy.'

'My editor used to tell us that if everyone's happy we're not doing our job.'

'Wise chap,' said Finn.

'A woman, actually.'

His smile held the hint of an apology. 'Of course.'

Their meals arrived and Chloe said carefully, as she spread a smear of wasabi over her salmon, 'It must have been a huge change for you, to come to a tiny paper like the *Bugle* after reporting on major world events.'

Finn paused in the process of cutting his steak and gave a small shrug. 'I guess I've joined the folk who want to stay out of the limelight.'

After everything he'd been through, Chloe could well believe this.

'I just needed to go off grid for a bit,' he said.

'Back-road therapy.'

'Yeah, more or less.'

Chloe wondered, though, if Burralea was a bit too quiet for Finn. Were there counsellors here, anyone he could talk to about losing his family? Just keeping to himself couldn't be healthy. Then she realised he was watching her rather keenly and she wondered if he'd surmised that her trek from Sydney was also a form of escape, of retreat. To her relief he didn't push the matter.

'But you're right,' he said instead. 'Coming here took a huge adjustment. I had real trouble at first finding anything I deemed newsworthy. It was like I needed my eyesight tested, the lenses adjusted.'

'I suppose there are triumphs and tragedies everywhere. It's just a matter of scale.'

'Well, yeah – and I also had to cut my ego to fit.' Finn grinned as he said this and he looked so attractive and downright charming, ridiculous flashes shot under Chloe's skin.

To her relief, he didn't notice anything. He was totally focused on talking about work.

'Running the *Bugle* has been a good lesson, really,' he said. 'It's brought me back to the basics. For any journalist, getting the details right is the important thing, whether it's Burralea's Junior Soccer results or a political crisis in Canberra.'

Chloe admired him for taking this low-key job seriously, even though most of his fellow journalists would have seen it as a major step down.

She couldn't help asking, 'Do you think you'll stay here?' But she wondered if she'd gone too far.

'Will you?' Finn shot the question straight back at her and his eyes gleamed as if he knew she was snookered.

'I —' Chloe hesitated. With every day she spent in Burralea, she liked the place, the people and her job more and more. She sensed that if she let it, the town could draw her in, encourage her to make deeper connections, to put down roots.

She had pretty much decided to take up Moira Briggs's offer of the flat above her office. Moira was happy to keep the arrangement flexible, however. And Chloe still saw this job as a stopgap; a chance to get away and earn a wage until she decided what she really wanted to do with the rest of her life.

She still longed for motherhood and that damn clock was

still ticking, but if she did decide to go solo, there were no fertility clinics in Burralea. Then there was the whole issue of Finn's drinking. She had no idea whether it would resurface and cause her problems.

'I don't know,' she told him. 'I haven't quite decided.'

His response was a slow smile. 'Neither have I.'

CHAPTER SIXTEEN

Moira Briggs seemed almost disappointed that Chloe's move into the flat above the Progress Association's office went very smoothly without her assistance. The ease of the move wasn't really surprising, however. The flat was fully furnished and Chloe had only a suitcase and a laptop to unpack. The rest of her things – sheets and towels, special books and her favourite smoky, two-toned coffee mugs – arrived in a box she'd left behind in Sydney and that her mum had efficiently forwarded.

Moira gave Chloe a potted maidenhair fern as a housewarming present, and Chloe's heart sank a little. She wasn't very good with pot plants and this fern looked scarily healthy but delicate.

She checked the gardening information on the internet and discovered that placing the pot on a water-filled pebble tray should help. This was now established in her kitchen. And her fingers were firmly crossed.

Shopping for groceries in Burralea was a cinch. The supermarket was just around the corner and it supplied almost everything Chloe needed. Extra luxuries, like ciabatta or salmon steaks or lavender tea, she could collect from stores in bigger towns while she was out and about, driving the *Bugle*'s vehicle.

To celebrate her very first evening in the flat, Chloe roasted a chicken breast with pancetta, leeks and thyme. She opened a bottle of chilled pinot gris and drank a glass while she cooked her dinner and had another glass with the meal. A bit flash for a week-night at home alone, perhaps, but after the upset over recent weeks of alternating between missing Jason dreadfully and wanting to punch him on his handsome nose, Chloe needed to fete her new independence.

The celebratory effect was somewhat spoiled by the fact that she ate her lovely meal on her lap in front of a TV quiz show, but she didn't fancy sitting at the table and listening to music alone. Unfortunately, the TV didn't really help either.

Annoyingly, her attention kept drifting from the screen to thoughts about her boss. Had Finn cooked his own dinner, or had he gone to the pub?

No doubt he was relieved that he could eat at the pub again whenever he liked without having to warn her in advance.

When she finished the meal, she washed the dishes and tidied the kitchen and gave the maidenhair a glass of water. The view through the window above the sink showed the night sky flecked with crystal stars, sharp and sparkling away from the loom of city lights.

She caught a movement below in the garden, a shadowy shape slipping into the shrubbery. A cat? Bandicoot? Possum? She couldn't be sure.

After the constant hum of voices and music in the pub, the flat was very quiet. The occasional motor vehicle rushed along the main road that skimmed the town, but Chloe only heard it if she really listened.

Loneliness threatened, but she cheered herself by taking photos with her phone of her lovely new bedroom, complete with a window seat, and the red sofa and chairs in the lounge. She sent the pics to Josie in Sydney.

My new pad. C xx

How gorgeous, Josie texted back. *Hope you're having fun. Our little Mischief is growing fast.*

Josie attached a photo of Eve, plump and bright eyed and sitting up, propped by cushions, with a broad grin that showed her toothless gums.

OMG, wrote Chloe, as she tried to ignore the sharp pang in her chest. *What a clever girl. Give her a big hug from Aunty* C *xx*

With this text message sent, the loneliness rushed back like air hurrying to fill a sudden vacuum. *Stuff it.* Chloe went to the fridge, extracted the wine bottle and poured herself another glass. She would end up like Finn if she wasn't careful.

And yet, Chloe knew that her issues were minor compared with her boss's, and she wouldn't be lonely for long. Greta Fairlie had already invited her back to the red claw farm for a barbecue on the weekend and as soon as she was properly settled, she would invite people over to the flat for a little dinner party. Jess and Willow were obvious starters, and Moira and Greta and their husbands.

Perhaps she would also join an art class or take up pottery. She just needed to be a bit proactive and she'd be fine.

In fact, Chloe allowed herself to imagine that if all went well here, if she settled into the new job, and into the town, and saved a bit more money, which shouldn't be difficult given the low rent, she might contact a fertility clinic.

The thought of single motherhood via IVF was both terrifying and exciting, but if she wanted her own little cuddly mischief, it was almost certainly her best option. And surely there had to be loads of advantages to raising a child in the country?

Fresh air, a lack of crowds, and a friendly community. What did they say? It takes a village . . .?

And how amazing to have playgroups, kindergarten and a primary school all within walking distance. Life had to be easier here than in Sydney. It would be like raising her little one in a cosy nest, a cocoon.

Warmed by that thought, Chloe took her wine and her book to bed. When she turned out the lamp thirty minutes later, she slept soundly.

Morning was as quiet as the evening, except for the crowing of a distant rooster. Chloe woke to a sense of unease, however. She'd been dreaming about Ben, the baker, who had walked into the rainforest and disappeared.

She had only ever seen one photo of Ben and he'd been suntanned with a gentle smile and streaky fair hair tied back in a man bun. In her dream, however, he'd had wild eyes and dreadlocks and he'd warned her that she was fooling herself if she thought life in a country town was safe and cosy.

The dream's after-effects hung over her as she made coffee and poured muesli into a bowl. Fortunately, by the time she'd listened to the DJ's chatter on the radio and then showered and dressed, she'd shaken off most of her edginess. Just the same, she would talk to Finn about Ben when she got to work.

The police weren't convinced that he'd been lost in the forest and perished. The fact that his cap was found near a hut with drug-making gear suggested foul play, or the far preferable possibility that Ben was now lying low, or on the run. And Chloe couldn't help thinking there must be more the *Bugle* could do to help his cause.

Outside, the day was warm and humid, the sky rimmed in the distance by fluffy white clouds. Chloe was, nevertheless, in an optimistic mood as she walked the few doors to the newspaper's office only to find Finn fuming as he stood, hands on hips, glaring at his computer screen.

'Good morning.' She spoke carefully, in case he was suffering from a hangover.

He glowered at her. 'What's this?'

Chloe stepped closer and saw a story she'd filed right at the end of the previous day. Finn had entrusted her to cover a couple of 'straight' news stories and her proposed header stood out in bold capitals on the screen. *AGGRIEVED VICTIM BLASTS COURT.* She'd thought it was rather attention grabbing.

'It's a story from yesterday's magistrates court hearing,' she said. 'A farmer's truck was stolen and the offender got off with a fairly lenient fine instead of a jail term.'

'Is that so?' Finn was obviously unimpressed. 'Was any word of that criticism actually spoken in court?'

'Well, not exactly,' Chloe admitted after a slight hesitation. 'If you remember, I also had to cover the School of Art's show at Ravenshoe, and by the time I got back, the hearing had finished.'

'So?' Finn showed no glimmer of sympathy.

'So I got the details of the case from the court staff and I was able to speak to the farmer in question.' She had found the fellow sitting outside on a bench, talking to a couple of other men, and she could tell he was really upset.

'And he gave you a sob story about the loss of his truck and the resulting loss of income and how the court system has a lot to answer for when an offender gets a mere fine that amounts to a couple of weeks' wages? And how magistrates are generally too lenient with criminals.'

'Yes, that's exactly right.' Chloe had quoted the man word for word.

Finn stared at her like she had told him the moon was made of Danish blue. 'You think we should publish this crap?'

Crap? It was the truth. She hadn't invented a single word. 'It should help to sell papers,' she suggested, but she did so with a sheepish smile. It was pretty darned obvious she was on shaky ground.

Finn's response was an eye-roll, followed by a shake of his head and then an exaggerated sigh. 'You know what this bloody well demonstrates, don't you?'

Chloe had no idea, but she was sure her boss was about to set her straight.

'It's a regrettable example of the stark difference between real-world journalism and a gossip magazine's fantasy beat-up.'

Damn him. He was far too self-righteous. Chloe squared her shoulders, gave a toss of her curls. 'And perhaps this is where a real-world news editor is supposed to kindly offer his brand-new journalist a little guidance. Or, at least, gently explain what's wrong with her story.'

'What's wrong, Chloe, is that you and I could end up in front of a magistrate for contempt of court. This amounts to criticism of the judiciary.'

Chloe decided it might be prudent to make no further comment.

'When you're covering a court story,' Finn continued with exaggerated patience. 'You don't report a single word that hasn't been actually stated in court, or presented in a document to the court. You most certainly don't report Joe Blow the victim's personal and potentially biased criticism of the hearing. The judiciary take rather a dim view of such cheek. And we – *this paper* – could cop a really stiff fine.'

'But can't journalists speak up for the little guy? Doesn't the farmer deserve to have his point of view heard?'

'There's an appeal process the farmer can follow if he thinks the penalty or the compensation have been manifestly inadequate.'

'I – I see.' Chloe knew the *Bugle* was on a financial knife edge and she'd been hired to help boost funds, not to deplete them. 'I guess I should apologise.'

For the longest time, Finn stood with his dark gaze locked with hers. Chloe willed herself to hold the eye contact, no matter how much she wanted to squirm, or look at her feet.

It wasn't as if she'd made *many* mistakes. She'd actually been pretty useful here until this morning. Yeah, she knew she'd been pulling her weight. She'd even managed to get an exclusive from a local councillor, generally known as Grumpy.

'That old bastard never gives me the time of day,' Finn had admitted. 'He's notorious for being ultra-conservative and suspicious of the media, but all you had to do was smile at him.'

Chloe hadn't stated the obvious – that female journos could actually be as effective as males.

Her boss had been extra pleased with another story she'd written about an elderly local who was forced to close down his sawmilling business due to limitations on rainforest harvesting.

When Chloe had investigated this, she'd discovered that the man's son had returned home from overseas to find his old dad deeply depressed, but with a huge shed of milled timber sitting idle.

The son had promptly begun selling these beautiful pieces of walnut, silkwood, cedar and flame oak to specialist cabinet-makers, wood-turners and boat-builders. The family's business was picking up again, and the son had also found a lucrative outlet for selling timber offcuts to craft markets in Melbourne. Better still, Chloe had tipped off Karen, who'd lined up an advertisement to accompany the story, and this had earned her high praise indeed from Finn.

She'd been on a roll, or so she'd thought, and had started feeling quite comfortable in her new job. Now, it seemed she was back to square one. In Finn's eyes, she was again the clueless Dolly he had never wanted to employ.

Without shrinking from his stern gaze, she readied herself for another verbal smack.

Instead of berating her, however, Finn looked away and ran a hand through his shaggy dark hair, making it stick up more than ever. 'I guess I should have checked whether you had court experience,' he said in a tone so unexpectedly conciliatory that Chloe almost missed its significance.

Was this an apology?

She probably looked a tad gobsmacked. Finn actually smiled.

Which was dangerous. He shouldn't smile like that, not without a warning.

She had no choice but to drop her gaze. She said, 'So I suppose you'd like me to rewrite this, with only the story the clerk of the court gave me.'

'You got it.' Finn turned to his desk. The smile was gone. This wasn't the right moment to ask him about Ben.

CHAPTER SEVENTEEN

Tammy, the hairdresser, looked very thin and tired, but she smiled as she welcomed Chloe into her salon.

'I'll just lock the door behind you and draw the curtains,' she said. 'Otherwise there's bound to be someone poking their nose in here, hoping for an after-hours haircut.'

Her small salon was very appealing and 'old world', with golden timber floors, ornately framed mirrors and a huge bowl filled with roses of every hue set on the glass counter beside a display of local jewellery and handmade soaps.

Tammy pointed to upholstered armchairs in the corner, grouped around a table with magazines. 'Take a seat,' she said.

Chloe smiled. 'Thanks for taking the time to see me.' It had been a long shot. In the end she hadn't consulted Finn. She feared he would consider this too delicate a situation to intrude on. And when she'd called in to the salon at lunchtime, she'd half-expected Tammy to flatly refuse to be interviewed but, while the hairdresser had been cautious, she hadn't said no.

'Can I get you a drink?' Tammy asked now. 'Tea? Coffee?' She sent a quick glance to the antique clock on the wall. It was five past six. 'Wine?'

'I'm fine, actually.' As Chloe said this, she caught a flash in Tammy's eyes that might have been disappointment. 'Unless you'd like something.'

'Well, it is wine o'clock.' Tammy's smile was wan. 'And after the day I've had, I could do with a glass.'

Chloe hesitated. She was still officially 'at work', but she knew that drinking alone wasn't much fun. 'Then I'd love to join you.'

'Excellent.' Tammy disappeared into a small alcove at the back of the shop. 'White okay?' she called.

'Yes, please.'

As Tammy returned, Chloe shifted the scattered magazines to make room on the table for her notebook and pen as well as the two glasses and a small dish of olives.

'I could easily provide you with an entire meal,' Tammy said. 'My freezer is full of casseroles. People just keep bringing them. Everyone's been so lovely.'

'I'll make sure I mention that in my story.' Chloe sent her a smile. 'Shows how popular you are.'

'I think it's a country town thing, though,' Tammy said. 'I'm not sure it would happen everywhere.' She took the armchair opposite Chloe, settling back into the cushions and crossing her long, thin legs.

She was wearing loose cotton slacks patterned in teal and pink paisley, echoes of the coloured streaks in her hair, and she'd teamed the pants with a tiny pink T-shirt and a floaty vest.

Chloe admired people who could carry off the layered look. Her own attempts at layering always made her look messy and as if she was merely playing at dressing up. Tammy clearly had flair and Chloe guessed she was probably an excellent hairdresser.

'So,' Tammy said as she picked up her wineglass. 'You'd like to write something for the paper about Ben.'

Chloe nodded. 'If you don't mind. I think it's important to keep Ben on the community's radar.'

'I guess.' Tammy looked less certain as she fidgeted with the glass's stem.

'I'd like to try for a new angle,' said Chloe.

'How? He's still missing. What else can you say?'

'I was hoping to write more of a character sketch,' Chloe explained. 'About Ben as a person.'

'Not a eulogy?' The hairdresser's eyes were suddenly round with worry, quite possibly on the verge of tears.

'Gosh, no,' Chloe hastened to assure her. 'That wasn't my intention at all. I was hoping that, perhaps, if we painted a broader picture of Ben, we might be able to trigger something. Jog someone's memory – or conscience.'

Tammy took a moment to consider this, and then she seemed to relax, much to Chloe's relief. 'I guess it can't hurt,' she said.

'I promise I'd show you the story first,' Chloe added. 'I don't usually, but I'd like to make sure you're comfortable before it goes to print.'

'Okay. I guess it's worth a shot. I certainly don't plan to give up on Ben.' With a weary smile, Tammy lifted her glass. 'Here's cheers, anyway.'

'Cheers.'

They smiled at each other and clinked their glasses. Chloe took a sip. The wine was crisp and cool and she realised this was the first drink she'd shared with another woman since her farewell drink with Josie in Sydney.

It was tempting to kick back and relax, but she had a job to do. 'So,' she said, setting the glass on the table and flipping open her notebook. 'What would you like to tell me about Ben?'

'The main thing is he's an incredibly gentle guy,' Tammy said, her voice warm with obviously happy memories. 'Honestly, he's just the sweetest, *nicest* fellow I've ever known. And he's funny. He loves to tell jokes and he makes me laugh. He makes his customers laugh. Everyone loves him.'

Chloe liked the way Tammy spoke about Ben in the present tense – as if he might suddenly reappear at any moment. 'I hear he's a damn fine baker as well,' she said.

'God, yes. He's been working so hard at his business and the bakery's been doing brilliantly. From the moment Ben set up shop here, his pies were a hit with the locals, and his bread's amazing, too. And just when this – this dreadful thing – happened, he was all set to expand. He was going to hire an apprentice, buy a van and sell to other places on the Tablelands – service stations, supermarkets, that sort of thing.'

Tammy paused, took a deep sip of her wine.

'Was – *is* – Ben involved with the community at all?' Chloe asked.

'Well, he coaches the under-8 soccer team and he's also a sponsor.' As Tammy said this, a smile that was almost cheeky brightened her face. 'Each week, the kids in the winning teams get a voucher for a free sausage roll.'

'That's clever. I bet it's good marketing, too.'

'It certainly helps.' Tammy took another drink of wine and sat for a bit, staring solemnly at her glass as she held it in her lap. 'Ben came here to make a fresh start.' She looked up, her mascara-rimmed eyes wary now. 'I suppose you know he hit a bad patch before he came here. When he was at the Gold Coast?'

'I did hear something, yes.' Chloe was aware that Ben had been involved in the drug scene on the Gold Coast and had ended up doing time. 'Sergeant Locke tells me Ben was very upfront about it. Apparently, he called in to the police station almost as soon as he arrived in Burralea. He knew his past would show up on his records, but he was determined to make a clean start here.'

'Too right.' Tammy said this with surprising vehemence. 'And that's exactly what he's done. A clean start. Squeaky clean.' She clenched a fist. 'That's why it bugs me so much that his disappearance seems to be connected to bloody drugs.' Her lips trembled now. 'There was gear for making ice in the hut near where I found his cap.'

If Chloe had known Tammy better, she would have hugged her. She put down her pen, leaned forward. 'I know that's terribly worrying, Tammy, but it doesn't mean Ben was actually involved in making drugs. The police certainly haven't drawn that conclusion.'

Tammy shrugged. 'Yeah, that's something, I guess.'

They sat for a bit in gloomy silence, sipping their wine, and Chloe wished she could produce a word of wisdom, some comforting advice. 'Is there anything else?' she asked gently.

'I'm not sure. You mean about Ben?'

'Yes. Maybe some little idiosyncrasy that people can relate to.'

'Like how he hates microwave ovens and refuses to use one?'

'Yes. That's interesting, given his profession.'

'Or the way he sings in the shower?'

As Chloe jotted this down, she found herself remembering how Jason used to sing along to the radio when he was driving. Unfortunately, he was always annoyingly off-key. 'What kind of singing?'

Tammy gave a small, giggling laugh. 'Would you believe reggae? He's actually quite good.' The laughter died and she let out a heavy sigh. 'The other thing . . . we'd started looking at houses around here. We were seriously thinking about buying a place together.'

'In Burralea?'

'Probably, or maybe just a bit out of town. We were also talking about starting a family.' As soon as she said this she threw up her hand, palm out, in a stopping gesture. 'Don't put that in the paper though.'

'No, no, don't worry,' promised Chloe, even though she could instantly imagine a host of attention-grabbing headlines.

Tammy drained her glass, then rose and went back to the little alcove, returning with a full glass and bringing the bottle to refresh Chloe's drink. She sat again with her legs crossed.

'This is off the record,' she said, dropping her voice as if someone might overhear. 'But for a while there, just after Ben went missing, I actually thought I might have been pregnant.' Now, her attempt to smile was a little crooked and sad. 'And you know, the crazy thing was, I was hoping I *was* pregnant.'

I totally get that, Chloe wanted to tell her.

Tammy sat a little straighter and added, defensively, 'Well, it would have been Ben's baby and – I don't know – maybe it could somehow have lured him back?'

Chloe's heart went out to the poor woman, but before she could answer, Tammy groaned and closed her eyes. 'I can't believe I just said that. I know it's crazy. Really, really dumb.'

'Not dumb,' said Chloe gently. 'I think most women's imaginations are a bit out of control when it comes to boyfriends and babies.'

Tammy opened her eyes again and stared at Chloe for the longest moment. 'You sound like you're talking from experience.'

I am, Chloe thought. And then . . . maybe it was the wine, or perhaps it was something about Tammy's cosy salon and her friendly, open manner that welcomed confidences – she was a hairdresser, after all. Or maybe Chloe just wanted to distract Tammy from her worries. Whatever the reason, she found herself telling Tammy about Jason.

'I was in a relationship for seven and a half years and everything was pretty close to perfect until I pinned my boyfriend down about starting a family.'

Tammy groaned. 'I know that type.'

'I guess a guy has a right to say he doesn't want kids,' Chloe went on. 'But he should have come straight with me years ago, instead of leading me on, letting me think – assume . . .' She took a breath to steady herself before she added the worst. 'The thing was, he didn't just tell me no, or give me a proper reason for saying no, apart from how expensive kids are. He asked me why I thought I'd be such a great mother.'

'Bloody hell!' It was gratifying to see the appalled look on Tammy's face. 'God, Chloe. After seven and a half years? That's such a low blow. What a prick!'

'Yeah.' *But I loved him for all of those seven and a half years.*

'I hope you sent him packing?'

Chloe nodded. 'Except I was the one who did the packing.'

'Good for you.' Tammy selected an olive from the little dish. 'It must have been a kick in the guts, though.'

'It hurt,' Chloe admitted. 'I was shattered, to be honest. But I think I'm finally "moving on".' She used her fingers to make air quotes around the phrase.

'That's great. Well done.' After a bit, Tammy asked, 'Would you consider IVF now? Becoming a single mother?'

'I've certainly thought about it.'

Chloe had, in fact, started her research, learning the necessary steps involved. Hormone injections, egg retrieval, clinical fertilisation and re-implantation. It was all a bit daunting, but it might be her only option.

'I'm thirty-seven and I do feel like I'm running out of time,' she said and then she closed her notebook. 'But I'm sorry. I got right off track. The last thing you need is my sob story.'

'But it's good to talk, isn't it?' Tammy said earnestly. 'And I appreciate you asking me about Ben. I think it's helped. I do feel a bit better. Most people avoid mentioning him. It – it's like he's already de—'

Tammy checked herself. 'Like he won't be coming back,' she said instead. With a tight, brave little smile, she added, 'And I refuse to believe that. I mean, it ain't over till it's over, is it?'

Chloe wondered if she could remain so optimistic under similar circumstances. But she wasn't about to question Tammy's faith.

'It certainly isn't,' she said and she stood and collected her things. 'Thanks for the wine and thanks for seeing me, Tammy. I should be able to show you a copy of the story tomorrow.'

'Let's hope it helps Ben somehow,' Tammy said.

She walked with Chloe to the door and they hugged as they said goodbye.

'It was great to meet you.' Tammy sounded as if she really meant it.

'You, too.' Chloe fingered her hair. 'I'll no doubt be back for a cut before long.'

'You have pretty hair. I'd love to cut it.'

'Thanks.'

Outside in the summer night, insects buzzed and as Chloe walked home, Tammy's words echoed in her head. *It ain't over till it's over.* She felt as if she'd made a new friend, but she was also more concerned than ever about Ben.

Chloe's meeting with Izzie Galbraith on the following day was an entirely different experience. She had been surprised when Emily had told her that her mother wanted a meeting. Now, as Chloe entered a nursing home for the very first time, she discovered that rooms filled with the frail and helpless elderly could be unexpectedly confronting.

This is a facet of life I really should face, though, Chloe told herself as she hurried past, conscious that she took her own youthfulness and fitness for granted. She vowed to come back again and write a story about the home. She knew that these folk, who were nearing the end of their lives and were often so easily dismissed, had lived busy and interesting lives, perhaps not as remarkable as Izzie's, but worth hearing about, surely?

She was directed to Izzie's room, and found the elderly woman out of bed and sitting in a chair. Izzie was as small and frail as any other resident in the home, but despite her stooped shoulders and age-spotted, knobbly hands, her bearing was surprisingly regal and she looked very alert, her dark eyes flashing behind pink-framed glasses. She was wearing a blue cotton dress, sensibly buttoned down the front, and her short white hair was neatly styled. Quite clearly, she had been waiting for Chloe.

'Hello.' Chloe smiled, thankful that she wasn't late. 'How are you, Izzie? I'm Chloe Brown from the *Bugle*.'

'Chloe, I'm very pleased to meet you.' Izzie spoke with a rather posh English accent. 'Come and sit down,' she ordered, gesturing to the only other chair in the room. 'Pull that a little closer, so we don't have to shout. That's right,' she added, as Chloe obeyed. 'Someone might bring us some tea soon, if we're lucky.'

'I've been so looking forward to meeting you,' Chloe said with another of her warmest smiles. 'I've heard so much about you and, I hope you don't mind, but I've done a little research, too. I was fascinated to learn that you were a pilot during the war and then you ran the *Bugle* virtually on your own.'

To Chloe's surprise, Izzie gave a dismissive wave of her hand. 'Yes, yes, but that feels like another lifetime ago. I suppose it was, really.' Leaning forward, Izzie said, 'I'm afraid *I'm* more interested in you, Chloe, and why you're here in Burralea. What you plan to do.'

Chloe hoped her shoulders hadn't sagged too visibly. No way could she admit to this heroic woman that she'd come to Burralea to recover from a sad romance. 'I felt like a change,' she said. 'Sydney can be rather —' She groped for a suitable word. 'Well, after you've lived there a while, Sydney can seem rather predictable. I was looking for a totally different experience.'

Izzie nodded, apparently accepting this. 'Did you always want to be a journalist?'

Oh, dear. Chloe had already been through one job interview with Emily, but now this felt like a second round. Again, she was uncomfortable about being totally honest. Truth was, she hadn't grown up wanting to be a journalist. Even when she'd started uni, she hadn't had any real plans for the future.

'I studied for an Arts degree at Sydney University and discovered I was good at English and Marketing,' she said. 'And after graduation, I managed to get a job in marketing with Hunter and Bromley, an engineering firm.'

'That's interesting.' Izzie gave a nod of approval. 'Did you enjoy it?'

'Yes, I quite liked it. My main task was to write ROI documents when the company was tendering for contracts and commissions. I had to present Hunter and Bromley in a positive and professional light, outlining their successes with previous projects, how they'd finished on time and under budget.'

'So the company could win or lose the job depending on how well you addressed their clients' criteria?' Izzie asked.

'Yes, that's right. I had to grow up rather quickly.'

The old lady smiled. 'And you enjoyed working there?'

'The engineers were brilliant, but they put all their focus into figures and formulas, so it was good for my ego to know I could help them to hit the right balance between honest information and marketing spin.'

'But I understand you also worked on a magazine for women.'

'That's right.'

'Was that a difficult transition?'

Gosh, this really was quite a grilling, but this queenly nonagenarian wasn't one to be argued with. Chloe drew a quick breath and ploughed on with her story. 'The move felt like a natural progression, actually. There was a young woman on the Hunter and Bromley staff, Tracey Bright, who was selected for the long jump in the Commonwealth Games. I wrote a story about her for the firm's in-house magazine. Then I also interviewed people in a small town near Broken Hill who were thrilled to finally get a stable water supply, thanks to our firm.'

'Let me guess,' responded Izzie with a smile. 'You realised you preferred to write about people rather than engineering projects?'

'In a nutshell.' Chloe smiled too. 'When Tina Jenkins from *Girl Talk* magazine contacted me, inviting me to develop the Tracey Bright story into a full-size feature for their magazine, I jumped at the chance. And it wasn't long afterwards that I heard about a job being offered at *Girl Talk*. I was thrilled when I got that position. I loved it.'

Chloe hoped Izzie wasn't about to quiz her about why she'd left *Girl Talk*. She was on the brink of directing a question to Izzie when they were distracted by a rattling sound outside. A plump, smiling woman with a tea trolley appeared in the doorway.

'Ah, good afternoon, Pam.' Izzie introduced Chloe, and Pam was instantly eager to tell her that a photo of her soccer-star nephew had been published in the previous week's *Bugle*.

'We were all so excited,' Pam said as she served tea and biscuits. 'And, Izzie, it's ginger nuts today. Your favourites.'

She left, with a smile and a wave.

Chloe, with her cup and saucer and ginger nut carefully balanced, tried to steer their conversation in a new direction. 'Izzie, I read that you were one of the Air Transport Auxiliary during World War II,' she said. 'I'd love to hear more about that.'

'Well yes, it was an interesting time,' Izzie admitted.

'You were like proper pilots, weren't you? Flying bombers and everything?'

Izzie nodded. 'But only to transport the planes from the factories to the military airfields. Once we delivered the planes, the men took over the real war work.' With a wry smile, she added, 'Even so, people were shocked that girls were allowed to fly those enormous planes.'

'You were trailblazers,' Chloe suggested.

'I suppose we were, yes. I think all the air forces have female pilots these days. But back then, people – especially men – found the idea of women flying ludicrous. Even the editor of an aviation magazine had a dig at us, complaining about the menacing women who thought they should be flying bombers when they didn't have the intelligence to scrub hospital floors.'

'Goodness,' exclaimed Chloe. 'Just as well there was no social media back then. Imagine the slanging matches on Facebook.'

'Yes, that's one mercy, I suppose,' Izzie said with a smile. 'And we proved them wrong, of course. Luckily, Churchill was on our side. He wanted an air force as strong as Germany's, and he was prepared to get it by any means.'

'It must have been incredibly exciting,' Chloe said. 'Scary, though.'

Izzie sat for a moment before she responded, as if she was thinking back through seventy-five long years.

Eventually, she said, 'It was a responsibility, being tasked with transporting very expensive, brand-new machines, but mostly we didn't have time to be scared. The flying required so much concentration, you see. But yes, it was exciting, no doubt about that. Flying Spitfires, oh, my goodness. They were wonderful machines. Incomparable. So streamlined, a cockpit barely wider than your shoulders, and the thrust equivalent of six super-charged racing Bentleys under its nose.'

Chloe, who had pretty much drifted rather aimlessly through her twenties, was entranced. She was itching to write a story about Izzie's experiences. Surely young people today would find it as fascinating as she did. But she was conscious of Emily's puzzling reluctance to print such a story.

Why? Wouldn't any daughter be proud of such a mother?

To Chloe's delight, Izzie reminisced a little more about her ATA days, about the comradeship of the girls, about the bombings and the shock of sighting a Luftwaffe Messerschmitt at close range. She was about to tell Chloe how she met her Australian husband when a nurse bustled in, wanting to take Izzie's blood pressure.

Chloe realised that she should probably leave.

'I hope you'll come again,' Izzie told her, as the nurse matter-of-factly tightened the cuff around her arm.

'I will, for sure,' Chloe promised. Her head was buzzing as she walked out, past those rooms of pale, sick elderly folk. She was trying to picture Izzie when she was young, in her smart navy uniform with gold braid, climbing into the cockpits of those enormous planes and facing danger on a daily basis.

CHAPTER EIGHTEEN

Great Britain, November, 1944

Izzie would never have taken off from South Wales if she had known the visibility would deteriorate so quickly. The weather closed in early, far earlier than the forecasts had predicted. But Izzie was not inclined to turn back.

She wasn't especially worried. She loved everything about flying, so of course she adored her job with Britain's Air Transport Auxiliary, especially knowing she was a vital part of the war effort. And this certainly wasn't the first time she'd flown through drizzling, cloudy conditions.

As she scanned the Welsh landscape below, valleys beckoned invitingly like tunnels in the clouds, and she recalled her orders for flying in bad weather. The rules were simple and straightforward: fly beneath the clouds whenever possible and stay on course, try not to fly above eight hundred feet, and don't try anything fancy. After all, she was transporting a Lancaster bomber, a hugely expensive, brand-new aeroplane, and she couldn't afford to make any mistakes.

Normally, she didn't mind that she and the other female ATA pilots hadn't been given the more sophisticated navigational training that was reserved for the men in the RAF. The women had only been shown how to use a plane's gyro compass, but this was next to no use to Izzie now, as the clouds hunkered closer, all around her, as thick as concrete.

Damn. She was completely alone and the valley she had been following had almost disappeared.

Izzie peered ahead, hoping for a promising circle of daylight. A small beacon of hope. Unfortunately, the other end of the narrow valley was also blocked by a wall of cloud and the weather showed no signs of clearing. She was trapped, surrounded by mountains she couldn't see.

For the first time in her flying career, Izzie was hit by a flash of real fear. Her responsibility weighed heavily and, like any of the ferry pilots, she was flying solo. This was expected of the ATA, even though the RAF flew similarly massive four-engined planes into combat with two pilots, a navigator and an engineer.

Now, getting out of this predicament rested on Izzie alone. Sweat broke out on her skin. A white-hot flare ripped through her stomach and chest. Izzie Oakshott was very close to panicking.

Her fear wasn't so much for her own life. She was desperately conscious of the huge effort that the production of this magnificent machine had entailed. All the fundraising, the building of the massive engines, the armaments, the thousands and thousands of rivets set in place by rows of women in factories, the miles of electrical cabling.

How terrible if she was the cause of its loss.

But no. She mustn't give in to such negative thinking. She had to stay calm, to concentrate on the task, on flying.

At the beginning of the war, her father had warned her and her siblings, 'In a family as large as ours, we shan't all come through this.'

Sobering as his words had been, Izzie, Jem and her sisters hadn't panicked back then, and she wouldn't panic now. It simply wasn't done. She knew the danger, but she had to push it to the back of her mind.

She was an excellent pilot and she was also an Oakshott, and everyone in her family was pulling their weight. Jem had joined the RAF and Vera's husband, Dave, had signed up for the Navy, while Betty and Jane had found themselves caring for ten evacuee children who'd arrived from London.

Her sisters had been rather wonderful, really, getting straight down to the business of giving all these children baths and washing their hair, letting them have the big bathroom, while the rest of the family used the tiny one. And they'd bought the children mackintoshes and wellington boots and had shown them how to help in the vegetable garden.

When the ATA had sent Izzie a letter, asking if she would help with ferrying planes from the factories to the RAF bases, her response had been fast.

Rather! Yes, please.

At the time, Izzie had been one of the small number of English women who already had their pilot's licence and she'd been thrilled to sign up. Of course, the decision to add females to the ATA had raised plenty of eyebrows. Even at Whitehall, there'd been quite a strong feeling that women shouldn't do this kind of job. They weren't suitable for the task and should never be employed in it.

Izzie could remember the poor red-faced fellow at Austin Reed tailors and how terribly fumbling and nervous he'd been when he'd had to measure the ATA girls' chests and waists for their smart navy blue uniforms. He'd only been used to male customers and he'd been incredibly careful not to touch the girls inappropriately. So they'd ended up with the crotch area in their trousers far too long and the chest area far too wide, and they'd had to make the necessary adjustments themselves.

Now, many more women had joined the service, offering their flying skills from all over the world. Like Izzie, they had proved their worth, flying everything from small, clever Spitfires that responded to the slightest touch, to whopping great Wellington bombers in which the tail seemed a mile away when you looked back. Despite the lack of navigation gear, the girls had mostly flown the planes safely, and in all kinds of weather.

Izzie certainly wasn't the first to face the gamble of how best to deal with sudden thick cloud and murk while flying without radio or instruments. She tried not to think about Amy Johnson, England's most famous female pilot, who'd lost her life in conditions very like this.

Today, Izzie had two choices: break the rules and fly higher in an attempt to get over the clouds, or fly lower and risk hitting the side of a mountain.

Really, there was no choice. Izzie rammed open the throttles, pulled the control column back and climbed steeply. Clouds swirled around the plane in a cold cocoon and forced her to climb even higher still.

At four thousand feet Izzie broke through, but all she could see was a carpet of cloud and bright sunshine. She was determined to remain calm, but she couldn't help feeling lonely and frightened up there. Desperately, she searched for a gap in the clouds, but as she flew on, the white blanket remained thick and impenetrable.

Eventually, of course, the petrol gauge began to drop dangerously low. Izzie couldn't stay up high forever, safe above the clouds. There was nothing for it but to throttle back and steer the Lancaster down. And hope and pray.

Descending slowly, Izzie's plane pierced the white, wet mist of cloud. She dropped to two thousand feet. Fifteen hundred feet. One thousand.

Six hundred.

She could only hope that when she finally got though she would find herself free of bloody hills.

The clouds broke. Below, Izzie saw rolling green countryside. Flat. Hill-less. Countryside.

'Thank you,' she whispered, and she was sure that her mother was watching over her that day.

There was no time for lapses in concentration, though. She had twenty minutes of fuel left, so now she had to find an aerodrome. Fast.

No touchdown had ever felt sweeter.

It was late in the day and drizzling lightly by the time Izzie had refuelled and taken off again and finally reached her destination RAF base in Lincolnshire.

As she taxied along the tarmac, a 'follow me' car guided her to the dispersal area. She gathered up her parachute, bundled it under her arm with her logbook and, while clutching the small overnight holdall she carried everywhere, climbed down through the hatch.

The ground crew were there to greet her. A nuggety, grey-haired fellow in overalls peered at her through the misty rain. 'Where's the pilot?' he asked.

Izzie used her free hand to brush an invisible speck of lint from her smart, navy blue uniform and she lifted her chin. 'I'm the pilot,' she told him.

The fellow stared at her, his mouth agape. 'You're one of them women we been hearing about.' His gaze roved over the towering aircraft she had just brought into land. Almost seventy feet long, the Lancaster stood at nearly twenty feet high, with wheels as tall as a man and a wingspan of over one hundred feet.

The plane was destined for strategic bombing in Europe and its belly was painted black to make it harder to see from below, while the upper surfaces were painted in camouflage colours. It was a formidable war machine, but Izzie had assumed that, by this stage of the war, most RAF bases were used to having bombers delivered by female pilots.

Clearly not at RAF Kelstern, Lincolnshire. Between exchanging shocked glances and shaking their heads, the ground crew were gaping at her.

'I'll need to take my delivery chit to the Operations Room,' Izzie said.

The grey-haired man blinked and seemed to snap to attention. 'Yes, of course, madam.' He shot a frantic glance to her left hand. 'Er . . . miss.' He pointed through the drizzle. 'It's the first of those Nissen huts.'

'Thank you.' Izzie favoured him with her sweetest smile before marching across the tarmac towards the row of ugly but practical half-cylindrical huts made of corrugated metal.

It was a relief to step out of the rain and into electric light and warmth.

'Here you are,' Izzie said, placing the chit in front of another surprised-looking man seated at the desk. 'I had a problem with clouds and visibility in Wales, so I ended up having to land and refuel, but there's nothing much else to report. No damage. No Luftwaffe sightings.'

Before the man at the desk could respond, the door behind Izzie burst open, letting in a gust of chilling rain.

'Hello there,' boomed a deeply cheerful masculine voice. 'I was in the Control Tower watching you land that wizard kite just now. I must say you did a jolly fine job.'

Izzie turned. The voice belonged to a tall chap, very pleasant looking, with wavy brown hair that flopped onto his forehead and skimmed his smiling hazel eyes.

'Thank you.' She offered her hand. 'How do you do, sir?'

'I'm Ian Forsythe,' he said. 'Commanding officer of this squadron.'

'Very pleased to meet you, sir.' Izzie could see by the insignia on his uniform that he was a wing commander. As he shook her hand firmly, she said, 'First Officer Isabella Oakshott, arriving somewhat later than expected.'

'Welcome to Kelstern.' Wing Commander Forsythe's smile was charming. 'But I'm afraid the taxi plane has already left for White Waltham without you.'

Izzie had half expected she might have to spend the night at this base. It wasn't the first time and she had brought pyjamas and a toothbrush. But finding her accommodation in this all-male preserve might prove tricky.

The wing commander didn't seem perturbed. 'Don't worry, we'll sort out digs for you. And a few of us are going into town tonight. Supper at the pub. You'd be very welcome to join us.'

He smiled again, such a handsome smile, but Izzie had no intention of being charmed by a wing commander's smile, or any other man's for that matter. At the beginning of the war, she had vowed that she wouldn't allow herself to fall in love, especially not with a serviceman. There was no point, surely?

So far, she'd gone out with several fellows in the RAF and she'd enjoyed plenty of good times, even a little 'fooling around', as they called it in American movies, but she'd kept her heart intact. It was timely to remind herself of this again now as she accepted yet another invitation.

Forty minutes later, Izzie was seated at a table in a corner of the Falconer & Frog, squashed between a pilot called Geoff Galbraith and an air gunner called Archie Bell. There were at least five airmen from Bomber Command dining with her, drinking beer and enjoying fish and chips, one of the few meal choices that hadn't suffered from rationing.

In a far corner of the pub, a woman with flaming red hair and a plunging neckline was lustily thumping out tunes on the piano:

'Run Rabbit Run' and 'Boogie Woogie Bugle Boy' and the sentimental favourite, 'The White Cliffs of Dover'.

Geoff Galbraith, a big shouldered, sandy-haired fellow with amazing blue eyes, seemed to be utterly intrigued by Izzie. Yes, he'd heard about the girls in the ATA, but he still found it hard to believe that she'd flown a Lancaster bomber all on her own.

'Aren't you too tiny?' he asked, letting his breath-robbingly bright gaze travel from the top of Izzie's dark hair to her toes. 'Those cockpits are made for long-legged male pilots.'

This was true, and Izzie had been asked these questions before. She might have shrugged the question away this time, but she was intrigued by Geoff Galbraith's strange accent, which wasn't American or South African and certainly not British. Perhaps he was from New Zealand. 'Where are you from?' she demanded rather cheekily.

'I'm an Aussie,' he responded with a slow, lopsided smile.

'An Australian?'

He nodded. 'From Queensland.'

She didn't need to ask how he'd ended up in the RAF's Bomber Command. She knew the British Air Force had commandeered the best pilots possible from all over the Commonwealth.

'You're a long way from home,' she said instead and she wished she didn't find him so instantly attractive, even more so than his wing commander. Perhaps it was the proximity. They were squashed so close together that their elbows had touched several times. Their thighs were almost touching too, and she was awfully conscious of his long muscular body, his ocean-blue eyes and something else intangible about the way he looked at her that set her buzzing.

It was very unlike her to react to a man so quickly. Very unsettling. She turned her attention to Archie Bell on the other side of her, but he was terribly shy and, apart from learning that he came from Cornwall, she could get little out of him.

Geoff soon won her attention again. 'Surely you must have trouble reaching the rudder pedals?' he asked, clearly bothered by her diminutive stature. 'Do the ground crew give you cushions?'

Izzie rolled her eyes. 'You've got to be joking.'

'So how do you manage?'

She shrugged. 'I roll up my parachute bag and my jacket and logbook and wedge them behind me in the cockpit seat.'

'Fair dinkum?' He looked amazed.

Conscious of the frank admiration in his delicious eyes, Izzie felt compelled to be totally truthful. 'I must admit I did run into trouble the first time I took off in a Hampden. The g-force was so powerful, it pushed me back and I lost control at the very worst moment.'

'Christ,' Geoff said irreverently. 'How did you get out of that?'

'I was jolly scared. The plane was wobbling badly, but somehow I wriggled into a hump and brought my left leg up and I was able to kick the throttle forward. The right engine roared back on full power, thank heavens.'

Geoff grinned and made a show of wiping his brow. 'Phew.'

'It was a tricky moment, all right. A very close call. I saw the windsock only inches below me.'

With another admiring grin, Geoff lifted his beer glass. 'But you made it and you're here now and I'm very honoured to meet you.'

'Well, thank you.' Izzie was sure she must be blushing. So much fuss over her small incident, when Bomber Command pilots faced the Luftwaffe and enemy flak on every mission.

'When do you have to fly back?' Geoff asked next.

'I imagine there'll be another delivery in the morning and then a taxi plane to take us back.'

'So we need to make the most of tonight.'

Oh, dear. Izzie could feel her resolve to be sensible evaporating faster than fog on a summer's morning. It was completely unwise.

She'd only exchanged a handful of words with the man. More importantly, she'd been determined not to risk her heart until this beastly war was over. And falling for a Bomber Command pilot was about as risky as it got.

It was another month before Izzie saw Geoff again, when she ferried another Lancaster to Kelstern. She'd been warned there would be no taxi plane until the next day and she would need to stay overnight, but she hadn't expected to be invited to a party.

She told herself there was no point in getting excited, but deep down she was longing to see Geoff again. When she arrived at the party, however, there was no sign of Geoff and it was Ian Forsythe who took her over. Good looking and charming, Ian was her partner for dance after dance.

A three-piece orchestra played and Ian was very good company, talking and laughing, shepherding her to the bar where the drinks and supper were served. Izzie desperately wanted to ask about Geoff. Was he away on a mission? Or worse, had he come in harm's way? But the questions felt dangerous, as if she were tempting fate, or at the very least, giving her feelings away.

At around nine-thirty, as she struggled to conceal her disappointment, Geoff suddenly appeared at Ian's side. Tall and suntanned, with those terrific blue eyes, he tapped the wing commander on the shoulder.

He looked so handsome. Indefinably different from Englishmen. Perhaps it was the suntan, or the way he held himself. Contained. Confident. At ease in his skin. Whatever the cause, the impact on Izzie was fierce.

'Thanks, mate,' he said to Ian with a smile.

'My pleasure, old chap.' With a very gentlemanly bow, Ian Forsythe excused himself. 'Enjoy yourselves, won't you?'

Izzie's jaw was probably sagging now. Had this been planned? The exchange between the two men had almost felt rehearsed.

'I knew I was going to be late and so Ian has been looking after you for me,' Geoff said. 'I'm sure he's done a good job.'

'Of course,' Izzie managed, after she'd regained her wits.

Geoff smiled down at her and took her in his arms and she was quite sure she shouldn't feel so happy. Quite sure, too, that dancing with Geoff shouldn't be so terribly different from dancing with Ian, who was also tall and handsome.

But from the moment Geoff took her hand in his and placed his other hand at her waist, Izzie's evening changed from pleasant to electrifying.

Once again, she tried to tell herself to calm down, to be sensible, but she was very much afraid that her fascination for this man and the giddy, reckless feelings he roused were beyond her control. It had never happened before, this happy buzz, this helplessness, but no matter how much she tried to warn herself against such weakness, she knew she was falling fast and hard. And she had no idea how to stop.

CHAPTER NINETEEN

Friday
Dad and I are making great plans for the school holidays. Dad has another journalist working on the paper now and so he can take time off. I'm going to fly to Cairns by myself. So exciting. He will meet me at the airport and drive us up the Tablelands.

Woohoo! I can't wait to see where he lives. At the moment when I try to imagine him living up in the mountains, the picture always goes fuzzy before I can see it properly.

His address is 15 Cedar Lane, Burralea, and I've tried to look it up on Street View on Google Maps, but there's a hedge in front of the house, so I couldn't see anything really. But now I'm actually going to stay there, so I'll be able to take photos on my phone. And afterwards, I'll still be able to picture Dad living there. In his lounge room, in his kitchen, in his yard.

I can't believe I'm actually going to be there with Dad. And we are going to do all kinds of cool things together.

Dad says we can go kayaking on the lake and camping. Proper camping in a tent by the lake and cooking over a fire.

I have fantasies about toasting marshmallows and eating sausages that have been cooked over a campfire. I've only ever read about sausages like that in books and they always sound so yummy – crunchy and a little black on the outside and juicy in the middle.

Dad's even going to try to organise horseriding lessons for me. I'm not actually all that keen on horses, but he thinks I'll love it, so I thanked him heaps and I'm reading Diary of a Horse Mad Girl.

Gran's taking me shopping for new jeans and a sweater. She says it can get cold up in the mountains, even in summer. I'm hoping I can get a hoodie. Problem is, Gran has very old-fashioned views about clothes.

Shopping for bras with her was SO embarrassing. OMG. To begin with she didn't even think I needed one, but when I told her I was the only girl in my class without one, she took me to Target. There were so many pretty ones in all kinds of styles and colours, but she would only let me buy two boring white bra camis. :(

Anyway . . . Dad says he might even have time to take me on a trip to the Barrier Reef. There's a glass-bottomed boat for looking at the coral and fish and you can go snorkelling, too. This is shaping up to be the Best Holiday of Bree Latimer's life!!

CHAPTER TWENTY

The Regional Gallery was last the place Finn wanted to be on a Saturday night, surrounded by art fanciers, and waiting for the mayor to finish her speech. It wasn't that he couldn't appreciate the local talent in the wide range of artworks on display, but he'd covered more than his fair share of such gatherings.

Before the mayor had stepped up to the microphone, he'd guessed exactly what she was going to say *and* he'd been right. He' also known that the wine in disposable plastic would be barely drinkable, and the cheese platters totally predictable. Not that he was snobbish about food and wine, but he wanted to be at home with a beer and a pizza with extra chilli. In front of the TV, watching the footie.

Standing well to the back of the crowd, with his camera looped over one shoulder, Finn covered his mouth with his hand to hide his yawn, and planned his exit strategy. As soon as he'd photographed the mayor and the requisite number of art lovers grouped in front of their favourite paintings and sculptures, he'd grab the necessary names, pay his respects to the gallery and art-society movers and shakers, and slip away. It wouldn't be the first time he'd told a white lie about needing to cover another function.

A round of applause signalled that the mayor had finished. Now Adele Pennington stepped up to the mike to give an overview of the art society's achievements for the past six months. Finn took out his phone. He would record her speech rather than taking notes.

As he flipped to the recording app, a new arrival caught his attention. In the doorway, a young woman appeared in a figure-hugging, short black dress that showed off miles of leg. She was wearing sheer black stockings, high heels, and a sleeveless dress with a low neckline, revealing smooth pale skin and a hint of perfect cleavage.

She was quite a stunner, but in a weird way, she reminded him of —

Finn blinked. Looked again.

Chloe? Surely not?

Staring like a gormless teenager, no doubt with his jaw somewhere around his knees, Finn realised the woman was turning, looking his way. It was Chloe, all right. She saw him, smiled and waved.

Whack.

This was Chloe Brown as Finn had never seen her before. At work, those long, shapely legs were always hidden by trousers and sensible shoes, and the blouses she wore had sleeves and collars. Tonight she'd done something with her hair, as well. It was swept up, leaving her pale neck bare, and glamorous earrings glittered. No doubt make-up also played a part in this transformation. Chloe's eyes, her cheekbones, her lips all drew Finn's fascinated attention.

Another burst of applause marked the end of Adele Pennington's speech. Thank God he'd remembered to hit the record button. As Finn pocketed his phone, Chloe made her way across the gallery, weaving between chattering groups.

'Good evening, boss.' She was smiling as she reached him.

Finn cleared his throat. 'Hey there. I wasn't expecting to see you here tonight.'

'I didn't know you'd be here, either,' she said. 'I could have covered this show for you.'

He shrugged. 'I gave you the weekend off.'

'Very generous of you, too.' Chloe smiled again and looked around her. 'I was interested in checking out the local art scene.'

'Yeah. Course.' Close up, she was even more arresting. Finn was *way* too conscious of the alluring curve of her bare neck, the smoothness of her skin, the sooty shadows on her eyelids that made her eyes even more attractive than usual. When she turned, he saw a small blue butterfly tattooed at her nape and he found it, instantly, the most fascinating piece of artwork in the room.

'Are you okay, Finn?' Chloe asked with a puzzled frown.

'Absolutely.' With an effort, he gathered his scattered wits and was instantly ashamed of himself. He was a grieving widower, not a young stud on the make. He cleared his throat. 'Let me introduce you to some of the folk here.'

'Thanks. That'd be great.' Chloe grinned. She seemed to be doing a lot of smiling. 'I assume this crowd is from the Burralea elite?'

'Some of them.' Finn almost placed a hand on her elbow, to steer her forward, but thought better of it. 'Come on,' he said. 'You need wine and cheese.'

As it turned out, Finn didn't slip away to watch the footie as he'd planned. After all, Chloe hardly knew anyone at this event and it was easy enough for him to make introductions. He learned that she'd studied art at high school and had a lingering interest in painting, which meant she was able to make insightful comments about the work on display. She also asked intelligent questions of the artists and Finn, trailing nearby, was able to collect info for his story that he would otherwise have missed.

'If I'd known you were an art lover, I'd have definitely allocated this job to you,' he admitted.

Chloe didn't point out that he could easily have quizzed her about her interests. She smiled forgivingly and murmured something about next time.

The crowd was thinning, people were leaving, and Finn told himself he should leave, too. But Chloe's glass was empty, so he fetched her another of the little plastic disposables. When he got back to her, she was being chatted up by a fellow with a Ned Kelly beard and the shoulders of a footballer. The fellow must have told her a joke and Chloe was laughing and looking utterly relaxed and, quite possibly, enchanted.

'Here's your wine,' Finn said to her.

She was still laughing as she turned. 'Oh, thank you,' she said. 'Finn, do you know Angus? Angus Richards?'

'No. How do you do?'

'Angus, this is my boss, Finn Latimer, the editor of the *Bugle*.'

Finn's hand was gripped in a vice-like handshake and after that, he was privy to Angus Richards' long-winded story about his family's blueberry farm west of Tolga and his sister's award-winning, best-selling, wheel-thrown pottery.

Finn supposed he should have excused himself and left Chloe and Angus to become congenially acquainted, but if Chloe was looking for male companionship, she could do way better than this bearded bore. A perverse stubbornness glued Finn's feet to the floor.

Eventually, the bearded Angus was called away by his sister the potter. He told Chloe that it was awesome to have met her and he hoped to see her around sometime. Chloe farewelled him with an extra warm, sparkling-eyed smile.

By now there were very few people left in the gallery.

'Would you like a lift home?' Finn asked her.

Chloe smiled again. She hadn't really stopped smiling since she'd arrived. 'That's gallant of you, Finn, but it's a lovely night and I don't have very far to walk.'

'In those heels?' He couldn't believe he'd asked this. Why hadn't he simply said goodnight?

'Well —' Surprise shone in her brown eyes and she studied him for an uncomfortably long time, as if she was trying to read him. Finn couldn't blame her for being confused. He was having a hard enough time trying to understand his own behaviour.

He shrugged, hoping to look casual. 'I'm using the company car and your place is on my way.'

Another smile. 'Then I'd appreciate a lift.'

The journey was brief, hardly more than two short blocks, and Finn kept his eyes strictly on the road and not on the girl beside him and the sheer filmy stockings covering her thighs.

When he pulled up outside the Progress Association's building, he didn't get out to open the door for her.

'Well, that was fun,' she said.

'Glad you enjoyed it.'

She should have jumped out then and he shouldn't have said anything more, but she didn't rush away and he found himself adding in a carefully nonchalant voice, 'By the way, there's a barbecue on tomorrow night, out at Seth Drummond's place. He's a mate of mine, has stud cattle. The farm's quite interesting and you'd really like his wife, Alice. Thought you might like to meet a few more people.'

'Oh.' In the car's darkened interior, Finn couldn't see Chloe's face, but she sounded surprised. A longish pause followed and he wished he could snatch back the invitation. There were lines to be drawn between work and recreation. What the *hell* had he been thinking?

'That sounds really nice,' she said at last. 'But Greta and Mike Fairlie have already invited me to a barbecue at their red claw farm.'

'Right. Sure. That's fine. No worries.' Finn spoke too quickly. What kind of dickhead was he? 'You'll enjoy that,' he said.

'Yes,' she said. 'I'm sure I will.'

'Goodnight then.'

'Goodnight, Finn.' Chloe opened the passenger door and the courtesy light came on, highlighting the blue butterfly on her neck, the soft, smooth skin of her arms and the short skirt creeping up her stocking-covered thighs. 'Thanks for the lift.'

He nodded. 'See you Monday.'

She closed the door and the light went out. She stepped onto the footpath and lifted a hand to wave as he took off. His place was a little way out of town and as he turned the next corner, he could see her through the rear-view mirror. In the yellow glow of a street-light, she was still standing on the footpath, watching him. He drove through the night grim-faced, cursing his stupidity.

CHAPTER TWENTY-ONE

Rolf's invitation came late in the afternoon. He had roasted a piece of beef in the fire pit and there was way too much for one. 'Why don't you come over?' he asked.

Emily hesitated. Now that they'd slept together, there would be an expectation.

'It's just a meal, Emily.'

But there would also be firelight and wine and conversation . . . and look how that had ended last time.

And yet, Emily couldn't deny she'd been dreadfully lonely since Alex had left. His continued lack of communication had been eating at her. The few evenings she'd spent at her book club or playing mahjong with her friends had not been enough to make up for the solitary nights spent at home, struggling to lose herself in a book or a TV program, with only her miserable thoughts for company.

'I'll pick you up in the canoe,' Rolf offered. 'And I can take you home afterwards.'

Afterwards . . .

He had diplomatically made a point of saying it was *just a meal*. 'You don't need to collect me, Rolf. I can row.'

'I don't like the idea of you rowing home alone in the dark.'

If she was honest, she wouldn't really enjoy that either.

'Perhaps I should drive then,' Emily said. It didn't really take very long to get to Rolf's place by car. She and Alex had done that so many times.

And of course, by then, she had committed herself, hadn't she?

They sat outside on logs Rolf had sawn and sanded into comfortable seats, enjoying a bottle from his excellent wine cellar. A glowing bed of hot coals heated the camp oven that held their dinner and an almost full moon was on the rise. Huge and lemon at first, it climbed the dusky sky and then turned silver and splendid with the arrival of night.

The beef was perfectly cooked and Rolf had prepared baked parmesan potatoes and steamed greens to accompany it. They ate the delicious meal on the paved terrace in front of the house where a view of the lake allowed them to watch the moon's path across the still water.

So very pleasant, it should have been relaxing, but Emily's brain was too busy. Would they, wouldn't they? What did Rolf expect? What did she want . . .?

She tried to keep the conversation light. 'These potatoes are divine,' she said. 'Did you find the recipe on the internet?'

Rolf shook his head. 'They're a tip I picked up from my chef son, David.'

She should have remembered about David. The youngest of Rolf's three sons, he was currently working in a restaurant in London's West End and apparently doing very well.

'How are your boys?' she asked. Rolf had stopped talking about his sons when Robbie died, which was considerate of him, but the silence shouldn't last forever.

'They're fine, thanks.' Rolf shot her a quick, searching glance and she smiled to show that she was okay with this conversation.

Perhaps satisfied, Rolf added, 'Nate seems to get himself promoted every five minutes.'

'He's into green energy or something, isn't he?'

'Yes, renewable energy trading. He works as a consultant, mainly with small businesses now. I can't quite keep up with it.'

'And what about Christopher?'

Rolf smiled broadly. 'Chris is still with the same engineering firm, and he finally seems to have settled down with a steady girlfriend.'

Emily managed to hold on to her own smile. *Don't think about Robbie.* 'That's great news. Have you met her?'

'Yes, she's lovely. A nurse. Perfect for Chris.'

'How wonderful.' To her relief, her voice didn't crack as she said this, but Rolf's answering smile was almost apologetic, as if he felt guilty for having three sons who were all alive and happy. But Emily knew that Rolf's life wasn't perfect. He'd been through an acrimonious divorce, and his former wife, Lisa, who had never forgiven him for giving up his business as a builder to become a writer, managed to annoy him on a regular basis.

'So how's your new novel progressing?' Emily asked next, determined to steer clear of the dangerous topics that might render her weeping in Rolf's arms. Besides, she loved hearing about his spy novels. She and Alex had read them all and enjoyed them immensely.

Her ploy worked. Rolf was happy to talk about his ingenious new plot and his plans to head over to Washington in a month or two for more research. Then he told her about an art-house movie he knew she would enjoy that was available from the local video store. Over coffee, Rolf also told her how to make the parmesan potatoes and Emily told him about the *Bugle*'s new female journalist, Chloe Brown.

'I've always thought it could be good to have a recipe column in the *Bugle*,' she said. 'I must mention it to Chloe. She might be interested. She could probably tie it in with the stories about local produce she's been writing.'

With their coffee finished and the moon now hiding behind the trees on the opposite promontory, she helped Rolf to clear the table and carry things into the kitchen.

'Don't worry about stacking the dishwasher,' he told her.

She wanted to keep busy. This was the difficult part, working out how to say goodnight without any awkwardness.

It didn't help that Rolf had taken up a casual pose with his solid arms folded over his chest and his hips resting against the kitchen bench. Emily couldn't read his mood. What was he expecting? Hoping for? She stood in the middle of the kitchen, twisting the rings on her left finger. The ruby engagement ring and the simple gold wedding band with Alex's and her initials engraved on the inside.

Quickly, she dropped her hands. The debris of their delightful meal reminded her of the recent morning at her place when she'd woken to find the unwashed dishes littering her kitchen.

It wasn't the mess that had bothered her then – she'd never been an especially fussy housewife – it was what the deserted dishes had signified. She'd taken Rolf to her bed. She'd committed adultery.

And now, tonight, she wasn't weeping and needy. But how terrible was it to have used this man, this friend, just once, and then to tell him he was no longer needed?

'Emily, stop stressing.' Rolf's gaze was gentle, almost reproachful.

'I'm sorry,' she said.

'And don't apologise.'

'But I feel bad. I feel as if – maybe – I led you to —' She cringed. She was making such a hash of this.

He was still leaning against the bench with his arms crossed. 'You didn't lead me anywhere I didn't want to go.'

Emily's cheeks flamed. If she was completely honest, she'd known that Rolf wanted her. So she really had taken advantage of him, which was unforgivable. But now —

'And now you're having regrets,' he said. 'It's perfectly understandable. I get it.'

'You do?'

'Of course.' Rolf's expression was so brimming with tender understanding it stole her breath. 'Don't forget how long I've known you, Emily. How long I've known both you and Alex.'

At the mention of Alex, Emily's guilt flared, hotter than ever, and she was very much afraid she was going to cry. But she couldn't give in to tears again.

She took a deep breath and held it before letting it out slowly. It helped to calm her, but she couldn't quite meet Rolf's gaze.

'Go home,' he said now. 'It's been a lovely evening and I've enjoyed your company immensely. I always do.'

Stepping away from the bench, he now stood, perhaps two feet from Emily, with his arms by his sides. He was wearing a crisp blue and white–striped shirt and old faded jeans, and she could remember how comforting it had been to slip into his arms, to rest her head against his solid chest.

Before she could do anything so crazy, she turned to find the handbag she'd left on a kitchen stool. She fished for her keys, slipped the bag's strap over her shoulder.

'Thank you, Rolf.' Her voice was little more than a whisper as she stepped towards him and kissed his cheek.

'My pleasure.'

Slipping an arm around her shoulder, he gave her a brief hug, dropped a kiss on her brow. Then, shifting his hand to the small of her back, he gently steered her to the open kitchen door. The cool night air washed over them and an outside sensor light flashed on. A possum scurried away from the light and up into a safely dark tree. Rolf walked with her to her car.

'Take care,' he said as she opened the car door and got in.

Emily was grateful to this man in so many ways, but she was sure she couldn't tell him so without breaking down. 'Thanks for a lovely evening, Rolf.'

He gave a curt nod and she fired the car's motor, switched on the headlights. Rolf held up his hand in a farewell salute before stepping out of the light and into the shadows, but he wasn't quite quick enough to hide the shadow that crossed his face.

The tears came as Emily drove home. She was on a winding, dark bush road, so she needed both hands on the wheel and couldn't do much about the tears as they slipped down her cheeks and dripped from the end of her chin.

She was crying from tension, from not wanting to hurt Rolf and knowing that she had. The poor man was being patient and a very good friend. But she knew that if she and Alex separated or divorced, Rolf would happily step into the role of her lover. And yet, he would never want to be the cause of their marriage breakdown.

As always, her grief for Robbie was there, too. Over time she'd learned to hide the pain of his loss, to put on a public face, but an underlying sadness remained that she would never be able to shake.

As she drew nearer to home, however, she saw the lights she'd left on in her empty house, and she knew the deepest part of her distress was caused by her husband's desertion.

It hurt so much to know that Alex could leave her and remain silent and distant when she so desperately needed him. Sadly, it didn't help that she understood why Alex had left, or that the true reasons reached way back into their past.

CHAPTER TWENTY-TWO

Cairns, 1987

Emily was pregnant again.

Four years earlier, she'd had a miscarriage on Red Hill station while Alex and the ringers were out mustering. It had been the scariest, loneliest, most heart-rending day of her life, until her second pregnancy ended eighteen months later.

Before that second sad occasion, Emily had been so hopeful. She had felt as fit as the proverbial mallee bull and on her visit to the antenatal clinic, she and the baby had been pronounced fine. She'd made it safely through the first scary twelve weeks and Alex had been as excited as she was.

He had spoiled her with cups of tea in bed in the mornings and had made sure she got plenty of rest. He had also hired a pensioner couple to help with the housework and gardening.

Together, Alex and Emily had dared to choose names. Kate for a girl and Alexander for a boy. Emily had insisted on the boy's name. Alex's father was also Alexander and she'd wanted to keep up the Hargreaves family tradition.

Alex hadn't been so sure. 'We don't want to end up with Alex the father, Alex the son and Alex the holy terror.'

Emily had merely laughed. She rather loved the idea of being mother to a cute little holy terror. She could picture him with a snub nose and freckles, and twinkling eyes peeking out from beneath a longish fringe. His hair would be dark like hers and Alex's. 'Maybe we could call him by his full name? Alexander?'

'Bit of a mouthful,' said Alex. 'Try yelling that from the back verandah.'

He had a point.

'What about Zander then?'

Alex pulled a face. 'Too hippie.'

'Well, maybe we'll just have to call him Chip – a chip off the old block.'

Tenderly, Alex stroked her tiny baby bump. Then he bent down and kissed it. 'And maybe we're having a sweet little Katie girl.'

That second time, when the cramping pains began, Alex had been home and he'd stayed by Emily's side, a solid, comforting presence while she'd waited for the Flying Doctor, but nothing could be done to save their tiny son.

So now, she had bravely embarked on yet another perilous journey towards motherhood, and this time she and Alex were taking no risks.

As soon as her pregnancy was confirmed, Emily left Red Hill, where she had made a little memorial garden with a cairn of river stones for the baby she would always call Alexander, and she had moved to her mother's house by the lake near Burralea.

Her husband was in total agreement, of course. Alex wanted only the best for his wife and his unborn child. He and Emily tried to be stoic about the separation, but almost nine months of being apart took their toll. Even during phone conversations, a palpable tension hung over them.

They didn't talk about names for this baby and they made no special preparations, even though the pregnancy progressed happily and problem-free into the final trimester. Emily would have loved to take a trip to a big department store in Cairns to buy a bassinet and a cot and a pram. And she entertained a wistful fantasy in which Alex pasted a decorative frieze around the nursery at Red Hill – sky blue with white fluffy clouds, a backdrop for floating multicoloured balloons and birds.

She was scared, though. She feared that to act on these fantasies would be tempting fate.

Matters weren't helped by the fact that whenever Alex came to the Lake House to visit Emily, Izzie was always there too. Very much in control.

Emily hated the tension of these visits. No outright arguments took place between her husband and her mother, but Izzie seemed to rub Alex up the wrong way.

Izzie Galbraith was the only woman in Emily's experience who remained immune to the impact of Alex's good looks. And she didn't like the way he fussed over Emily, taking her cups of tea in the mornings and making sure she had her feet up for a rest after lunch each day.

Izzie sniffed at such cosseting. She'd always taken pride in being a strong, independent woman. Not only had she ferried fighter planes in England during World War II, but she had married an Australian Bomber Command pilot and settled in North Queensland with him, only to be widowed less than ten years later, when he rejoined the RAAF and was killed in the Korean War.

'I have enormous respect for your mother,' Alex confided to Emily. 'Heaven knows she's heroic in every sense of the word, but we're a different generation and we're not at war now. I think she should ease off. She's too hard on you.'

Naturally, Izzie had tried to raise her only daughter to be like herself, with a British stiff upper lip, but although Emily also admired her mother's strength, she actually adored the way Alex worried and fussed over her. Sometimes she felt as if he was making up for the loss of her father, who had died before she was born.

Of course, Emily also felt defensive about Alex. Consequently, she was super-conscious of her mother's critical eye-rolls and sniffs. She was also aware of her husband's answering tension in the clenching of his hands beneath the dining table, or in the subtle roll of his shoulders. She had seen that shoulder roll and neck stretch in the past – especially on one memorable occasion, soon after she'd arrived at Red Hill, when Alex had come within inches of punching a ringer who'd tried to give her cheek.

At least, despite the tensions at the Lake House, Alex remained a perfect gentleman. He didn't snap at his mother-in-law when she chided him and, throughout his regular visits, they grudgingly tolerated each other. The months rolled on, and when Emily was six weeks away from the due date, she moved down to Cairns to a hostel right near the Base Hospital.

She phoned Alex. 'I'm here safe and sound. No sign of early contractions and the baby's kicking like mad.'

'That's wonderful, Em, darling. I wish I could see you.'

'Me, too. I miss you so much.' She longed to see Alex's smile, to bury her face in his chest and breathe in the scent of his skin, and she yearned to have him beside her through the long, lonely nights.

'I'm planning to be there with you at least two weeks before D-day,' he told her.

'That would be great.' Emily had been to another set of antenatal classes and all the women in her group had husbands who planned to be with them for their babies' births.

She wanted to be just like them, with her baby's father at her side, calming her fears. They both so desperately needed this baby to be pink and healthy, lusty and yelling.

Two days before Alex was due to arrive from Red Hill, Emily's labour started. The contractions were mild and twenty minutes apart, but she went straight to the hospital and instructed her mother to telephone Alex. He needed to leave Red Hill immediately. It would be best if he could catch a ride on a private plane. They knew several graziers who had their pilots' licences.

But when Izzie found Emily in the labour ward, she had bad news. 'I couldn't speak to Alex, I'm afraid. I could only leave a message with the housekeeper.'

'But you told Sandy to send Jim straight out to find Alex, didn't you?'

Izzie shrugged. 'I assumed the woman would have enough common sense to think of that for herself.'

'Oh, *Mum*!' Emily slammed clenched fists into the mattress.

'Don't upset yourself, Emily. Women have been having babies for centuries without their husbands hanging about and getting in the way.'

'But *I* want Alex. I *need* him.' Her husband had been with her for tiny Alexander's miscarriage and, despite the sadness, Emily knew that their bond had deepened more than she'd ever thought possible. In the three years since, she and Alex had supported and buoyed each other. They'd become partners in every sense. A team. And now it was vitally important to share the triumph of this baby's safe arrival. Together.

It felt wrong to go ahead and have their baby without Alex. Emily didn't try to stem her tears.

'Don't make such a fuss.' Izzie was firm in her disapproval.

'You're more than capable of delivering a baby without your husband holding your hand.'

Emily pleaded with the midwife. 'Can we slow things down?'

'Now why would you want to do that?' the midwife retorted with a bemused smile.

Alex was still hours away and the contractions were getting stronger and closer. 'I want to hold on,' Emily said. 'To give my husband time to get here.'

'Don't start stressing about timetables, m'dear.' The midwife gave Emily's hand a reassuring pat. 'I'm sure your husband will forgive you if he finds you already sitting up in bed with a bonny baby in your arms.'

It was dark when Emily woke.

Alex was sitting beside her bed. 'Hello, my darling girl.'

She was no longer in the labour ward, but in a private room. A night light allowed her to see him. Around her wrist was a plastic bracelet with her name and on a cabinet beside her stood a vase of pink roses with a card attached. *Love, Mum xx*

She remembered everything that had happened. The birth had seemed pretty torrid to her, but the midwife had declared that it was quite, quite normal.

'It's a boy,' she told Alex. 'A healthy baby boy.'

'I know,' he said. 'I'm so proud.'

But it was Izzie, not Alex, who had witnessed the precious birth. Apparently, the midwife had found Emily's mother hanging about outside the delivery room and had assumed her presence was prearranged. So she'd invited her in.

'I'm sorry I couldn't hold on a bit longer,' Emily said now as Alex kissed her. 'But he's beautiful, Alex. Have you seen him?' She looked around the room. Where was the little cot on wheels? 'I thought they were going to leave him here with me.'

'Your mother suggested you needed to sleep,' Alex said in a quiet, hard-to-read voice.

'Really? But have you seen the baby? He's still okay, isn't he?'

'He's fine, sweetheart. Izzie took me to the nursery and I saw him through a window.'

'He's so beautiful,' Emily said again.

'From what I could see, he looks strong. A real bruiser.' But there was something missing in Alex's smile, in his voice.

'Where's Mum now?' Emily asked.

'I believe she's gone back to her hotel, somewhere nearby.'

Emily nodded and released a small sigh.

'And you want to call the baby Robert?' Alex added.

This was a shock. Her mother must have told him. 'What do you think?'

Alex shrugged. 'It's as good a name as any, I guess.'

'It was my father's second name,' Emily explained. 'But Mum shouldn't have told you, Alex. She knew I wanted to discuss the names with you first.'

'You must have confided in her.' His voice held a gentle reproach.

'She caught me at a weak moment. You know what she can be like.' Emily felt terrible. She had wanted everything about this birth to be perfect. For her and for Alex. 'I'm sorry, darling.' She would never tell Alex that Izzie had suggested they call the baby Jeremy – Jem for short – after the big brother she'd adored. 'And, honestly, I had no idea they were going to bring Mum into the delivery room for the birth.'

Alex made no comment, but his throat rippled as he swallowed and Emily knew then that he was hurting. Her mother, no doubt with the best of intentions, had bulldozed in where he belonged.

She reached for the buzzer beside her.

Alex stiffened. 'What are you doing?'

Fortunately, Emily didn't have to answer. Almost immediately, a nurse appeared in the doorway.

'How can I help you?' the nurse asked.

'Could you please bring my baby back to this room?'

'But it's past midnight and you need to rest.'

Emily, however, was adamant. She needed to share this night with Alex, to celebrate the wondrous miracle. To let the truth sink in that this baby, their son, was here to stay. Like every other healthy baby, he would learn to crawl, to toddle and eventually to run. In turn, he would be a schoolboy, a teenager, a man.

'I want him here.' Emily spoke so firmly she surprised herself. 'My husband has only just arrived from a cattle property out west. He hasn't seen his son yet.'

'Well . . .' The nurse's gaze switched to Alex and lingered. Even in the soft glow of the night light he was looking his tanned-and-handsome best, dressed in moleskins and a pale-blue shirt with button-down pockets, his thick, dark, fashionably long hair curling at the collar. The nurse offered him a dimpling smile. 'I'll see what I can manage.'

***

Showered and changed into a fresh nightgown, Izzie eyed her reflection in the hotel's bathroom mirror. Her dark curls were heavily streaked with grey, and deep wrinkles fanned out from the corners of her eyes. The lines seemed fitting for her newly acquired status as grandmother. Her throat was wrinkled, too, as were her hands, the finger joints swelling with the beginnings of arthritis.

So different from her grandson's smooth little fingers.

In the delivery room, she had offered the baby her finger and he'd clasped her with such a firm little grip. In fact, his hand had closed around her finger so tightly she'd been quite overcome. She had found it necessary to leave the room before anyone noticed her tears.

Outside, on the hospital verandah, she had stared at the moon, at the waving palm trees and the dark, silent tropical sea and had blinked hard till her emotions were under control. She had forgotten the heart-tugging perfection of a newborn babe.

Becoming a grandparent was a privilege, of course, a gift denied her own mother, who'd died far too young, while her poor husband hadn't even survived long enough to know he was a father.

Izzie had been tempted to remind Emily of this when she was making such a fuss about Alex missing the baby's birth. Really, the younger generation had no idea.

CHAPTER TWENTY-THREE

England, 1945

Izzie had assumed she understood about happiness. Before the war happiness had meant having family and friends around you, and life had been pretty much carefree. Since the war's outbreak, happiness had become a matter of practicality, a roof over your head, enough food to eat and a job that kept you busy and stopped you from thinking too hard about the crazy world beyond your little sphere of responsibility.

When suddenly, in the murky depths of the war, she had met Geoff Galbraith, the Australian pilot, she had rocketed, in a blink, to an entirely new and unimagined level of happiness.

It was completely unwise and against all of her self-imposed rules, but Izzie was helpless. To see Geoff's smile was like drinking stars. To see the heat in his eyes when he caught sight of her, across a tarmac or a crowded pub, made her feel she was flying too close to the sun. At his touch, she was soaring. Flaming. Giddy and boneless with longing.

They married quickly. There was no point in dallying. Izzie didn't need her father's permission and she didn't want to hold things up by travelling home to ask him. Besides, she wasn't sure her father would be thrilled with the idea of her marrying an Australian, and she couldn't bear to have an argument over Geoff.

They fitted the registry office ceremony in between her taxi flights and Geoff's Bomber Command duties. Izzie's friend Olive Wise and Geoff's wing commander, Ian Forsythe, were their witnesses. Izzie didn't have a wedding dress, but she had a nice 'sort of' bouquet of white roses and they had a little party for just the four of them, with champagne, supplied by Ian, and ham salad and tinned fruit bought with food coupons.

Their honeymoon was an exciting and magical three days in the Cotswolds, but in the weeks that followed, they saw each other rarely. By this point in the war, Geoff was flying in bombing raids over Düsseldorf.

During this time, they managed occasional telephone calls and one or two letters, and a miraculous weekend where they hardly left their hotel. In those precious hours they didn't talk about the war, or even about flying.

Lying in the hotel bed, with Izzie nestled in his arms, looking out through a high window to a pale-grey English sky, Geoff told her about his home in North Queensland where his father had a farm on the edge of a lake. Izzie told him about her home in Cambridgeshire and about her sisters and Jem. Geoff added that his older brother would take over the farm.

'And thank heavens,' Geoff said. 'I've never wanted to be a farmer.'

'So what do you want to do?' Izzie asked, even though it felt reckless to talk about life after the war.

'This probably sounds crazy, but I'd like to start a newspaper.'

'Goodness.' Starting a newspaper was the last thing Izzie had expected her pilot husband to announce, and it did sound a little crazy.

'A small country newspaper,' Geoff said. 'With its own printing press. Country towns need to have their own stories told.'

'Are you trained as a journalist?' Izzie didn't want to be pedantic, but it did seem pertinent.

He merely smiled. 'No, but I wasn't trained as a pilot until this bloody war.'

Then he promptly changed the subject by drawing her close and kissing her so comprehensively that all thought of conversation was abandoned.

Too soon – way too soon – the very next month, in fact, brought the news Izzie never wanted to hear. After a flight over the Ruhr, Geoff was missing, presumed killed. His plane had taken a direct hit. It had been reported by others in his squadron as spiralling to the earth in a blaze of fire.

Izzie asked her commanding officer, June Brightman, if she could go to the Red Cross in London, to see if they had any more information.

It was the worst journey of her life. The Red Cross had no news.

Back at Hamble, Izzie rang June. 'I couldn't find out anything, I'm afraid.'

'Oh, my dear,' said June. 'I'm so very sorry. Not knowing is so difficult.'

Izzie was trying desperately to be brave. Despite her new married name, she was still an Oakshott by birth. It helped that, in spite of the dire reports, she had a strong conviction that Geoff was alive. Surely, if he was really dead she would know? She would feel the emptiness, the utter hopelessness, deep inside her.

'I'd like to get back to work,' she said.

After a beat, June replied. 'I think that's probably the best thing to do.'

'I'm so glad you agree.' Sitting around waiting for news was impossible.

Izzie's housemates were wonderful. They arranged things between them so that someone was always around to keep her company whenever she wasn't working. But even with their help, Izzie might have given in to grief if she hadn't been so sure, deep inside, that she would see Geoff again.

She didn't talk about this certainty, but she clung to it in secret, even when she received an official letter from the War Office telling her that her husband was missing, believed killed. Her stubborn belief and the flying kept her going. At least when she was flying she was so occupied with what she was doing, so busy concentrating on the task at hand, she had no room to worry or focus on other things.

And in the end, Izzie's belief and trust were rewarded. Another month later, a postcard arrived, addressed to her, care of Ian Forsythe. Ian passed it on to her as quickly as he could. The card was from Geoff.

Such brilliant news. Geoff and three of his crew had managed to use their parachutes to jump free of the crash. All of them were still alive, although Archie Bell had been badly injured. Geoff was in a prisoner-of-war camp for officers in Münster, Germany.

Izzie allowed herself to cry with relief and she even did so in front of her friends. But the next day she was back to work. It was only a matter of weeks later, she heard on the BBC Home Service news that Allied troops had reached Geoff's camp. The POWs were transported to Brussels and then flown home.

She was working at Hamble when Geoff phoned.

'Izzie?'

His voice. At last. Her heart jolted so hard she felt dizzy. Gripping the receiver in two hands, she had to lean against the nearest wall. 'Hello, Geoff.' So this was yet another level of happiness, so strong it made her numb. Izzie couldn't think what to say. 'Where are you?'

Geoff laughed that wonderful, easy-going laugh of his. 'To be honest, I'm not sure. I'm just so bloody glad to be back on English soil, I didn't ask. Somewhere near the coast. I'm going to have to find a train.'

The girls who shared the house with Izzie wanted to put out bunting and a welcome mat. She wouldn't let them. 'Geoff would hate it,' she said, although she couldn't be sure about that. She suspected that she was the one who would hate it. It was, after all, the way she'd been brought up.

CHAPTER TWENTY-FOUR

On the day Ben's story was due to appear in the *Bugle*, Chloe rose early. She planned a morning run down to the lake and back, a new routine she'd started as an antidote to the nerve-jangling edginess that had plagued her ever since Saturday night. She was still trying to shake off distracting memories of the way Finn had looked at her, his eyes burning, and then the surprise of his invitation to the Drummonds' barbecue.

It was crazy the way her emotions had seesawed. She had known the invitation wasn't a date, and her reaction was totally over the top. And yet now, whenever Finn was around, she felt as if she was standing too close to the edge of a cliff.

Naturally, she had given herself several stern lectures.

Okay, so maybe she'd finally conceded that her boss was hot. But she wasn't looking for a new relationship, thank you very much, and she was absolutely certain that he wasn't either. Finn was grieving a truly terrible loss, and while Chloe's issues were minor by comparison, her scars from Jason were still tender and painful.

These days, she was a relationship cynic. So yeah, even if there was a bit of a vibe happening between her and her boss, they were both too wounded and too wary to act on it.

Chloe hoped that, in time, the lectures would sink in. Meanwhile the running was part of her de-stress strategy and she planned to call in at the newsagency on her way home.

After more than a decade in journalism, she was used to seeing her stories in print, but this morning she was keener than usual to see Ben's story on the page alongside the great photo that Tammy had provided.

She was sure it was important to keep Ben on the Burralea radar. As Tammy had said: *it ain't over till it's over*.

Chloe went to the bathroom, splashed her face with cold water, then changed into running shorts and a singlet and tied her hair back before heading to the kitchen for a glass of water. Her first coffee of the day would be her reward on her return.

The flat's kitchen and living area were open plan and as Chloe crossed the space, she sensed something different about one of the red armchairs.

She turned to check. Froze.

Screamed.

The *something different* on the chair was olivey-brown. It was also coiled and scaly. *Oh, God.* The snake was *huge*. And it was staring at Chloe with evil eyes.

Panic flashed, making her heart pound and her skin crawl. At any moment, the snake would slide off that chair. And it would probably slither towards her. Bite her?

One thing was absolutely certain. She couldn't possibly deal with this.

And, really, there was only one person she could turn to for help. Without taking her eyes from the coiled monster that was trying to disguise itself as a chair cushion, Chloe backed into the bedroom. Then she shoved the door shut and dashed to grab her phone from the bedside table.

Her fingers were shaking as she scrolled to find Finn's number and she prayed that he would answer.

The phone rang and rang and Chloe's desperation mounted, along with her terror of what might be happening on the other side of the door. She could picture the snake slithering over the furniture, the floor, hiding somewhere, waiting to strike at her. As she listened intently to the phone's ringing, she inched the door open again, hoping the wretched thing hadn't moved.

To her relief the snake was still coiled on the chair. At what must have been the very last ring, she heard Finn's voice.

'Is that you, Chloe?' His question ended in a sleepy yawn.

'I need your help,' she said, not caring how wimpy and girly she sounded. She'd lived her whole life in Sydney and she was used to snakes remaining in the wild. In her experience, at least, they'd never scaled walls and crawled into her lounge room.

'What's happened?' Finn asked.

'There's a snake. It's here, in my flat. It's huge.'

'Is it upstairs? It climbed in?' Finn didn't sound nearly as concerned as he should have under such dire circumstances.

'Yes!' Watching the snake from the doorway, Chloe saw it lift its long skinny head. She saw the flicker of its ghastly tongue. She squealed. 'It – it's moving!'

'Okay. Don't panic.'

How could she *not* panic? 'I *hate* snakes.'

'Yeah, fair enough. What colour is it?'

'I don't know. Olivey-green, I guess, with yellow splotches.'

'Sounds like a jungle python. They're not really dangerous.'

'A snake's a snake, Finn.'

'But yours isn't likely to be deadly. The really poisonous snakes don't usually climb. And they don't have those markings.'

Chloe supposed she should feel a measure of relief, but it wasn't easy to stop freaking when the thing was still there in her lounge room. And anyway, a fear of snakes was natural. It was universal, wasn't it? Part of human DNA.

'I'll come over,' Finn said at last. 'Stay cool and I'll see you soon.'

For the next five minutes, Chloe hovered in the bedroom doorway, not daring to move as she watched the dreaded intruder. During this time, the snake also remained motionless and kept its beady eyes pinned on her.

It was a stalemate of sorts, but Chloe knew that when Finn arrived, she would have to move. She would have to cross that room, passing within a metre of *that* chair before she could head downstairs to let him in the front door.

Was she brave enough?

She was still wondering this when she heard the doorbell ring. Her heart skidded.

Just do it. Run.

With a terrified whimper, she took off, barefooted. Why hadn't she thought to put on shoes? Scurrying across the room, not daring to look at the snake, she reached the stairs in safety, but she was breathless with terror as she opened the door.

Finn. Unshaven, dressed in tattered jeans and even more battered sandshoes and a thin grey T-shirt with a hole in one shoulder. He held up a sugarbag and offered her a smile. 'Good morning. Latimer's Snake Removal Service.'

'Thanks for coming.' Chloe was so grateful to see him she almost hugged him.

Finn continued to smile at her, but then clearly changed his mind. Perhaps he'd realised how scared she was. 'Is it still upstairs?' he asked.

Chloe nodded and stepped back to let him in. She closed the door and, without another word, Finn followed her through the Progress Association's office and up the stairs to her flat.

'It's right there, in that armchair.' Chloe pointed as they reached the top of the stairs. But then —

'Oh, crap! It's gone! Oh, God, Finn! It was right there on that chair.'

Primal instinct took over. Chloe dashed the short distance to the dining chairs and leaped onto one, her legs shaking so badly she almost missed her footing. 'Where can it be?' she wailed.

'You're sure it was definitely still here before you came downstairs?' At least Finn wasn't panicking.

'Yes, I swear,' Chloe vowed. 'It was right there in that armchair. Coiled up. I didn't imagine it. You've got to believe me.'

'Okay. Don't freak. I'll find it.'

She supposed Finn's calmness came from the years he'd spent living in Africa and Asia with God knew how many scary creatures. Chloe watched in fearful admiration as he moved carefully around the lounge area, checking behind the chairs and tipping them to see underneath.

'How big was it?' he asked.

'Huge. At least, I – I didn't see it stretched out, but I think it was huge.'

A corner of his mouth twitched. He looked behind the TV cabinet with no apparent luck. 'It may have gone into your bedroom,' he said. 'Do you mind?'

Chloe shook her head. 'No, of course not. Go ahead.' The bed was unmade and she'd left her nightie flung over a chair, but now wasn't the time to be coy. Still perched on the chair and clinging to its back for balance, she leaned as far as she dared, craning to watch Finn as he investigated her room. He looked under the pillows and sheet, under the bed, the wardrobe, the cushions on the window seat.

He went into the bathroom.

'Aha!' she heard him cry. 'There you are, you cheeky bugger.' There was a sound of bumping, of something being knocked over. 'Got you.'

It wasn't long before Finn emerged, gripping the now-closed neck of the sugarbag. He lifted it triumphantly.

'You can get down now,' he told Chloe with a grin.

'You swear you've got him in there?' She had to make sure, even though she could see an obvious bulge in the bag.

'Yep. He was in your shower, trying to climb the taps to the high window. Wouldn't have done him any good, though. It's fly-screened.'

Chloe kept her eyes glued on the sugarbag as she stepped down from the chair.

'I'm afraid he knocked over a bottle of shampoo. A fair bit spilled.'

'A small price to pay,' she said. She could feel magnanimous now the snake was in the bag. 'What are you going to do with it?'

Finn shrugged as he took a piece of rope from his pocket and tied it around the mouth of the bag. 'Guess I'll take him a kilometre or so away and let him go in the rainforest.' He glanced towards her kitchen. 'Did you leave that window open last night?'

'Um . . . yes.' Chloe turned to the gaping window and winced. 'Do you think that's how it got in?'

'I'd say so.' Finn crossed the room. 'There's a handy tree right outside.'

'It was a hot night. I was trying to catch a breeze.'

'Might be worth closing it in future before you turn in. Or asking Moira Briggs to fork out for a flyscreen.'

Chloe nodded emphatically. 'Don't worry. I won't make that mistake again.'

She looked again at the safely secured mouth of the bag. 'I suppose it's not cruel to leave it in there for a little while?'

'No, it's fine. Why?'

'Well . . . I was thinking I owe you breakfast.'

It seemed the least Chloe could do, but when Finn didn't respond immediately, instead regarding her with a complicated smile, she started to have second thoughts. And then she remembered she was wearing skimpy running shorts and a singlet. Not the best apparel for offering her boss an impulsive invitation.

And not the brightest move, given the tension that had been zinging between them over the past few days.

'Or maybe that's not such —' she began.

'I'd love breakfast,' he said before she could complete her retreat, and it was hard to tell if he was pleased, or simply amused.

'Right.' Chloe flashed a smile that probably looked way more confident than she felt. 'Bacon and mushrooms okay?'

'Brilliant.' Finn held up the bag. 'I'll just duck downstairs and stow this in the vehicle.'

As Finn disappeared, Chloe considered dashing into her bedroom to change into something more 'suitable'. But it was a bit late now. Finn had already seen her in this gear and time was ticking away.

She told herself this was no big deal. Finn had simply done her a good turn and she was repaying the favour. Nothing more.

She needed to chill and try to produce a half-decent breakfast.

Grabbing the bacon rashers and a paper bag filled with mushrooms from the fridge, Chloe set them on the bench and tried to quell the stupid buzzing inside her.

Finn's footsteps sounded on the stairs and she found a chopping board and knife and began to dice the bacon as if her life depended on it.

He came into the kitchen. 'How can I help?'

'Um —' *Concentrate, girl.* 'I only have plunger coffee. But perhaps you could take care of it?'

'Sure.'

Without hesitation, he filled the kettle and set it to boil and after that, their morning was relatively plain sailing. Chloe told him where to find the coffee and the plunger and she set the bacon in a pan to fry while she sliced the mushrooms and chopped thyme. He offered to make toast and she told him about the ciabatta in the freezer.

They shared the butter – she added a dollop to the pan of mushrooms, while he attended to the toast.

Chloe sprinkled the thyme. Finn found the coffee mugs hanging on hooks. It was all ridiculously domesticated and in no time they were sitting down to breakfast. Like a couple.

Except they weren't, of course, and Chloe suspected that Finn was even more definite about this than she was, which no doubt explained why he remained quite casual and relaxed.

'This is sensational,' he said, tucking into a small mountain of mushrooms and bacon piled onto toast. 'If I bother to cook breakfast, the best I manage is a boiled egg.'

'I usually make do with muesli and yoghurt,' Chloe admitted.

'But you had all these ingredients in your fridge, just ready to go.'

She shrugged. 'If I hadn't used the mushrooms for this, they probably would have gone into a risotto. But it was a good excuse for me to cook one of my favourite breakfasts.'

He grinned. 'Well, you can count me as impressed.'

Despite her best efforts to quell any reaction, her cheeks grew distressingly hot. Quickly, she said, 'Would you like marmalade for your other piece of toast? It's local. I bought it at the markets. It's cumquat.'

Finn ended up having two slices of marmalade toast and a second cup of coffee and they chatted about safe things, about the colourful locals they'd met on their rounds, and about life in general in Burralea: the convenience of having a supermarket just around the corner, the variety of products at the farmers' markets, the peacefulness of life away from the city and its traffic.

'There's something about being close to the earth,' Finn said. 'Having your feet on the ground, rather than under a desk. Nothing really beats sitting on a log or a big mossy rock.'

'I'm sure the snake would agree with you,' Chloe teased.

He grinned.

'But seriously,' she said, to make up for the dig, 'the thing that really blows me away is the birdsong in the morning.'

'I totally agree.

'And then there's the stars, so bright at night. They're so awesome, so clear.'

Finn nodded. 'The night skies are something else.' He said this quietly and, as he did so, his gaze connected with Chloe's and held.

Foolishly, she found herself wondering if he was thinking about a starry night – or *something else*. His eyes seemed to shimmer with unexpected emotion, while the air around them condensed, robbing her of breath.

The moment might have become awkward, but Finn saved it by taking out his phone and transferring his attention to the small screen in his hand. 'It's getting late,' he said. 'I'd better make tracks if I'm to drop off our friend on the way home.'

'Of course.'

They both stood.

'Thanks for breakfast, Chloe.'

'Thanks for your help.' She lifted a hand to wave. 'See you soon.'

So . . . they'd negotiated breakfast successfully. Chloe let out a breath of relief as Finn descended the stairs. Apart from the brief, confusing night-sky moment, they'd behaved like friendly associates, which was how things ought to be.

Finn was almost at the bottom of the stairs when she heard the sound of the front door opening.

Moira Briggs's voice called, gleefully, 'Finn!'

Damn. Chloe winced. Finn would hate being caught coming down from her flat at this early hour by the ever curious and talkative Moira.

'Morning, Moira,' she heard him say. 'How are you?'

'Very well, thank you, Finn, and I'm sure you must be, too.' Moira's voice positively trilled with barely suppressed innuendo.

Chloe swore softly. Moira was sure to leap to all sorts of incorrect conclusions.

Tiptoeing closer to the top of the stairs, she strained to hear Finn's explanation about the snake, which was regrettably out of sight in his car.

Chloe had a problem with a python, she imagined him telling Moira. *Climbed through the kitchen window.*

Perhaps Moira would instantly offer to put in a flyscreen.

'I'll see you around,' she heard Finn say. And silence followed, apart from a small sound that might have been a chuckle from Moira.

Chloe listened carefully, anxious to hear the rest of Finn's explanation, but a moment later, from outside in the street, came the sound of the Forester's motor starting up and taking off.

Huh? Chloe couldn't believe it.

Surely Finn must know that Moira Briggs would jump to all sorts of terrible conclusions? She would assume Finn had spent the night here in the flat. And he was well aware of Moira's tendency to gossip. What was wrong with the man? Surely it was in his own interests to set Moira straight.

Chloe almost tore downstairs to deal with Moira herself, but then she remembered she was still in her skimpy shorts and singlet top, and she curbed the impulse. If she wanted to take the moral high ground, she would find it easier to do so after she'd showered and dressed demurely for work.

By then she might also have calmed down, and she needed to be totally cool and reasonable when she explained this situation to her landlady.

Frustratingly, the explanation about the snake didn't go nearly as well as Chloe had hoped.

Moira's eyes were almost popping with excitement and no matter how clearly Chloe made her point, she couldn't wipe the woman's delighted, cat-that-got-the-cream grin.

'Of course, my dear,' Moira soothed. 'You don't need to justify anything to me.'

'But you do understand about the snake?'

'Well, I have to admit it's a brilliant excuse.' Moira almost giggled as she said this.

'Excuse?' Chloe stared at her in dismay. ' Moira, it's no excuse. There really was a snake. I got up this morning and walked into my lounge room and there it was, curled in the armchair.'

'Yes, dear.' Moira might have been trying to sound sympathetic, but her efforts were spoiled by her gleeful grin.

Somehow, Chloe resisted the urge to stamp her foot or to groan aloud, but she was furious with Moira for being so stubborn, and even more furious with Finn for leaving her in this damned awkward predicament. Surely if he was any kind of gentleman he would have made sure Moira understood the innocence of his early morning presence in her flat.

Now, it probably wouldn't matter what she told Moira, the woman would continue to smirk and smile.

Chloe was curt as she bade her good morning. She didn't even bother to make enquiries about a flyscreen, and she was fuming as she hurried outside. She was still fuming as she stomped into the office, all set to launch into her attack. Until she saw a copy of the latest edition of the *Bugle* spread open on Finn's desk.

Her attention was immediately caught by Ben's story and photo.

The headline on page three was bold and eye-catching, the photograph large and clear.

'You did a good job with that.' Finn appeared in the doorway to the little storeroom.

'Thanks.' Chloe was ever so slightly disarmed. 'Let's hope it helps.'

'Yeah.' He leaned a bulky shoulder against the doorjamb and frowned at a spot on the floor. 'I would never have thought to write a story like that. And yet I know what it's like when people avoid you because you're grieving.'

Chloe took a sharp breath. Finn had never hinted at his own grief before.

'It's a bit different for Tammy,' she said gently. 'She's not really grieving. She won't give up believing that Ben will come back.'

Finn still looked pensive. No doubt he was thinking about his family and, at any other time, Chloe would have been dripping with sympathy. But damn it, she'd been geared up to seize the moment, to let fly with her fury.

'I have a job for you,' he said, beating her to the mark. 'I'd like you to cover a story about new equipment for the children's ward at the hospital.'

By lunchtime, Chloe's anger had almost dissipated. She was even beginning to see it as an overreaction – until she ducked into the Lilly Pilly café to grab a salad sandwich and Jess rushed up to her with a grin as wide as a slice of watermelon.

'I hear you found a visitor in your flat this morning?' Jess's amused expression was an annoying replica of Moira's.

'An unwanted visitor,' Chloe corrected her tartly. 'An enormous snake.'

Jess laughed. 'Lucky you.'

'A python,' Chloe added in exasperation. 'It was huge.'

'Must have been scary,' her friend said, still with a huge smile. 'I'm so pleased Finn was there too.'

'Yes, so was I, but he only came after I called him for help.'

'Mmm.'

'Honestly.' Chloe leaned closer and hissed in Jess's ear in a desperate whisper. 'He didn't spend the night.'

Jess's expression was reproachful. 'Me thinks she doth protest too much.'

Chloe glared back at her. The last thing she needed was a café waitress quoting Shakespeare. 'You've been talking to Moira, haven't you?' she said.

'Moira Briggs? No.'

'Then who told you about the snake?'

'Emily Hargreaves,' Jess said with a cheeky shrug.

Chloe's jaw dropped so hard she was sure it must have dislocated. 'I didn't know you were so pally with my employer.'

'I'm not really, but she pops in here quite regularly. We get to know most of the locals.'

And to hear all the gossip, Chloe thought with a weary sigh.

CHAPTER TWENTY-FIVE

It was late in the day when Emily called into the *Bugle* office. Finn had been out for half the afternoon and the rest of the time he'd been busy on the phone, so Chloe hadn't had a chance to share the news from the café.

All afternoon her tension had gathered steam, and by the time Emily strolled in, she was about ready to burst a valve.

Fortunately, Emily didn't seem to notice the way Chloe jumped when she saw her and, although she was smiling, there was no sign of a smirk. 'How are you both?' she asked.

Finn and Chloe both assured her they were fine, although Chloe's assurance may have been a little too emphatic. Emily complimented them on this week's edition and the ensuing conversation was exceedingly convivial.

Emily even offered an invitation. 'I've been meaning to have you both over to dinner some time,' she said. 'I was wondering if Friday night might suit?'

Chloe couldn't help thinking this was some kind of litmus test, but Finn seemed totally at ease. 'Friday night works for me,' he said without so much as glancing Chloe's way.

'And I'm free,' said Chloe. 'Thanks, Emily.'

Emily looked delighted. Chloe was beginning to relax. Perhaps their super-discreet employer wasn't going to mention the snake episode after all.

They talked a little more about Ben Shaw and the latest reports from the police, as well as about plans for more feature articles. Emily told them she was really pleased with the increase in advertising and Finn acknowledged this was mainly thanks to Chloe's input.

Emily's smile was warm and smacked of sincerity. 'I'll see you on Friday night, then.'

They thanked her and said they were looking forward to it, and Emily crossed the office to leave.

Phew. No embarrassing moments after all.

In the doorway, Emily turned back and said, with yet another smile, 'It's just as well you were on hand to help Chloe with that python, Finn.'

Chloe was too surprised to respond before Emily made her quick exit. Which left Finn to receive the full vent of her fury.

She rounded on him. 'Why didn't you say something?'

'What about?' His expression was all innocence, like a choir boy on a Christmas card.

Chloe groaned with frustration. 'Don't pretend you don't know. The bloody snake, of course. Now just about everyone in this town seems to believe you spent last night at my flat. *All* night.'

He gave a careless shrug. 'So what? Let them think what they like. We don't owe them an explanation.'

'But —' Chloe spluttered. 'Don't you care? Everyone's talking about us. Moira. The women at the café. God knows who else. And now our employer.'

'Emily was just teasing,' Finn told her smoothly.

'So? Maybe I don't appreciate being teased about something so personal.' Chloe glared at him, and when he made no response, she grabbed her bag and headed for the door. She was fed up. With everyone and every*thing*.

How on earth had she ever thought she might enjoy living in a small country town? At least she now knew the reality – that snakes invaded high-set windows and gossipers were thick on the ground. As for bosses who were too sexy for their T-shirts —

'Chloe.' She was almost at the doorway when Finn lunged after her and grabbed at her wrist, halting her in mid-stomp.

She held her breath, way too conscious of his touch, of the warm pressure of his fingers encircling her skin.

'Don't let a little thing like this get to you,' he said.

Chloe wasn't quite sure why she was angrier than ever. Maybe because the 'little thing' he referred to was their reputations and the question of whether or not they were lovers. The fact that he didn't care one way or the other maddened her beyond reason.

Yanking her arm free, she fixed him with a venomous scowl. 'If you don't understand why I'm angry, you're even dumber than I thought.'

With that, she marched off, hurrying along the footpath as quickly as she dared without drawing unwanted attention. To her relief, Moira had already closed the Progress Association office and gone home. She was fumbling with her keys when Finn caught up with her.

'Chloe.'

She found the key quickly and shoved it into the lock. 'You're too late, Finn. There's no point in making this worse.'

The door opened easily and she slipped inside, spinning around to slam it in his face. Finn's foot was too fast for her.

'Let me in,' he said. 'We need to talk.'

'No, thanks.' Not with his unhelpful attitude.

'I'd like to understand why you're so worked up.'

'Can you really pretend you don't know?'

'I'm not pretending anything.' Finn shouldered the door open and stepped inside, letting it swing closed behind him with a solid click.

Chloe swallowed to ease the sudden tightness in her throat and in her chest, while Finn towered in front of her, his gaze assessing her, his hands resting lightly on his hips. A non-verbal challenge?

'So what's this all about?' he asked quietly.

'I told you.'

'I don't think so. I know you're obviously pissed off with me, but I don't really get why.'

Wasn't it obvious? She let out a huff of pure frustration. 'You could have avoided all of this if you'd simply told Moira the truth this morning. If you'd set her straight about the damn snake as soon as you saw her, you could have stopped the gossip before it started.'

A crooked little smile tilted Finn's mouth. 'You think so?'

'I'm sure of it.'

'So let me get this straight.' He nodded towards the staircase. 'Moira Briggs sees me walking down those stairs at half past eight in the morning and I'm supposed to immediately jump in with apologies and explanations, like I'm ashamed of having breakfast with you? Or I'm shit-scared of her?'

When he put it like that, it did sound rather lame.

Finn's dark eyes gleamed. 'And even if we had spent the night together, so what?'

'I —' Chloe couldn't finish the sentence. Her brain had turned to mush at the thought of spending an entire night with Finn.

'Is that what you're angry about?' Finn asked, and somehow he seemed to be closer to her now. 'You're mad because we didn't sleep together, but everyone thinks we did?'

'Perhaps.' She gave a dazed shake of her head and realised her mistake. 'No, no, that's not what I meant.'

'Are you sure, Chloe?' He was even closer to her now and he was speaking so quietly, she had to lean towards him. In fact, if she leaned the tiniest bit closer —

She could no longer focus on her argument. In an attempt to do so, she closed her eyes and found herself back at the edge of the cliff. In danger of falling.

'Chloe.'

She heard the tense roughness in his voice, felt the heat of his body moving closer, and she knew if she opened her eyes, his gaze would be burning. The attraction vibe was back in full force. Or maybe it had never left.

When Finn touched her cheek, just the gentlest, whispering caress, she didn't flinch or pull back. With his thumb, he traced the shape of her chin – and she let him.

'We can sort this out,' he said. 'But it may mean that I have to kiss you.'

Chloe knew she was supposed to protest, but his lips brushed against hers in the lightest of teases and she forgot that she was angry. And when he deepened the kiss and slipped his arms around her, gathering her in, she didn't resist. She foolishly snuggled closer and kissed him back.

With gentle fingers, he traced the nape of her neck, under her hair. 'And I'm going to have to kiss that damn butterfly,' he murmured.

Even as she melted, Chloe couldn't hold back a triumphant little smile. The butterfly tattoo had been her first act of independence after she'd left Jason. Her gift to herself, and a part of her that Jason knew nothing about. Now, already, Finn had found it . . . claimed it . . .

He pressed a trail of warm, sensuous kisses over the vulnerable skin on her neck, and she was lost.

*

They made it up the stairs without tripping or stumbling – a miracle, Chloe suspected, given how little attention they paid to where they put their feet.

Very few words were exchanged. Certainly not a civilised, pre-coital discussion or negotiation, befitting a cautious couple well past the first flush of youth. This evening, need and longing ruled. Chloe was a knot desperate to unravel.

Later, she could only vaguely recall the way they'd helped each other out of their clothes. All she could really remember was the feverish urgency of their kisses and the breathtaking thrill of first contact. Of his skin meeting hers. Of seductive hands and teasing lips embarking on an intimate trail of discovery.

Somewhere in the hazy mists of desire, it occurred to her that they should perhaps slow down, linger a little, but there was a danger they might also come to their senses. It seemed Finn was as unwilling as she was to take that risk.

Afterwards, they lay side by side, spent, panting like swimmers who'd finally made it to shore.

By then, darkness had fallen completely. Delicate starlight showed the outline of the wardrobe, the silver glimmer of its oval mirror, the white wrinkled sheets and their naked bodies.

Wow . . . Chloe's body was still thrumming from her sensational climax, and she wasn't sure what to do or say now. This had all been so unexpected, and although she'd written articles for *Girl Talk* with guidelines for casual sex, she had spent seven and a half years with one guy, so she'd never put the theory into practice.

At least Finn had remembered, in the heat of the moment, to mention that he'd had a vasectomy. So that was one of the basics covered.

She pulled the sheet up so they weren't quite so exposed and wondered if thanks or apologies were in order. But the sex had been too amazing to be diminished by either of these responses. And yet, she was quite sure it was time to talk, to clear the air, et cetera, but without too painful a postmortem.

To her relief, Finn spoke first. 'In case you were wondering, that wasn't planned.'

Chloe nodded. 'And in case you were wondering, I won't get all emotional or clingy. I mean – I know it was only sex.'

'A-huh.' The tone of his response was hard to read.

She tried again. 'It's not like the start of a relationship, or – or anything.'

'Yeah, of course.'

'I guess we were both just —'

'Ripe for plucking,' he suggested.

She turned to him and saw the amusement in his eyes and the flash of his sudden smile. They both laughed.

The laughter helped to lighten the mood, but she still felt a bit out of her depth. She wondered if there'd been other women in Finn's life since his wife died, or was she the first? It wasn't a question she could ask.

'Would you like a drink?' she asked instead. 'Although I'm afraid I only have white wine.'

'Maybe I should leave. I know you're worried about gossip.'

Chloe had certainly made a huge fuss about gossip, but she realised now that she didn't want him to go. It would feel too rushed. *Too* casual. And she would be left with a tangle of confused thoughts. But she'd also just promised him that she wouldn't cling.

Finn swung his legs over the side of the bed and sat with his back to her. His shoulders were broad, his back nicely toned with a very masculine V shape that tapered to slim hips, and she wondered if he was a swimmer.

He turned and looked back at her, his expression a little sad, or perhaps worried. 'I don't want you to feel this was *wham, bam, thank you, ma'am.*'

'I won't.' She'd enjoyed herself far too much to start thinking negatively. Perhaps there would be another time when they each shared a little about their past. She would like to understand more about Finn as a man. And it would be helpful to know if this evening had been a one-off, a full stop – or some kind of stepping stone.

He leaned over, touched a finger to her wrinkled brow. 'What are you stewing over now?'

'Nothing in particular.'

He watched her for a moment or two. 'Yes,' he said.

She frowned. 'Yes, what?'

He didn't answer immediately. Then, quietly, while no longer meeting her gaze, 'Yes, this is the first time – since my wife —'

'Oh.' Chloe couldn't think of anything to say. This news was *big*. Bigger than she'd expected.

She watched him reach for his clothes. It seemed he wasn't ready to add any more to his statement and she wondered if he felt guilty, somehow disloyal to his dead wife.

She felt absolutely no guilt about Jason, she realised. If anything, this evening had brought a huge sense of relief, even triumph. Which no doubt illustrated that she and Finn Latimer were on vastly different emotional journeys.

Moving out of bed, she picked up the cotton dressing gown she'd left draped on a nearby chair. She was hungry, but she didn't offer to make dinner. After a day that had started with the snake and breakfast and had ended with sex, she was sure another meal would be taking things too far.

Finn buckled his belt and pulled on boots. 'Don't forget to keep that window closed tonight,' he said.

'Don't worry. I'm not likely to forget that ever again.'

'Great.'

Together they left the bedroom, both careful not to tread on her clothes, which still lay scattered on the floor, evidence of their lust-crazed haste.

Already that blaze of passion was beginning to feel unreal, like something that might have happened in a dream.

At the top of the stairs they stopped. 'I'll let myself out.' Finn touched her lightly on the elbow and his eyes held a shimmer of unexpected emotion. 'Are you okay, Chloe?'

'Yes,' she said. 'Absolutely.' And then, 'What about you?'

He nodded, chanced a wry smile. 'I don't want to embarrass you, but perhaps thanks are in order.'

'No, don't thank me.' He was right – she was embarrassed – and if anyone owed thanks, she probably did. She'd been so incredibly turned on and that climax had been —

'And I won't make a habit of this,' he added.

Her disappointment was ridiculous.

'For very practical reasons, I'm going to be preoccupied,' he said next. 'The school holidays start this weekend, and my daughter's coming to stay.'

His daughter?

Chloe gasped as if he'd winded her. How could Finn have a daughter and never have mentioned her? 'You have a daughter?'

'Yes. Bree. She's twelve.'

Surely this was impossible? Chloe reached for the stair railing for support. 'Where is she?'

'In Townsville. At boarding school. She's a weekly boarder and she stays with my parents on the weekends.'

'But —' Chloe wanted to protest. This girl, this twelve-year-old Bree, had lost her mother and her little brother. But instead of keeping her close and giving her his fatherly support, Finn had simply dumped her in a boarding school? How could he be so heartless?

Chloe's own longing for a child was so strong she found such negligence beyond her comprehension.

'Aren't the schools up here good enough?' She couldn't keep a bitter edge from her voice.

'I don't know,' Finn admitted. 'That's not the point. I – I thought Bree would be better off down there.'

'Away from you?'

His gaze was steady, as if he dared her to challenge him. 'Yes,' he said.

'Is it because of the drinking?'

He frowned. 'The *what*?'

'Well, you do have a bit of a problem with alcohol, don't you?'

'No. Why would you —' Then he must have remembered. 'Oh, you mean the day you arrived. Fair enough.' He shook his head. 'But that was a one-off. An – an anniversary. I don't make a habit of wiping myself out.'

Once upon a time this might have been good news, but right now Chloe wanted to thump Finn. How could the same man who had just made sensational love to her suddenly floor her with such a disappointing revelation?

Here she was, desperate for a child, while Finn had a daughter he practically ignored. Was she forever doomed to be attracted to men with hopeless attitudes to fatherhood?

No doubt her own feelings were skewed by her deep longing for a baby, but she was sure she wasn't the only woman who would find Finn's offloading of his daughter unfathomable.

'I've been meaning to tell you about Bree,' Finn said. 'Over the next few weeks, I'll probably need to take the odd morning or afternoon off, so I can entertain her.'

'I daresay,' Chloe replied tartly. 'I would expect you'd need a good amount of time off. I'm surprised you didn't take proper holidays.'

His eyes narrowed. He probably didn't appreciate being reprimanded. 'I'm sure we'll sort something out.'

Obviously he hadn't been prepared to leave the paper in Chloe's tender care. She realised she was in danger of landing back at square one – dead angry with her boss. But then again, she couldn't begin to understand the suffering and grief he'd dealt with over these past few years.

Chloe decided to rein in her disapproval. She even managed to smile. 'I hope I get to meet Bree.'

'I'm sure you will.' Finn glanced down the stairs, clearly keen to leave, but when he looked back at her, there was no sign of hostility in his dark gaze. 'I'd better say goodnight.'

For a tantalising moment, he looked as if he was going to kiss her, but he must have thought better of it. He tapped her on the elbow and then turned and went down the stairs quickly. Disappeared. She heard the front door open and close. Then silence.

***

As Finn started up the Forester, he took a deep, very necessary breath.

So. He'd taken a step. A step he'd thought, many times during the past three years, that he might never take again. And it hadn't been mindless sex with a stranger. He'd made love with a work colleague. His only work colleague, who just happened to have bewitching brown eyes and an even more tempting pink mouth.

Was he crazy?

Or was this step a sign of progress?

For the second time in a week, Finn's thoughts were rioting as he drove away from Chloe Brown. He'd become so used to floundering in deepest grief. For three years now, sorrow had been an ever-present weight he'd learned to live with. He hadn't dared to imagine he'd ever get back to normal life.

And, yeah . . . it was the normality of this evening that had come as a total surprise. Despite the high-voltage sparks and unreasoning haste that had sent him racing Chloe upstairs, the impulse had felt amazingly rational and normal. And the sex had been bloody fantastic.

Absolutely.

Sensuous, responsive Chloe was another surprise. How had he ever thought of her as mousy? If he wasn't careful she could become a new addiction.

Then the final surprise – he wasn't now plagued by guilt or remorse. And it seemed the world hadn't come to an end.

The road ahead took a dogleg turn over a narrow bridge that spanned the creek. Slowing to take the turn, Finn saw the sheen of rounded rocks and little splashes of white foam where the water rushed around them. He saw a slender moon hanging like a silver charm between the branches of a rainforest fig.

The sight was a familiar one. He had encountered many versions of it since he'd come to live in the country, but he never tired of the unexpected beauty of nature in the raw.

Chloe had mentioned the night sky in their conversation at breakfast. She'd loved how clear and bright the stars were away from the city lights. And Finn was reminded of an inescapable truth: darkness was necessary to appreciate the light.

He had experienced his own share of darkness, so perhaps it made sense that tonight had been out-of-this-world amazing. Not that he would allow himself to get carried away. Hell, no. He certainly wasn't going to lose his head over the first girl he'd slept with since he'd been widowed. He would take this – whatever *this* was – super, super slowly.

For that reason alone, Bree's imminent arrival was probably a godsend. A perfect reason to avoid further complication with Chloe. Bree would need his undivided attention. He only hoped he was up to the task.

CHAPTER TWENTY-SIX

Rolf arrived early on Friday evening. Emily knew he would enjoy the company of fellow writers, even if the writers were journalists rather than novelists, so she had invited him to join her for dinner with Chloe and Finn.

'I came a bit early because I thought you might have a job for me,' he said, after he'd exchanged cheek kisses with Emily and followed her into the kitchen.

'That's very thoughtful, Rolf, but apart from frying the lamb cutlets at the last minute, I'm more or less organised. I've kept everything simple, with things I could do ahead.'

'And I know from experience it will all be delicious.'

The mix of fondness and desire in his smile made Emily's breath catch. It was flattering to be wanted, and in the absence of her husband's love, Rolf's affection was exceptionally comforting. Perhaps more comforting than she'd realised.

To her horror, her eyes brimmed with tears. She blinked hard, forcing her thoughts to practical matters.

'It would be great if you could look after the drinks,' she said, eyeing the wine that he'd once again brought. 'There's champagne and beer in the fridge, and the usual spirits over in the bar. I've set the table, but you know where I keep the rest of the glasses.'

'It would be my pleasure.' Rolf set the bottles on a side table and, with his arms free, he reached for her. 'Come here. You look badly in need of a hug.'

Emily didn't protest. She sank against his chest with a grateful sigh, savouring the closeness and his strength. She smelled his freshly ironed shirt, caught a whiff of his aftershave.

'Thanks,' she said softly as he released her. 'I did need that.'

'So Alex still hasn't made contact?'

She shook her head.

'The man's a fool.'

A shuddering sigh escaped her. 'Perhaps I didn't try hard enough.'

'Excuse me?'

'I know everyone grieves in different ways. Maybe I should have tried harder to understand Alex.'

'Rather an uphill battle if he won't talk,' Rolf suggested.

'That's true.' Emily squared her shoulders. 'Anyway, this evening isn't about me and my troubles.'

'I'm looking forward to your guests,' Rolf said, smoothly accepting her change of subject. 'I've met Finn Latimer on several occasions, of course, but I've never had the chance for a decent conversation. I'd like to hear more about his time overseas.'

'If he's prepared to talk about that.'

'Well, yes, I won't push.' Rolf smiled gently. 'Between you and your editor, you've had your share of sorrows.'

'Indeed we have. But I think Chloe is good for Finn. I'm sure I made the right decision when I decided to hire her. She's efficient and creative and rather lovely in an understated kind of way. I believe Finn's been happier since Chloe arrived.'

Rolf eyed her shrewdly. 'You wouldn't be trying your hand at matchmaking, would you?'

Emily chanced a coy smile. 'I suspect I don't need to.'

'Really?'

'There's talk around town, but I shouldn't be adding to the gossip, Rolf. And you'll be able to decide for yourself very soon. Now, let me check that everything is ready. I think I need salt and pepper for the table.'

Emily loved setting the table for a dinner party. She was fortunate to have rather a lovely collection of tableware and cutlery, and tonight she'd combined vintage pieces that her mother had brought out from England with newer crockery. She enjoyed the layered, collected look of antique green dinner plates under floral entree plates, and she'd added green napkins and candles to complement touches of coral in the flowers.

Beyond the dining table, views through the enormous plate-glass windows showed the trees and the lake and the sunset. The green and hot-pink tones of the outdoors were echoes of her table setting and she found this artistically satisfying, even if nobody else noticed.

***

The sun was a burnished, glowing orb suspended above the western hills as Finn and Chloe headed towards the lake in the *Bugle*'s Forester.

Chloe had opted to wear her brown linen. It was stylish yet safe, which seemed a wise choice if she and Finn were to spend another social evening together.

Not that Chloe was uptight. Finn's revelation about his daughter had proved a helpful distraction in recent days. Chloe was confident now that her disappointment over Finn's offhand attitude to Bree had wiped any lingering romantic fantasies.

Which meant she could relax this evening. She had her relationship with the hot editor sorted. Their blazing encounter had been an aberration. A one-off, not to be repeated. And Chloe could live with that. Really, she could.

For the next several weeks, Finn's out-of-office time would be devoted to his daughter, a move Chloe totally approved of.

And now, as they left behind the newer houses on the outskirts of Burralea and drove past freshly ploughed paddocks, she turned to Finn, who was driving. 'I guess you must be looking forward to Bree's arrival.'

He nodded. 'She's a great kid.'

'She's twelve, did you say?'

'Yeah. Just had her birthday.'

'A pre-teen.'

'Tell me about it.' Finn let out a heavy sigh. 'I'll probably be totally out of my depth.'

Chloe was tempted to suggest that he might have been more at ease with his daughter if he hadn't kept her at such a distance, but she held her tongue.

'I tried,' Finn said suddenly, shooting her a quick, sharp glance.

'You mean you tried with Bree?' Could he read her mind?

'Yeah. I guess you think I'm a shit of a father, but I *did* try. At first, after the – ah – incident, Bree wouldn't let me out of her sight. We had every meal together. I walked her to school and, at the end of the day, I was there at the door to pick her up. I slept on the floor in her room for weeks.'

'Gosh,' Chloe said softly.

'Some mornings I would wake to find her curled there on the floor with me.' Finn slowed the vehicle to take a sharp corner. 'I decided I had to get away from Thailand,' he said as the road straightened out once more. 'I managed to get a job in Sydney with Channel Nine. Bree was living with me and going to school nearby. I hoped it would be okay, but we were both still too shattered. Barely functioning. Nothing felt right. I knew Bree was falling behind at school and then one day she came home with a black eye.'

'God, Finn. The poor kid. Was she being bullied in the school yard?'

'Yeah. A girl in her class. And I had to accept I was failing her.' Finn stared grimly at the road ahead. 'I'd already failed to protect her mother and her brother. I was failing everyone I loved and I was so scared I'd lose Bree too.'

Chloe's heart swelled with sympathy and she was a little ashamed of how quickly she'd jumped to judge Finn. His choices made so much more sense now. 'But Bree loves her new school?' she asked.

'Well, she's certainly a hell of a lot happier there than she was in Sydney and she seems to be doing well academically. And my parents are there for extra support.'

'And now she must be really looking forward to spending her holidays up here with you.'

At this, Finn smiled crookedly. 'She says she can't wait. I suppose she sees it as an adventure. Now I just have to hope the reality lives up to her expectations.'

Chloe could scarcely believe the rush of emotion his story had roused. If she wasn't careful, her defences would crumble and she'd find herself once again vulnerable around this man.

It was only sex.

She wasn't falling for him.

It was time to remind herself of her own goals. She'd continued her research into IVF options on the internet and had discovered fertility specialists in Cairns. Only an hour away. From that point, it was a simple step to dreaming of her own baby. Right here in Burralea. A little playmate for Jess's Willow, perhaps.

'You'll love the Lake House.' Finn's voice broke into her thoughts as they approached the forested area that rimmed the lake.

'Emily's parents built the place in about 1950. They hired some famous architect and it still feels modern today.'

'Wow. It must have caused quite a stir around here at the time.'

'Yes. From what I've heard, Emily's parents were innovators.'

Chloe nodded. 'Izzie, her mother, was certainly quite amazing – being a pilot during the war and then later running the paper. I wanted to write a story about her and she didn't seem to mind when I spoke to her, but I sensed that Emily had strong reservations. It's a pity. It seems such a waste of good local content.'

'I'm not really surprised,' Finn said as he turned onto a dirt track that wound through the trees. 'I'm sure Emily's trying to keep out of the spotlight. Do you know about her son?'

'No.' Chloe could remember that Moira had hinted at something, but, surprisingly, she'd never been forthcoming.

'He was a pilot with the RAAF and he was killed in Syria a little over a year ago.'

'Oh, no. How awful.' Chloe wasn't sure she could bear more bad news. Compared with Finn's and Emily's heartbreak, her despair over Jason seemed so very minor.

'Emily was shattered, of course,' Finn went on. 'Robbie was their only child. I don't think her husband's handled it very well. He seems to spend a lot of time on their property out west.'

'So he's not around to support her?'

'Doesn't seem to be.'

Chloe couldn't hold back her heavy sigh. 'Bloody men!' she growled, not quite under her breath.

Finn sent her a cautious glance, but she didn't bother to explain, and she was feeling rather subdued as they pulled up in front of a stunning house. All timber and glass, it was surrounded by trees and had the shining waters of the lake as its backdrop. And then Emily, smiling and serene, came to the front door to greet them.

Dressed in an aqua silk kaftan over slim white slacks, she looked lovely, as always, and she welcomed them with a warm smile.

'How lovely to see you both. Oh, Chloe, how thoughtful. Thank you,' she said as Chloe offered the locally made chocolates she'd brought. 'Now, come and meet my good friend Rolf.'

Emily ushered them inside. 'This is Rolf Anders, the author,' she said with a beaming smile as she gestured to her companion, a wide-shouldered fellow with greying red hair and beard, who looked to be about her own age.

'How do you do, Rolf? I've read one of your books,' Chloe blurted excitedly as they shook hands. 'I'm trying to remember the title. It was something about snow. '

'*First Snow*?'

'Yes, that's the one. It was set in Japan.'

'I've read several of Rolf's books, too,' Finn said. 'He knows I'm a fan.' He smiled at Rolf. 'Good to see you again,' he said as he also shook hands.

'This is amazing,' gushed Chloe. 'I had no idea you lived up here.'

'Why wouldn't I?' Rolf grinned. 'It's so beautiful.'

'Rolf has a house on the other side of the lake,' Emily explained.

'Did you come by boat?'

'Yes, I did, actually. By canoe.'

'Like *Swallows and Amazons*.'

'Indeed.'

There were smiles all round and the evening got off to a very convivial start. Champagne was poured. A platter of delicious canapés was handed around and they settled down to chat, and to enjoy the view through huge glass windows where the sunset and then dusk spread a gently changing palette of colours over the lake.

Everyone present was interested in writing and authors, newspapers and books, so the conversation flowed very smoothly. Rolf told them about the quaint nineteenth-century Japanese fishing port of Otaru where the novel *First Snow* was set.

'I seem to remember that the main action took place during some sort of festival,' Chloe said.

'That's right.' Rolf grinned. 'The Snow Light Festival in February, when the canal is lined with glowing snow lanterns and it's all incredibly beautiful and romantic. So naturally, it was the perfect setting for a murder.'

This brought a round of laughter, and when they moved to the exquisitely set dining table to enjoy Emily's first course of homemade pâté and toast, Chloe realised she'd stopped fretting about the tragedies Finn and Emily had suffered.

Right now, in this moment, she felt happier and more relaxed than she had in a very long time. She supposed the excellent champagne helped. Her mellow mood certainly wasn't caused by the hot editor sitting opposite her. It must have been the company in general, the excellent food and the ambience of the lovely house. Clearly, Emily was a first-class hostess, and tonight she seemed to be enjoying herself as much as anyone.

Emily really likes Rolf, Chloe decided. *And I think he might be in love with her.*

Or perhaps the champagne is going to my head.

When Emily excused herself to finalise the main course, Chloe asked if she could help.

Emily smiled. 'There's really no need. I'm just frying lamb cutlets.' Then, perhaps she had second thoughts, 'But you're very welcome to come through to the kitchen. You can collect the salad, if you like.'

'I'd love to,' Chloe said, rising.

Rolf spoke up. 'In that case, may I be a crashing bore and take a quick squiz at the TV news to catch the cricket score?'

'Of course,' Emily told him, smiling good-naturedly even as she sent an eye-roll in Chloe's direction.

Emily had already coated the cutlets in herbed breadcrumbs, and there was a bowl of bean and parsley salad in the fridge.

'If you could take the cling wrap off that salad and give it a bit of a toss, that would be helpful, Chloe. The servers are right there on the bench.'

From the nearby living room came the murmur of the men's voices and the background patter of a female news anchor. Chloe tossed the salad, enjoying the scent of lemon and parsley as she did so.

'Does it need a little more dressing?' Emily asked as she added a little oil to a pan. 'I have it here in this little —'

She broke off, interrupted by Finn's voice. Yelling. Animated. 'Look, that's Ben Shaw! Bloody hell, it's got to be him! Yes, I'm sure it is.'

CHAPTER TWENTY-SEVEN

Across the kitchen, Chloe and Emily turned to each other with wide-eyed surprise, before simultaneously dropping what they were doing and rushing into the living room.

Finn was on his feet, his eyes huge with shock. 'I just saw Ben Shaw,' he said, waving towards the TV. 'It was a story from Thailand. Something to do with the tourist beaches. And Ben was there, coming out of the water.'

'Are you absolutely sure it was him?' asked Emily.

Finn lifted his hands in a gesture of helplessness. 'Look, it was only a flash, but I'd swear it was him. I think I recognised the beach as well – Kata Noi in Phuket.'

'Maybe we can catch the same story on another channel,' Rolf suggested helpfully.

'There's no need.' Emily had already picked up the remote.

'Is this a smart TV?' Finn asked. 'Can you rewind?'

'I can indeed. Not that I've used the facility very often, but it's one of Alex's favourite toys.' She found, after a little searching, the appropriate button. 'If I go back about seven minutes, that should be far enough, shouldn't it?'

'Yes, it should be plenty.'

They waited patiently as a reporter in Brisbane explained the latest fracas in the state government, and then there was a cross-over to the colour story from Thailand. Almost immediately, scenes of crowded beaches appeared on the screen, with scantily clad tourists reclining on sun loungers beneath brightly coloured umbrellas. A pretty, suntanned journalist in a tangerine shirt reported earnestly on a smoking ban on the tourist beaches.

'The measure aims to tackle the issue of thousands of discarded cigarette butts at popular resorts,' she said.

Chloe didn't hear anything more. She was completely distracted by a figure striding out of the sea behind the journalist. Tall, tanned, with his long, wet hair slicked back from his face, the young man was a dead ringer for the photographs Tammy had shown her of Ben.

At the last minute, the fellow seemed to notice the camera pointed in his direction and he turned abruptly, as if he was keen to get out of range.

'That was definitely Ben,' Finn declared. 'I'm certain of it now.'

'Yes, I think you're right.' Emily rewound again and managed to freeze the shot of the figure on the screen. 'It's so weird, though,' she said. 'How on earth did he walk into a rainforest in North Queensland and end up in Thailand? How could he have got through the airports and Customs without anyone knowing? *Why* would he have done that?'

'To hide?' Rolf suggested.

'But why?' persisted Emily. 'He was so happy here. His business was doing so well.'

'I think we can safely assume that he didn't have a choice,' said Finn. 'Or at least, he believed he didn't have a choice.'

'And if that was the case, there's almost certainly a criminal element involved,' added Rolf.

'And we should tell the police,' said Emily.

Finn narrowed his eyes. 'I'm not sure about that.' His gaze was distanced, thoughtful. 'I wouldn't rush to tell the local coppers. After all, Ben obviously didn't turn to them for help and he must have had a good reason. If he's in trouble, I wouldn't want to make things worse for him.'

'What about Tammy?' asked Chloe. Throughout this discussion, Tammy had been front and centre in her thoughts. She kept seeing her worried face, the hollowed cheekbones and the fear that lurked in her big blue eyes, even when she was smiling. 'Should we ring her?'

She wondered what the chances were that Tammy had been watching the same news program. It was such a little story and the moment with Ben on the screen so fleeting, but surely others in Burralea had seen it.

'Yes, we'll need to let her know. She's been so stressed,' said Finn.

Straight away, he pulled out his phone, while the rest of them stood around feeling helpless. 'Tammy,' he said a moment later. 'It's Finn. We've just seen Ben on the TV. Yeah. Honest. It looks like he's in Thailand, of all places, and he's alive and well.' Silence followed. Finn listened, then nodded. 'Yes. Okay. All right.'

When he disconnected he pulled a strange face. 'Well, that was a weird conversation. She didn't sound nearly as excited as I expected.'

'She's probably just too stunned,' suggested Chloe.

There were nods of agreement all round. Of course Tammy would be stunned. Soon she would be ringing other people, friends, asking if they'd seen Ben too.

'I still have quite a few contacts in Thailand,' Finn said next. 'I reckon I'd have a good chance of tracking Ben down and maybe getting to the bottom of all this.'

Rolf gave a thoughtful nod. 'I'm inclined to agree with that line of action. Whatever's happened to Ben is bound to be quite serious.'

'It sounds like something out of one of your novels, Rolf,' said Emily.

'I can grab a flight from Cairns.' Finn was clearly warming to the idea. 'I'd have to get a transfer in Singapore, but I reckon I could be in Bangkok in twenty-four hours, or close to it.' He looked directly to Chloe.

She knew the light in his eyes was merely a reflection of his enthusiasm for this mission, but her cheeks grew hot nevertheless.

'You could manage the *Bugle*, couldn't you, Chloe? It should only be for a few days and there's nothing much happening this weekend.'

'Of course I can.'

'Just so long as you remember —'

'To get all the sporting results.' Chloe grinned. 'I know. I have your list of contacts.'

'And with any luck I'll be back before Tuesday's deadline.'

She shook her head. 'Don't rush. I'm sure I could manage that, too.'

'And I could probably help,' volunteered Emily.

The two women exchanged smiles.

'Yes, Emily can keep me in line,' Chloe agreed.

'Oh, hell,' Finn cried, smashing a palm to his temple. 'I've been totally forgetting about Bree's visit.'

Oh, God. In the excitement of the moment, Chloe had forgotten her, too.

Emily frowned at him. 'You mean your daughter is coming here?'

'Yeah.' Finn was the very picture of despair. 'She's due to arrive tomorrow morning for the start of the Christmas holidays.'

'Oh, Finn.' Emily looked almost as distraught as he did.

Silence fell as everyone stared at him, their sympathy transparent.

'I could look after her,' Chloe volunteered, before she had time for second thoughts.

Emily opened her mouth and looked as if she was on the verge of volunteering herself, but then she caught Rolf's eye. Something passed between them, a silent exchange, and she seemed to change her mind.

'How about I get those cutlets on?' she said instead. 'I'm assuming we still want to eat?'

'Yes, of course.' Finn made a flustered gesture. 'I'm sorry for the interruption. I guess I got carried away, but I'd hate to spoil your delicious meal.'

As Emily departed, Finn sank into an armchair, elbows on his knees, his hands hanging loosely as he frowned at the polished timber floor.

'I mean it, Finn,' Chloe said. 'I'm sure it's important that you try to find Ben quickly, and I could look after Bree for a few days. We already have quite a few stories lined up for next week's edition. And I'm a whiz at doing the rounds now.'

He looked up at her, his dark eyes brimming with emotion. 'Thanks, Chloe. But maybe I should try to hold Bree off for a few days. It will mean changing her flights, but that shouldn't be a problem.'

Chloe imagined the child with her bags packed, excitedly looking forward to her flight in the coming morning. Then, the crushing disappointment of her father's phone call.

'Let her come,' she said. 'You know what it's like to be a kid on the first day of your summer holidays. We don't have to cover any important events this weekend, so I'll think of some fun things to do. I know I'm no substitute for her dad, but —' Chloe was fast losing confidence in her ability to back up this impulsive offer.

Finn still looked worried. 'Are you sure?'

'Absolutely sure,' she said without flinching. She could hardly retreat now.

'Well . . . thanks. I'll certainly owe you one.'

For a beat, their gazes held and Chloe was sure Finn was remembering, as she was, the amazing passion-fest they'd shared. Just in time, she realised that Rolf was watching them with unmistakably keen interest and she flicked her gaze elsewhere – *anywhere* – but she knew she was blushing. *Damn it.*

Emily's meal was indeed delicious. The cutlets and salad were followed by icy concoctions of pineapple, passionfruit and coconut, enlivened with segments of finger lime and a splash of Malibu.

The dessert's flavours were sensational, and everyone tried to change the flow of conversation to safe, stress-free topics. Chloe asked Rolf about his new book and he politely replied. But although she was extremely interested, her distracted thoughts were churning and tumbling like balls in a Lotto machine, and she knew everyone else was having the same struggle.

It was pointless, however, to go on, talking round and round in circles about Ben. This was, Chloe decided in the end, yet another example of how an exceptionally pleasant evening could turn in the blink of an eye.

***

'You were right about that pair,' Rolf told Emily as her guests drove off. 'There's a definite vibe between them.'

'I know. It's so good to see Finn coming out of hibernation.' Emily was smiling as she began to clear the table. 'It was also very brave of Chloe to take on the *Bugle* and Bree.'

'Yes, it'll be quite a juggling act.'

'I hope she'll let me help.'

'With the paper?' Rolf asked as he gathered up glasses.

'Actually, I was thinking more about helping with Bree. I miss —' Emily drew a sharp breath. 'I miss contact with young people.' She didn't meet Rolf's gaze as she said this and she hurried away, carrying dessert dishes to the kitchen.

'Thanks,' she said as Rolf followed and set the wineglasses on the bench beside a pile of dirty plates.

'You should let me help you with this lot.' He gestured to the mess.

'Oh, the dishwasher will take care of it.'

Once again, they had arrived at the tricky end of the evening. And again, Emily felt bad about sending him away. She felt especially bad about sending him out into the mist-filled dark to row across the lake.

'It's late and there's a mist,' she said. 'Why don't I drive you home?'

Rolf smiled and the silent message in his eyes was clear. He wanted her. Quite possibly, he loved her, but the choice was hers. He would not overstep the boundaries of friendship a second time, unless she issued an invitation.

Heaven knew, she was sorely tempted to enjoy the comfort and pleasure Rolf offered. She stood, hesitant, trying to sort out the conflicting cues from her head and her heart. Rolf was a good man, an exceptionally pleasant companion, clearly willing and ready to step into the shoes that, to all intents and purposes, had been abandoned by her husband.

Her husband. Alex.

Unfortunately, Emily's heart still rocked with a violent, inescapable longing whenever she thought of him. And Rolf was too fine a man to be regarded as some sort of consolation prize.

Her car keys were at the far end of the bench, next to her handbag. 'Let me drive you,' she said.

She had taken a step towards the keys when Rolf stopped her with a hand on her arm. 'I'm quite happy to take the canoe.'

'But it's so dark and misty.'

'I have a headlamp. I'll be fine.'

From outside came the haunting hoot of an owl. 'All right, then,' she said. 'But ring me when you're safely home.'

He smiled again. 'Or perhaps I could flash a Morse code signal?'

'No use. I wouldn't be able to read it. I couldn't tell the difference between an SOS and an All's well.' But she was smiling now, too, and that was another thing about Rolf – he never failed to make her smile.

Small wonder she was tempted.

He stepped forward, slipped his arms around her waist and kissed her. His lips were warm, his kiss fearless, as if he were staking a claim, asking a final question. It was now or never.

Emily remained very still, unable to surrender. With the softest of sighs, Rolf released her.

'Take care, beautiful one,' he said and then he turned and left by the back door.

She heard his footsteps on the stairs, heard him say goodnight to Murphy and then the dog's soft yelp in reply. She told herself this must never happen again. She must be totally honest with Rolf. No questions, no doubts.

From an open window she watched. The night air was cool and damp on her cheeks and she followed the narrow beam of his torchlight as it flashed and zigzagged with his movements. She heard the scrape of the canoe's hull on the gravelly shore and the soft splash of oars that signalled his departure.

She remained at the window watching the beam of his light grow smaller and smaller. When it eventually disappeared, the loneliness she'd been fighting for weeks descended.

She was crying now, as she turned away from the window, and the worst of it was, her tears weren't for Rolf.

Damn you, Alex.

CHAPTER TWENTY-EIGHT

1973

Like so many other young Aussies, Emily spent a glorious year abroad in her early twenties, first visiting her mother's relatives, and then working, travelling and partying in the UK and Europe. Not so surprisingly, she found the prospect of returning home a great deal less tantalising than setting sail from Sydney had been.

The other girls who shared her cabin for the return journey felt much the same way. Sally was moping over a man she'd left behind in Liverpool and Roslyn was already missing London's theatres and art galleries.

'Back to flies and sheep dip,' Bev complained as their ship pulled out of Portsmouth.

Over the dinner table that first night, there were a few optimistic comments. More than one fellow claimed he couldn't wait to get back to hot sunshine, cold beer and steak and eggs. But the overall mood was definitely more subdued than on the outward voyage.

On leaving Australia, there'd been Tahiti, Panama and Curaçao to discover, and the whole exotic spectacle of Europe. Now, it was Portsmouth, Cape Town, then Fremantle . . .

Back to work, in other words. And the result? The young Australian passengers set out to party harder than ever.

After the first twenty-four hours, however, Emily was bored. She didn't particularly enjoy evenings with too much drinking, clouds of cigarette smoke and raucous laughter. The days weren't much better, lying around by the pool, sunbathing, while fending off offers from young men to rub suntan oil into her back.

Not to mention the tediously boastful tales of adventure. Or misadventure. Cringe-worthy stories of Aussie yobbos in Earl's Court, vomiting in taxis or stealing a policeman's helmet.

Emily consoled herself that at least she'd found her sea legs much more quickly on this return voyage. On the third night, she slipped away from a drinking competition between Aussies and Germans and wandered alone on the deck.

It was a lovely evening with the ship ploughing through clear seas. The lighting on the deck was subdued and showed the moon shimmering on the water, and when she leaned on the railing, she could feel the comforting vibration of the ship's motor.

She drew a deep breath, enjoying the breeze on her face and the clean, salty tang of the air. While she stood there, watching the rise and fall of the sea, a school of flying fish leaped out of a wave in a shower of silver.

Utterly entranced, Emily almost missed the footsteps behind her. When she swung round, she half expected to find one of her cabin mates come to fetch her, to urge her back to the party. But it was a man who stood a few feet away. He was wearing a penguin suit, complete with bow tie, and his white shirtfront gleamed in the moonlight.

'I hope I didn't startle you.' His accent was British, rather cultured and charming, a good match for his finely cut suit.

'I don't startle too easily,' Emily told him.

'But you like to be alone.'

She hesitated, and then smiled. 'It was just too noisy down there.'

He came to stand beside her at the railing. 'Do you mind if I join you?'

'I don't suppose so.'

Beside her, he was taller than she'd realised. He had fair, wavy hair and light-coloured eyes, which were possibly blue, and he was, in fact, extremely handsome. She was surprised she hadn't noticed him earlier.

'Have you been dining at the captain's table tonight?' she asked.

'Yes, but I excused myself when it came to the cigars.'

So he wasn't a smoker. Emily knew his personal habits shouldn't matter. She wasn't sure why she cared – unless he planned to kiss her.

He told her his name was Toby Bryce and he was travelling to his sister's wedding in Armidale. His sister was to marry a sheep farmer, a man with considerable holdings, and the wedding was to be a very swish affair, hence his dinner suit from Savile Row.

As he spoke, the sounds from the disco below drifted upwards. A saxophone was playing 'The First Time Ever I Saw Your Face'.

'Would you like to go down there for a dance or two?' Toby asked.

Emily shook her head. 'Not now.' She was happy to talk, to stay here on the deck with the night sky and the silver-tipped sea and this handsome stranger.

And so it began – one of those shipboard romances that grew out of boredom as much as anything. Mostly a matter of kisses stolen on shadowy decks, but on several evenings, Toby engineered to have privacy in his cabin for an hour or two. Emily felt absolutely no inclination to resist his charms.

It was a final fling, before her boring old life resumed. Her cabin mates were in total sympathy.

'You're a lucky one, Emily. He's a dish.'

'Yeah, he's drop-dead handsome without being stuck up.'

Bev wasn't quite so certain. 'But he doesn't seem to get on with the other fellows. Not even the Pommy chaps. I'm not sure that's a good sign.'

It wasn't too long after Bev's stern observation that Toby arrived at breakfast with a black eye.

'Wasn't it rough last night?' he said as he poured his coffee. 'I fell out of the damn bunk.'

Not everyone at their table was as sympathetic as Emily expected. And then, mid-morning, when she was heading for the deck where she was due for a game of shuttlecock with the girls, a tall figure stepped forward, blocking her path.

Emily had seen this Australian fellow before. She couldn't help it. He was another eye-catching chap. Tall, dark haired, dressed casually today in a navy blue shirt, faded jeans and deck shoes, he wasn't merely blocking her way, he was also frowning at her.

'Can I have a word?' he said.

Emily gave an impatient shake of her head. 'I'm in rather a hurry, actually.'

'Spare me a minute.' His expression was serious. 'It's important.'

She glared at him. 'Why?'

'I need to talk to you about your boyfriend.'

To her dismay, her face burst into flames. How dare this man stick his nose, unasked, into her private life? 'I'm sorry,' she responded in her most regal tone. 'But that's none of your business.'

'Well, I'm making it my business for a very good reason.'

If Toby Bryce hadn't so recently appeared at breakfast with a black eye, Emily might have pushed past this busybody and stormed off. But Bev's comment about Toby's unpopularity with the other men niggled, and the black eye was an unmistakable reality. Besides, there was something about this Australian that commanded Emily's attention. Something in his voice, something in the way he held himself that hinted at mental toughness. And honesty.

Emily straightened her shoulders. 'All right. What do you want to tell me?'

'It might be best if we go up on the deck. Somewhere we won't be interrupted.'

At this, she sighed. 'Perhaps you'd better tell me your name first.'

'Alex Hargreaves.'

'Right, Alex.' She didn't offer her hand. She was feeling a little sick. What was this all about? 'You'd better make this quick. I'm already late for shuttlecock.'

Momentarily, he looked as if he was going to smile, but his face remained deadpan as he nodded. 'This way.'

So, Emily followed Alex Hargreaves up a companionway to the deck, to a corner near the lifeboats that was private. Here he leaned against the railing and fixed his keen, grey-eyed gaze on the sea below. Emily was forced to step closer so she could hear whatever he had to say and she was far too conscious of his height and size, of his compelling masculinity.

'Look, this isn't easy,' he began. 'And you're not going to like it, but you need to know.' He met her gaze directly, his grey eyes as serious as a heart attack. 'Toby Bryce is treating you very badly. I know it's hard to hear, but the bastard's been bragging about his conquests on board this boat, as well as the fact that he's got a wife and kids waiting for him in Sydney.'

Just in time, Emily gripped the railing before her knees gave way. She had never felt so humiliated, so foolish. So angry. Fighting tears, she asked, 'Are you quite sure? About the wife?'

'He's shown off the photos in his wallet. I'm afraid you can ask just about any of the blokes on our deck.'

Emily had no intention of quizzing other men. At this point, she would have preferred to enter a nunnery than to communicate with any member of the male sex.

Alex had spoken of Toby's conquests. Plural. Which must mean there were other women as foolish as she had been. Somehow, that made the situation even more unbearable.

'Did you hit him?' she asked. 'Is that how he got the black eye?'

Alex shook his head. 'Someone else, a mate who had a sister involved, took care of that. But he baulked at talking to you.'

'You drew the short straw?' Emily asked, bitterly.

'I volunteered. I thought you deserved to know.'

At least Emily didn't cry, which was one small mercy. 'Do you plan to speak to the other women?'

Slowly, Alex shook his head. 'I don't really know them. But I heard your name mentioned.'

'I suppose I should thank you,' she said tightly. 'But I'm not exactly grateful.' In that moment, she hated Alex Hargreaves.

'You're okay?' he asked with an admirable attempt at sincerity.

How could she possibly be okay? He had just exposed her to be the silliest and weakest of females. But she said, 'Yes, of course.'

He gave a grimly courteous nod. 'I'll let you get back to your shuttlecock then.' And he walked away down the deck without looking back.

For weeks, Emily hated Alex. Yet, deep down, she was also secretly grateful. It would have been appalling to have kept up the affair all the way to Sydney and then to have watched Toby Bryce's wife and family greet him at the dock.

And at least none of her girlfriends seemed to have twigged.

They accepted that she'd broken up with Toby. These things happened. It had never been serious.

Emily's biggest problem was that she was now excruciatingly aware of Alex. As the voyage continued, he seemed to be suddenly, always, there in her peripheral vision, talking to others, dancing with others, flirting with others.

She wished she could ignore him, but her self-control was shot to pieces. Her gaze was constantly swinging in the tall, dark Australian's direction, as if he were due north and she a helpless arrow on a compass. Fortunately, Alex never seemed to notice, but Emily knew the exact lines of his profile, the measure of his shoulders, the shape of his hands.

The voyage continued with the usual social activities – trivia nights and fancy-dress balls and silly horse and jockey competitions with girls on guys' shoulders, tapping at helium balloons. There were always plenty of girls keen to be Alex's partner. Emily was very careful to keep her distance.

It was after their stop in Cape Town, when a group of Australians held a ceremonial burning of eucalyptus leaves and felt instantly homesick, that Emily began to think differently. By then, Toby Bryce was moving in entirely different circles and her pain and humiliation were lessening. She felt moved to let Alex know she was grateful for the way he'd handled her silly mistake.

It was some time, however, before she found the courage and the right moment to approach him. Their ship was due to reach Fremantle within twenty-four hours and Emily had no idea if Alex was about to disembark. With some urgency now, she searched for him and found him sitting cross-legged on the deck, fortuitously quite alone, with his back against a bulkhead.

His hair was somewhat messy and curling at the ends and he was wearing a blinding white T-shirt and washed-out denim shorts. He was working with rope, his tanned, long fingers deftly tying a rather elaborate ornamental knot.

'Hello.' Emily was quite hopelessly nervous.

Alex set the knotting aside, rose easily to his feet and smiled. 'Hi.'

She couldn't tell if he was pleased to see her, or merely amused.

'I thought you might be leaving the ship tomorrow,' she said.

He shook his head. 'I won't be disembarking till Sydney.'

'Oh? Right.' She swallowed. She was here now, so she should just get it over with. 'Anyway, I – I wanted to thank you. You know – for warning me about —'

'That dickhead Pom?'

'Yes.'

'No worries.' His smile faded. 'I didn't want to see you badly hurt.'

'Yes, and I'm grateful.'

Emily looked up and, when their gazes connected, lightning flashed. Or, at least, that was how it felt to her. Like a scene straight from Hollywood with an orchestra playing.

Except that it was broad daylight on a rolling deck and the only sound was the hum of the ship's engines. Embarrassed, she gave a little shrug. 'Well, I just wanted to make sure I thanked you.' Then, before he could reply, she turned and fled.

CHAPTER TWENTY-NINE

After finally admitting her gratitude, Emily managed, with a supreme effort, to keep her gaze averted whenever Alex was within eyesight. Their ship docked at Fremantle and then in Melbourne, and there were numerous farewells and good wishes for the travellers and the excited migrants who were about to embark on a new life in Australia. Only Sally was left in Emily's cabin when they sailed through the Heads into Sydney Harbour.

There was no one to greet Emily as she disembarked, but she did see Toby Bryce being embraced by a strawberry blonde, with two little girls tugging at his coat.

As soon as Emily's luggage was unloaded, she took a taxi to the airport. She had an evening flight booked to Brisbane and from there she would fly, the next morning, to Cairns.

She felt flat, which was annoying. She wanted to feel triumphant after her travels and pleased to see Australian sunshine and to be surrounded once more by Aussie accents. But she was too aware of the mundaneness of returning from adventure to a very ordinary life in a deathly quiet country town.

At the airport, she found a trolley and loaded it with her

luggage, then joined the queue in front of the Ansett desk.

'Well, hello.'

Emily recognised the deep voice close behind her and her heart gave an unhealthy skip as she spun around.

Alex Hargreaves, with a similarly loaded trolley, smiled at her. 'Long time, no see.'

'Yes.' She was smiling too. She was stupidly pleased.

'Where are you headed?' he asked.

'Brisbane.'

'That's a lucky coincidence. So am I. Are you on the six-thirty flight?'

'Yes.' By now, Emily might have been beaming, and she felt as light and fluttery as a butterfly.

'Next!' called the woman at the check-in desk.

Emily sent Alex a quick smile before shoving her loaded trolley forward. To her surprise, he followed, arriving at the desk alongside her.

'We're travelling together,' he told the woman.

Emily swallowed a choked gasp. The woman's eyebrows shot high, but Alex smiled so charmingly, she accepted their booking papers without a murmur.

By now Emily's heart was drumming. In a blinding instant, she realised that she wanted, more than anything, to get to know this man, to make up for all the time she'd lost on the ship by deliberately avoiding him.

Their luggage was forwarded onto the conveyor belt and they were given their boarding passes – seats 12A and 12B – and there was another hour to fill in till they boarded. Alex took her to a bar where he ordered a cold XXXX beer and a glass of riesling. They sat at a small table with a dish of peanuts and a view of the aerodrome and the busy spectacle outside, which they ignored while they talked and talked, their faces lit by happy, sappy smiles, like two long-lost lovers reunited.

Emily asked, 'What do you do when you're at home?'

'That's a good question,' Alex said. 'I've finished a law degree and I was all set to join a law firm in Brisbane, but I've just heard, while I was in England, that my uncle has died and left me his property in northern Queensland.'

'Goodness. I'm sorry to hear about your uncle, but lucky you.'

'It was a shock.'

'I live in North Queensland.'

His dark eyebrows rose. 'I knew it.'

'You knew where I lived?'

'No, I knew —' He stopped and looked away to the busy tarmac where a plane was whizzing down the runway, gathering speed for take-off. When he turned back to her, his smile was almost shy. 'I knew you were going to be important to me.'

It was as if a gong had been struck inside Emily. She was used to flattery from men, but this, coming from Alex, seemed different. Felt so much more significant.

'What sort of property did your uncle own?' she asked when she regained control of her breathing.

'A cattle property. Out near Cloncurry. It's called Red Hill.'

'Have you been there?'

'Many years ago, when I was about ten.'

'Did you like it?'

'I loved it, actually. I learned to ride horses. And to drive a ute. It was amazing, tearing across those endless plains on horseback, or in the ute.' He gave a light laugh. 'I came close to killing myself a couple of times.'

She could well imagine the allure of such youthful recklessness. It sounded like the sort of thing her mother would have loved.

'Would you want to live out there?' she asked.

'I might,' Alex said. 'I've been asking myself why my uncle left the place to me and not to my father, his brother. I have a feeling he was worried Dad would just automatically sell it. I think he hoped I might take over and run it.'

'How do you feel about that?' Emily couldn't quite believe she was asking a man she'd virtually just met so many personal questions, but after avoiding him for weeks, she now felt extraordinarily comfortable, as if they were already . . . friends.

'I'll admit I'm tempted to turn myself into a cattleman,' Alex said. 'But I need to get back out to Red Hill to take a good look around. I'd have a hell of a lot to learn. I know next to nothing about cattle.'

He turned to her with another of those smiles that made creases at the corners of his eyes. 'Enough about me. Where do you live in North Queensland?'

Emily told him about Burralea, about the Lake House and about her mother running the *Bugle*.

'That's impressive.'

'Yes.' Her mother's story always impressed.

'And you?' he asked. 'What do you do?'

'Oh, I try my hand at this and that. I've spent the past year working on and off, in shoe shops, mostly, in London. I travelled, of course. Scotland, Europe. I suppose you might call me a dabbler. I'm nothing like my parents. Sometimes I think I must have been a changeling.'

He looked amused. 'Why do you say that?'

In truth, Emily wasn't sure why she'd been so brutally honest. Perhaps it was the sense that she and this man had spent too much time *not* getting to know each other. She found herself telling Alex extra details she never usually talked about. Her parents' heroism during the war, and then, her mother taking over the newspaper after her father's death.

'She's so strong,' Emily said. 'It's a lot to live up to.'

'Yes, it would be. But you've been travelling on your own and that takes courage.'

'I suppose so.' But Emily had been hoping that her travels would bring her a new awareness of life's possibilities. It was disappointing to realise she was no closer to 'finding herself' than she'd been before she left home.

'And you're an excellent listener,' Alex said. 'That's a gift in itself.'

They talked throughout their flight to Brisbane, sitting close together, leaning closer still and keeping their voices low. They talked in more detail about their travels. Emily had fallen in love with Scotland and Spain. Alex had been very impressed by Norway where he'd travelled above the Arctic Circle. Neither of them had been to Ireland. They agreed they would have to go back one day.

They talked about the people they'd met, the food they'd eaten, the sights they'd seen. It wasn't till they were about to land in Brisbane that Alex told Emily he needed to see *her* again, that he would like to catch up with her when he came north.

She did her best to appear nonchalant, but it was exactly what she wanted to hear.

In Brisbane they shared a taxi and Alex accompanied her to her hotel and left the cabbie to wait, while she checked in and organised for her luggage to be stowed, and he walked with her to her room.

Of course, she told him there was no need for such gallantry.

'Who's being gallant?' he asked as she pushed her door open. 'I'm here because I need to kiss you.'

Emily's heart tumbled a slow, happy somersault. 'Thank heavens for that. I was worried you just wanted to talk.'

Alex laughed and, despite the waiting taxi, he took his time, closing the door behind them and drawing her close. His kiss was deep and tender and perfect. Everything about him was so right. She couldn't believe she'd spent so long avoiding him.

'I've waited a long time for this,' he said.

'You have?'

'Since I first saw you in Portsmouth boarding the ship.'

Breathless with surprise, Emily tried to remember that day. She'd been busy organising the pieces of her luggage that went into the hold and those which she kept in the cabin.

And Alex had been watching her. *All that time.*

'But you ignored me.'

He shook his head. 'Never.'

Now, she lifted her hands to his shoulders and they kissed again, with fresh urgency.

'You have to go,' she told him with great reluctance.

'I know.' His arms tightened around her and he brushed his mouth over hers as if he needed to remember the taste and the feel of her.

Finally, he released her. 'Okay, I'm leaving now.'

She couldn't quite hold back her disappointed sigh, but then he took something from his pocket and pressed it into her hand.

It was a knotted circlet, made of white rope, similar to the knot he'd been fashioning on the ship.

'Thank you,' she said softly as she fingered it, feeling the small bumps and smooth lines.

'It's a knot bracelet,' he said. 'In the old days, the sailors used to make them for their sweethearts.'

She was blushing and ridiculously pleased. She slipped it over her wrist.

At the door, he paused and looked back. 'Do you think you might like to come out to Red Hill with me?'

Already, at that early point, Emily knew that he was actually asking her so much more.

'I'd love to,' she said.

She had travelled to Europe to find herself and she'd come home and found Alex instead. Feminists and her mother might not be impressed. Emily was brimming with happiness.

A month later, Alex arrived at the Lake House. Emily had primed her mother, and Izzie had said that of course Alex was welcome to visit. She hadn't even seemed to mind that her daughter planned to take off on a trip to western Queensland with a man she'd only just met.

This was a huge relief for Emily, but she was still nervous about a meeting between her mother and the man she'd fallen for. She was even a little scared that when she saw Alex again on home soil, she might no longer find him quite so attractive.

Luckily, her heart wasn't the least bit fickle. From the moment Alex emerged from his car, hot, dusty and tired after his long journey, Emily was lit from inside with incandescent joy. Everything about him was as perfect as she'd remembered. With this man by her side, she felt ready to take on any challenge.

Izzie, small, slim and straight-backed, greeted Alex warmly enough. He had brought her chocolates and a bottle of wine, but she wasn't a woman to be won over by gifts. It was the cut of the man her daughter had chosen that mattered most and, to Emily's relief, Izzie seemed to approve. Alex was good looking, well mannered and he had clear goals to make a success of his life, whether he went into law or the cattle business. He would do.

'Mind you,' Izzie said, addressing her daughter over the dinner table that evening. 'If Alex decides to take on the cattle property, your life won't be easy.'

Emily gasped in shocked embarrassment. 'Mum, for heaven's sake. Alex and I are only friends. He hasn't proposed marriage.' She was too mortified to catch Alex's eye.

Her mother gave no hint of an apology, however, and after the meal, she cornered Emily in the kitchen, knowing full well that Alex was within hearing distance.

'It's worth being forewarned, Emily,' she said. 'There's no point in having romantic notions about life on a cattle station. It won't be a matter of sitting around enjoying afternoon tea with other graziers' wives. You'll have to pitch in and help. You'll be running the household, cleaning and cooking for the stockmen, growing vegetables – there are no handy shops nearby – *and* you'll be supervising your children's education.'

Her smile for Emily had been almost taunting. 'It could be the making of you, my dear.'

Alex had overheard this of course, and he was incensed. That night, he stole through the darkness to Emily's room.

'Your mother's wrong,' he whispered fiercely as he drew Emily into his arms. 'How dare she forecast the life I might provide for you.' Wrapping her close, he continued. 'If I go ahead with the cattle, I wouldn't ask you to do anything you didn't want to do. I would hire a housekeeper, a cook, a governess, a gardener. Whatever you needed. And if I couldn't manage all that, I would go back to law. I won't have you slaving just to keep your mother happy.'

He sounded so indignant and so gorgeously protective, Emily loved him more deeply than ever. 'I wouldn't mind pulling my weight,' she assured him. She was sure she was ready for a challenge.

Alex lifted his head, so he could read her face in the faint moonlight. 'I promise you, my darling, that whatever we decide, if *she* doesn't like it, I'll stick up for you.'

Looking back with the benefit of hindsight, Emily wished she had been stronger, tried harder, right from the very start, to ease the niggling tensions between her mother and Alex. While there had never been open warfare, the tension had simmered away throughout their marriage. It seemed so obvious to her now that instead of relishing the way Alex had stood up for her, she should have made an effort at the very beginning to smooth the way for the decades ahead.

Now, Robbie's death had churned that tension into a deep, dark, painful chasm and Emily was riddled with regret.

CHAPTER THIRTY

A thick white mist shrouded the track as Finn drove away from the Lake House. Of necessity, he was silent, concentrating on the barely visible path that wound through the trees, while Chloe huddled in the passenger seat, wrapped in a pashmina, and tried to picture the days ahead.

It was settled. Finn would go to Thailand. Using his mobile phone, he had already booked his flights, and Chloe would look after the *Bugle*, as well as Finn's daughter.

Chloe wasn't nervous about the newspaper. Lately she'd felt she had a good grasp of what was expected. Caring for Bree was another matter entirely.

She tried to remember what it was like to be twelve, but she had been the youngest of three and her life had been safe and suburban and ordinary. At twelve, her major concerns had centred on being picked for the school's netball team, or finding books in the library by her favourite authors.

A year earlier, Chloe's grandmother had died and Chloe had been sad, of course, but it had been a gentle kind of grieving, shared with her entire family. In other words, her life couldn't have been more different from Bree's.

It was only when Finn turned onto the bitumen where the driving was easier, with clear white lines marking the centre and edges of the road, that he spoke. 'Chloe, I hope I'm not dumping too much on you.'

'You really shouldn't worry about me,' she said. 'But I can't help wondering how you were planning to entertain Bree and keep running the *Bugle* at the same time.'

In the dim interior of the car, she saw his grimace. 'I must admit, I was relying on Moira Briggs for inspiration. She seemed to have a whole list of ideas about how to keep Bree occupied.'

'Well, yes, Moira's certainly resourceful.' And then, because she was actually rather worried, 'I hope Bree isn't too upset about the change of plans.'

Finn's heavy sigh sounded above the purring of the car's motor. He'd rung his parents to try to talk to Bree, only to learn that she'd gone to bed early without any prompting or arguments, because she was *so* looking forward to her early morning flight. 'I'll try to catch her in the morning. If not, I'll phone from Singapore to reassure her it's only for a few days.'

'You hope.'

He didn't respond to this. After a bit, he said, 'You should probably stay at my cottage. Your flat only has the one bed.'

This was true. Chloe had been wondering how comfortable her sofa was for sleeping, but she wished her skin hadn't zapped the very instant Finn mentioned the word *bed*. 'All right,' she said cautiously.

'How about I take you back to my place now, so you can check it out?'

It was a simple question, so why did it feel complicated?

Chloe told herself she was being an idiot, reading double meanings where there were none. She nodded. 'Just a quick look, I guess.'

Finn's cottage was in Cedar Lane, the other side of town, on the very edge of farmland, and set back behind a brunfelsia hedge. A light on the front porch showed the hedge's pale flowers and a sweet scent followed them up the short, uneven brick path.

'It's very basic,' he said as he pushed the front door open and turned on a light.

The building might have been basic, but Finn had given it a touch of the exotic with bright silk cushions and throw rugs and interesting pieces of pottery.

'You've made it very nice,' Chloe said, trying to ignore the tension that had gripped her from the moment she'd walked through the front door into his private domain. 'I suppose you've collected these interesting bits and pieces from all over the world?'

'More or less.' He looked almost as tense as she was. He nodded to a doorway. 'I'm putting Bree in that room.'

Chloe crossed to the room's entrance and Finn came behind her, reaching around to flick the light switch.

'It's nearly all second-hand stuff,' he said.

The little room held a single bed covered with a white chenille spread and a bright-red batik throw. A multicoloured rag mat brightened the floor and a chest of drawers, painted white, stood against the opposite wall. Above it hung a mirror with an enchanting frame made from driftwood twigs. Hooks on the walls took the place of a wardrobe and a little timber bookcase painted a distressed green held a tantalising collection of books and magazines.

'I think Bree will love it,' Chloe said, genuinely impressed. She pictured a vase of flowers on the chest of drawers. Something bright, yellow daisies, perhaps. She should try to get some tomorrow. 'You have a secret flair for interior decorating.'

Finn gave a smiling shake of his head. 'Alice Drummond helped. She's the expert.'

'Alice Drummond?' Chloe tamped down the stupid spurt of jealousy.

'My mate Seth Drummond's wife. They were hosting that barbecue I mentioned.'

'Oh, yes, of course.' Ridiculously, she found it hard to breathe. She was far too aware of Finn standing close behind her, reminding her, in vivid detail, of what happened when he got too close. The heat of his kisses, the delirious pleasure of his hands on her skin, of their bodies locked and urgent.

It might have been *only sex*, but right now it was all Chloe could think about. She tried to remember the reasons why sex between co-workers might be unwise. Finn was her boss – except that he wasn't really. Only Emily could hire and fire her. Finn was simply her immediate superior. Were there rules about that?

'So – the kitchen?' she asked and her voice was way too breathy.

When Finn didn't answer, she turned to find him staring at her, which only increased her breathing difficulties. It was almost as if a spell had been cast, freezing them both into statues.

He swallowed. 'Yes, right, the kitchen.' Abruptly he turned. 'It's through here.'

A crazy zinging strummed inside her as she followed him. His kitchen was old-fashioned with yellow laminex bench tops and a free-standing, glass-fronted cupboard filled with mismatched crockery. It reminded her of her grandmother's kitchen from years ago. If she opened the pantry door, she would probably catch remembered scents from childhood . . . nutmeg and cinnamon . . .

'The stovetop is gas and the oven's electric. I think you'll find the freezer is reasonably well stocked.' Finn paused. 'So – any questions?'

Chloe knew there must be a host of things she needed to know, but her brain had completely stalled.

Finn waited, his gaze intense, his eyes once again burning.

She shook her head. 'All good.'

'Ohhh-kay.' He drew the word out. 'There's not much else to show you. The bathroom's at the back. And then there's – my room.'

'Right.'

'As I said, this place is basic.'

'But with a certain rustic charm.'

He smiled, then seemed at a loss. After what felt like an age, he asked, 'So – would you like to see my room?'

It wasn't necessary. Not necessary at all.

'It's a bit of a mess,' he said.

'I don't mind.' Why on earth had she said that?

A beat passed and it was her chance to turn back, to ask him to drive her home. Finn was watching her closely. Waiting. She knew her response was vitally important. She could go home now, or she could risk ending up in bed with him. Again.

She didn't move, didn't speak.

'It's this way,' he said quietly and he led her down a short passage to another doorway.

The mess wasn't too bad. The bed was unmade, exposing rumpled charcoal-grey sheets. On the floor in the corner, discarded clothes lay in a heap. A dresser was littered with books.

'I'll make it up with clean sheets for you,' Finn said.

'Don't bother.' He had more important things to get on with, like packing for Thailand. But right now, Chloe didn't want to distract him with practical concerns.

From the moment she'd left the car, her common sense had been peeling away like petals from a flower. Her needs had shifted. She wanted Finn Latimer to concentrate on her.

She knew from experience he had wonderful focus.

'So,' he said quietly. 'I should take you home.'

No, her mind wailed.

'Yes,' she said softly.

But neither of them moved and Chloe was so filled with wanting she thought she might burst.

'Maybe later?' Finn asked.

She gave the smallest nod.

It was enough. To her relief, he drew her to him, wrapping his arms around her as he kissed her.

His focus was perfect.

'I should go. You need to pack.' Chloe was sitting in Finn's bed. She had no idea of the time, but it had to be late – probably *very* late – and she was trying to remember where her clothes were.

'You don't have to rush.' Finn reached for her hand.

'But you have an early flight and you need —'

'I need a moment.' Finn pulled her hand towards him, lifted her wrist to his lips and pressed a kiss to the fine veins on the inside. And then another kiss.

The sweetness of this was almost too much. Chloe was a cloud of confusion. Happy and exultant. Shy and uncertain. Overtaken by emotions that seemed to come out of nowhere.

This was supposed to be *just sex*, but it felt like so much more.

'I keep thinking this shouldn't be happening,' she said.

'Because we work together?'

'I suppose.' But this wasn't tawdry office sex. Finn wasn't a predator and she wasn't using her body to get a promotion. They were simply work colleagues who fancied the pants off each other. Literally.

The fact that Finn was also a grieving widower and she had plans for single motherhood should have made this even less complicated. They had separate lives and this truly was *only sex*. Her confusion was unnecessary. And yet —

'I've never really asked you about your relationships,' Finn said as he lifted a stray curl and tucked it behind her ear. 'I suppose, I just assumed you were – *free* – for want of a better word.'

'Oh, don't worry, I'm free. I broke up with my – with someone before I left Sydney.'

'Would this someone be the other half of Mr and Mrs Very Brown?'

Chloe was surprised that he remembered. 'Yes.' She was also surprised that talking about the breakup with Jason no longer gutted her.

'Had you been together for long?'

She might as well confess the sorry truth. 'Way too long. Seven and a half years.'

A small silence passed before Finn spoke. 'Breaking up after that amount of time would be as painful as getting divorced. Dare I ask what happened?'

'Nothing happened really. Jason didn't cheat on me, as far as I know. The decision was pretty much mutual.' This wasn't quite the truth. Jason had sulked a bit like a teenager, but Chloe had realised by then that he didn't really love her. She'd become a comfortable habit he wasn't ready to give up.

Meanwhile, Chloe's feelings for him had crumbled with astonishing speed after he'd asked that fateful question about her fitness for motherhood.

'I think Gwyneth Paltrow coined the term "conscious uncoupling" when she divorced Chris Martin,' she said. The dorky term had given the journalists at *Girl Talk* a good chuckle at the time. 'And that pretty much describes Jason and me.'

She gave a deliberate little shrug. 'So you shouldn't have me on your conscience, Finn. If you get tired of – of *this*, you won't break my heart. I'm pretty much a romance skeptic these days.'

'I'll bear that in mind,' he said dryly, but he was still holding her hand and his grasp tightened, warmly possessive. 'But just for the record, you're a classy woman, Chloe Brown.' Leaning closer still, he brushed his lips over hers in an unhurried, lazy caress. 'Smoking hot in bed.'

A shaky laugh escaped her. 'Thank you, sir.' She should probably return the compliment, but before she could find the right words, Finn released her hand and swung to his side of the bed.

'And you're damn right,' he said. 'I have packing to do.'

CHAPTER THIRTY-ONE

When the line of travellers streamed into the arrivals hall at Cairns airport, Chloe recognised Bree Latimer immediately. Finn had shown her a photo on his phone. And now, here she was, accompanied by a young female flight attendant.

Dressed in denim jeans and a purple T-shirt, Bree was tall for her age and slim, with straight hair, as dark as her father's, falling past her shoulders. In the photo, however, the girl's face had been lit by a bright, mischievous smile. This morning, unfortunately, Bree's hunched shoulders and tragic expression told a very different story. Chloe, although nervous, felt an instant pang of sympathy.

When she stepped forward to greet Bree, Finn's daughter looked right past her and kept walking.

'Bree,' Chloe said.

The girl stopped and turned, as did the attendant.

Chloe smiled at them. 'Hi,' she said. 'I'm Chloe Brown.' Finn had rung the airline to warn them that a different adult would be collecting his daughter. To Bree, she said, 'I work with your father.'

Bree's face was bleak as she held up her phone. 'He just told me.'

The attendant gushed as she farewelled Bree. Clearly she was keen to get away.

'I'm sorry about the lousy timing,' Chloe told the girl. 'I know your dad was really looking forward to your visit. He's planning to get back here as quickly as he can.'

Bree merely rolled her eyes at this. 'He said he's in the international terminal.'

'Yes, that's right.'

'Where is it? Can I see him?'

Chloe wished with all her heart that this was possible. 'I don't think so,' she said. 'I'm almost certain he's already through Security and Customs.'

Bree obviously knew enough about international flights to accept this, but she did so with a deeply despondent sigh.

'I'm really sorry this has happened,' said Chloe again. 'But he was called away on an emergency.'

'I thought he'd stopped doing that sort of work.'

'Well, yes, he had, but something important came up, out of the blue, and Finn – your father – really was the only man for the job.'

'Yeah, whatever.' Bree was looking around her at scenes of happy families greeting each other. Two small boys were waving and rushing excitedly towards a tall man who was probably their father. A plump grandmother in an pink kaftan and silver bangles was hugging a girl about Bree's age.

Chloe said, 'We'd better go through to the luggage carousel. What does your suitcase look like?'

'It's a backpack. Navy blue.' As Bree said this, she lifted her chin, as if she was proud of the fact that her luggage wasn't just an ordinary suitcase. But as Chloe set off, she followed with an air of deepest gloom.

The backpack was large and quite heavy, but when Chloe fetched a trolley, Bree looked appalled.

'I can carry my pack,' she said.

'But it's heavy and there's no need.' Chloe offered her a smile that she hoped was encouraging. 'That's why trolleys were invented.'

Bree's response was a mutinous glare as she heaved the pack onto her narrow back.

Chloe drew a deep, patient breath. 'Okay.' She pointed to the huge sliding glass doors. 'The car's this way.'

They headed out into blazing sunshine and a wall of humid tropical heat, Bree following with her load, a few steps behind, like an obstinate turtle.

'Would you like to have a look around Cairns before we leave?' Chloe asked as she fed notes into the parking meter. 'We could go down to the pier. It's lovely, with views over the water. You might like a soft drink? A little morning tea?'

Bree shook her head. 'I had something on the plane. I want to see my dad's house.' She shot Chloe a worried glance. 'I can still stay at his place, can't I?'

'Yes, of course. I'm going to stay there with you until he gets back.'

The girl's chin jutted forward as if she wasn't happy with this news, but she must have realised she couldn't do much about it. 'Are you my dad's girlfriend?

'No. I just work with him at the *Burralea Bugle*.' To Chloe's relief, she managed to say this without the slightest hesitation.

They reached the Forester and Bree deposited her pack in the back with a little help from Chloe, who quickly got the car's air conditioning going.

'It's sweltering down here on the coast,' she said. 'But you'll find it cooler up on the Tablelands.'

But Bree, now settled in the passenger seat beside Chloe, was busy looking at her phone and didn't bother to respond. Chloe wondered if she was hoping for a final message from her father.

'Would you like the radio on?' she asked as they headed north on the Captain Cook Highway towards the turn-off to Kuranda.

Bree shook her head and muttered, 'I'm right, thanks.' With that, she pulled a set of small earphones from a pocket in her shorts, connected them to her phone and sat with her head turned away, slumped in her seat and staring, forlornly no doubt, through the passenger window.

Chloe suppressed a spurt of irritation. She knew the girl was only twelve and still coming to grips with a massive disappointment, but after very little sleep, Chloe was feeling the strain. Still, she hadn't expected this assignment to be easy.

She was doing this for Ben Shaw's girlfriend, Tammy, as much as for Finn. The poor woman needed answers. The Burralea community needed answers. And it was possible that Ben needed rescuing. Chloe could only hope that at some point Bree would thaw.

The journey continued in silence, apart from a short period halfway up the thickly forested Kuranda Range when Bree pulled off her earphones in disgust, demanding to know why she couldn't hear her music.

'We must have lost the network,' Chloe suggested. 'Because of these high mountains. Wait till we get to the top and you should be fine.'

Which proved to be the case. For the rest of the journey through Mareeba, Walkamin, Tolga, Atherton, Bree continued to listen to music on her phone and Chloe drove in stoical silence. It was only when they reached a sign proclaiming *Welcome to Burralea* that Bree finally removed the earplugs and looked about her with a degree of interest.

'I think you'll like your dad's place,' Chloe said, as she took the first turn. 'It's on the edge of town and it looks out over farmland.'

'Where do you live?' Bree asked, almost aggressively.

'In a little flat, right in the centre of town,' Chloe said. 'Near the *Bugle*'s office.'

'Oh.' Apparently placated, Bree continued to look at the passing scenery. They passed a plant nursery and then a strawberry farm with a stall on its front footpath. On a small rise, a glimpse of a shimmering lake shone in the distance.

'Dad said we could go canoeing on Lake Tinaroo,' Bree said.

'And I'm sure you will. I know he was really looking forward to it.'

Bree merely wrinkled her nose.

'And here's the house,' Chloe added, as she pulled up in front of the hedge that shielded Finn's cottage from the road.

Bree was definitely curious and perhaps a little eager now. Chloe thought she caught a hint of a smile. As they hefted her backpack out of the Forester, Bree kept looking over her shoulder to the house.

In the daylight, it was rather sweet, with a low sweeping roof and a yellow front door with sets of six-paned windows on either side, shaded by quaint, timber-framed awnings. Chloe found the correct key in the bunch Finn had given her and pushed the door open, then stepped back to let Bree enter first.

'Oh,' the girl said, letting her backpack slide to the floor with a hefty thump. And she stood, staring at Finn's small lounge room with its bright cushions and rugs and pottery pieces.

The kid was swallowing hard and a hint of silver tears glittered in her eyes. 'It's ages since I've seen these things,' she said in a small voice that threatened to crack.

Chloe felt her own eyes growing moist and she decided it might be wise to divert Bree, before she became too swamped by sad memories. 'Your bedroom's through here,' she said.

Leaving her pack on the floor, Bree crossed to the bedroom doorway. She stared for quite a while before she eventually smiled. 'This is actually quite cool,' she said, but almost immediately she frowned and shot Chloe a glance laced with suspicion. 'Did you do all this?'

'Decorate your room?' said Chloe. 'Of course not. It's all your dad's handiwork.' Which was almost the truth.

Bree still looked doubtful. She was staring at the vase of bright yellow cosmos sitting on top of the chest of drawers.

'Apart from the flowers,' Chloe corrected. 'I'll admit they were my contribution.' This morning, she'd found the clump of cosmos growing in an old concrete wash tub in Finn's backyard.

At last, there was a small smile from Bree. 'I knew Dad would never think to put flowers in my room.'

'But he did everything else. I believe he even painted the chest of drawers and the bookcase.'

Another warmer smile transformed Bree's face, making her look extraordinarily pretty. 'That's kind of awesome, isn't it?'

Rather than sitting around in the cottage, Chloe took Bree to the Lilly Pilly café for lunch. She decided it would be best to keep the girl busy and occupied, seeing new sights, having new experiences.

The café was extra popular on weekends. Even so, there was plenty of chatter and laughter coming from the busy kitchen.

'Hi there,' beamed Jess as Chloe fronted up to the counter to order. Jess's eyes widened with curiosity as she flashed Bree an extra-bright smile. 'Hello.'

'This is Bree, Finn Latimer's daughter,' Chloe said. 'Bree, this is Jess. She has the most gorgeous little baby called Willow.'

'Nice to meet you,' Bree responded politely.

Jess wasn't quite so polite. Her mouth gaped as she stared at Bree. 'Am I hearing right? This is Finn Latimer's *daughter*?'

'That's exactly right.' Chloe kept her voice deliberately matter-of-fact and hoped Jess wouldn't make too much fuss.

Another of the café's staff, Gina, ducked out from behind the coffee machine. Her eyes were also popping. 'Finn has a daughter?'

'Really?' cried another woman, who'd been busily buttering bread at a central bench in the open-plan kitchen. And she promptly left her task and joined Jess and Gina at the counter.

'Hello,' the trio chorused, grinning madly at Bree.

'Wow, I can see that you look like your dad.'

'What's your name, love?'

'Bree.'

'Bree? Oh, isn't that perfect?'

'Your dad's a dark horse. He never told us about you, but hey, lovely to meet you, Bree.'

By now, Joyce, the café's owner, who'd been busily cutting up a new slab of quiche, was glaring at them. 'What's going on over there?'

Gina turned back to her. 'We're just saying hello to Finn Latimer's daughter.'

'Really? Finn has a daughter?' Now Joyce was as intrigued as the others and came to join them at the counter. 'Oh, wow! Don't you just look like him.'

Chloe was worried it would all be too much for the poor girl. Bree probably wasn't used to being treated like the daughter of a rock star.

Luckily, she didn't seem to mind all the attention. Quite possibly she was lapping it up. And at least the women didn't mention Ben's reappearance on TV, or ask about Finn's whereabouts. But perhaps it was just as well that another group of customers entered the café and the women returned to their posts.

'Is everyone super friendly up here?' Bree asked, once they'd ordered their meals and were seated at a table beneath a vine-covered pergola in the courtyard at the back of the café.

'Pretty much,' said Chloe. 'It's a very friendly town. I hope you didn't mind all the fuss?'

'Not really.' Bree gave a sheepish smile. 'They seem to like Dad, don't they?'

Well, he is the hottest guy in town. Chloe hastily binned that thought. 'When you're the editor of a small country newspaper, you get to know everyone,' she said.

Bree seemed to accept this. 'Do you like working here?' she asked as she stirred her chocolate milkshake and prodded the scoop of ice-cream with a long-handled spoon.

'Yes, I must admit I haven't been here very long, but so far I'm really enjoying it.' Chloe was pleased that she could say this quite honestly.

'I think I'd like to be a journalist when I grow up. I'm better at writing than just about anything else.'

'Why wait till you grow up? You can probably help me. I'll be putting the paper out by myself until your dad gets back.'

Bree gave an astonished huff of laughter. 'No way. You wouldn't let me write a news story.'

'I might.' Chloe knew she would have to find a way to keep the girl occupied.

'Like a proper journalist?' Bree looked both thrilled and horrified.

Chloe was sure they could manage to write one or two small stories together. 'Absolutely,' she said in her most assuring tone.

'You know I'm only twelve? I'm tall for my age.'

Chloe swallowed an urge to smile. 'Yes, I know that, Bree, and I wouldn't ask you to write the lead story for the front page, but there's bound to be something you can tackle with a little guidance.'

'That's so cool.'

Chloe knew Bree's happy grin wasn't merely because their hamburgers had arrived.

*

'I need to grab a few things from my flat, while we're in town,' Chloe said, as they finished lunch. She felt a bit guilty about admitting this. It wouldn't have been necessary if she hadn't slept over at Finn's.

Bree was obviously curious as she followed her into the Progress Association's office, which was fortuitously closed to the public after 1 p.m. on a Saturday, so they escaped Moira's eagle eyes.

'This is nice,' the girl said when they'd climbed the stairs and she was looking around at the red lounge chairs and the neat little kitchen. She seemed happy enough to wait, while Chloe ducked into her room to grab extra clothes and toiletries.

When Chloe returned, Bree was at the sink, filling a glass with water. 'Your maidenhair fern is looking pretty sick,' she said.

'Oh, God.' Chloe had forgotten all about the pot plant. She'd been so preoccupied this past week, she couldn't remember the last time she'd watered it. Now she could see that a vast quantity of its delicate green leaves had turned brown and dry.

'It's not too late to save it,' said Bree with impressive gravity, as she carefully poured water into the pot.

'You sound like an expert.'

'My gran's an expert with ferns. She's always nursing her friends' maidenhairs back to life.'

'Wow, that's a handy skill. What does she do?'

'Cuts off the dead bits and soaks the pots in a bucket of water, and then she uses a little bottle with a spray pump to mist them every day.'

'Sounds logical,' said Chloe. 'Then I guess we'd better do that. I'd rather not risk this plant dying, so I'll take it back to your dad's place. Do you mind carrying it?'

Bree didn't mind at all and back at Cedar Lane, they duly used Chloe's manicure scissors to tidy the dead fronds and she found a bucket to soak the pot. Miraculously, after that, their Saturday continued with relative ease.

Bree unpacked and set up her bedroom the way she wanted it, and then Chloe took her to Lake Eacham for a swim in the deliciously deep, crystal clear rainwater. Back at the cottage, they cooked spag bol together, with Chloe showing Bree how to tear basil leaves and to crush garlic with the side of a knife blade and a little salt.

While the sauce was simmering, Bree rang her grandmother and she didn't disappear into her room to do so. She happily related details of her day, including Finn's interior decorating skills and his fan club at the Lilly Pilly café, as well as Chloe's inadequacies in the pot plant department. She sounded happy enough as she spoke, much to Chloe's relief.

When Finn rang from Singapore airport at around seven, however, Bree did go through to her room and close the door.

Nervous now, Chloe tried to keep busy, grating parmesan cheese for their spaghetti and choosing colourful bowls to eat from. She found half a bottle of red wine and poured herself a glass. She was taking a first sip when she heard Bree's bedroom door open.

The girl came into the kitchen, looking somewhat down in the mouth. She held out her phone. 'Dad wants to speak to you,' she said in the subdued voice of a child who'd been told off.

'Okay.' Chloe squared her shoulders as she took the phone. 'Hello, Finn.'

'Chloe.' His voice was clipped and businesslike, with no hint of the seductive lover of the previous night. 'What's this Bree's telling me about you letting her write for the *Bugle*?'

Chloe sighed. The last thing she wanted was an argument with Finn in front of his daughter, especially when said daughter was the subject in question and was watching her with big, worried eyes.

In her smoothest voice, she said, 'Yes, I'm delighted that you have so much faith in me. Thanks.'

'Chloe, don't play games. Be sensible. The kid's twelve, for heaven's sake.'

'I know.' Chloe bristled. What right did Finn have to lecture her? He'd kept the girl at arm's length in a boarding school, and then abandoned her, breaking his promise to his daughter and, consequently, her heart.

'It's amazing what they teach them at school these days,' Chloe said. 'How to write haiku, book reviews, little news stories. I'm always amazed at what my nieces and nephews produce.'

A frustrated *harrumph* sounded in her ear. 'You're determined, aren't you?'

'Yes, I think I am,' Chloe said sweetly.

Another, heavier sigh. 'I can only hope you know what you're doing.'

'Thank you, Finn. And all the best to you, too.' Chloe sent Bree an encouraging wink.

'By the way,' he said as she was about to disconnect. 'I rang Tammy again.'

'Oh, good. I meant to ring her, but I've been rather distracted. How is she? Has she seen the TV news yet?'

'No, but someone else rang her about it.'

'Is she freaking?'

'Yeah, she's pretty tense. She told me to be careful.'

Chloe's heart gave a strange little clunk. Until this moment, she hadn't allowed herself to think of Finn being in danger. It was big of Tammy to consider his welfare when her own worries were so huge. 'Well, I'm sure that's good advice,' she said.

'Don't worry. I'll be fine.'

CHAPTER THIRTY-TWO

As the plane began its descent into Bangkok, Finn watched the pattern of blue and green rectangles way below delineating fish farms and rice paddies. Before long, these gave way to buildings, scattered at first, and then gradually denser, criss-crossed by expressways and overpasses. Finn's stomach tightened.

With every metre's drop in altitude, the painful memories he'd been fighting forced their way back. Sweat broke out on his skin.

Sarah and Louis had died in this country, in Thailand's southern city of Betong. And he hadn't been with them. A car bomb had exploded outside their hotel, just as they were leaving through the front doors.

They'd died alone.

He should have been there.

If he'd accompanied them, he might have seen something, alerted them, saved them.

Guilt struck again, as it had a thousand times, and Finn tortured himself by replaying those final days. Sarah had been desperate to get away from the heat and drenching humidity of

Bangkok. She decided they needed a few days in Betong, a city surrounded by mountains and mist.

He could remember her shining-eyed smile as she'd showed him the tourist brochure. 'They call it the City in the Fog with Beautiful Flowers. Isn't that gorgeous, Finn? We can take Bree out of school for a day or two. It can be a birthday treat. We all need a break.'

At the last minute, Finn had received word that an Australian federal minister would be passing through Bangkok on his way back from trade talks in Europe. Finn was certainly overdue to take leave, but the chance to interview the minister about the latest changes to the Thailand–Australia Free Trade Agreement was too good to pass up.

Disappointed, and more than a little fed up with him, Sarah had travelled alone to Betong, taking Louis but leaving Bree in school after all, because the girl didn't want to miss a swimming carnival. Finn flinched now, as he remembered collecting Bree from school and giving her the heartbreaking news.

Bree. The surviving daughter he'd now deserted.

Fresh emotion whacked him. What the hell had he been thinking? What if something happened to Bree now, while he was away? How had he ever imagined that looking for Ben Shaw was more important than keeping his promise to his daughter?

To Finn's horror, his eyes filled with tears. Abruptly, he closed them, willed himself to get a grip. If he wasn't careful, the friendly American businessman seated beside him would notice something was wrong and try to help.

To calm himself, Finn replayed the phone conversation with Bree from Singapore in his mind. She'd sounded so different from the forlorn pre-teen who'd landed in Cairns. On this second call, his daughter had been super excited, talking fast as she told him everything she'd done that day, everything that she and Chloe planned to do.

Then Chloe. *Wow.* She'd refused to argue with him on the phone in front of Bree and had instead, politely, smoothly, put him in his place.

Chloe was obviously managing just fine. Bree was once again happy, and excited about being in Burralea, and his damn newspaper wasn't going to collapse if she had a hand in writing one little story.

Having reassured himself on this point, Finn found, to his surprise, that he could smile. Damn it, before Chloe Brown had arrived in Burralea, he'd been smugly convinced that the woman would be a lightweight.

And yet, Chloe had not only proved to be a valuable work colleague, but a beguiling temptress who'd unwittingly lifted a corner on the blanket of grief that had shrouded him for the past three years. And now, it seemed, she'd also rescued his daughter from the hugest of disappointments.

No question, Finn owed Chloe big time. But, in his own defence, his rash impulse to jump on a plane to find Ben Shaw was only partly crazy.

He still had good contacts here in Thailand and he was confident he could track Ben down. So, yeah, he had set himself a mission and, for now, he had no choice but to file away his personal issues and get the job done.

As always, the taxi ride from the airport was a nerve-jangling business of dodging tuktuks, motorbikes, lorries and the other brightly painted taxis. Eventually, Finn checked in to his hotel, then headed straight for Bangkok's ABC office.

He'd known Doug Brady, an ageing journo, formerly from Melbourne, for many years. Doug still headed the Bangkok office and his face broke into a deeply creased grin when Finn walked in.

'Good to see you, old son,' he said as he gripped Finn's hand. Doug knew, of course, all about Finn's history and the reasons he'd left Thailand. 'How are you faring these days?'

If there was anyone Finn could talk to comfortably about what had happened in Betong, that person was almost certainly Doug. The men agreed to catch up for a good chinwag, later in the day, at their favourite watering hole, a rooftop bar on Ratchadamnoen Klang Road.

'But right now,' Finn said, 'the person I need to speak to, if possible, is the young female reporter who covered a story about the new smoking bans on tourist beaches.'

Doug's shaggy white eyebrows rose. 'No kidding?'

'Dead serious,' Finn replied.

'It was a young stringer, Tania Moore, who reported that story.' Doug couldn't hide his curiosity. 'But why would you come all this way just to sniff around a little piece like that?'

There was no point in beating about the bush. Finn showed Doug a photo of Ben Shaw. 'This man went missing in the rainforest in Far North Queensland. They've been searching for him for weeks without any luck. His girlfriend's on the verge of a nervous breakdown, and suddenly he turns up in your footage on Kata Noi beach.'

'Blow me down.' Doug took the photo and studied it hard. 'You know we got word from Sydney to kill that story?'

Fine hairs lifted on the back of Finn's neck. 'Sydney killed it?'

'Yeah. Word came from head office within hours of it going to air.'

'You have any idea why?'

Doug shook his head. 'They wouldn't or couldn't say. I doubt our mob really knew the guts of it, but I'm guessing some government agency doesn't want people to know where your boy is. Probably the AFP.'

'That makes sense,' said Finn. And if the Australian Federal Police were involved in this, he knew exactly where he had to go next.

Jack O'Brien, known to almost everyone as Jacko, didn't look like a federal agent. A small man with a narrow foxy face, he could easily be mistaken for a bank johnny or an accountant, but he'd worked for the Feds in Southeast Asia for the past decade.

He was predictably cagey when Finn rang, but he agreed to a meeting. The address he gave was for a café in the ground floor of an apartment block in the Ekkamai district.

When Finn arrived, Jacko was already there, seated at a table that afforded him a view of the entries to both the café and the apartment block's foyer.

'Long time no see,' he drawled as he shook Finn's hand. Then with a wave, he summoned a waiter. 'Get yourself a coffee or something,' he told Finn. Jacko had always been a man of few words.

Finn ordered a pot of jasmine tea and while it was being prepared, he pulled Ben's photo from his wallet and set it on the table between them.

Jacko was outwardly calm as he picked up the photo between two fingers, but after a quick glance, he dropped it again and fixed Finn with a stony-eyed glare.

Okay, so the Fed wasn't happy. Finn expected a comment, however, and he waited. Jacko merely took a sip of his coffee and then lit a cigarette.

The jasmine tea arrived in a pot shaped like an elephant with a trunk for a spout. Finn poured it into a small white cup, savouring the remembered scent. In Australia, even in good Thai restaurants, the tea never smelled quite the same.

He shot another glance to Jacko. The man was playing hardball, but Finn hadn't slept in twenty-four hours and he was fast losing patience. 'You know who this is, don't you?'

'I might.'

'What the fuck's going on, Jacko?'

A fine stream of smoke was exhaled before the policeman spoke. 'You tell me your story first.'

'Fine.' Finn shrugged and kept it brief. 'This guy's a friend,' he said, tapping Ben's photo. 'His name's Ben Shaw, a popular baker from a little town in North Queensland. About six weeks back, he went missing under mysterious circumstances. No sign of him anywhere, despite big-scale searches. Then two days ago, there's a news story from Thailand on Aussie TV with a visual of Ben in the background.'

Jacko's foxy face remained blank.

'And now I hear that story's been killed.' Finn returned the other man's steady stare. 'That sounds to me like your mob.'

Time crawled as Jacko tapped his cigarette, letting the ash drop into his saucer. 'What are you going to do about it?' he asked. His voice was raspy, the voice of lifelong smoker.

Finn decided that two could play at this game. Leaning forward, elbows on the table, he spoke with cool determination. 'Unless you come up with a rational explanation, I'd be of a mind to contact my old colleagues at *The Australian* or the Fairfax press. I reckon they'd be intrigued to hear my story.'

At last, a reaction. Jacko tilted back in his chair, gave an exasperated sigh. 'Jesus wept, Latimer. Give me a break.' A coughing fit followed and Jacko used a handkerchief to wipe his mouth.

When he was finished, Jacko glared at Finn with watery eyes. 'Just my bloody luck. You, of all people, end up in Far North Queensland, poking your nose into the biggest investigation of my career.'

Finn sat straighter as Jacko glared at him.

'You have no bloody idea how much is at stake here,' Jacko growled. 'The undercover agents I'm running back home have been on this case for years. And now, Hawk, my man in Far North Queensland, is in a high-risk situation.'

'I – I see. But what does this have to do with my friend?'

Jacko rolled weary eyes to the ceiling, then let out a heavy sigh. 'Who have you spoken to about this?

'Doug Brady.'

'Who in Australia?'

'No one. Well, I rang Ben's partner, Tammy Holden, to see if she'd seen the story.'

'And?'

'She hadn't, but it had only just aired. She seemed too it stunned to say much.'

'What about your local coppers?'

Finn shrugged. 'I've no idea. I didn't speak to them. It was pretty obvious that Ben hadn't contacted them, so I thought it would be best if I acted independently.'

'Okay,' Jacko said quietly. 'That all lines up with our intel.'

'So you've spoken to Cameron Locke in Burralea?' Finn asked, surprised.

Jacko nodded. 'He knows to keep right out of this.'

'Right.' Finn inhaled as he digested this interesting information. 'And Ben?'

Jacko didn't answer. Instead, he picked up his phone, scrolled till he found what he was looking for, and pressed.

'Mate,' he said when the phone was answered. 'It's time for you to make an appearance.'

Finn found himself sitting on the edge of his seat and, scant moments later, he saw Jacko's gaze flick to the doorway behind him. Finn turned and Ben was there.

CHAPTER THIRTY-THREE

Chloe took a while to get to sleep in Finn's bed with Bree in the other room at the far end of the hallway. She couldn't help remembering the previous night, and now she was worrying that she and Finn had been reckless to jump into bed for a second time.

Surely the excuse that it was *only sex* could not hold indefinitely? And what about the murmured conversation afterwards, in the dark? Surely that had indicated a deepening sense of intimacy?

Chloe suspected she was in danger of falling hard for Finn. But falling for a man who was emotionally unavailable was not part of her plan. She had already wasted far too many years with the wrong guy. Her time was limited if she wanted to have a baby, her own little Willow or Bree – or Brad, for that matter – and getting entangled with her boss would not be helpful.

She would have to be super careful when Finn returned from Thailand. At least there would be no more leaping into bed while Bree was staying here with him, so that was a good thing.

And at least she could feel okay about the way Finn's daughter was settling in. Bree's transformation in a matter of hours from a sullen pre-teen to a pleasant companion was a huge source of relief.

Tonight, Chloe and Bree had rather enjoyed eating their spaghetti from bowls on the couch, while watching a rerun of *The Princess Diaries*. Chloe told herself she'd be fine as long as she stopped worrying about the future and concentrated on the twin tasks for the next few days of supervising the *Bugle* and Bree.

In fact, if all went well, Finn's return would be the perfect time for Chloe to make an appointment at the IVF clinic in Cairns. By then, she would be owed some time off.

Happy to have these thoughts sorted, Chloe finally relaxed, and settled to sleep.

A small knock on the bedroom door woke her. It was only just daylight as far as she could tell. Through sleepy, squinted eyes, she saw Bree in the doorway. She was wrapped in a blue cotton dressing gown and her feet were bare, but despite the subdued early light, Chloe could tell immediately that the girl was upset.

'Sorry to wake you,' Bree said in a small voice.

'That's okay.' Chloe propped herself up on one elbow. 'What's the matter?'

Bree came a little way into the room, her expression even more woeful than it had been yesterday when she'd arrived at the airport. 'I think —' She bit down on her lip and she looked as if she was about to cry.

'Bree, what is it? What's happened?' Chloe hoped she didn't sound as alarmed as she felt.

'I think I've started my period.'

Oh, God.

Dual reactions of relief and dismay rendered Chloe speechless. She knew she must have looked shocked, but she couldn't help it. This was a situation way above her pay grade.

'Is – is this your first time?' she asked.

Bree nodded, her eyes huge and shiny. She had lovely eyes, grey with a hint of blue, so that they appeared almost violet. But now they were brimming with tears, clear evidence that she was quite overwhelmed by yet another new challenge.

'You poor darling.' Chloe swung out of bed, awash with sympathy. For Bree. And for herself. The poor girl needed her mother, not a babysitter she'd met the day before.

Bree didn't have a mother.

'There's some on the sheets.' Bree's voice sounded close to cracking.

'Don't worry, sweetie. We can easily fix that.' Slipping her arm around the girl's shoulders, Chloe gave her a hug. 'If it's any consolation, it happens to all of us girls.'

A sob did break from Bree then, but she quickly stifled it, swiping at her eyes and rubbing at her nose with the sleeve of her dressing gown.

'Come on,' said Chloe. 'Luckily, I've got just what you need. And after breakfast, I'll duck up to the supermarket and get more supplies.'

Bree nodded and managed a wan smile.

In the bathroom, Chloe handed her a slim packet of pads. 'This will get you started. Do you know how to use them?'

Bree nodded again. 'We had a sex education night at school and the nurse kept waving them around. It was so gross.' She smiled crookedly. 'I – I didn't really think it would happen yet. Gran didn't say anything.'

'Well, I guess your gran's past having to worry about such things.' Chloe offered her an encouraging smile. 'You know this is probably happening to most of your girlfriends around now.'

'I know Maisie Green started last year,' Bree said, with an accompanying eye-roll. 'She's got massive boobs too and she never stops bragging.'

'There's always one like that.'

'Yeah.' But Bree still looked shocked and miserable.

Chloe gave her shoulder another squeeze. 'You'll soon get the hang of it,' she said. 'It's a girl thing we all get to share. I started my period on the bus on the way home from school. It was *so-o-o* embarrassing. When I got to my bus stop, I had to try to walk with my schoolbag covering the spot.'

Chloe acted it out, using a bath towel in place of her school bag.

'Noooo,' wailed Bree. 'Shame.' But she was smiling now.

'Worst day of my life.'

They were both smiling.

Chloe was glad she'd brought her favourite indulgent muesli to Finn's place. With the sheets and undies sorted in the laundry, she and Bree ate their breakfast on the small back verandah, overlooking the backyard with its random clumps of cosmos and a view of a farmer's newly ploughed field.

The muesli was laden with nuts and coconut flakes and Chloe added dollops of creamy, berry-rich yoghurt and a sliced banana.

'Yum,' said Bree. 'This is amazing.'

'I know, it's hard to believe it's still healthy,' said Chloe, tucking in.

They finished their meal with coffee – very milky coffee for Bree – while watching white cockatoos swoop and peck in the newly turned earth. And, out of nowhere, Chloe was struck by a brilliant idea.

'We should have an all-girls party,' she said. It seemed the perfect way to mark this occasion. 'We could keep it simple. Maybe pizzas,' she told Bree. 'And everyone can choose their own toppings.'

'That might be fun. No pineapple for me.' Bree frowned. 'But do you know many girls around here?'

'Well, that's the catch,' Chloe admitted. Her invitation list would be pretty much limited to Jess and Willow, Tammy and Emily. 'The girls would actually range in age from a baby to a sixty-something.'

'Oh.'

'Sorry.' Chloe smacked a palm to her forehead. 'That probably sounds more like a punishment for you than any kind of fun party.'

'No,' Bree said, shaking her head. 'It sounds okay.'

Perhaps, Chloe surmised, any kind of party sounded okay to a kid who went to boarding school and spent her weekends with her grandparents.

Bree was frowning again, though. 'These people wouldn't have to know about – *you know what* – would they?'

'Your period? No, no,' Chloe assured her. 'That's our secret. But at least *you'll* know we're all girls in the same boat. Even baby Willow has this ahead of her.'

Bree looked suddenly solemn. 'It means I can be a mother some day, doesn't it?'

'Yeah,' Chloe said softly. *If you're lucky.*

Without warning, she felt the sting of tears, as her own desperate yearning for motherhood spiked, hard and sharp. Almost immediately, her self-pity was eclipsed, though, by the tragedy of Bree's mother, missing not just this landmark day in her daughter's life, but everything that lay in her future.

Terrified of upsetting Bree, Chloe blinked. Hard. Took a deep breath. 'Right,' she said. 'I'd better do a ring around and see who's free to party.'

It was only when she looked up Tammy's number that she realised, with a guilty start, that she'd been so caught up with managing Bree that she hadn't yet contacted Tammy about Ben's dramatic appearance on TV.

Tammy arrived at their little impromptu party with a bottle of chilled white wine, a jar of sundried tomatoes and a very tense smile.

'Have you heard from Finn?' she asked almost as soon as Chloe opened the door.

Chloe shook her head. 'Not today,' she said. 'Not since he arrived in Thailand.'

Tammy grimaced. 'I'm not sure I can bear the suspense.' She thrust the bottle of tomatoes into Chloe's hands. 'Thanks for inviting me. I've been climbing the walls at home. You might be able to use these on your pizzas. One of my clients made them.'

With her free hand, she reached out to Bree and smiled. 'It's really nice to meet you, Bree. You look so much like Finn. All that lovely dark, glossy hair.'

'Watch out, Bree, or you'll be going home with a new hairstyle,' warned Chloe with a grin.

'I wouldn't mind,' said Bree, fingering the end of a long dark tress.

'You'll wait till your father's here, thank you,' Chloe intervened. 'Come through to the kitchen, Tammy, and I'll pour you a glass.'

The route to the kitchen took them through the lounge room, where Emily was sitting cross-legged on the carpet, playing a hand-clapping game with baby Willow. They made a very enchanting picture and Chloe did her best to crush the pang of longing she still felt every time she saw a cute baby.

'Hi, Tammy,' called Emily. 'You must be so relieved about Ben.'

'I guess,' Tammy said uncertainly.

'At least we now know he's alive,' suggested Chloe. 'And Finn's fairly confident about these contacts of his.'

Tammy gave a worried nod and followed Chloe to the kitchen where Jess was making a start on the pizza toppings.

'Willow and Emily are getting on like a house on fire,' Chloe told her after she'd greeted Tammy.

Jess nodded, but Chloe thought she looked rather tense. Was everyone tense today?

'Can I help with these?' Tammy asked as she surveyed the pizza bases waiting for further adornment.

'No, this kitchen's so small, we'll fall over each other,' said Chloe.

'It's cute, though.' Tammy looked about her. 'I like old-fashioned stuff. It reminds me of my grandmother's place.'

'Yes, I had the same reaction when I saw it.' Chloe handed her a filled glass.

Tammy raised it in a salute. 'Lovely to be here, but if I'm not needed, I'll go back and talk to Emily and Bree.'

'We won't be long,' Chloe assured her as she began to slice salami. 'But before you go – any special pizza requests?'

Tammy shook her head. 'I eat anything except anchovies.'

'Righto. We're only doing one base with anchovies.'

Tammy left and, almost immediately, the chatter from the lounge room rose a decibel or two, as her voice chimed in. Laughter quickly followed, which no doubt meant that Tammy had told them one of her jokes. She was, by all reports, a talented joke-teller.

Then Emily's voice could be heard, sounding especially happy, followed by a delighted little squeal from Willow.

'You're missing the fun,' Chloe told Jess.

Jess shrugged. 'I'm fine. Honestly.'

As they worked side by side, Chloe said in an undertone, 'It's so sad that Emily lost her son. She would have made a lovely grandmother.'

Jess gave a distracted nod. She was dotting mushrooms onto a pizza at careful, evenly spaced intervals and her mouth was pinched and tight, her expression uncharacteristically serious. Not at all the smiley and confident Jess, who usually relished a bit of gossip.

'Are you okay, Jess?' Chloe asked.

'Of course.' But Jess almost snapped the words. 'Why?'

'You seem —' Watching her, Chloe tried for a joke. 'Let me put it this way. I've never thought of you as being OCD.'

'Obsessive compulsive? Me?' Jess looked up from her task, frowning. 'What makes you say that?'

'Well, if I didn't know better, I'd swear you'd used a micrometer screw gauge to measure the distance between those mushrooms.'

'Oh.' Jess dropped her gaze back to her work. 'I see what you mean.' Her mouth quirked in a rueful smile. 'Sorry.'

'There's no need to apologise. I just hope you're okay.'

'Yes, I'm perfectly fine. Why wouldn't I be?'

'I don't know. You just seem different tonight.'

A brief flicker of emotion came and went in Jess's eyes, like the shadow of a fast-moving cloud. For a moment, Chloe thought Jess was going to confide in her, but then she shrugged. 'I think I'm just a bit tired. The café was full on till mid afternoon.'

'So you shouldn't be slaving here now. You should be out there with the others with your feet up, enjoying a glass. Go on.' Chloe shooed her. 'Go and play with your baby. Bree can help me with these. They're nearly done, anyway.'

'No, I'm fine.' Jess was, again, quietly but unmistakably insistent. 'Honestly.'

Chloe didn't push the matter, but she was definitely puzzled.

***

'This has been a lovely evening, Chloe,' said Emily. 'Maybe we can do it again some time and you can all come to my place.'

The 'girls' were relaxing after their meal. Willow had gone to sleep on Bree's bed, surrounded by a safety wall of pillows, and now, the others were replete with pizza and mellowed by wine, or lemon squash, in Bree's case.

Emily was still sitting on the floor with a cushion at her back and braced by a bookcase. She was wearing stretch denim slacks and had kicked off her shoes, and she was actually quite comfortable, but she wasn't sure she could get up again without assistance.

Earlier, she had removed some of the more delicate pieces of pottery out of little Willow's fumbling reach and she'd had such a lovely time playing with the little girl. It was amazing, really, that such a simple evening could be so pleasant. The conversation had been easygoing, with everyone keen to offer Bree advice on the best activities to enjoy while she was staying in Burralea.

Bree, in turn, had quizzed them about the schools in the district, which Emily found interesting. She wondered if Finn would come home to find himself under pressure to allow his daughter to move here full time.

Jess and Tammy had also asked Bree about her boarding school, and it was pretty clear that she was happy enough there, but of course, she missed her father.

Chloe, after only a little prompting, had told them a few gossipy stories from her days at *Girl Talk* magazine. All in all, given the diversity of the group, they seemed to have found plenty to chat about, which had moved Emily to offer her invitation.

'I don't think I've ever been to your place,' said Tammy. 'In fact, I know I haven't, but I've heard about it, of course. It sounds lovely, down by the lake.'

'Then you must come,' said Emily. 'We can try for another girls' night in.' Life was so much less complicated without men. 'Although I don't suppose that will work once Finn's back,' she mused.

'And hopefully, Ben will be back soon, too,' added Tammy.

'Yes, of course,' Emily averred, and for a moment or two there was silence as everyone wondered . . . and hoped . . .

It was important to have the men safely home, of course it was, but when Emily thought of her own man, Alex, she couldn't quite manage a smile. So she drank some more wine.

'Will your husband be back soon?'

This question came from Jess, which surprised Emily. If only it was easy to answer.

'I hope so,' she said. 'He's busy with supervising the muster on his cattle property at the moment.' She added a quick smile. 'But that won't last forever, of course.'

Tammy was listening to this with evident interest and she quickly pounced on Jess. 'While we're asking nosy questions, what about your man?'

'My man?' Jess gave a fair imitation of a deer caught in headlights.

'Willow's father?' clarified Tammy. 'Are you expecting a visit from him?'

'No.' Jess answered quickly, perhaps too quickly, and a tide of red flooded her face.

Tammy's eyes grew even wider. With unabashed curiosity, and a fair dose of impertinence, she continued to stare at Jess, who was curled on a beanbag in the opposite corner, chewing on a thumbnail. Obviously, Tammy was waiting for more information about Willow's mysterious father.

'He's totally out of the picture,' Jess said, at last, but she refused to look up.

Emily could readily sympathise. She suspected Jess might be in the same difficult position as she was, of having to make up a story to cover a private disappointment.

'All right, my turn to confess,' she said, wanting to break the tension. 'My hip is going on me, and someone's going to have to help me up.' She held out a hand and Chloe promptly took hold and helped her to her feet.

'Oh, dear,' Emily moaned as her hip complained, but at least her ploy worked. Everyone was smiling again.

As she drove home, however, she couldn't help wondering how long Tammy could keep up her brave face. The poor girl must have been going out of her mind with worry about Ben. His sudden reappearance in Thailand was bizarre, to say the least, and although Emily had imagined a host of explanations, not one of them was reassuring.

CHAPTER THIRTY-FOUR

When Ben Shaw heard that Finn Latimer was in Bangkok, phoning Jack O'Brien and making enquiries, his reaction, for all of five seconds, had been one of elated incredulity. He was chuffed to know that good old Finn had turned up here to try to rescue him. But almost immediately, the deeper implications of Finn's appearance had dawned on Ben and he was scared. Shit-scared.

He knew it could mean only one thing. Finn had seen, or at least had heard about, the television footage of him on Kata Noi beach.

Jacko had managed to have the story killed after just one airing, but Finn had seen it, so no doubt half of Australia had, too. It could only be a matter of time before the news reached the entire drug ring that Jacko had spent years trying to shut down.

This knowledge made Ben sick to the stomach. For weeks now, he'd been living on a knife edge, lying low in the flat Jacko had rented for him at Kata Noi. On the rare occasions he'd ventured out, he'd done his level best to blend in with the tourist crowds. He thought he'd managed pretty well until he'd come out of the surf to find a TV camera pointed directly at him.

Ben's first fears had been for the man who had saved his life.

He'd known that Hawk could now be in grave danger and so he'd called Jacko straight away, of course, and the brilliant Fed had sprung instantly into action.

Jacko had put in years of patient, meticulous work gathering info on Norman Chrysler and the wider drug ring that was spread throughout the eastern states of Australia. It would be a disaster of epic proportions if those crims were alerted now, at this final stage, just when Jacko's network was poised to close in.

Unfortunately, Jacko hadn't been able to stop that first news segment from going to air. As an extra precaution, he'd moved Ben down here to Bangkok, into the spare room in his own apartment, no less. And ever since, his agents and contacts both in Australia and Thailand had been in a state of constant vigil, their eyes and ears alert for the first sign that the ring had wised up.

So far there hadn't been a ripple.

Then Finn's phone call.

Ben had never seen Jacko look so scared and angry. The last thing the Fed had needed was a journalist sticking his nose in where it most desperately wasn't wanted.

'And not just any journalist,' Jacko had moaned. 'But a damn clever one, who knows me too bloody well. And just when we're on the bloody brink of closing this damn operation.'

Jacko had agreed to meet Finn, but he had also sent out another round of alerts and he had paced his living room, smoking, coughing and spluttering until, thirty minutes later, he'd been reassured. Norman Chrysler and his connections appeared to be none the wiser. They were carrying on as usual. Not a hint of suspicion. The AFP agents' plans were still safe.

And now, with the signal to join Jacko and Finn in the café on the apartment block's ground floor, Ben knew it was crazy to be excited, but it had been weeks since he'd had any contact with Burralea.

As he stepped through the doorway into the café, the good-looking dude who was the town's newspaper editor rose to his feet, smiling, holding out his hand.

'Ben, it's so good to see you.'

'You, too, Finn,' Ben said as they shook hands.

Finn was grinning, shaking his head in amazement. 'My mind's spinning, of course, trying to work out what the hell's going on.'

'I know,' Ben agreed as he lowered himself into the spare chair at their table. He would take his cue from Jacko. 'Crazy, huh?'

'I hope you guys are going to explain all this now,' Finn said as soon as a waiter had taken Ben's order.

Jacko, in the process of lighting another cigarette, waved in Ben's direction. 'Tell him your story.'

Ben lifted his eyebrows. 'All of it?'

'May as well. Finn's an old hand and this is still operational. It'll be off the record until we make the arrests.'

'Right.' Ben drew a deep breath as he tried to get his thoughts in order. So much had happened since that fateful afternoon when he'd veered off the rainforest track. 'I guess you realise by now that I stumbled on a little ice-cooking operation.'

Finn nodded. 'The local police could tell us that much. The hut was abandoned by the time they found it, of course.'

'Yeah, well, Norman Chrysler wanted me dead. But lucky for me, he didn't know that the guy he'd told to shoot me was actually an undercover cop.'

'Working for the Feds, I assume?'

'Yeah. So this guy – I've only known him as Hawk – took me off into the bush, but instead of topping me, he helped me to disappear. At first, I couldn't see why he didn't just arrest Chrysler and be done with it. After all, he had the gun, but he assured me it couldn't work that way. He'd invested years on this case and he couldn't risk anything rash. He gave me a phone and Jacko's number here in Thailand. Wrote the number on my wrist and told me to memorise it then wash it off.'

Ben smiled as he admitted, 'Numbers have never been my forte, but I sure managed to learn that one. And Hawk gave me the code word "Sunshine" as well. Worked like magic.'

He flicked his glance towards Jacko, who was watching him carefully, despite the smoke reddening his eyes. 'I simply gave Jacko the word and he seemed to understand the whole situation,' he said.

Finn turned to Jacko as well, no doubt expecting a comment, but the Fed remained deadpan and took another drag on his cigarette. Finn returned his attention to Ben. 'I suspected you hadn't spoken to the local police.'

'No chance. Hawk warned me to steer clear of them, or anyone in the Federal Police in Australia. Said it was too risky. For him and for me. The only person I was allowed to speak to was Tammy.'

Finn's jaw dropped. 'You spoke to Tammy?'

'Just the once. To put her in the picture.'

'You mean she's known all along that you were alive?'

Ben nodded. 'I had to swear to Hawk that she could be trusted. I wasn't happy, putting that kind of pressure on her. I knew it would be a terrible strain, but it's hard to argue when a bloke's pointing a shotgun at you. And, of course, I had to make Tammy promise not to tell anyone else.'

'The poor girl. No wonder she's been looking so tense and anxious. We all thought it was grief.'

As he had constantly, throughout these past lonely weeks, Ben let his thoughts settle on his bubbly, talkative Tammy. Her clients were always confiding in her, sharing their troubles and their personal secrets. She must have found it so damn hard to keep his secret to herself. But he'd known that, in this case, Tammy would be super careful. Of course she would. She was smart and he had made sure she understood how serious the situation was.

'I couldn't go home,' Ben said. I couldn't risk being seen in town, and I could only phone Tammy and tell her as much as I thought she needed to know.'

'Amazing,' said Finn with a shake of his head. 'Well, I guarantee, you can be proud of Tammy, mate. She's done a great job of keeping your secret. Fooled the whole town. My new journalist even interviewed her, specifically trying to dig deeper, but she never let on.'

Ben smiled. 'My girl might not look especially strong, but she's smart and she's tough.'

And I love her, he thought, with a stab to his heart primed by both joy and fear. It was hard to believe it might not be long now before he could see her again.

CHAPTER THIRTY-FIVE

The lake was like a mirror in the early morning, reflecting the pale-blue perfection of a cloudless sky. The only ripples on the surface were made by Emily's oars as she rowed towards home, working fluidly in a seamless motion, now as familiar to her as breathing.

Already, the sun had climbed fast and the day threatened to grow hot before it was too much older. But for now the air on the lake was cool.

There was even a breeze as Emily approached the shore. She feathered the oars over the glassy surface and allowed the boat to skim past the reeds to the bank, expecting to see Murphy waiting, sitting in his usual spot, eagerly alert with his golden tail waving.

For the first time in her memory, her dog wasn't there to greet her.

Emily frowned, scanning the bank. Murphy's absence was worrying, but not completely alarming. Perhaps he'd been distracted by a particularly enticing smell and was off chasing a bandicoot or some other unfortunate small creature.

In the shallows, Emily alighted and pushed the boat forward, edging it gently onto the sand. Carefully, she gathered up the long, thin oars, and once again scanned the tree-studded bank that sloped all the way up to the house. Still no sign of the dog.

'Murphy!' she called.

No response.

She called again, more loudly, 'Murphy! Where are you, boy?'

At last, a happy bark. The flurry of worry in Emily's breast eased. Obviously, her loyal dog had been captivated by something incredibly important.

Now, sure enough, the golden lab came bounding down the back steps and over the slope, his tail thrashing. Emily grinned at him as he raced towards her. Then she saw something else that made her happy smile freeze.

At the house, the back flyscreen door had opened and a figure appeared. Tall, masculine and heartbreakingly familiar. She almost dropped the oars.

Alex.

His name was a mere whisper on Emily's lips. Her heart thumped so hard she could feel it banging against her ribs.

Murphy scampered excitedly back and forth, expecting her customary greeting. She gave him a distracted pat. She was too busy watching as Alex continued, without haste, down the back stairs.

She supposed she must have known that he would eventually come back, but she had expected a warning, a phone call at least. Stupidly, she wished she was dressed in something more glamorous than the spandex T-shirt and shorts she wore for rowing.

Alex was, of course, wearing the usual attire that suited him so perfectly, a blue striped shirt with long sleeves rolled to the elbows, pale chinos and brown leather riding boots. His silver hair glinted in the morning light as he came with long, easy strides to where she stood, anchored, clutching the oars.

A storm broke in her chest. Longing for the man she'd fallen for all those years ago and whose love she had never doubted. Till lately. Anger for the way he'd walked out on her and his subsequent prolonged silence.

But guilt was there, too. Guilt for her indiscretion with Rolf. And pain when she recalled the horrendous fight with Alex, still unresolved since the night he left.

Such dreadful insults they'd hurled at each other. Insults born out of the deepest pain and grief. Such hurtful, unspeakable things they'd said.

'Good morning, Emily,' Alex said now as he came to a stop a metre from her.

Was there a hint of a cautious smile in his eyes? She couldn't be sure. His mouth remained firm.

'Hello, Alex.' Everything about him was painfully familiar and dear, and yet, after weeks of silence, also strangely distant. This morning, there was no welcoming kiss, no smiling, no rushing into each other's arms.

Murphy, however, continued to scamper blissfully around them, as if he was ecstatic that his master and mistress were together again.

'When did you get here?' Emily asked her husband.

'About ten minutes ago.'

'You haven't come straight from Red Hill, have you?'

'I have, actually.'

'You must have driven all night.'

After all this time, what on earth could have brought him hurrying home at such an unlikely hour?

But Alex merely gave a curt nod and held out his hand for the oars. 'Let me take those for you.'

Mutely, Emily handed them over. She thought of the many times she'd imagined a reunion with Alex. Foolishly, she'd pictured an emotional, teary scene with hugs and profuse apologies, followed by something akin to a second honeymoon. Yet here they were, behaving like polite strangers.

Given the current mood, she half expected Alex to make a superficial comment now, to mention the beautiful morning, perhaps. She would hate it if he did, when the important things had been left too long unsaid.

It was almost a relief when he remained silent as they walked back to the house. Without further word, he stowed the oars as carefully as Emily would have done, while she took off her wet rowing shoes and dried her feet, pulled the elastic from her hair and gave it a hasty finger-comb.

'I've started the coffee,' he said.

'Oh, good.' Her response was automatic. This morning, nothing mattered but the reason for her husband's return. Everything else, even the first coffee of the day, had lost its attraction.

Once they were in the kitchen, Emily let Alex fiddle with the coffee plunger and mugs while she fussed over Murphy, petting him and giving him his breakfast, then washing her hands at the sink.

Alex slid a full mug across the counter towards her.

'Thank you.' But she didn't take the mug and she didn't sit on a stool at the bench.

She was over the first shock of seeing her husband, and she was beginning to feel rather annoyed with him for waltzing into the house and trying to act as if everything was normal, as if their terrible row had never happened, as if he hadn't shunned her for weeks.

'Is the mustering over?' she asked.

Alex nodded. 'Yes.'

So, was this his reason for coming back? He'd run out of excuses to stay away? Surely he could have just lingered at Red Hill for as long as he liked? 'Did it go well?' she asked tightly.

'Very smoothly, thanks. And prices are up. We should make a good profit this year.'

Another annoying response. Why mention money now? Anyone would think they were still young, desperately anxious to make a go of their cattle business. For more than a decade, they'd been comfortably off.

Emily took a deep breath. 'So what happened? Any particular reason you came back?'

Alex lifted his gaze to meet hers. 'I'm not exactly proud of the reason.'

He certainly looked rather abashed. Despite her annoyance, she felt a small spurt of sympathy.

'I had a phone call from Rolf,' Alex said.

Emily changed her mind about not sitting down. She was too shaky to remain standing. Her thoughts were racing now, trying to imagine the conversation between Rolf and her husband. Clearly its impact had been significant.

A thousand possibilities flashed through her mind. None of them good.

She forced herself to ask, 'What did Rolf say?'

'Not a lot.' Alex dropped his gaze to his untouched coffee mug. He picked it up, set it down again.

Emily's hands clenched. She wanted to scream. *Just tell me.*

Still without looking at her, he said, 'Rolf told me I was being a bloody fool and if I wasn't careful I would lose you, or words to that effect.'

'I – I see.'

'I gather the two of you have had some rather in-depth conversations.'

'Yes.' Emily swallowed. 'Yes, we have.'

Alex looked up at her now and his gaze was a complicated mix that might have been suspicion, or blazing emotion. 'He's in love with you, isn't he?'

'Rolf?' Her cheeks flamed. 'I – I don't know.' She should have felt guilty then. But Alex couldn't claim the moral high ground when he'd taken no responsibility for his part in their separation.

A new flash of anger quickly cleansed her conscience. 'Is that why you came back, Alex? To grill me about my relationship with Rolf Anders?'

Her husband sighed, closed his eyes. 'No, Emily.' His voice was unexpectedly quiet.

Now, even with his eyes closed, she could see the pain in his handsome face. It showed in the hollows beneath his cheekbones, in the deep creases that ran from beside his nose to the edges of his down-turned mouth. When he opened his eyes again, the torment was almost too much for her to bear.

'I came back to —'

The phone on the kitchen wall rang shrilly, making Emily jump. She tried to ignore it. She couldn't answer it now, but of course it wouldn't give up.

Alex was closest. 'I'll get it,' he said.

'It's bound to be for me.' Emily wriggled off the stool and hurried across the kitchen. 'It's probably Chloe, the new girl at the *Bugle*.' She grabbed the receiver. 'Hello?'

'Hello, Emily?' The young woman's voice wasn't Chloe's.

'Yes, Emily here.'

'It's Jess.'

'Jess?' Emily repeated, momentarily puzzled. 'Oh, *Jess*,' she said again, as she remembered the girl from the café with the sweet baby girl. 'Yes, of course, Jess. Sorry, I was a bit distracted here for a moment.' She looked at Alex, lifted her eyebrows, offering an apologetic shrug. 'How are you?'

'I'm fine, thanks. I hope I haven't rung too early.'

This was Emily's chance to get rid of the interruption, but her deeply ingrained manners delivered an automatic response. 'No, this is fine. How can I help?'

'Well, I was wondering —' The girl stopped, but before Emily could become too impatient, she said quickly, 'I was wondering if

I could visit you. If I could bring Willow to see you, too. There's something I – I need to tell you. We wouldn't take up much of your time.'

On any other morning, Emily would have been delighted. For weeks she'd been so terribly lonely, and at Chloe's party, she'd loved the chance to connect with another generation. Little fatherless Willow had stolen her heart.

But now? The timing couldn't have been worse. She glanced towards Alex. 'I – I'm afraid I'm rather busy this morning.'

'Oh? Sorry. That's okay. Some other time then.'

'What about later in the day?' Emily had been conscious of the note of disappointment in Jess's voice.

'Only if it suits. I finish work at the café around three-thirty.'

'That would be fine. Come for afternoon tea.'

'Oh, thank you. That's lovely. But please don't go to any trouble. I'll bring something to eat from the café.'

'All right, Jess. That's a deal. I'll see you then.'

As Emily hung up, she felt extraordinarily weary. Perhaps she could blame the lack of coffee.

She turned to Alex. 'Now, where were we?'

For the first time since he'd arrived, her husband smiled. 'I believe I was about to offer you an apology.'

CHAPTER THIRTY-SIX

Since Finn's earliest days in Bangkok, the Pranakorn Bar had been a favourite watering hole for the expat journos. Positioned a short walk from the busy tourist strip on Khao San Road, the bar left behind the budget guesthouses, mid-range hotels and internet cafés and offered something more authentic.

It was also where the hip, local Thai people ate and drank. With no special dress code, the ambience was laid-back and the prices pocket-friendly. Quality live music played and the view from the rooftop provided glimpses of old-world Bangkok – government buildings hundreds of years old and the Phra Prang temple, shimmering and golden.

Finn was running late when he arrived for his promised meeting with Doug Brady. He had grabbed a few moments to ring Tammy Holden, to let her know that he'd met with Ben, that Ben was now in Bangkok, fit and well, and hoped to be coming home very soon.

The poor girl had shrieked so loudly Finn had needed to hold his phone well away from his ear. She had asked him to say it all over again, so she could be sure it was true. And then, when he had done so, she'd wept buckets. But between her sobs, she'd been profuse in her thanks.

'No worries,' Finn had assured her. 'As we speak, the Feds are closing in on an Australian drug network that has links here in Thailand.'

'Does that mean I can start telling people at last?' Tammy was pleading.

'No, you'll have to hold off until Ben's safely home, but you won't have to wait too long.'

He'd been pleased to pass on such a positive message, but now, as he entered the bike shop that took up the ground floor of the Pranakorn building, he felt as if he was stepping back in time. Without warning, his old enemy grief came sweeping back, in wave after painful wave.

Time to get a grip. To put on a brave face, despite the underlying sadness that was so hard to shake.

Resolutely, Finn climbed four flights of stairs, passing the busy kitchen that smelled just as it always had, of curry paste and fish sauce. Then finally he stepped out to the dark little rooftop bar.

Everything about the place was achingly familiar. Cosy and dimly lit, the space was filled with customers seated at small round tables. Live music – guitar and violin – played the Etta James song 'At Last'. No waiters stepped forward to guide him to a table. It wasn't that kind of place.

Finn saw Doug in a dim, candlelit corner, nursing a glass of whisky. He was about to make his way towards him when he was gripped by a cruel rush of memories.

The phone call with the news of his wife's and son's deaths. The ghastly journey to Betong. Identifying Sarah and Louis. The gut-wrenching stillness of their lifeless bodies and the numbing grief that followed. Raw. Cavernous. Smothering.

Sometime in the haze of days that had followed, his friends had brought him here to this bar for a kind of wake. They had been hoping to help him, to cheer him in some small way. For Finn, the evening had been intolerable.

And now . . .

He was back. In that place and time. Experiencing every detail of the loss. Sharp, vivid and immediate. The guilt, so unforgiving.

To Finn's horror, his eyes welled with tears. Next moment he was shaking and tears were streaming down his face, so that he could barely see Doug rising from his seat, obviously worried.

But Finn knew that another step towards his old friend would spell disaster. He would break down completely, make a fool of himself and spoil the evening for everyone present.

Abruptly, he made a sharp gesture to Doug, somewhere between a wave and a salute, and then turned on his heel and hastened away, sobbing, stumbling blindly down the stairs, scrubbing at his tears with the heels of his hands.

'Finn!'

He was halfway back to Khao San Road when Doug caught up with him.

'Finn,' Doug said again as he grabbed him by the elbow.

Finn stopped. The portly old guy was red-faced and puffing from his exertion. 'I'm sorry, Doug. I don't know what happened.'

'It's called grief.' Doug pulled a handkerchief from his trouser pocket and mopped at his shiny brow. 'I guess I should have known better than to suggest the same old venue.'

Finn nodded, let out a heavy sigh. He was calmer now, thank God.

'I'm sure you still need a drink,' Doug said. 'There are plenty of places just round the corner.'

They found a bar crowded with noisy, hard-drinking tourists, who happily ignored them. There was one rickety table left, with two equally wonky bamboo stools.

'I hope this will take my weight.' Doug smiled as he gingerly settled himself.

They ordered whisky and as Finn took his first few sips and felt its warming glow, he realised that Doug, whisky and the anonymity of a noisy bar filled with strangers were exactly what he needed.

'I'm sorry about what just happened,' he said.

Doug shook his head. 'No need for apologies.'

'I thought I'd finished with feeling like crap. I was pretty sure I was coming out the other side.'

'I'm afraid that's not how it works,' Doug said gently.

Finn stared at him. 'You know how this grief thing works?' But even as he asked the question, he remembered – of course Doug would know. Finn had never met Doug's partner, Clive. He had died of AIDS twenty years ago. From all accounts, he'd been a talented and flamboyant musician. Popular and loads of fun.

'I know it won't leave you – ever,' Doug said. 'But then, you wouldn't want it to.'

Finn wasn't so sure about that. Back in Australia, he'd begun to believe he might finally move on with his life. Tonight, in Bangkok, he knew he had taken several major steps backwards.

Doug rocked his glass a little, making the ice cubes clink. 'The way I see it, grief slams back every so often to remind us of how much we loved the people we lost. It makes us remember how much they loved us, too. And why we miss them.'

'That's true.' Finn sighed. 'I just wish it didn't hit so damn hard.'

'The pain is a measure of how much you loved.'

That was certainly true. There'd been times when Finn almost wished he hadn't loved his wife so deeply. He might have let her go more easily.

'The way I see it,' Doug went on. 'The pain is also a reminder of how important life is.'

'You think?'

'Absolutely. You're still alive, Finn, and the world around you is a beautiful place.' Doug looked around at the raucous, carousing youngsters and rolled his eyes. 'Well, maybe not this place.'

Finn almost smiled. 'And I still have Bree, of course.'

'Of course you do. And what a great little kid she was when she was here. How's she doing these days?'

Finn wished he could answer this honestly. Wished he could tell Doug that he'd kept his daughter close, that he knew exactly how her height measured against his. That he knew what she liked to eat for breakfast, and what kind of friends she had.

Instead, all he really knew about his daughter were the scant details she cared to share with him over the telephone. Sadly, he'd kept Bree almost as distant as Sarah and Louis. But he was too ashamed to admit this.

'She's great,' he said. 'She's twelve now.' He managed a lopsided smile. 'Apparently, she's trying her hand at journalism while I'm away. My offsider, Chloe Brown, is taking care of her.'

Doug was watching him now with keen interest. 'This Chloe Brown must be a good sort.'

'Yeah, Chloe's great, actually.' Finn almost smiled again, as he thought about the *Dolly* reporter who'd turned out to be so much more.

'Young, is she, this Chloe?'

'No, ancient. Almost as old as me.'

Doug laughed, a huffing bellow.

Finn found his smile expanding too. 'Chloe reckons she's going to let Bree help on the paper. I can't see it working, myself, but —' He gave a helpless shrug.

'What paper is this again?'

'The *Burralea Bugle*.' Finn held up his hand. 'I know, I know, you don't have to tell me.'

'Tell you what?'

'That I'm crazy to bury myself in a tiny country town no one's ever heard of.'

'Is that how you feel?'

Finn thought about Burralea, about the surrounding landscape of rolling farmland, of pink dawns over soft hills and silver lakes, so easy on the eye. He thought about the friendly, undemanding locals, and the personal friends he'd made. Honest, hardworking rural types, laconic humorists, fun to be with. Solid, reliable. He thought about Chloe. 'I don't mind it there, actually.'

'You're enjoying it, aren't you?' Doug sounded intrigued.

'To be honest, going north was, most definitely, an escape at first. I had to get out of Sydney. And a country town can be a place to hide. But the town has a way of growing on you, too. And then there's the challenge of keeping a small newspaper viable against the odds.'

'Quite a decent challenge, I should imagine.'

'It's surprising how you can winkle out stories when nothing seems to be happening.'

'Like a story about a local baker who's taken undercover by the Feds?'

Finn grinned. 'But even when everything's quiet, a small town is still intimately part of a bigger world. Events that affect the state, the nation, still affect us. And when you think about it, even in a big city, you're still just a dot on a speck in the universe.' He grinned again as he got to his feet. 'But before I get too philosophical, I believe it's my shout.'

CHAPTER THIRTY-SEVEN

In the *Bugle* office, Chloe let out a huff of relief as she put down her phone and turned to Bree. The girl was sitting at her father's desk, diligently refining her touch-typing skills on his computer.

'A great little news story has just come in,' Chloe told her. 'And I reckon it's right up your alley, Bree.'

Bree's eyes widened with instant excitement. After a morning at the *Bugle* office, spent mostly fetching coffee, sweeping the floor and answering the landline phone, Bree was still bursting with enthusiasm, and desperate to start work as a real reporter.

'What kind of story?' she asked.

'A little dog went missing from the local nursing home and now he's been found.'

'Cooper?' Bree sat up straighter.

'Yes, that's his name.' Chloe stared at her in surprise. 'How did you know about him?'

'I saw the *Lost Dog* signs in the shop windows. At the café and the supermarket.'

'That's very observant of you, Bree.' Chloe smiled at her. 'Well done.'

'I love dogs. Who found him?' Bree was obviously trying to be businesslike, despite blushing at Chloe's praise.

'Two children who live on a farm out on Wetherby Road.'

'Kids? Wow!' Now Bree almost jumped out of her seat with excitement. 'Can I come with you when you interview them?'

'That's my plan. I've just checked with their mother and they're available this morning. But you should be the one who does the interviewing.'

'Really? You'd let me?'

'I don't see why not.'

For a moment Bree looked worried, but then she smiled. 'Awesome!'

Moira Briggs had been very keen to supervise Bree, and Chloe knew she would be grateful for Moira's assistance if Finn was away for much longer, but for now Chloe was happy to keep the girl with her. Secretly, she was enjoying Bree's company.

See, Jason? I would make a good mum.

It was a very happy discovery.

On the drive to the farm, however, Bree's nerves seemed to return.

'I'll have to ask lots of questions, won't I?'

'You will,' Chloe agreed. 'It helps to start with the basics – who, what, when and where.'

'I'll try to remember, but you'll stay with me, won't you? In case I miss stuff?'

'Of course I will.'

'I brought a notepad and pen, but I might be a bit slow getting it all down.'

'That's where my trusty recorder comes in handy.' Chloe held out her phone. 'But you should try to take notes as well.'

'Right.'

'Don't worry, Bree. This is going to be fun.'

The girl's smile was clearly one of relief.

*

Their destination was a dairy farm set high on a hill. The milking sheds and fences were quite close to the road, while the red-roofed, white-walled farmhouse sat on the hill's crest and was shaded by a huge flowering jacaranda.

Bree leaned forward, straining against her seatbelt as she took in the vista of steep green hillsides dotted with black and white cows and the well-worn dirt tracks leading to the corrugated iron milking sheds, which were no doubt churned to mud when it rained. 'Wow!' she whispered.

Chloe understood. There was something otherworldly about these isolated, windswept farms perched so high above the rest of the world.

'Wouldn't it be cool to live somewhere like this?' Bree said as Chloe drove in through the open farm gates and a flock of guinea fowl scattered in front of them.

Chloe smiled. She could remember visiting a farm, as a child, and being entranced by the chickens, ducks and horses, and wishing she could live there. But then, at that age, she'd also wanted to live in a lighthouse and on a riverboat and in an igloo.

As she pulled up on a gravelled drive in front of the house, the door opened and a boy and a girl appeared, both redheads, tall and skinny, with the kind of well-scrubbed wholesomeness that seemed natural to country kids. The boy was probably around Bree's age and his sister a little younger. They were smiling shyly.

Bree, however, looked rather solemn as she climbed out of the Forester, clutching her notepad and pen. Chloe hoped she wasn't too overawed by her new responsibility.

'Hello,' called the boy. 'Mum said to come in. She's just taking something out of the oven.'

'It's a date loaf,' his little sister informed them self-importantly.

'What are your names?' Chloe asked them in her friendliest manner.

'Sam,' said the boy.

'And I'm Milla,' added his sister.

'Hello Sam. Hello, Milla. I'm Chloe and this is Bree.'

'Hello,' they chorused.

'Hello.' Bree smiled nervously.

'Come this way,' Sam told them.

They were led through a modestly furnished living area to a side verandah where a table had been set with a floral tablecloth, a teapot, cups and saucers, as well as glasses and a jug of juice covered by an old-fashioned lace doily.

'You can sit down,' Sam said. 'Mum'll be here in a minute.'

As he said this, a woman came onto the verandah, bearing a china plate piled with buttered slices of date loaf. Like her children, she was tall and slim, with red hair, although her freckled face looked tired and her hair was starting to fade. Chloe supposed life on a dairy farm wasn't always as idyllic as it looked from the outside.

'Hi, I'm Mary,' she said, brightening and offering a friendly smile. 'I thought you'd probably like a spot of morning tea.'

'That's very kind of you, Mary.' Chloe had previously noted that farming women seemed to stay slim, even though they were always baking delicious things to eat. Probably because they worked so hard.

As they sat at the table, Bree carefully set her notepad and pen beside her plate. From here there was a breathtaking view of green hills and valleys rolling away for ever. Tea was poured and the children were given glasses of pineapple juice, freshly squeezed. The date loaf was handed around. Somewhere behind one of the farm sheds a tractor roared to life.

'I should warn you, Bree,' said Chloe as she gestured to the table. 'Journalists don't usually get such delicious extras.'

'Are you a journalist, too?' Sam looked seriously impressed as he asked Bree this.

Bree blushed again. 'Kind of.' Then quickly she corrected herself. 'Well, no, I'm not really. Chloe's the real reporter, and I'm just helping her, because my dad's away. He's the editor.' This last was said with a marked note of pride.

'And are you her mum?' Milla asked Chloe.

'No,' Chloe and Bree answered in unison.

'I'm a journalist at the paper,' Chloe explained, but to her secret dismay, there'd been more than one occasion in the last few days when she'd fantasised about having a daughter like Bree. In the past, her focus had been on babies, but Bree had proved that kids could be endearing and fun at any age.

And now, as Finn's daughter turned to her with wide, worried eyes, Chloe felt awash with genuine fondness.

'When do I start asking the questions?' the girl whispered.

'In a minute or two, when you've finished eating,' Chloe suggested and then, in a bid to relax her protégé, she asked Sam and Milla about their plans for the Christmas holidays.

Milla immediately pulled a mournful face. 'We can't go away, because Dad has to keep milking every day.'

'Oh, dear.' Chloe tried to rustle up another question. Clearly this was a sore point.

Sam stepped in, however. 'Give it a miss, Mill. You know we're going to camp down near the lake, and Dad and me will slip home for the milking.'

His sister pouted. 'Yeah, but we can't go to the beach or anything fun.'

'I'm going to go camping at the lake with my dad when he gets back,' Bree announced brightly.

'Really?' Sam was clearly interested in this prospect.

'Yeah.' Bree shot a quick glance in Chloe's direction. 'He promised.'

This was news to Chloe, but she wisely held her tongue.

Sam grinned. 'We might see you there.'

Bree nodded and went a little pink again. She picked up the notepad. 'So – um – maybe I should start asking you about the dog, Cooper.'

Chloe clicked the recording app on her phone and set it on the table. 'No one minds if I record this?'

The others shook their heads.

'We found Cooper down by the creek,' Milla told Bree eagerly.

'Yes, that's fantastic. So what sort of dog is he?'

'A black and tan bitser,' said Sam.

Oh, good for you, Bree! Chloe was proud of the way the girl had brought the interview straight back to where she wanted it, starting with the basics.

'And when did he go missing?'

'Last —' Sam frowned and seemed to be counting back the days in his head. 'I think it was Thursday.'

'That's right, Thursday,' confirmed his mum.

Bree conscientiously noted this down. 'And do you know what happened? How he got lost in the first place?'

Milla piped up again. 'Our grandma said one of the old people from the home took him for a walk and then forgot about him and walked back without him.'

'Oh, dear, poor Cooper.'

'I'm surprised he didn't just go home anyway,' said Mary.

'Maybe he was confused about what he should do,' suggested Bree.

'Perhaps.'

Sam said, 'Someone told Dad they thought they saw him under the bridge on Sheoak Creek. Dad went down there looking, but he'd disappeared again by then.'

'And Grandma told us that everyone at the home was really sad and worried,' added Milla. 'Father Jonno even said a prayer for Cooper at church.'

'Gosh,' Bree said with a laugh. 'Maybe that's what saved Cooper? And thanks, you're already answering the questions before I can ask them.'

Milla gave a cheeky little grin and shrugged.

'So you found him yesterday, is that right?' asked Bree.

Sam nodded. 'We went back to the creek and found him limping along the track.'

'But there's no creek up here, is there? Did you walk all that way?'

The children grinned. Milla said, 'We were riding our horses.'

'Oh!' Bree's mouth hung open as she took in the prospect of kids her age exploring these hills and valleys on horseback.

'This has been great,' Chloe intervened. 'I think you've just about covered all your questions, haven't you, Bree?'

Bree turned back to the children. 'Where do you go to school?'

'Burralea Primary,' said Milla. 'Are you putting that in the paper?'

'No.' Bree smiled shyly. 'I just wanted to know.'

'I'll be going to high school, next year,' said Sam. 'What about you?'

'I go to a boarding school in Townsville. It has both primary and secondary.'

'Oh.'

There seemed little more to be said after that. Chloe took a photo of Sam and Milla and then she thanked Mary for the interview and the morning tea. 'We'd better get back to the office and write this up so it makes this week's edition,' she told them.

As they got into the car, Bree seemed a little subdued, but then Sam called, 'Might see you at the lake.'

'Yeah!' She was smiling again as they drove off.

CHAPTER THIRTY-EIGHT

Lying in bed beside her husband, Emily stretched luxuriously. She and Alex had made love in broad daylight, which seemed quite risqué for a pair of sixty-somethings. And, after so many weeks of misery, Emily was almost happy again.

Now, already, she found it hard to believe that she had been so scared when she'd first seen Alex this morning. In the kitchen, when he'd suddenly told her that he wanted to apologise, she'd almost laughed. When it was nearly too late, she'd realised he was serious.

'An apology?' She had found it necessary to repeat this to make sure she'd heard him correctly.

'I owe you a thousand apologies,' Alex had said. 'I've been stupidly selfish, caught up in my own grief, as if my pain was bigger and more important than anyone else's.'

Emily had to admit the argument that had sent Alex retreating to Red Hill *had* felt like a kind of pain contest.

But of course there had been terrible heartache. They were Robbie's parents. He was their only child. They had both adored him and his death had left them utterly bereft. Rudderless.

'I shouldn't have laid the blame on you and your mother,' Alex said. 'That was cruel.'

'We both said cruel things. I've wanted to say sorry too. I never meant things to get so – so —'

Her husband smiled sadly. 'So *mega*?'

It was a word Robbie had often used and, almost instantly, they were both blinded by tears. Both reaching for each other. Clinging. Sobbing their apologies.

Such a release to finally cry and to hug. Their coffee had been cold when they finally released each other and sat down to talk. They drank it anyway.

'I've had time to think more rationally,' Alex said then. 'I know I blamed your mother's heroics for inspiring Robbie to join the Air Force. And I do believe that was a factor. But he might just as easily have wanted to fly helicopters to muster cattle.'

'And you wouldn't have objected then.'

'That's right. I probably would have been thrilled.' Alex sighed. 'And the crazy thing is that I really do admire Izzie. She's always been an amazing woman and a wonderful role model for Robbie.'

'He adored her.'

'They had a great relationship.' Alex managed to smile. Then, with an unhappy grimace, he added, 'We both know there've been plenty of helicopter-mustering accidents. So, if Robbie had stayed in the cattle business —'

He didn't finish the sentence, but Emily knew he was thinking that even if Robbie had followed his father's wishes and stayed in the cattle industry, the result might have been the same. As always, she was fighting the wall of sadness that threatened whenever she thought about her son's death.

Alex sighed again, more heavily. 'It tears me apart to think that Robbie died believing I was mad at him for joining the Air Force.' His jaw trembled. 'I mean, I didn't go into law the way my father had hoped. I gave up an expensive education and took off into the outback to raise cattle and my father let me go without reproach. I – I should have known better. I didn't want to be the kind of man who held his son back from his dreams.'

'You didn't hold him back,' Emily said gently. 'When we were fighting, I might have suggested, in the heat of the moment, that you tried to stop Robbie from joining the RAAF. But that was the grief talking. I'm sorry I said that, Alex. I knew you were always going to back down, to give Robbie your blessing to do whatever he felt was right.'

She reached for her husband's hand, felt it tremble, and she wrapped her fingers around his, desperate now to reassure him. 'I'm sure Robbie knew it, too.' She squeezed his hand more tightly. 'Alex, Robbie did know. He always knew you loved him.' Her voice cracked as she said this and then she was weeping again and Alex was pulling her into his arms and holding her close.

'My dearest, dearest girl.'

Looking up at him through her tears, she tried to smile.

'I hope you know I'll always love you, Emily.'

'When you were away for so long, I was beginning to wonder.'

'I'm sorry. I was a stubborn jerk. It was easier to spend long days on horseback than it was to come home and admit I was wrong.'

With a guilty start, Emily thought of Rolf. She wondered if Alex would mention their friend's role in his decision to return, and she was rather relieved when he didn't. As far as she knew, Rolf had left yesterday, flying to Brisbane first, en route for Washington.

Perhaps Rolf had rung Alex from Brisbane. Obviously, he had said only enough to shake Alex without revealing everything. And that was how it should be. Must be. Some secrets were never meant to be shared. She was confident that Rolf would never betray her and she would have to come to terms with the choice she'd made that night.

She reached for her husband's hand, linked her fingers with his and squeezed. 'I'm so glad you're back, Alex.'

'So am I. We'll stop quarrelling now, won't we?'

Emily smiled. 'I hope so.'

Like someone coming out of a long sleep, she drew a deep breath and looked around her. They were still in the kitchen and the day outside was now bright and hot, the lake the same bleached blue as the sky. 'Would you like breakfast?' she asked. 'Or should we just wait till lunch now it's getting so late?'

But Alex wasn't worried about breakfast or lunch. He had a better idea, which was how they had ended up here in bed. In the middle of the day.

So they had behaved like honeymooners after all, Emily realised with amused satisfaction.

Alex rolled towards her now, traced the line of her shoulder. 'This seems like the perfect occasion to take you out to lunch.'

The suggestion had instant appeal, but Emily couldn't help feeling as if she'd forgotten her responsibilities – at the *Bugle*, or the CWA. And then she remembered. 'Oh, gosh. I almost forgot that Jess is coming this afternoon.'

Alex frowned. 'Who's Jess?'

'A new girl in town. The one who phoned this morning. A single mother. She works at the Lilly Pilly and she's made friends with Chloe, our new journalist.'

'And she wants to visit with you?'

'Yes.' What had Jess said? *There's something I need to tell you.*

'When's she coming?'

'A little after half past three.'

'Then we've plenty of time for lunch.'

***

Finn had no idea what to expect when he pulled up outside the *Bugle* office. His short trip to Thailand had been a roller-coaster, the tension of the events there made so much worse by the knowledge that he'd abandoned Bree at the crucial start to their promised holiday together.

So much had happened in such a short time – the meetings with Ben, with Doug Brady and Jack O'Brien, who was putting the finishing touches on plans for the final arrests. It was surreal to be back so soon, looking down the familiar street with its quaint shops and cottages and carefully tended footpaths.

From here he could see kids, freed from school for the long summer holidays, playing cricket on the spare allotment beside the Community Hall. He saw old Ernie Cruikshank walking his dog past Ben Shaw's bakery, which still had the closed sign on the door. A middle-aged woman, her hair freshly coiffed, emerged from Tammy's salon.

Finn wished he could feel more triumphant. He had finally found Ben and there would soon be an end to the baker's disturbing disappearance and exile. But these victories were small compensation for the painful truth that he had deserted his daughter and had landed the entire responsibility for her onto Chloe.

He felt like a heel. A tired heel at that. He'd had little sleep in the past few days, but it was time to face the music.

With no idea what to expect, Finn wearily climbed out of the small hire car. He had not warned Chloe of his arrival. She would have felt obliged to come down to Cairns to pick him up, losing precious hours out of her day, and he'd already made her life difficult enough.

'Dad!'

A delighted shriek reached him, even before he got to the office door. His daughter burst onto the footpath and launched herself at him like a small missile.

'You're back,' Bree cried, hugging him hard.

Finn hugged her in return, but his throat was suddenly so tight and raw he couldn't speak. Through the open doorway, he saw Chloe, inside the office, still sitting at her desk, watching them.

'How've you both been?' he managed to ask Bree when he'd cleared his throat. He hoped the news wasn't bad.

'We've had the *best* time ever.' Grabbing his hand, Bree pulled him into the office. 'Chloe and I have been swimming in the lake and we had a party and we've done an interview. *And* I've written my first ever news story and Chloe says it's *good*.'

Finn had never seen his daughter so excited. 'Your first news story, eh?'

'Yep.' Bree was clearly bursting with pride. 'Chloe says it's fine and I've written the headline and everything. Come and have a look.'

Now, with two hands at his back, Bree pushed him towards his own computer where a story on the screen was headed: *JOYOUS REUNION FOR COOPER*.

'Headline looks great.' Finn felt somewhat winded. 'Who's Cooper?'

'The cutest little black and tan dog. He went missing from the Burralea Nursing Home. Two kids found him – Sam and Milla Peterson – and Chloe and me went and interviewed them. They live on a farm, Dad, way up on top of a hill and I asked all the questions.' Bree paused to catch her breath. Her face was flushed, her eyes shining. 'It was so cool.'

'Seems like Chloe's taken very good care of you.'

As Finn said this, his gaze met Chloe's. Her warm brown eyes were shimmering. With tears? Once again, he was sideswiped by unexpected emotion.

But then Chloe smiled. 'Welcome home,' she said.

'Thanks.' Finn dredged up a shaky smile of his own. 'It's good to be back.'

And he realised, for possibly the first time, that returning to this small office in this tiny country town really did feel like coming home.

***

It was almost four when Jess arrived at the Lake House in the little yellow bubble of a car that she had recently bought. She was looking surprisingly transformed, with her brown hair freed from its usual ponytail and hanging to her shoulders in a shining fall. She had also replaced her habitual jeans and T-shirt with a slim-fitting shift of green linen that brought out sea-green depths in her eyes.

The baby was dressed up, too, in a cute little pink floral dress with puffed sleeves and sweet smocking.

'Oh, don't you both look lovely,' Emily said as she greeted them.

She had the tea things ready on a tray and Alex was downstairs tinkering with the outboard motor of his little sailing boat. He hadn't used the boat in ages, of course, but now he wanted to get it going again and to make the most of opportunities to sail before the wet season arrived.

'Sorry I'm a bit late,' said Jess. 'Willow was asleep when I went to collect her from day care and then I needed to feed her.'

'That's fine.' Emily grinned at the rosy-cheeked, bright-eyed baby. 'You look wide awake now, don't you, Willow?' Then to Jess, 'Come inside and make yourselves comfortable.'

'Thanks.' Jess took a plastic container from her capacious shoulder bag, which no doubt held all the paraphernalia that young mothers found necessary. 'I brought some baklava.'

Emily laughed. 'That's very wicked of you. Wicked in the best sense, of course. I'm very partial to baklava.'

'Ellen at the Lilly Pilly made it. It's become her specialty,' Jess said as she followed Emily into the lounge room. 'Oh, wow!'

Like many previous guests, Jess stood in open-mouthed admiration of the view provided by the floor to ceiling windows of the tree-dotted shore and the lake beyond.

'I knew it would be lovely here, but that view's beyond amazing.'

'Yes, we're lucky,' Emily murmured as she had so many times before. 'It's a pity it isn't a nicer day, though.' Thick grey clouds loomed, darkening the normally silvery water to a dull gunmetal grey.

Emily tapped the box Jess had brought. 'I'll just pop this on the tea tray in the kitchen.'

She wasn't sure if the 'talk' Jess had planned was serious enough to start without waiting for the kettle to boil, so she returned quickly to find Jess still admiring the view. With Willow in her arms, Jess had moved a little closer to the window. From this angle, Alex could be seen leaning over the stern of his boat, wrangling a fixture on the outboard motor with a spanner.

Jess turned, looking suddenly worried. 'Is – is that your husband?'

'Yes.'

'I thought he was away.'

'He's come back from out west. Just arrived this morning.'

As Emily said this, Alex straightened and glanced towards the house.

'He's very distinguished-looking, isn't he?' Jess said, watching him.

Emily smiled. 'I've always liked to think so.'

'Your son looked like him.'

'My son?' Emily had to reach for the back of a chair to steady herself. 'You – you knew Robbie?'

'I did, yes.' Jess hugged Willow a little more tightly. Her mouth worked as she struggled to smile. 'That's why I've come. I wanted to tell you that I met Robbie in Sydney. I – I knew him quite well, actually.'

Emily stared at her in stunned amazement. This was the second shock she'd received today and she now felt as if she'd fallen into a kind of stupor. Several seconds must have passed before she gave a dazed shake of her head. 'But – but you've been here for weeks and you've never said anything.'

'I know. I'm sorry. You must think I'm very strange. It's just —' Jess swallowed and then blinked, as if she were fighting tears. 'I – I wasn't ready to talk about it.'

Emily recalled the telephone conversation this morning. *There's something I need to tell you.*

Watching the young woman as she stood there now, with her baby, both so smartly dressed, while nervously delivering this startling news, Emily was stirred by an unsettling presentiment. Goosebumps broke out of her arms. Afternoon tea no longer mattered.

'If you're going to talk about Robbie, I think my husband would like to hear it, too,' she said. 'Do you mind if I fetch him?'

'No, I guess not.' Jess gave a shrug, but her demeanour was anything but casual.

'I'll be back in just a moment.' Emily indicated an armchair. 'Take a seat.'

It wasn't a command, but Jess obeyed rather meekly and Emily left, her heart racing as she hurried through the house and down the back stairs. Outside, a wind had picked up, rustling through the trees and tossing clouds across a darkening sky.

'Alex,' she called, but he had his head down, tinkering with the motor again, and he didn't seem to hear her. Emily crossed the grass. 'Alex.'

He turned, looked back over his shoulder.

'Can you come upstairs for a moment?' she asked him. 'Jess – the young woman who's come to visit me – she says she knew Robbie.' Emily came a little closer and lowered her voice even though Jess couldn't possibly hear her. 'She's come to tell me something about Robbie, but it's a little weird, Alex. I've known her for weeks and this is the first time she's mentioned Robbie. I just thought I'd like to have you there, too, to hear whatever she has to say.'

Alex was frowning as he wiped his hands on an old piece of rag. 'It does sound rather strange.'

'Will you come?'

'Of course.'

'She has a baby.' Emily couldn't hold back the note of warning in her voice.

'A baby?' The creases in Alex's forehead deepened. 'You don't think —'

'I don't know what to think. I'm trying not to think, actually.' Emily nodded towards the house. 'Come on. We'd better not keep her waiting.'

A chilly numbness descended as Emily returned to the house with Alex following close behind. In the kitchen, he stopped to wash his hands properly at the sink, but he didn't bother to remove his boots.

When they came into the lounge room, Jess was in the armchair and Willow was sitting on the floor in front of her, surrounded by a scattering of brightly coloured plastic toys. The baby grinned when she saw them and lifted her arms.

'Gaaa!' she cried, showing two little white teeth in her lower gum.

Alex halted for a moment and eyed the child with wary reserve, then he took command, striding across the room. 'Hello,' he said warmly. 'I'm Alex. And I believe you're Jess.'

'Yes.' Jess looked a tad intimidated, but she held out her hand.

'Pleased to meet you, Jess.' They shook hands. Then Alex looked down at the baby. He was well over six feet and, to Emily, the distance between the man and the little one seemed enormous. 'And this is your daughter?'

'Yes,' Jess said again. 'Her name's Willow.'

'Willow?' A reaction that might have been surprise or amusement flashed in Alex's eyes. No doubt he was out of touch with recent trends in baby names, but he quickly covered his response. 'Hello, Willow.'

The baby had spied Alex's brown leather riding boots, and now she was crawling towards them.

'I don't think you want to play with those,' he said, stepping quickly away from her chubby, searching fingers. 'God knows what they've brought back from the cattle yards.'

But with the delicious prospect of the boots suddenly removed, Willow looked around her, opened her mouth and gave a lusty wail.

'Oh, dear, what a noise,' Jess soothed, swooping down to gather up her daughter and drop a kiss on her cheek.

Emily found herself chiming in, keen to rekindle the little girl's smiles. 'Hey, Willow, why don't you show us how you can clap hands?'

Miraculously, the crying stopped. Tears still glistened on Willow's lashes, but already she was beaming as she patted her little palms together.

'Clever girl!' Emily cried, and despite the strain of the occasion, she found herself once again enchanted, just as she'd been at Chloe's party.

Jess sat down again, with Willow now restrained on her knee. She gave her a toy zebra to play with, while Emily and Alex sat on the sofa opposite her.

With peace restored, Emily took a calming breath. Outside, however, the weather was growing wilder. Leaves were flying through the air and the wind whipped small whitecaps on the lake. Thunder rumbled. A storm was very close.

'So,' Emily said to Jess. 'You were going to tell us how you knew Robbie.'

Jess nodded and patted Willow's back, an action that Emily suspected calmed Jess as much as it soothed her daughter.

'My father's in the RAAF,' Jess said. 'So I've been to plenty of social events at the base over the years. I – ah – met Robbie at a Christmas party two years ago.'

Emily deliberately avoided doing calculations in her head, but with the baby there in front of them, she couldn't help wondering.

'Robbie and I got on really well,' Jess said. 'Actually, we got on *incredibly* well. I thought he was – wonderful.' Tears shone in her eyes and she tried to smile. 'It seemed we just clicked right from the start and it wasn't long before we were seeing each other as often as our jobs would allow.'

A stone lodged painfully in Emily's throat. Robbie had mentioned a girl, but he'd spoken so casually she'd assumed it wasn't serious. Beyond the window, the rain arrived in a grey wall, scudding across the lake towards them.

With her lips pressed together, Jess drew a deep breath and released it. She said, 'When I realised I was pregnant, we were going to announce our engagement, but then Robbie's deployment order came through, so we decided to wait until —' Now her mouth pulled out of shape as she struggled to keep control.

Emily, poised on the edge of the sofa, felt the lump in her throat swell to bursting point. Beside her, Alex was as still as a mountain.

Jess blinked several times before she managed to continue. 'We decided to wait,' she said again. 'It was Robbie's decision. He wanted to wait till he was back from Syria, so he could bring me up here. He was only supposed to be away for two months and he wanted me to meet you, and vice versa, before we made any kind of official announcement.'

Now rain lashed at the windows, almost obscuring the view, and Emily's urge to weep was so strong, she had to press a fist to her mouth to hold the sobs back. She was thinking of Robbie, falling in love with this girl and flying off to Syria, knowing he was to become a father. Never seeing his daughter, just as her father had done when he'd gone to Korea. History repeating itself.

'So Willow is our granddaughter,' said Alex, stating the obvious, as Jess searched in her huge bag and found tissues.

Jess nodded and wiped at her eyes. 'I'm sorry. I know it must be a shock for you.'

'It certainly is,' he said.

Emily was still too choked to speak. She was remembering the evening at Chloe's party, when she'd got down on the floor to play with Willow. Most especially, she was remembering the instant rapport she'd felt, the delightful connection to the engaging little girl. At the time, she'd fiercely wished for a grandchild of her own.

Now, the knowledge that this sweet, cheeky cherub was Robbie's daughter brought joy and heartbreak in equal quantities. Her longing to sweep across the room and gather Willow into her arms was almost overwhelming.

She looked to Alex to see how he was coping, but his face was a stern mask, giving away nothing.

'I don't believe you came to Robbie's funeral,' he said.

Jess shook her head. 'I heard that you wanted a very private funeral up here.'

'Perhaps if we'd known about you —' Alex began, but then he stopped, possibly aware that he was pushing.

'I'm sorry I didn't get in contact at the time,' Jess said.

'You've been in Burralea for several weeks now? You have a job here? In the local café?'

Jess swallowed. 'Yes.'

Alex was frowning again. 'And you previously had a job in Sydney?'

'I was a physiotherapist in Sydney.' Quickly, Jess added, 'I know it must seem very peculiar to you. You must be wondering why I've only approached you now, when I met Emily some weeks ago.'

This was, of course, the question Emily had been dying to ask.

'My parents thought my plan was crazy, too,' Jess went on. 'Dad wanted to get in touch with you even before Willow was born, but eventually, he and Mum backed off and let me do things my way. You see – I felt I needed to know a bit more about you before I introduced Willow. I'm afraid I – I was scared about how you might react.'

For the first time, Emily spoke up. 'You were worried we'd be terribly possessive and make all sorts of demands?'

'Something like that, yes. But I think it was also because of how much I loved Robbie.' Again, Jess tried to smile, but couldn't quite manage it. 'What we had was special and private,' she continued bravely. 'When he was in Syria I was writing to him every day, and he was writing to me, and then it just stopped.' Her lips trembled again. 'I used to have my phone out all the time in case he rang. When I – I lost him, I felt so cheated. Willow was all I had left, and I wasn't sure I could be generous enough to share her.'

To Emily, it made an awful kind of sense.

She looked to Alex, who no longer appeared so stony, and she could see that he was starting to accept the astonishing news. Then she looked again to tawny-haired Jess with her dear little dark-haired baby daughter, and her heart gave an unexpected little skip.

But oh, poor, darling Robbie.

The new knowledge that her wonderful son would never meet his sweet little girl overwhelmed her and she couldn't hold back her tears.

'I'm sorry.' Jess was weeping now, too.

'No, don't be sorry. We're grateful to you, Jess. Aren't we, Alex?'

To her relief, her husband nodded.

'I miss him so much.'

'Of course you do, my dear.' This came from Alex and was spoken with surprising gentleness.

Wiping her eyes again, Jess took another deep breath. 'It's such a relief to have told you at last. You're not angry?'

Emily managed, despite the tears, to smile. 'How could we be angry, when you've brought Willow to us and she's so adorable? I really am very happy, Jess.' Her smile collapsed. 'But, oh, my God, this is also so sad.'

Almost in unison, they rose – Alex, Emily and Jess, with Willow in her arms – weeping, hugging and smiling all at once.

Jess handed Willow to Emily and, for the first time, she hugged the little girl, cherishing her baby-fresh smell and warm chubbiness. Her granddaughter. *Their* granddaughter.

She handed Willow to Alex. 'Meet your grandpa, Willow.'

Tears glittered in her husband's eyes as he hugged her and kissed her plump cheek. 'She's a little cutie,' he told Jess. Then he hugged Jess and kissed her cheek as well.

Jess smiled as she wiped at her eyes yet again. Soon they were all smiling. Willow wriggled to be allowed back on the floor. Alex let her down, then he went outside to remove his boots.

Coming back into the lounge in his socks, he said, 'Surely this calls for a celebration?' He looked towards Emily. 'Do we have champagne?'

'We do, indeed,' Emily said. It was supposed to be for Christmas, but he was right. They needed to open it now. Then she remembered. 'Jess, can you drink champagne if you're still breastfeeding?'

'I've been good for months,' said Jess. 'But I think this feels like an occasion when champagne is compulsory.'

So their afternoon tea became champagne and baklava and, while the storm wore itself out and rolled away, the trio talked and talked.

Jess told them more about her family and the job she'd left behind in Sydney. She explained that she was living with a second cousin here in Burralea.

She talked about Robbie, telling his proud parents how popular he'd been with his RAAF mates. How she and Robbie had both loved the outdoors. Whenever they could, they'd escape the city, often sailing on Sydney Harbour, or hiking in the Blue Mountains.

'My plan is to stay in Burralea for six months,' she told them. 'After that, I'm not sure. My parents expect me back in Sydney, of course, and I hadn't really expected to like it here, but —' She smiled wryly. 'Nobody warned me about country towns and how they find a way into your heart.'

Emily invited Jess to stay on for an early evening meal, but Willow was tiring and starting to whinge.

'Little madam can become ear-splitting if she gets too worked up,' Jess said. 'And we wouldn't want to outstay our welcome.'

So, with promises to come again, she drove off, while Emily and Alex stood together, watching her little car trundle along the dirt track that wound through the trees.

'My goodness,' Emily said as the car finally disappeared around a bend. 'What a day it's been.'

'Extraordinary.' Alex slipped an arm around her shoulders. 'You must be exhausted.'

'So must you. You were driving all night.'

'Yes, I'm tired, all right.'

Emily sank her head onto his shoulder. 'Thank heavens you came back. I'm not sure I could have coped with this afternoon without you. And you might have missed meeting Willow.'

'Funny name, isn't it?' he said.

'I rather like it. I suppose I'm used to it now, but willows are beautiful trees. I've always loved them. And the name has a certain poetry.'

Alex smiled. 'I can see you're quite smitten.'

'I believe I am.'

Their smiles were broad as they walked, with their arms around each other, back to the house.

'I wonder what your mother will make of this?' Alex asked as they reached the top step.

'I don't know,' said Emily. 'I've been wondering about that, too. She adored Robbie. I hope it's not too much of a shock for her.'

'If it is, she probably won't let on.'

CHAPTER THIRTY-NINE

By six the following evening, the latest edition of the *Burralea Bugle* had been emailed to the printers.

Finn stretched as he rose from his chair. 'That's a good job well done. I owe you one, Dolly.'

Chloe frowned. She knew Finn was probably still tired from his whirlwind trip, but surely he wasn't so wiped he'd forgotten her name? 'Dolly?'

He offered her a rueful smile. 'Every so often I need to remind myself of how damn supercilious I was when you first arrived here.'

Chloe was, actually, quite aware of Finn's change of heart regarding her journalistic abilities. Today, he'd told her several times that she was a lifesaver, that the paper was in really good shape. He'd also mentioned that Bree had raved last night about how wonderful she was.

'And I'm sure I haven't thanked you properly for taking such good care of Bree,' he said now. 'After we dropped you home, last night, all I heard from Bree was Chloe says this, and Chloe says that. And Chloe does it this way, Dad.'

'Bree's a sweetheart, Finn. She's so enthusiastic about everything, and fun to be with. I couldn't help liking her. It's no wonder we got on well.'

'She told me how you helped with – you know —' He stopped, looked a tad embarrassed.

'The poor girl,' Chloe said. 'The period was such a shock for her.'

'Yeah. I can't believe you copped that.'

'It worked out fine, thankfully. And it seems to be all over already, for now.'

'You handled everything so brilliantly, Chloe. Hell, you even threw a party. I'm so grateful. I'm sure I owe you dinner. How about the pub?'

This was unexpected.

'Will Bree join us?' Bree had spent the day on the Drummonds' cattle property with Alice and their little boy, Charlie. Apparently, Finn had been inundated with offers to help entertain his daughter. Not only Alice Drummond, but Emily Hargreaves, Moira Briggs and Gina from the Lilly Pilly had all called to let him know they were happy to help.

'She's sleeping over at the Drummonds',' Finn told Chloe now. 'They have ducklings due to hatch at any hour and she couldn't bear to leave.'

Chloe was relieved to hear that it was Bree's choice to sleep over. She knew how absolutely overjoyed the girl had been by her father's return, and she was a little worried that Finn might have offloaded her far too readily.

She teased him gently. 'You'll have to watch out. Your daughter's being seduced by country living. She loved it when we went out to the Petersons' dairy farm, too.'

'Yeah. I suspect she's already fantasising about marrying a farmer or a grazier when she grows up.'

'Or having a farm of her own.'

At this, he gave a sheepish smile. 'Of course.' Then he picked up his phone, checked it and slipped it into his pocket.

Chloe wondered if she should warn Finn that Bree might not be thrilled to leave Burralea at the end of the summer holidays, but she decided he was astute enough to work that out for himself.

Now he slid her a lazy smile. 'So, how about dinner?'

It took considerable effort to drag her gaze away from that tempting smile. Chloe knew she had to keep her wits about her now. While Finn had been in Thailand, she'd decided that their casual arrangement must come to an end.

For one thing, sleeping with him no longer felt casual, which was a pretty clear danger signal. More importantly, Finn needed to concentrate on his relationship with Bree.

Chloe had seen the girl's thin arms clinging so very fervently to Finn's waist as she'd greeted him yesterday. Bree adored her dad and, after years of mistakenly believing he wasn't fit for fatherhood, Finn needed to devote these summer holidays to rebuilding his confidence, establishing a loving connection with his child.

He certainly didn't need the complication of an office affair. Which, sadly, was all his out-of-hours dalliance with Chloe really amounted to.

'You were going to give me the full story about Ben,' she said. Today, there had only been time for Finn to pass on the barest details. 'But you wouldn't want to do that at the pub where we might be overheard.'

'I thought we could save that for later.'

Later. Chloe's skin flamed as if Finn had already touched her, and her mind raced ahead, anticipating the bliss of spending *later* in the evening with him.

But no, she had just vowed to be sensible. Even as her imagination tempted and teased, she shook her head.

He frowned. 'Bad idea?'

'A very bad idea,' she said quietly.

She saw the rise and fall of his chest as he took this in. She hoped that she didn't have to spell it out that she wasn't really the right candidate for casual sex. She didn't want to admit that for her, their relationship had reached a kind of tipping point. If she wasn't careful, she would find herself in too deep and once again broken-hearted.

It was time to step back.

'You're worried about Bree,' Finn suggested.

Bree was only part of the problem, but Chloe said, 'Of course.'

'I've already told you she adores you.'

'Bree likes me as a friend, Finn, as a companion perhaps. But that doesn't mean she'd like to find me in her father's bed.'

Pushing away from his desk, he stood, hands on hips, staring at a spot on the opposite wall. Eventually, he let out a heavy sigh. 'You're right, of course.' He said this quietly, and then he turned back to her and smiled, sadly. 'Damn it.'

And damn him for smiling at her like that. 'At least it was nice while it lasted,' she said.

'Nice, eh?'

Finn looked affronted, but Chloe wasn't about to pander to his ego.

'That's the word I'm choosing, yes.'

For the longest time, he stared at her, his dark eyes sober and thoughtful. Eventually, he said, 'I definitely owe you one, Chloe, so if it can't be dinner – how about Ben's story? You can write the exclusive. Sell it to one of the major syndicates.'

She almost choked. She couldn't believe Finn would trust her with such an important story, a story he'd scooped.

'That – that's incredibly generous.' Too generous, surely?

He shrugged. 'It'll be quite a coup to have on your CV.'

Her CV? A shiver skittered down her spine. 'I wasn't planning to leave just yet.'

'No, but one day . . .'

Chloe couldn't think of anything sensible to say. It was crazy that she felt utterly wretched, as if she'd suffered a terrible loss. Finn was making a casual observation about the future and he was being sensible about their relationship. And so was she. They weren't having dinner. There would be no *later*.

It was exactly what she had asked for.

But now she realised with a sudden chilling clarity that calling things off with Finn had achieved very little. The tension, the memories of those blissful nights, would always be there. Perhaps he realised it too.

She half thought he might go all alpha male on her, ignore their sensible agreement, and haul her into his arms. Instead, he lifted a hand and ran his fingers through his thick, dark hair.

'Look, we're both tired,' he said. 'This probably isn't the right time to have this discussion. We'll set aside time tomorrow and I'll give you the lowdown on Ben's story. Okay?'

'Yes, sure.' After a longish beat, Chloe remembered to add, 'Thank you.'

Chloe had to pass Tammy's salon on her way home. The curtains hadn't been drawn and through the glass in the shop's French doors, she could see Tammy at the counter, pen in hand, leaning over a hefty book, no doubt checking her appointments for the lead-in to Christmas.

Chloe tapped on the glass and Tammy spun around quickly, her posture rigid, her eyes huge and tense. After peering for a second or two, she must have recognised Chloe and her shoulders relaxed. She gave a quick smile and a wave and came to open the door.

'Hi.' Tammy looked thinner than ever and her eyes were pink and red-rimmed.

Chloe opened her arms. 'Oh, Tammy, you poor thing. This tension must be killing you.'

'Almost.' Tammy sank into Chloe's hug, clinging to her for a moment or two before stepping back to let her inside.

'Finn says it should be all over in another day or so,' Chloe said.

'I know, I know.' Tammy closed her eyes and her mouth twisted into a rueful smile. 'I keep telling myself that, over and over, but it's scary. Almost too good to be true.'

'Yes, I imagine it must feel like that, but you've been strong for so long, Tams, you just have to hang in there for a few more days.'

Opening her eyes again, Tammy said, 'So you know I've had to keep everything under my hat all this time?'

Chloe nodded. 'Finn hasn't had time to tell me everything yet, but I think I've got the gist of it.' She'd been floored to hear that all along, Tammy had known where Ben was. It was incredible.

'There've been times when my poor head nearly exploded,' Tammy said.

'I can imagine. And I'm sure I didn't help, coming to you with my nosy questions.'

'I very nearly told you the whole story that night. I felt I could trust you and it was so tempting to just spill my guts. But then I realised it might have made me feel better, but it wouldn't have been fair to burden you with my awful secret.'

Chloe wondered if she would have been so considerate under such difficult circumstances. 'You've been bloody amazing,' she said.

'And thank God I can talk about it with you now.' Tammy smiled. 'Thanks for popping in.'

'Actually, I was going to ask you if you had plans for dinner. I wondered if you might like to have something at my place?'

'At your flat?'

'Yes.'

'So you're living there again, now that Finn's home?'

'Yes, of course.' Chloe hoped her ridiculous disappointment didn't show, and she was grateful when Tammy didn't persist with this line of questioning. 'I was just going to throw together a simple vegetarian pasta. And I thought you might like a little company.'

'I'd adore *your* company,' Tammy said warmly. She looked back to the books she'd left open on the counter. 'I was about to make a list of products I need to order, but I can leave that till the morning.'

'No, you finish what you need to do, and I'll get started on a sauce. Pop down whenever you're ready.'

'Okay. Lovely. I'll grab a bottle from the pub.'

'No need.' Chloe grinned. 'I have all the essential supplies.'

Twenty minutes later, Chloe's little kitchen was redolent with tomatoes and herbs. Softly, in the background, a compilation of popular music played.

Tammy, wineglass in hand, was perched on a stool at the kitchen bench, talking at first about Bree and Finn, asking questions and sharing observations about how important this summer reunion must be for them. To Chloe's relief, Tammy didn't quiz her too hard about her own relationship with Finn. And it wasn't long before the conversation veered to Ben.

'The thing that's got me puzzled about Ben's story,' Chloe said, 'is why he had to be whisked away to Thailand. Why couldn't he have just been hidden in Australia?'

'Apparently it was just too dangerous for the Feds to leave Ben in Australia. Not only dangerous for him, but for the undercover cop who saved his life.'

'Wow. So his appearance on TV must have really worried them.'

'Yeah, I imagine they were shitting themselves.'

Chloe dropped a good handful of spaghetti into a large pot of boiling water. 'But how did he actually get to Thailand? I mean, how on earth did he slip through Customs and everything?'

'Seems it was all very hush hush, a bit like something out of a movie,' said Tammy. 'Ben was given this code – "Sunshine". He had to ring a number they gave him and simply say "Sunshine" and the Feds knew exactly what to do next. They told him where they would pick him up, and he was allowed to ring me, as long as he was sure I could be trusted.'

Tammy rolled her eyes at this, then took a quick sip of her drink before she went on. 'Ben was allowed one more phone call from Thailand and that was when he told me the rest. Apparently, some middle-aged guy drove up from Cairns. He arrived on the rainforest road in a truck like a delivery van and beeped his horn three times. Ben came out of hiding and was told to climb in the back. It was set up with a couple of beds and a little kitchen. And Ben had to stay hidden there, while the guy drove him all the way to Darwin playing country and western music the whole way. Poor Ben.'

'I take it he doesn't like country and western?'

'Can't stand it. He's a beach boy at heart.'

They both smiled.

'At least he was safe,' said Chloe.

'Yeah, he reckons he was so relieved he wasn't going to be shot, he climbed into that van and bawled like a baby.'

This was a sobering thought.

'So, what happened in Darwin?' Chloe asked next, as she gave the softening pasta a stir.

'Some kind of Malaysian cargo boat was waiting for them and it took Ben all the way to Thailand. That was the best bit, apparently, because Ben loves the sea and the weather was fine. He had a small cabin to himself and he helped the cook in the galley, so he had a pretty good voyage, really.'

While the whole of Burralea fretted and searched. Chloe kept that unhelpful thought to herself. 'Arriving in Thailand must have been tricky, though.'

Tammy nodded. 'Someone from the Federal Police was there to meet the boat. Ben reckons you'd never pick the guy for a Fed – he looks more like an accountant or some kind of desk jockey. But he had a Thai official with him in an impressive military uniform, and they just walked Ben through Customs and Immigration and no one tried to stop them.'

'So he didn't need any paperwork?'

Tammy shrugged. 'I might be wrong, but that's the way it seems, as far as I can tell. Ben was driven to some beachside hotel and told to keep to himself, but otherwise, he could act normally, like a tourist.'

Chloe nodded. 'Ben certainly looked like he'd been in the surf when we saw him on TV.'

'Yeah.'

'Finn told me it's all connected to one of the largest ice-producing rings in the country. Apparently, there's one crim, Norman Chrysler, who has a particularly murderous reputation, but I think he's already in custody. So there's just a bit more work to weed out a corrupt low-level officer and they'll be able to wrap up the operation.'

'I bloody well hope so.' Tammy inspected her empty wineglass. 'Mind if I help myself to a drop more?'

'Of course not, but don't get up. I'm closer.' Chloe fetched the chilled bottle from the fridge and topped up their glasses. Turning back to the stove, she added a small mountain of chopped parsley and basil to the simmering sauce of tomatoes, olives and capers.

'That smells amazing,' said Tammy.

'The spaghetti's just about ready.'

'Are you going to throw it against the wall to test it?'

Chloe laughed. 'I've done that once or twice, in my old flat in Sydney, just for fun. But with Moira Briggs as my landlady, I think I'll show these walls more respect.'

'Fair enough. Moira works her butt off for this community, but I'm sure it pays to keep in her good books.'

'That reminds me,' said Chloe. 'Moira gave me a maidenhair fern and I left it at Finn's place. I'll have to make sure I remember to get it safely back.'

Tammy leaned forward, elbows on the kitchen bench, her smile conspiratorial. 'So, if you don't mind me asking, what's the story with you and Finn?'

Chloe hesitated, which she knew was a dead giveaway, but she couldn't help it. She was feeling rather fragile about Finn this evening.

'Sorry.' Tammy winced. 'I'm getting too nosy.'

'No, it's okay.' Chloe was sure she would feel better if she told the truth, but she concentrated on lifting out a strand of spaghetti as she spoke, so she could avoid looking Tammy in the eye. She broke the strand to test it. 'This is cooked. How about I serve up first?'

'Sure, what can I do?'

Chloe handed her a couple of place mats and a handful of cutlery. 'Would you mind putting these on the table?'

Tammy jumped to oblige and the subject of Finn was dropped – for the time being, at least. The background music had moved onto Eva Cassidy singing 'Fields of Gold'. Chloe heaped spaghetti and sauce onto her favourite pottery dinner plates, and added shaved parmesan.

'Oh, wow.' Tammy patted her flat stomach. 'I've just realised I'm starving.'

They settled at the little dining table with their laden plates and glasses of wine, and for a while their chatter was reduced to murmurs of appreciation from Tammy. Chloe, also enjoying the simple pasta and wine, took a deep breath and consciously relaxed, as she let the breath go.

Watching her, Tammy said, 'Are you okay, sweetie?'

'Yes, thanks.' Chloe tried for a convincing smile.

'Is this where I dare to ask again about Finn? You can tell me to pull my head in.'

'It's okay.' Chloe was sure it was best to satisfy Tammy's curiosity and be done with it. 'There *was* a bit of a "thing" happening with Finn and me, but it wasn't serious, and it's over now.'

Tammy's mouth twisted into a thoughtful grimace as she wound her fork into the spaghetti. 'I guess it could be tricky while Bree's staying with him.'

'Exactly. Bree needs Finn's full attention. But he's also had huge issues to deal with since his wife and little son died. It's the sort of thing you can never get over, really, and I honestly don't think Finn's ready for anything but a casual fling.'

'Which is not much help for you, if you're hoping to start a family.'

Too true. And after spending just a few short days with Bree, Chloe's mothering instincts had come rushing, like a geyser, to the surface. She and Bree had got on exceptionally well, and Chloe knew that she'd done a good job of caring for her.

As a bonus, now, her ex-boyfriend's cruel and taunting question about her suitabilty for motherhood no longer had the power to hurt.

Of course, no mother was perfect, but most women tried their very best, and Chloe knew she could answer with confidence. *Yes, Jason, I'd be a fine mother. Damn you, I'd be a bloody great mum.*

And she desperately wanted a baby. In her arms, in her life. Keeping her awake at night. A tiny person who needed and loved her without question.

Now, more than ever, her longing to be a mother was deep and urgent.

And Tammy was still waiting for her answer.

Chloe tried for a smile, but it felt a little strained. 'I really want a baby,' she said. 'But I certainly wouldn't be starting a family with Finn. Even if we were serious, which we're not, and even if he didn't already have one daughter, which he finds more than enough to handle – he's had the snip.'

'Oh, well —' Tammy seemed, for once, to be lost for words. 'I guess that brings you back to IVF?'

CHAPTER FORTY

Ben Shaw arrived home without a fanfare. Tammy had been pre-warned by telephone and was waiting for him at Cairns airport, and their reunion was both tearful and joyous. They drove up the range and slipped quietly into town, closed the doors and drew the curtains.

Tomorrow there would be fuss with celebrations to follow. Finn would publish a spread in the *Bugle*. His agreement with Jack O'Brien not to break the story and jeopardise the investigation had resulted in an exclusive for the little country newspaper. Chloe, meanwhile, had prepared a story for the bigger newspapers, and radio and TV exposure could no doubt be expected. Emily Hargreaves had already volunteered the Lake House for a 'welcome home' party. An official and festive reopening of Ben's Bakery was also planned.

For this evening, however, Tammy and Ben wanted only each other's company and the chance to savour the peace of knowing a miracle had most definitely occurred. Their ordeal was finally over and they would be forever grateful to a brave young policeman codenamed Hawk.

***

Outside, it was a perfect starry night, and on the edge of town, in Finn's backyard, a crackling fire glowed. A pan of fried onions was being kept warm on the coals, while Finn and Bree cooked sausages over the flames, using long forks made from fencing wire. They planned to eat their sausages and onions slathered in tomato sauce and wrapped in bread.

Bree was beside herself with excitement.

'This is the best fun,' she enthused. 'So much better than cooking inside on a boring old stove in a boring old kitchen. And we don't even have to eat veggies. Gran would never let me eat sausages without veggies.'

Finn felt obliged to defend his obvious slackness. 'Onions are vegetables.'

'But they're so yummy, they don't count.'

He was well aware that his pre-teen daughter was testing the boundaries, but he decided he would tackle the veggie issue another time. 'Boring stoves in boring kitchens have their uses,' he countered.

'If it's raining, I guess.'

'Yes, you'll soon change your tune when the wet season arrives.'

But this evening, nothing could dampen Bree's enthusiasm. When she wasn't extolling the merits of cooking over an open fire, she chattered about her busy day.

Moira Briggs had come into her own, lining up a team of willing participants to entertain Bree. Moira had even photocopied a roster of engagements for Bree, keeping one on her desk and another taped on a wall in the *Bugle*'s office, so Finn knew where his daughter was at all times.

Bree seemed more than happy with the arrangement, especially as there was a little pocket money involved. Yesterday, she had tidied all the tourist brochures in the Progress Association office, and had then stuck stamps on a mountain of Christmas cards for

Moira before delivering them to the letterbox outside the post office. In Tammy's hairdressing salon, she'd swept floors and polished mirrors with bunches of rolled-up newspaper – 'not the *Bugle*, Dad' – and a little spray bottle of methylated spirits. And at the Lilly Pilly café, she'd gleefully helped Gina and Jess to put up Christmas decorations.

The town had embraced his daughter, and Finn's original fears that he would never be able to keep her occupied were a thing of the past. Even Emily had wanted to be involved. Today, she had arrived in her silver Volvo and had taken Bree away to Atherton for a Christmas shopping spree. And this evening, Bree had shared with her father the astonishing news that little baby Willow, belonging to Jess from the Lilly Pilly, was actually Emily's granddaughter.

Bree couldn't supply details of how this amazing relationship had come to light. It was something Finn would have to discreetly investigate.

'But we had the best time, Dad. It was so much fun buying Willow's Christmas presents. We got this toy smartphone with all kinds of buttons to press. It plays music and makes animal sounds and everything. And we got these little ducks that flash coloured lights when they float in the bath. And the cutest little dress with red and white spots for Willow to wear on Christmas Day.'

Guiltily, Finn remembered that he had given little thought to Christmas gifts. His parents had opted to stay in Townsville, happy to pass the festive season very quietly, but he would make sure to send them gifts. And he should buy something for Bree. And for Chloe.

Chloe.

Finn's normally clear thinking clouded whenever he considered Chloe. He knew she'd been sensible to hold him at bay. An office romance was fraught with complications. But already, he felt that stepping away from such a liaison was not as easy or straightforward as it should have been.

Fortunately, Bree's arrival and the Christmas break offered him the perfect excuse to defer a close examination of his finer feelings for his work colleague. But he certainly owed Chloe for the way she'd so brilliantly looked after Bree, and his Christmas gift should reflect his appreciation.

Perfume would be easy, but probably too personal. Flowers, perhaps? Something exotic? Orchids or lilies? *But not a pot plant*, Finn thought with a wry smile, recalling the story of how Bree had been required to rescue Chloe's maidenhair fern.

In the past he had bought jars of gourmet chutney or marmalade for Emily and she'd always seemed delighted. But Chloe deserved something special. *French champagne?*

This was going to take some thought.

'What would you like for Christmas?' he asked Bree.

Sitting on the grass beside him with her thin arms wrapped around her bent knees, Bree grinned. 'A puppy?'

Oh, Bree. Finn saw his daughter's eager face and his heart sank. She couldn't take a puppy back to boarding school. 'Not this Christmas,' he said gently. 'What else would you like?'

Obviously disappointed, she shrugged. 'I don't mind. We're still going camping, aren't we? Down by the lake, like you promised?'

Bree turned to Finn, her eyes wide and searching, and he caught a flash of Sarah in the intent look on their daughter's face. His heart rocked, but not in the sickening way it might have done in the past, whenever he remembered his wife. A new kind of peace had settled in him since he'd been back to Thailand and, for that, he was extremely grateful.

'We'll definitely go camping,' he assured Bree. He couldn't break another promise. 'We can take the week between Christmas and New Year's. There's no edition of the *Bugle* that week.'

'The whole week?'

'Yes. The camping ground will probably be crowded, though.'

'That doesn't matter. Will we take your canoe?'

'Yes, of course.'

She hugged herself with excitement. 'Sam and Milla will probably be there.'

Finn frowned. 'Who are Sam and Milla?'

'The kids I wrote the story about. The ones who found Cooper, the lost dog. Sam told me he'd be camping at the lake.'

Finn felt a stirring of fatherly concern. 'How old's this Sam?'

''Bout my age.' Bree said this without a hint of coyness, and Finn supposed he should calm down. 'Will there be lots of kids, Dad?'

'Bound to be.'

'Cool!' Leaping to her feet, his daughter promptly performed a series of cartwheels over the lawn, demonstrating surprising athletic grace while heading, to Finn's relief, well away from the fire.

'Wow! How long have you been able to do that?' he asked, suitably impressed.

Bree gave another shrug. 'Ages.'

More than ever, he was painfully aware of his need to make up for lost time.

A rickety garden seat had come with the house, and they sat there now to eat their simple repast. The sausages and onions were suitably blackened and Bree declared them 'fantabulous'.

Finn marvelled that his daughter was so easy to please. He was sure pre-teen girls were supposed to be notoriously difficult and he feared this must be a passing fad. At any moment, Bree would turn into a sulky adolescent, who was bored by *everything*.

No doubt, he was currently enjoying a kind of honeymoon phase, where she saw Burralea as new and exciting. Soon she would wake up, the scales would fall from her eyes and she would see this place as a dull little town where nothing happened.

'Can Chloe come camping with us?'

To Finn's dismay, the mere mention of Chloe sent a shock wave zapping through him. The thought of her sharing a tent with them made his breathing snag.

'Dad?'

Bree was waiting for an answer.

'Chloe's going home to Sydney for Christmas.'

'That's a pity. I really like her. I'll miss her.'

'Yeah. Chloe's great.' Finn managed, with some effort, to keep his tone casual.

'I mean, I *really* like her,' Bree insisted and she was frowning at him now, watching him with a shrewd glint in her eyes that made him uneasy.

'That's . . . great.' Finn wasn't sure where this conversation was heading and he felt his way cautiously. 'She was wonderful, the way she looked after you.'

'She was amazing.'

'I'm trying to think of a decent thank-you present.'

'Jewellery,' Bree promptly announced, as if this was the obvious solution.

Finn shook his head. 'Bit over the top.'

'No way.'

'Don't worry,' he said before Bree offered more outlandish suggestions. 'I'll think of something.'

'Word on the street, Dad —'

'Excuse me? What did you just say?'

'Word on the street.'

'Where'd you hear a term like that?'

'I don't know.' Bree widened her eyes, innocent as a flower. 'It's what people say, isn't it?'

Not twelve-year-olds, surely? Finn sighed. 'So what's this word?'

'That you and Chloe are an item.'

Another zap ripped through Finn. Bloody hell. One minute his kid was doing cartwheels. The next she was talking like a thirty-year-old. 'I'm not going to ask who told you that,' he said sternly. 'But let it be a warning about country towns. You hear all sorts of gossip and half of it's nonsense.'

'Which half are you and Chloe in?'

Finn groaned. 'It's time you stopped asking questions that are none of your business.' He stood. 'And it's high time you had your shower and got ready for bed.' He knew he sounded like a parent who was losing control. He was out of practice at this fathering gig.

Abruptly, he began to collect plates and cooking gear to take inside. 'Come on,' he said over his shoulder.

To his relief, Bree didn't argue.

***

'Finn, I was hoping to take a day off next week, before I leave for Sydney.'

Chloe posed her question at the end of a busy week filled with Carols by Candlelight, Christmas markets, the launch of an activities program in the park for kids and celebrations for Ben's return. But while pre-Christmas wasn't the best time for her to squeeze in a visit to the fertility clinic in Cairns, she had reached a new desperation point.

If Finn was surprised by her request, however, he covered it quickly. 'Sure,' he said. 'Which day would you like?'

Chloe had, in fact, already rung the clinic and found there were only a couple of appointment slots available, so she'd made a tentative booking, hoping it would suit, and had even teed up with Jess to borrow her car. 'Next Wednesday?' she asked.

Finn nodded. 'Should be fine.' He smiled at her then. 'Christmas shopping?'

It was silly to feel nervous. 'Among other things, yes.'

Perhaps she wasn't convincing. Finn was watching her closely. 'Is everything okay, Chloe?'

'Of course,' she said too quickly.

His dark eyes narrowed and he continued to study her in nerve-racking silence. Eventually, he said, 'I can't help feeling that you and I have skipped an important conversation.'

Chloe tensed. She knew full well what Finn was referring to. Over the past week, the strain and edginess between them had been palpable. In the office, or when they had inadvertently met on the street, or at social events like Emily's 'welcome home' party for Ben, she had ducked and weaved, keeping as much distance between herself and Finn as possible.

Now, she had little choice but to try the same tactic again. 'Well, you know what it's like at this time of the year,' she said, as she gathered up her bag and her phone, preparing to leave. 'And it's even busier for you now that you have Bree here.' She shot him a smile, which was, regrettably, shaky. 'How is Bree? I've hardly seen her these past few days.'

'She's fine, thanks, having a ball.'

'Do you think she'll find it hard to leave Burralea when the time comes?'

'She's already begging me to let her stay. I've told her we won't make any decisions until after New Year's. She might get bored yet and change her tune.'

'That sounds like a good plan.'

Finn was standing now with his feet comfortably apart and his arms folded, positioning himself in the middle of the small office, more or less blocking Chloe's exit. 'Bree's also been begging me to invite you over for a meal sometime. A barbecue, perhaps. I thought maybe tomorrow night?'

In a perfect world, Chloe would have adored a Saturday evening at home with Finn and his winsome daughter. Even now, when she knew how very unwise it would be to become more emotionally entangled with that pair, a foolish inner voice also whispered how much fun it could be.

But it was time to be strong. 'I don't think that's a good idea, Finn.'

He frowned. 'If I remember correctly, this is where our conversation stalled last time. I was inviting you to dinner and you were back-pedalling madly.'

Chloe dropped her gaze, before her eyes gave her away. 'That was because of Bree,' she said. 'I didn't want to give her the wrong idea.'

'Apparently she already has the quite definite idea that we're an item.'

Chloe gulped. 'But we're not. We shouldn't be.'

'Is that how you really feel, Chloe?'

She knew he was watching her intently.

Now her throat constricted, making it hard to breathe, and she also knew she was in danger of weakening. Facing Finn now, it was hard to remember why they shouldn't fall back into their deliciously exciting romance. But she had promised herself she wouldn't just drift indefinitely. It was time to take control of her future.

'I think it's sensible,' she said bravely. 'Office flings are inevitably a mistake.'

Finn stood rock still, but Chloe saw the movement of his throat as he swallowed. Her heart hammered and she longed to forget common sense, to sink against him, to have his arms come around her, holding her close.

Tears threatened.

A beat later, Finn moved towards her and she thought he might pull her into his arms. Instead, he touched her cheek – just one gentle brush of his knuckles – and his eyes betrayed a tenderness that tore at her heart. He said, 'I'd feel much better about being sensible if you didn't look so upset.'

Don't, she wanted to tell him. *Don't be lovely. Don't make this harder.* She drew a ragged, noisy breath and knew she could retreat no further. It was time to be brave, to be honest and tell him exactly how she felt. She only hoped she could do so without dissolving into a weeping puddle.

Another deep breath was necessary. 'The thing is,' she said. 'I assumed I'd be fine with a casual affair, but I've discovered I'm not very good at it.' When Finn looked puzzled, she clarified. 'At the casual part, I mean.' Then she blushed. She wasn't managing this very well, but she forced herself to continue. 'But – but I understand you're not ready for anything more – than casual.'

There. At least she hadn't burst into tears.

She didn't expect Finn to jump to correct her, to declare that a 'casual' arrangement didn't suit him either. But when he remained silent, Chloe was hit by a terrible sense of déjà vu. She found herself recalling her breakup with Jason. Jason hadn't wanted children. Finn was wary of a new commitment – *and* he had taken steps to ensure he could never be a father again.

It seemed she was forever doomed to need more from her lovers than they were able to give.

Several seconds ticked by before Finn spoke. 'Look, I hear what you're saying,' he said at last. 'And if you really want to call it quits, I won't argue. But —' A sigh escaped him. 'Things have been pretty crazy around here lately. Perhaps we could take the same advice I gave Bree?'

Chloe frowned. 'Sorry?'

'Maybe it wouldn't hurt to wait till after Christmas. See if you still feel —'

He left the sentence hanging and, in the silence that followed, Chloe knew that breaking up for the second time in one year was going to be even harder than the first. But she also knew that a few weeks couldn't change their insurmountable hurdles.

In the new year, she planned to embark on an IVF program. Her eggs would be fertilised by some unknown donor. Finn, meanwhile, would still be a grieving widower, working to forge a happier future with his daughter.

But she felt too emotionally exhausted to argue with him now, and although she was sure that nothing would change, she nodded. 'Okay.'

'Good.' Finn smiled. 'And you should definitely rethink tomorrow night's barbecue. If nothing else, it will get Bree off my back.'

CHAPTER FORTY-ONE

Bree was beside herself with excitement when she heard that Chloe was coming to their barbecue. She was dead keen to help with the preparations, had accompanied her dad to the supermarket and had been his kitchen hand, shelling peas and peeling carrots. And she'd even raked the leaves that had fallen in the backyard, marring the perfection of his newly mowed grass.

As the evening grew closer, Bree washed her hair and put on the new denim shorts and red and white–striped top that she'd bought during her shopping expedition with Emily. In a drawer in the kitchen dresser, she found a batik print tablecloth to cover the folding camp table that her dad set in the backyard near the fire pit. To decorate the table, she picked a fresh bunch of the yellow flowers that grew in the old concrete washing tub in a corner of the yard and she put them in a blue jug that she found on a shelf in the kitchen.

'Hey, that looks great,' Finn said when he saw what she'd done. 'You've got the decorating knack, Bree.'

Her chest swelled with pride.

And now, at last, the preparations were complete and it was time to pick up Chloe. Bree was bouncing with excitement as she bundled herself into the passenger seat in the Forester. She adored Chloe and she loved her dad deeply, and she was thrilled that her dad was different these days. Happier, calmer and much more willing to chat.

She suspected Chloe was somehow involved in this transformation. And so it seemed logical to Bree that her future could only be better and brighter if her father spent more time in Chloe's company.

Now, as they pulled up outside the Progress Association office, Chloe was ready and waiting just inside the door. She looked beautiful in a Christmassy green halter-neck dress, with her legs bare and her feet clad in sandals with sparkly green stones. Bree was out of the car as soon as it stopped, rushing with open arms to hug Chloe.

'You look fabulous,' she told Chloe.

Chloe laughed. 'So do you.' She touched a little shoulder frill on Bree's striped top. 'This is cute.'

'I bought it when I went shopping with Emily.'

Now her dad had come around the front of the car. He was looking pretty good too, with his hair neatly combed, and dressed in jeans and a navy-blue shirt with the sleeves rolled up to his elbows.

He kissed Chloe politely on the cheek, which was a bit disappointing for Bree, but they both did rather a lot of smiling, she was pleased to note. When they got back into the car, Bree insisted on having the back seat, leaving Chloe to sit in front with her dad for the short drive back to Cedar Lane.

Once home, they went inside. Chloe had brought a bowl of creamy French onion dip that she'd made and a box of crackers. Bree found a plate for the crackers. Finn took another plate from the fridge with the lamb chops that he planned to barbecue and they moved out to the backyard.

It was a perfect summer's evening. Shade from the trees along the fence line stretched over the grass and a gentle breeze wafted. Crickets hummed in the shrubbery and, above the whole scene, a spectacular sunset spread its pretty bloom over the sky. The camping table looked smart with its batik cloth and gleaming glasses waiting to be filled. A bucket of ice held white wine for Chloe, lemon squash for Bree – she would have liked Coke, but squash was fine – and beer for her Dad. The fire in the pit ringed by stones glowed and flickered.

Bree knew she was happier than she had been in a long, long time. Properly happy, all the way through. She loved her grandparents and she enjoyed their company, but in Townsville she had always been conscious of the father-shaped hole in her life.

Losing her mother and Louis had been beyond terrible, but somehow Bree had been just as sad to know that her father, her personal hero, was alive and had chosen to be absent.

But now he was here. Or rather she was here, living in the same house as him every day. Her dad was the last person to wish her goodnight and the first person to greet her in the morning. He hugged her often and at night they read her favourite books together.

During this past week, even though her dad was busy and Bree had spent more time with Mrs Briggs from the Progress Association or Gina at the Lilly Pilly, she had heard all sorts of wonderful comments about him. It seemed everyone in these parts seemed to have a good word for Finn Latimer, which was wonderfully reassuring.

Best of all, when Bree had told her father that she didn't want to go back to boarding school, he hadn't said that she must. He had given her another lovely hug and said he was going to think about it and he would make a decision in the new year.

So now, each night, Bree lay in bed and looked out at the stars and made a wish, always the same wish.

The barbecue meal was delicious – lamb chops with mint jelly, a yummy brown rice and pea salad, and steamed and buttered carrots smeared with Dijon mustard.

'I had no idea you were such a good cook,' Chloe told Finn.

Bree piped up, 'He spent ages and ages looking up recipes on the internet.'

With that, she took off, dancing excitedly over the grass, but as she spun past her dad, he caught her by the elbow.

'As the father whale said to the baby whale – just remember you're more likely to be harpooned when you're spouting.'

'Huh?' Bree stopped and stared at him as she tried to compute this. 'But it's wrong to hurt baby whales.' Then it dawned on her and she grinned. 'You mean I'm talking too much?'

'Exactly.'

But she simply laughed and danced away to perform a series of cartwheels over the grass.

Behind her, she heard her father say, 'I have no idea where she gets her energy from.' But his smile was fond as he said this, and Bree could see that he was happy. Bree only hoped that Chloe was happy too. Mostly Chloe seemed fine, but every so often she looked a little worried.

The evening darkened quite quickly and Finn lit a couple of fat candles. He hadn't made a proper dessert, but there was a dish of scrumptious chocolates wrapped in shiny paper in different pretty colours. Chloe had one chocolate and Bree had three, while she told Chloe all about their plans for camping at the lake between Christmas and New Year's.

'We might see Sam and Milla.'

'Yes, you probably will. That'll be fun.'

'And we'll take Dad's canoe.'

'How lovely.'

'Have you ever been camping?'

'No I haven't, actually. Well, only on a school camp and that doesn't really count.'

'Wish you could come with us.'

'Bree.' Her father's voice held a warning note. 'You know Chloe needs to see her own family for Christmas.'

Bree shrugged. It had been worth a try. Every so often her father and Chloe talked about boring grown-up stuff, mostly to do with the paper. Bree usually drifted away and practised her handstands, or did a cartwheel or three. When there seemed to be a break in their conversation, she danced back to them.

She flopped down on the garden bench beside Chloe. 'Guess what, Chloe?'

'What?'

'Dad and I found the most awesome house yesterday.'

'You've been househunting?' Chloe directed her question to Finn, who had moved to the barbecue to lift the uneaten chops onto a plate to take inside.

'We weren't exactly hunting,' he said. 'We more or less stumbled on the place by accident.'

Bree's jaw dropped. 'But you already knew the address, Dad. You saw it on the inter—'

'For Pete's sake, Bree —' For the first time, he looked annoyed.

Confused, Bree frowned at him. 'But can't I tell Chloe about the house?'

'We were just driving past,' he told Chloe now. 'And the house happened to be open for inspection.'

This was sort of true. 'So we went inside,' Bree chimed in blithely. 'I can tell Chloe that, can't I, Dad?'

'I think you already have.'

Bree took this as consent. 'The house was so cool,' she continued, avoiding her father's watchful eye. 'It's on the side of a hill and when you walk in off the street and through the front door, you can see right through to a deck that looks out at the view.'

'How lovely.'

'It's beautiful. You can see a little bit of the lake in the distance.

And there's four bedrooms and two bathrooms and the most perfect yard with a fence for having a dog.'

'Well, that's important, I'm sure.' Chloe smiled with her mouth, but her eyes looked sort of sad. 'It's fun to look at houses and to imagine yourself living there.'

'Yeah.' Bree had been imagining herself living there ever since she'd seen the house. She'd imagined having a dog to play with. A bitser would do – she wasn't fussy. She would take it for walks.

She had also pictured herself going to school here in Burralea and having friends like Sam and Milla Peterson. Once she started school she could have girlfriends for sleepovers in one of those lovely big bedrooms. And her dad would always be there. And perhaps Chloe could fit into the picture too.

'Would you like a top up?' Finn asked Chloe as he retrieved the wine bottle from the bucket of ice.

Chloe looked at her glass, which was empty. 'Actually, I don't think I will, thanks. I've probably had enough.'

'Maybe we could go inside and watch a movie now,' Bree suggested, remembering the movies she'd enjoyed with Chloe.

Her dad looked surprised.

Chloe looked worried. 'I'm not sure about a movie tonight, Bree. I'm actually a bit tired,' she said. 'It's been a big week.'

Bree was shocked. It wasn't much past eight-thirty.

'I can take you home any time you like,' her father was saying.

Dad??

'Thanks, Finn. It was a lovely meal. I really enjoyed it.'

This sounded, to Bree, as if Chloe was being polite, but really, she wanted to go home. And her father hadn't tried to talk her out of it, which was worrying. Bree had hoped that Chloe and her dad might relax and have a little more fun together, even become a bit romantic. But there was no sign tonight that they were anything more than people who worked together.

'If you don't mind, I will go now,' Chloe said. 'And grab an early night.'

Bree was watching the two of them carefully. It was hard to tell how her dad felt about this early departure. His face was kind of blank, but Chloe was biting at her bottom lip and looking strangely nervous.

Her dad collected the car keys from the kitchen counter. 'You coming for the ride, Bree?'

She made a quick decision and shook her head. 'I'll stay here. I think there's a movie just starting on TV.'

'Okay,' he said. 'I'll only be ten minutes.'

'You don't need to rush back. I'll be fine, Dad.'

He frowned at her severely, and looked as if he wanted to reprimand her. But he didn't.

Chloe came and kissed her. 'Goodnight, Bree. Thanks for a lovely evening.'

Bree threaded her thin arms around Chloe's neck and hugged her hard. 'I've missed you.'

'I know, sweetheart. I've been so busy. But I hear you've been incredibly helpful to all sorts of people.'

'But soon it will be Christmas and you're going away.'

'And then I'll be back straight after New Year's.'

Bree nodded. 'All right.'

'See you then.' Chloe kissed her again and Bree could smell her rather glamorous scent. She hoped her dad got to smell it, too, when he said goodnight to Chloe.

She followed them to the front door and stood in the pool of light that spilled onto the path and watched as they walked to the Forester that was parked out the front. Her dad opened the passenger door for Chloe. She got in and then he walked around to the driver's side.

As far as Bree could tell, they weren't talking at all. The motor roared, the lights came on and the Forester took off into the night.

Bree closed the door and went inside, found the remote and flicked on the television. She didn't mind if her dad took ages before he returned.

To her dismay, he was back in less than ten minutes.

CHAPTER FORTY-TWO

It was a Sunday afternoon when Emily and Alex met Jess, Willow and Chloe in the parking area outside the nursing home. Letting Izzie know that she had a great-granddaughter had required a certain amount of courage on Emily's behalf. There was no gentle way, really, of sharing such astonishing news.

As Alex had predicted, Izzie reacted calmly – on the surface, at least – although Emily was sure she had been rocked by the revelation. It hadn't been long, though, before Izzie asked to meet Jess and Willow. And then, somehow, Chloe had become involved. Izzie had, apparently, struck up quite a friendship with Chloe, had even agreed to let Chloe write a feature story about her wartime experiences for the *Bugle*.

'There was a time when a story about my pilot days might have annoyed Alex,' Izzie had commented to Emily. 'Rubbed him up the wrong way, you know. But your husband seems to have mellowed.'

Emily suppressed an urge to smile when she heard this. Perhaps the mellowing had been mutual, she decided. Her mother had even agreed to Chloe's suggestion that she should publish a photo of Izzie with her new great-granddaughter, as part of a series of little stories she was writing about the nursing home.

So. Here they were. It was to be quite an occasion. A proper afternoon tea. Everyone in the group, especially Willow, was smartly dressed, and Emily had made her mother's favourite ginger fluff sponge. Now she carried this carefully, as the little group processed down the hallway to the dining room, which had been chosen as a suitable venue for such a gathering.

Izzie was ready and waiting, sitting in her chair, dressed in her best pink jacket and skirt. Tammy had called in earlier to do Izzie's hair and she had pinned a small posy to her jacket, and had given her a little rouge and lipstick, so that she looked quite perky and bright, as if she might, indeed, live forever. A table was set with a pretty cloth and teacups, saucers and plates.

Jess was clearly a little nervous, but Chloe's easy chatter helped to ease the way and soon everyone was relaxed and smiling. Willow was at her cherubic best, smiling and clapping her hands and showing off her little teeth.

Although, when she was placed in Izzie's bony lap, the baby looked a bit uncertain. She stared up into the ancient face, so different from her mum's, and her lower lip drooped, as if tears were imminent.

Then Izzie, to everyone's amazement, quacked like a duck, and Willow forgot about crying as she stared solemnly at the old lady with round, surprised eyes.

'Do you like ducks?' Izzie asked her in her cultured English voice, adding a smile and an extra, 'Quack, quack, quack.'

Willow's lip drooped lower.

'What about pussy cats?' asked Izzie. 'Meow?'

'Oh, yes, she *loves* cats,' enthused Jess. 'Don't you, pumpkin? She's always trying to pull my cousin's cat's tail.'

Perhaps her mother's approval did the trick. To everyone's relief, Willow smiled again and she continued to smile happily as Chloe snapped photos of her with her great-grandmother.

As they eventually settled Willow and her toys on a rug on the floor, while the adults tucked into the tea and cake, Chloe asked Emily, 'Have you decided who Willow looks like?'

Emily had indeed searched Willow's little face for a likeness to Robbie, but she hadn't really found one. 'To be honest, I thought she reminded me of —' She paused, aware that her answer might not be welcome.

Alex piped up. 'Were you going to say that she looks like Izzie?'

'Well, yes, I was, actually.' No doubt it seemed a ridiculous comparison to anyone who hadn't known her mother when she was younger, but there was something about the baby's face, about her eyes, especially, an expression that seemed incredibly familiar to Emily.

'That's what I thought, too,' said Alex.

'You think she looks like me?' asked Izzie. 'Really? But I'm almost a hundred.'

'Still, I can see it,' Alex said and he smiled. 'I've known you for a long time now, remember.'

'Goodness.' Izzie seemed quite taken aback.

'That's lovely,' joined in Chloe.

Even Jess was nodding. 'I've never been able to decide who Willow looks like,' she said. 'But I think you're probably right. Isn't it amazing how these likenesses can pass down through the generations?'

'There you go, Izzie,' said Alex. 'A glimpse of immortality.'

'Oh, dear.' Without warning, Izzie's eyes filled with tears.

Emily gasped at the sight. Her mother never cried. She never allowed herself to give in to such weakness.

'Mum, are you all right?' She slipped quickly to her mother's side.

Izzie managed a small smile through her tears and she nodded. 'It's just so wonderful, isn't it? Robbie's baby here with us.' Tears streamed down her cheeks as she turned to Jess. 'Thank you, my dear. You've made an old lady very happy.'

Of course, they were all a bit teary then. Teary and smiling. Willow, oblivious to all the emotion, crawled to play with Alex's shoelaces and, as his shoes were clean this time, he let her. She tugged at the laces until she finally got one completely undone, and Emily thought how fitting it was that Izzie Oakshott Galbraith's determined spirit might live on in this cute little descendant.

CHAPTER FORTY-THREE

The next week passed in a blur for Chloe. It was a week of many small tasks, both at work and at home, of jobs that just seemed to keep mounting. At the *Bugle*, a surprising number of end-of-year events needed to be reported. And outside office hours, Chloe dealt with all the usual pre-Christmas fever of gift-purchasing and wrapping, of cards to be sent or responded to, of packing for her return to Sydney.

Chloe had also found it necessary to try a little Christmas baking. She had received a host of unexpected gifts from people she'd met in the course of her work and she wanted to give something back. This had resulted in an evening spent making shortbread cookies cut into tree and star shapes, and nougat filled with dried cranberries and pistachios for a Christmassy look. These, wrapped in cellophane and tied with a tartan bow, had been well received.

On top of these tasks, there had been the trip to Cairns for the nerve-racking interview and assessments at the fertility clinic. Chloe made the journey down from the mountains in some trepidation. She had never enjoyed visiting doctors, and this time she'd felt as if her entire future happiness depended on the visit. If her body proved unsuitable for motherhood, she had nothing to look forward to.

Of course, a large part of her low mood was caused by a need to distance herself emotionally from Finn. In the new year, he would almost certainly agree to let his daughter stay in Burralea. He and Bree would settle together in some lovely home, like the one on the side of a hill that Bree had enthused about. If Chloe was to be any part of that picture, it would be as Finn's bit on the side.

No, thank you.

Chloe had tried to be sensible. At the barbecue she had been pleased to see Finn and Bree so happy together. It really was wonderful to know that they had discovered a new and deeper bond, and that they seemed to be finally moving on after their terrible tragedy. Despite Chloe's best efforts, however, her common sense had not been strong enough to lift her deepening sadness. She'd spent a miserable night after the barbecue and a horrible Sunday, crying and feeling extremely sorry for herself.

On Monday morning she had emerged from a grey haze of wretchedness and decided that her choices were clear. To continue a casual affair with Finn was out of the question. And, while she had the rest of her life to find another man, the right man – even though she had her doubts about ever finding anyone who suited her better than Finn – she did not have the rest of her life to have a child.

She still wanted a child. A child of her own. Her own Bree or Willow. Now. Before she ran out of time.

To her relief, the visit to the clinic had gone well, and she had been given the all clear and sent home with a cooler bag of medication and instructions to inject herself daily in order to stimulate her egg production.

Unfortunately, this had posed a major challenge. Chloe was dead scared of needles and had no partner to help her. But this challenge had also been her reality check, an important test of her motivation. If she wanted to have a baby on her own, she had no choice but to get used to doing all manner of things without help.

For all these reasons, it had been a huge week, an exhausting week. Chloe had only to look in the mirror to see how strained and tired she was.

If she arrived on her parents' doorstep looking like this, they would start fussing and worrying and muttering about the terrible mistake she'd made in moving so far away. Clearly, a restorative hot bath and a facial were in order.

Ten minutes later, Chloe lay in a deep and blissfully hot bath, with her hair wrapped in a towel and her face covered in a lavender mask. It was *so good*. The scent of lavender always calmed her and she could feel her limbs relaxing in the hot water. She drew a deep breath and let it out slowly. Then another.

Yes, this was a great idea. Already, she was beginning to feel so much better.

She began to plan. Tomorrow she would drive back to Cairns airport with Jess and Willow, who were also having Christmas with family in Sydney. Chloe was looking forward to a good long chat with Jess, who had managed so brilliantly as a single mum and under tragic circumstances. Jess was seriously considering returning to the north in the new year and resuming her career as a physiotherapist, which would be wonderful.

Lying there now, in the warm, scented suds, Chloe thought about the friends she had made since she'd arrived in Burralea. Jess, Tammy and Emily had all dealt with very real stress and heartbreak. Beside their problems, Chloe realised that her own boyfriend issues were quite pathetic by comparison.

I really should count my blessings. I have my health, a fun circle of friends, a steady job and —

From below came the annoying ring of the doorbell.

Nooo!

Immediately tense, Chloe sat up, willing whoever it was to go away. Perhaps, if she was very quiet, the caller would think she wasn't home. She waited, sitting very still and not making so much as a ripple in the bathwater. The bell rang again.

Damn. She tried to think who it might be at this hour. She wondered if it could be Moira, coming back for something important that she'd forgotten, only to realise she hadn't brought her key. She supposed she had better peep through the bathroom window and try to see who was down below.

With a heavy sigh, Chloe heaved herself out of the tub, grabbed a towel to catch the worst of the drips and padded, with wet, bare feet, to the window. From this angle, an awning blocked her view of the front door. At least the street was empty at this time of night, so she pushed the window wider and leaned out as far as she dared.

Finn was standing on the footpath.

Whack. Chloe's heart slammed hard.

What on earth was he doing here? They had said goodbye in the *Bugle* office and she had given him a jar filled with nougat and a gift for Bree.

Now he was back.

If she'd been thinking quickly enough, she would have ducked out of view. Unfortunately, Finn had already seen her. He grinned, lifted a hand to wave. 'Chloe!'

It was a wonder he recognised her with her head wrapped, turban style, in a yellow towel, and her face covered by a gooey purple mask. 'What do you want?' she called.

'To see you.'

Her impulse was to tell him to go away. She was supposed to be relaxing, and already he had made her pulse rate skyrocket. But if she refused to see him now, she would spend the entire Christmas break wondering why he'd come, what he'd wanted to say. Even so, she certainly wasn't going downstairs to meet him in a towel and a purple mask.

'I'll need a moment or two,' she called.

'Take your time.'

Of course she rushed, scraping at the creamy mask with tissues and then washing her face with warm water to get rid of lingering traces of purple. She looked a bit pink and blotchy after the scrubbing and she considered using make-up, but then asked herself why she should bother. It was only her editor.

All her good clothes were packed, so she pulled on a faded grey T-shirt and a pair of capri pants that had once been white, but were now also closer to grey. A hasty brush through her hair would have to do. Slipping her feet into thongs, she went down the stairs, taking her time to inhale a few deep, calming breaths.

She opened the door. Finn was still waiting. He had changed out of his work clothes and his dark hair was damp and tamed, as if he'd had a shower. He now wore a white shirt open at the neck and left to hang loose over pale-blue jeans. *Ordinary clothes*, she told herself, *should not look so breathtakingly attractive.*

'How can I help you, Finn?'

His smile was charming. 'I was hoping I could come in.'

Chloe hesitated.

'I brought you this.' He held out a small gift wrapped in expensive-looking red and gold paper.

'Oh. Thank you.' She was still standing in the doorway as she accepted his gift.

'So —?' He smiled at her again, lifted a questioning eyebrow.

Chloe swallowed. He was waiting to be invited inside and it was ridiculous to feel so nervous about a man she worked with every day.

She stepped back. 'Come in.'

'Thank you.'

He smelled clean, of soap, or perhaps a little aftershave. As Chloe turned and led him upstairs, she tried not to think about that other time when they had kissed each other senseless as they'd made this ascent. This was the first occasion Finn had been back in her flat since that night. But surely, after their recent conversations, he wasn't expecting a repeat performance?

In the kitchen, she set his gift, unopened, on the bench top. 'Can I offer you a drink?'

'Were you planning to have one?'

'Perhaps a small one. Jess and I have an early start in the morning. I'm afraid I only have white wine. Will that do?'

Finn nodded. 'Thanks.' He stood by the counter as she fetched the bottle and glasses.

She felt ridiculously self-conscious and she kept her eyes lowered as she poured, watching the chilled wine frost the glass.

'Chloe, what's this?'

Looking up, she discovered Finn holding an orange with a hypodermic syringe stuck into it.

Oh, shit. Her face flooded with heat. 'Um – I – um – I'm just practising.'

'Dare I ask what you're practising?'

'Giving myself needles.'

He frowned. 'Do you have diabetes?'

'No.'

Finn continued to frown and look worried.

'It's just that I'm scared of needles, and I need to give myself injections to stimulate my hormone production, so I'm practising on oranges.'

'I – I see.' He still looked confused, which was understandable.

'I want to have a baby. So I'm going to try for IVF.' Chloe couldn't believe she had actually told him this, but now that it was out, she felt better. Stronger. Perhaps he would finally understand why she wasn't available for a casual affair.

'Wow.' He spoke very softly, still looking at the orange, turning it over slowly. When he looked up, his dark eyes held a suspicious sheen. 'You'll be a wonderful mother, Chloe.'

Oh, Finn.

Of all the things he might have said, this compliment was Chloe's undoing. Her lips quivered, her mouth pulled out of shape. She lifted a hand to try to hold back the sobs welling in her throat.

'Don't say that,' she pleaded, and a moment later she was weeping. Helplessly.

Finn reached her in an instant. His arms came around her, holding her close while she wept against his clean white shirt.

'I'm sorry,' she blubbered.

'Don't be.' Gently, he stroked her hair. 'I mean it. You'll be a fantastic mum.'

She felt compelled to explain her tears. 'It's just that the fellow I lived with in Sydney more or less told me I'd be a terrible mother. It hurt so much. And now – to have you say this —' Her lips trembled again and more tears spilled.

She swiped at her eyes. 'I have to do it, Finn. I'm thirty-seven. By the time I get through the IVF process, I'll be thirty-eight. And then there's the nine months of pregnancy. I've waited so long and I feel like I'm running out of time.'

Strands of her hair had fallen across her face and now Finn tucked them behind her ear. 'You don't have to justify your decision, Chloe. It sounds perfectly reasonable.'

'Does it?'

'Yes.' His mouth tilted in a rueful smile. 'Unfortunately.'

Now it was her turn to frown. 'Why unfortunately?'

'Because I came here to try to change your mind.'

'What about?

'Us.'

Chloe gulped. 'You want to keep me as a sort of mistress?'

'No, actually. I'd much prefer to keep you as a sort of partner.'

Her knees almost gave way. Surely she wasn't hearing correctly? 'Partner? Not to live with you?'

'Yes.' Finn's smile was a tad sad. 'I know you think I'm commitment shy, but I'm not, really.'

'But you're – you're grieving. You're not ready for —'

She was still searching for the right word when Finn continued.

'I'll admit it's taken me a while to get over losing Sarah and Louis. I still miss them terribly and I imagine I'll always miss them. They're an important part of my life, of my past, so they're also a part of who I am.' Finn took Chloe's hand in his, threaded his fingers with hers. 'But I can't live in the past forever.'

His eyes shimmered again as he smiled. 'I've already lost one woman I loved and that time it wasn't my fault. I'd hate to lose the woman I love now because I didn't speak up.'

Love. He'd used the word 'love'.

'I want to look to the future now, Chloe, and I was hoping you might think about sharing it with me.'

Chloe was glad he was holding her hands or she might have stumbled. This still seemed too good to be true. She couldn't help asking, 'Are you sure?'

'Couldn't be surer. I've been thinking of little else but how clever and kind and damn sexy you are, and how much I need you.' He lifted her hand to his lips and pressed a warm kiss to her knuckles. 'Bree and I both need you, Chloe. Believe it or not, I've even been thinking about the possibility that you might want a child of your own.'

She let out a huff of shock, of incredulous relief. 'So – so you wouldn't mind if I still went ahead with the IVF?'

'No,' he said with reassuring promptness. 'Although it might be even better if we could organise to have our own child naturally.'

'But – you can't. Haven't you had the snip?'

'I have, but at the time, the doctor made it clear that the procedure is almost certainly reversible.'

'Oh, my goodness.' Quite overcome by surprise, by unbelievable joy, Chloe had no choice but to throw herself into Finn's arms.

As he held her close against his warm, solid chest, she heard his heart beating beneath her ear and she savoured a moment of perfect happiness.

'I can't quite believe this,' she whispered.

'Neither can I,' said Finn. 'I thought I could never be happy again, but you've worked a kind of magic, you clever, clever girl.'

She lifted her face to look at him, to try to explain the true depth of her feelings, but there was no need for words, for Finn kissed her now. And she returned his kiss, fervently, with open lips and a singing heart and with her arms wound tightly around him.

She had never known a kiss so filled with joy, with perfect sweetness and promise. It was ages before they finally paused for breath, and she was grinning madly, while her eyes brimmed once again with tears.

'I can't believe I'm so hopelessly soppy,' she said with a shaky laugh.

Finn smiled and kissed her forehead. 'Soppiness suits you.'

She brushed at the tears with her fingers. She supposed she should search for a tissue. On the kitchen bench beside them, their wineglasses sat untouched beside Finn's Christmas present. She eyed the pretty wrapping.

'I should open that, Finn.'

'Later.' With sudden impatience, he pulled her back to him. 'I can tell you what it is.' He trailed sweet kisses over her neck.

'What?' she asked in a breathless whisper.

'A coloured-glass-bead necklace made by a local artist.'

Closing her eyes, she pressed closer to him again. 'It sounds lovely.'

'I hope you'll like it. Bree said I should give you jewellery.'

'Clever Bree,' Chloe murmured. Then, with a uneasy prickle of guilt, she opened her eyes and looked up. 'Where is Bree?'

'At Emily's. Jess and Willow are there as well. They're having a final visit before Christmas.'

'Oh, that's great. Perfect.'

'Emily asked me to invite you to join them, but I think she was rather hoping we'd be better occupied here.'

'Emily knows – about us?'

'She seems to have an inkling.'

Chloe grinned. Soon the whole of Burralea would have more than an inkling about her and Finn, and the best thing was, she knew the townsfolk would be almost as happy as she was.

They kissed again, and now she felt peace settle alongside their fever and urgency, the confident knowledge that their new life started from this moment.

EPILOGUE

The school bus pulled to a stop beside a paddock perched high on a hill. From here, sloping green dairy land spilled, offering views to the east, all the way to the majestic purple peaks of Mount Bartle Frere.

'Bye, Bree,' youthful voices called, as the gangly teenager alighted from the bus, sidestepping a muddy puddle left by recent rains.

'Byeee,' she called back, waving and grinning to her friends.

The bus took off and a rusty-headed boy turned to look back through the rear window, sending Bree a smile and a thumbs-up salute. As he did so, she felt a strange little flip in her chest. Then she bit down on her lip to stop herself from grinning too happily.

If her friends knew she was sweet on Sam Peterson, they would be onto her like sniffer dogs. Any whiff of romance and the gossip would go viral.

This was a minor problem though. Generally, Bree was loving her new school. She'd been relieved to discover that the teachers were excellent, the kids friendly, and there was even a debating team, which she adored. Of course, the fact that Sam Peterson was also in the debating team was in no way connected to her enjoyment.

Now, as the bus disappeared, Bree heard the beep of a text message, the regular text message she received every afternoon from either Chloe or her dad.

Hope you're home safe. Can you check the slow cooker and perhaps turn it down to low? Still at work, but home soon. C xx

Bree smiled and sent back a quick reply.

Will do. C u soon. B xx

As she loped the last few metres along the road to her house, she could see her half-grown puppy, Black Velvet, waiting at the five-barred gate, her tail wagging so fast it was a blur.

'Hey, gorgeous girl!' She greeted her dog with a cuddle and allowed herself to be enthusiastically licked. 'Walkies later, okay?'

Bree needed her afternoon tea first. By the end of the school day she was always famished. Chloe said it was because she was growing so fast.

Bree checked the letterbox. Along with a couple of bills, there was a letter addressed to her – and it wasn't from her grandma, but from her old school. Curious, she let herself into the house and went straight to the kitchen, the heart of their new home that she especially loved, with views out through a wall of windows all the way down the valley.

Leaving the mail on the kitchen counter, she checked the slow cooker, as Chloe had asked, turned it down and then made herself a cheese sandwich and a glass of Milo. Settling on a kitchen stool, she slit open the envelope addressed to her. It was from her old English teacher, Mrs Marlowe.

Just as Mrs M had promised over a year ago, she had forwarded the letter that Bree had written in class to herself. The letter was still safely sealed inside another envelope addressed to Bree in her own handwriting. And there was a note.

Dear Bree,

I hope you are now happily settled in your new school, and I hope you enjoy this little glimpse into your past. It can be helpful to think about how much you've changed in just one year. I'm sure you're doing very well and your new English teacher is very lucky to have you in his (or her) class.

Keep writing,
and kindest regards,
Jenny Marlowe

Bree's throat felt a bit tight as she thought about Mrs M and her boarding roommate Abbey and the other friends at her old school. Before nostalgia took hold, however, she slit the envelope and pulled out the handwritten pages, took a bite of her sandwich and began to read.

Dear Bree,

Hey, dude, if you're still alive when you read this, you'll be a teenager by now. Do you have pimples yet? I hope not.

Do you feel any different? More grown up? It sure would be good if your mood has improved.

Yikes. Bree read on, but she was struck, after just a few paragraphs, by how sad she'd been back then, and what a baby, too, worrying about whether her boobs would grow and whether Joshua Cook even knew she existed.

Joshua Who? she thought now with a bemused smile.

Reading the letter brought it all back – how badly she had missed her dad and how hard it had been to tough it out at school, to pretend she was as happy and carefree as the other girls. A year ago, shecould never have imagined she would be so truly happy now. She actually felt sorry for the girl who'd written that letter, especially the bit about her mum and Louis and how she hadn't wanted to go to the cemetery . . .

Last week, on that same sad anniversary, Bree and her dad had taken his canoe out into the middle of the lake. They'd gone at night, after dinner, when the sky was filled with a gazillion stars.

The stars were reflected in the water, so the lake had looked as if it was filled with them too. And sitting there, with the canoe rocking gently in the sparkling darkness, Bree and her dad had talked about her mum and Louis. They had shared their favourite memories – especially their holiday on Magnetic Island when they'd snorkelled among coral fish and then built a barbecue on the beach, and her mum had strummed her guitar while the moon rose over the sea.

They remembered Louis as a cheeky toddler discovering the joy of playing with a hose, spraying water over everyone and making them squeal. They remembered him dancing with over-the-top excitement when he got a robot dog for Christmas.

Bree told her dad of her shame that she'd yelled at Louis just before he died, for something as silly as messing up the icing on her birthday cake. Her dad told her that he had regrets, too.

'But we shouldn't let our regrets spoil our happy memories,' he said.

And then he recounted one of Bree's favourite stories, of how excited he and her mother had been when she was born.

'Mum thought you were the most beautiful baby ever created,' he said. 'She wanted you to be happy, Bree. It's all she ever wanted for you. And I know, she would want us both to be happy.'

It was a big thought to take in, because just thinking about her mother always made her sad. But Bree did understand that staying sad forever was a waste of the life her mother had given her.

As this thought settled inside her, she scooped a handful of water, making the stars shatter into tiny glittering shards of light. She said, 'Mum would like Chloe, Dad. I think she'd be pleased to know we have someone as lovely as Chloe making us both happy.'

At first her father didn't answer and Bree was terrified that she had said the wrong thing, that she'd made him cry. When at last he spoke, his voice was rough around the edges.

'Chloe's going to have a baby, Bree.'

'A *what*?' Bree was so stunned and excited she almost rocked the canoe and sent them tumbling into the water.

'You don't mind, do you?' her dad asked, as if he was worried.

'No. Of course I don't mind. That's amazing. It's wonderful.'

Suddenly Bree remembered the clues she'd overlooked – the fact that Chloe had stopped drinking wine some time back, and there had been mornings when she couldn't face breakfast. Wow! It really was happening. She would be a big sister again. And Chloe would be a mother. An absolutely awesome mother to some lucky little kid.

'It's just the most perfect news ever, Dad.' Then, in case she had missed another important clue, Bree asked, '*You* don't mind, do you?'

In the faint light, she saw his happy smile. 'Of course I don't. I'm over the moon.' Gently, he added, 'I love, Chloe, Bree. So much.'

'Yeah, Dad, I know,' she said. 'So do I. I'm so over the moon for her.'

They laughed then and looked up at the moon, shining like a silver queen, with the many stars as her subjects. The night was so beautiful with its lake of shining stars, as if the heavens had reached down to touch them with a promise of beauty and hope.

'Do you know whether it's a boy or a girl?' Bree asked.

Her dad shook his head. 'Chloe's had scans and tests to make sure everything's okay, but we've decided we don't want to know the baby's sex. It's kind of fun to keep it a surprise.'

Bree grinned. 'A surprise! That makes it even more perfect.' She reached for her oar. 'But we'd better get back, don't you think?'

This news was way too exciting to remain sitting sedately in a canoe. She needed to dance a happy jig, to hug Chloe, to make sure she was okay.

'Good idea,' her father said, and they rowed for the shore, eager to reach home.

***

Time to go home.

In the *Bugle* office, Chloe was smiling as she shut down her computer. At any moment, Finn would arrive back from covering the council meeting and together they would drive home to their house perched on a misty hillside where Bree and Black Velvet and a slow-cooked casserole awaited them.

It still spun Chloe out at times that her life had taken such a one-eighty-degree turn, bringing her so far from Jason and the Coogee flat and the hectic pace of *Girl Talk*.

'And you're happy, darling, aren't you?' her mother had asked, when Chloe had rung last week, with her exciting news about the baby.

'I am, Mum, truly, truly happy,' Chloe had assured her, as she had previously at Easter, when she, Finn and Bree had travelled to Sydney for a meeting with the Browns that had gone, to her relief, quite seamlessly. Like a patchwork square added to a quilt, another little corner of Chloe's life had felt settled.

Now, as she tidied her desk, preparing to leave, a knock sounded on the office door. 'Chloe!'

Tammy was there, wide-eyed with excitement.

'You've escaped early,' Chloe said with a smile. Tammy was nearly always working late, squeezing in one last customer.

'Gina French's colour needs five more minutes. So I popped out to tell you. I couldn't wait. I did the test at lunch time.'

Chloe grinned. 'And?'

'Two blue lines!' Tammy announced, adding a triumphant squeal and a fist punch into the air.

'Oh, Tams!' Leaping out of her chair, Chloe rushed to hug her friend. 'That's fantastic. The best. I'm so happy for you.'

'Yeah. So we're going to be yummy mummies together.'

Chloe laughed. 'With Jess and Willow, and Alice Drummond and her new little Jasper, we'll have enough to form a playgroup.' Her thoughts were already racing ahead, imagining the playdough and finger painting and daisy chains and morning tea with her girlfriends. Simple pleasures she had once feared she might never enjoy.

'Anyway, I'd better dash back to Gina,' Tammy said. 'But I wanted you to be the first to know. After Ben, of course. Oh, my God, you should see him puffing out his chest like he's won an Olympic gold medal.'

With a grin and a wave, Tammy was off and as she darted back down the footpath, the Forester drew into the curb. From the doorway, Chloe watched Finn emerge from the car. He smiled his special smile, just for her, and a slow wave of happiness rolled through her.

The summer's evening was glowing, soft and dusky gold, casting gentle shadows. This was her favourite time of day, when the world was washed in beauty and she was going home with Finn. With a satisfied sigh, she closed the door and walked towards him.

ACKNOWLEDGEMENTS

I dedicated this book to you, my readers, because you are truly important to me. Storytellers have always needed someone to 'listen', and I imagine you in all the different circumstances that life throws at us, taking time out to slip into another world, just as I do when I read. Some of you have taken the trouble to email me, or to make contact via Facebook, or to write a review, and for that I am exceptionally grateful. Your messages and your thoughtfulness are my inspiration. To those readers I've never 'met', just knowing you're out there is enough to get me started on yet another story.

As with every book, my husband, Elliot, was incredibly helpful while I wrote *The Summer of Secrets*. This time, his role was especially inspirational, as he has also been an editor on a country town newspaper and this was a story I've been wanting to write for some time.

My fictional town of Burralea is modelled on the real-life town of Yungaburra on the Atherton Tablelands, and I'm grateful to the Yungaburra community, who take such pride in keeping their beautiful village picture perfect for all to enjoy.

I'd also like to thank Judith Ryan, who has served with the Australian Defence Force, and helped me to make sure that important story details were accurate.

Special thanks are also due to Ali Watts for her perceptive guidance, to Nikki Lusk for her keen editorial eye, and to the rest of the team at Penguin Random House: Amanda Martin, Nerrilee Weir, Jo Baker, Ali Hampton, Emily Cook and Chloe Davies.

BOOK CLUB NOTES

1. Chloe is devastated when Jason asks: 'What makes you think you'd be such a great mother?' How are the different perspectives on parenthood and its challenges explored throughout the novel?

2. What do you think are important qualities in a parent? Does this story perhaps ask whether any of us really knows?

3. Several characters are impacted by grief. Who are they and how are their steps towards healing revealed?

4. Bree's story is told mostly through her diary extracts. Discuss other novels where letters and diaries play a major role.

5. At a very early age, Izzie learns to put on a brave face. What were the circumstances that caused this? How did her courage and her British 'stiff upper lip' affect her relationships with others?

6. What, if anything did you know of the women who flew huge bombers for the Air Transport Auxiliary during World War II? Do you think they deserve wider recognition?

7. The author paints an idyllic picture of life in a small country town. Do you think this is realistic? Do you imagine Finn and Chloe staying in Burralea after Bree finishes school?

8. The history of Emily and Alex's relationship is told in reverse. Do you think this is an effective literary device?

9. Why do you think this book is called *The Summer of Secrets*? Discuss the many secrets the story contains. Are some secrets more justified than others?

10. Discuss the similarities between this novel and other books by Barbara Hannay.